A Customary

Obsession 2: Power

Jane Creelman Graiko

"The great question which, in all ages, has disturbed mankind and brought on them the greatest part of their mischiefs... has been, not whether be power in the world, nor whence it came, but who should have it."

-John Locke, Essay on Human Understanding

A Customary Obsession 2: Power

Greystone Prose

Printed in the United States of America

Literature & Fiction / Mystery, Thriller & Suspense / Contemporary
Vermont / Eugenics / Genetics / Romance / Women in Law
Enforcement / Survivors of Assault

Third Edition: August, 2014

ISBN-13: 978-0-9907369-0-5

Dedication Page

To my husband Ron, for too many reasons to list.

To my parents:
James Edward Creelman, Jr. (April 22, 1921 - to June 5, 2012)
Constance Beauregard Creelman (April 23, 1923 - July 17, 2012)

Married in Albany, New York on September 8, 1944 shortly before James left for the Pacific Theater in the US Army Air Corps.

Partners in life for more than 67 years.

Military nomads for decades with assignments in Sembach Air Force Base, West Germany; Darmstadt Army Post, West Germany; Misawa Air Force Base, Japan; Johnson Air Force Base, Japan; and Fort Meade, Maryland.

Civilian travelers through Europe: Germany, Austria, France, Holland, and Italy with four children (Connie, Jane, Jim, and John).
Civilian travelers to Japan with three children (Jane, Jim, and John – Connie stayed Stateside).

Until we reach retirement age, many of us never realize how the values instilled and habits encouraged in childhood continue to shape us as adults. I thank my parents for my appreciation of other cultures, books, music, a rounded education, and travel to new places. All of that seemed so ordinary until as an adult, I learned how rare my experiences truly were.

My first novel was published while they were alive. I asked for and received honest feedback, not always positive. Though they passed on before the second, I felt grateful for the opportunity to discuss the general theme as I moved along. I wish them peace.

To Dr. Reena Kavilaveettil of Tampa, Florida, for erasing two years of tests and struggles to reach a diagnosis of my condition. The Lynette Delorange character struggles with the same.

Spring

Prologue

In a cold sweat, Mel bolted upright, ran his fingers through his damp hair, and pressed his palm against his pounding heart. He pulled a robe on, headed into the living room, and rebuilt the fire. As he settled into his reading chair, he stared blankly at flickering flames, transfixed by a vision of his beloved as a child. Mel understood the true essence of love rested in the memories of those who moved beyond physical pleasures into an unbroken spiritual bond. Across the mountains and over more than a hundred miles, Mel heard Laurette Marie scream out to him in her moment of panic.

Mel grabbed the phone. "Something dreadful has happened, Gilbert. Utilize your network and discover if a factual basis exists for a vision of my beloved Laura in pain."

"For Christ's sake, Mel, the sun's not even up yet."

"Young man, do not take our Lord's name in vain!"

"Sorry."

"Do as instructed."

"Yes, sir."

Mel hung up and waited. When the phone rang 11 minutes later, he grabbed. "She lives, yes?"

"She's in surgery to remove two bullets. Mel, how could you know that? The state police haven't issued a statement yet."

Mel closed his eyes. "Such is the unending love I feel for that child. If our good Lord looks upon you so favorably, someday you too shall experience such a connection."

Mel hung up, crossed to his desk, and scanned notes for a guest sermon. In light of Laura's predicament, the words seemed like meaningless drivel. He crumpled pages, threw them into the fire, and sat to pen a sermon so masterful—create a message so glorious—hearts, souls, and voices of the Chosen would reach Heaven where He would spare her life and return her body, heart, and soul to the only man who truly adored her.

1.

The instant she opened her eyes, Laura felt bored. She needed rest and continued care but an extended stay in the hospital left her edgy. She hated the smells, sounds, and food, hated the way she heard TVs in the background, and hated when a cleaning crew came through, spread a smelly mixture, and pushed a floor polisher in arcs. She hated murmured voices of staff, hated how nurses tracked bathroom functions, and hated how a nurse arrived at 8:59 PM to scoot Steve out the door. No matter how hard she tried, Laura couldn't control her moods and snapped for the smallest of reasons. When Laura heard squeaky wheels of a cart toting another slopped-together bland breakfast, she rested her hand in her lap so the diamond sparkled in morning sun. She forced herself to finish dry scrambled eggs and wheat toast. She grabbed crutches, hobbled to the window, rested on the sill, and imagined at that moment, sun shone through Steve's bedroom window. When her attention shifted, a crutch clattered to the floor and a nurse stuck her head around. Laura groaned, "Dr. Paige has to let me out of this prison during my lifetime!"

The nurse scanned her clipboard. "How does tomorrow morning sound, Trooper Delorange?"

"Great!"

When Steve arrived for visiting hours, Laura felt a flush. "Scolarzski, this is your last chance to change your mind."

He plopped into a chair. "About what, Delorange?"

"Your invitation to recuperate at your house; I get sprung tomorrow." He lunged forward for a hug.

2

In the morning, Ed Granger heard Delorange was scheduled to be released and headed to the hospital. After he breezed through expected niceties, he made his pitch. "There's an ongoing investigation the VSP could use help with." He stopped when Scolarzski rushed in, shot off a half-assed insult, and faced Delorange. "Need help packing?"

"I'm all set; I couldn't sleep and finished around 3:00." She glanced sideways. "Um, Granger's here on official business."

Scolarzski snorted, "Laura resigned, sir; remember?"

Ed shrugged, "In all the confusion, I never forwarded her letter to Middlesex. That's better since she stays on the payroll and medical plan, plus has a chance to make a real difference."

Scolarzski turned to Delorange and chuckled, "I guess almost dying from multiple gunshot wounds isn't enough of a contribution yet." On his way out, he sneered, "I'm still under suspension so I'll leave the two of you to finish your *official* discussion in private."

Ed turned to Delorange with a smile. "The old loyalty variable strikes again. Years ago I finished an MBA researching partnership loyalty. I'd be happy to let you read my thesis."

"Do you have a point, Lieutenant?"

Ed stated statistically speaking, the first pair-up stayed strongest if it lasted a year with shared danger. "Despite such obvious differences, that's why Barber and Scolarzski stay close. It's obvious for you, too, but for him? I see a first repeated in a different flavor."

"For God's sake, leave the file, sir. I'll read it and call you."

Ed held the folder. "Don't let that maniac paw through it."

"Give it to me then take your pop psychology with you."

Ed grinned. "When will you be back at work, Trooper?"

She stared at the door. "My doctor recommends two weeks of limited activity—after that, half days at a desk. Sir, let's be clear I won't stay more than 320 hours. No matter how intriguing this case is, you have the equivalent of eight weeks coming to you."

Ed handed the file over. "I predict you'll see it through."

She stuffed the file in her suitcase and snapped it shut. "Don't bet on it, sir; I'm done. I'll share my work on the MacClure - Orsini investigation and testify in court but that's it."

"I predict you'll follow through." When Ed passed Scolarzski leaning against a wall, the sergeant grunted something undoubtedly hostile under his breath but Ed waved and headed to the elevator.

3

Laura watched Steve rush in and grab a suitcase. "Let's go."

When a nurse arrived with a wheelchair, Laura mumbled, "I don't need that. I'm gotten pretty good with crutches."

"It's hospital policy, Detective."

When Laura banged her left leg and struggled to lift her foot onto the rest, Steve helped. "Did that hurt?"

"It's just the same dull ache."

When she trembled, Steve whispered, "Are you okay?"

"It hurts but mostly I'm nervous. You had six weeks to hear me whine like a baby. Is that enough to regret what happened that night?"

Steve asked the nurse for a moment alone. "I spent the time reliving that night and loving every second."

Laura smoothed hair above his ears and noticed he needed a haircut; it appeared he lost weight, too. "It's sad to see how much you focused on my recovery so be honest."

"I have no regrets, kid. I've loved you for a very long time."

"Okay, let's go." In the car, Laura reached across to squeeze his hand. "After so little privacy lately, I can't wait to be alone."

Steve shrugged, "Your father's not pleased with our plans, thinks you should go his house until the wedding."

"He'll come around."

At a stop sign, Steve shifted into neutral and grabbed. "I can't believe you didn't boot me out of your life once and for all."

Even though it hurt, Laura hugged back. "Never, but please drive; I ache to be alone with you."

4

Steve drove slowly so she could see how everything changed in six weeks: tiny buds on trees, pale green grass in muddy pastures, newly-plowed fields. She rested her cheek against his shoulder and drifted to sleep. When Steve pulled into his driveway and turned the ignition off, he rolled a window down to sniff a rich scent of mud and yesterday's rain. The brook ran fast and he heard sounds from the woods—birds mostly or a squirrel. He waited patiently for Laura to open her eyes and when she did, she peered in every direction and gasped, "It snowed that night and now look how everything changed!"

"Spring's my favorite season in Vermont. I survive winter and mud season knowing everything will be like this." Steve lifted her out, carried her inside, and lowered her to a chair. "I'm sorry it took so long to recognize how dangerous Stephanie was."

"Let's not waste a minute on that woman," Laura muttered and glanced around a familiar kitchen. "It's always the little things that get to me first—buds on trees after a long, cold winter and your half-dead plants lined up along your window sill like wounded soldiers."

Steve knelt on the floor. "I know you only agreed to recuperate here while I'm on suspension but you could move in now. Say yes and I'll go to your apartment later and bring everything here."

"Do you have to do it today?"

"You don't want to move in with me?"

Laura squeezed his chin. "Packing can wait, mister. After six weeks, you may not remember a promise made in the dark, but I do. The sun is shining. Remember?"

Steve cleared his throat. "We can't; your back is…"

Laura licked her lips. "I'll be uncomfortable for a while but you're gentle; surely we can be creative."

Steve considered her offer yet answered, "It's too soon and not a good idea, anyway. Your mother will be here soon."

Laura grinned. "Leave a note on the door: *Lynette: while we make love, have a seat on the porch or come back later.*"

Steve chuckled, "Tacky," lifted and carried her to the bedroom. In seconds, she fell asleep. Steve studied her face and whispered, "An intelligent, idealistic, beautiful, young woman like you deserves more than an old fart like me." He tucked a blanket under her chin and stood. "Dear God in Heaven, I don't deserve this gift."

"Oh, but you do," she mumbled softly.

Overnight, Steve slept soundly for the first time in six weeks. Even as Laura tossed and turned, he relaxed because her restlessness proved she lay beside him, alive. In the morning, he dressed and left a note on the dresser *I'll call later.* After breakfast, he grabbed the note and added *I place my heart and soul in your hands, Laura—willingly place them there for safekeeping. If this isn't forever, tell me now. Hurt me now.* In early morning drizzle, Steve drove his pickup to her place to pack belongings. He felt acutely aware of Laura's presence in her apartment and felt deeply touched by her trust. For two years with the Vermont State Police, she lived there alone surrounded by her possessions, independent and sure of herself as she progressed through life, a strong woman who survived without a needy man like him underfoot.

Her mother called the apartment at 9:00. "I said I'd be there by now but it's an off day. When I feel like this, I won't drive."

"If you want, I can come get you."

Lynette sighed, "Thanks; I hoped you'd offer."

By noon, furniture stood ready to schedule for pickup by experienced movers while smaller items came in boxes, ready to be carried out to the truck when rain stopped. He stared at piles of towels, sheets, and clothes, counted seven boxes of books and whispered, "Laura, thank you for inviting me into your life."

Lynette glanced up from taping. "And thank you for loving her like you do."

5

Laura opened her eyes to an odd combination: a sound of rain on the roof and sun through a window. She stared at a shockingly blue sky with dark, rushing clouds and called, "Steve?" At no response, she noticed he left breakfast on the bedside table and when he called, laughed, "Not smart to spoil me, mister."

"If you like that little gesture, wait 'til you get pregnant, kid."

Laura felt the flush. "I may not be able to; does that change your mind about marriage?"

"Nah; who'm I kidding, anyway? I had the old vas deferens snipped years ago and the thought of reversal unappealing."

"If that means what I think it does, why did you use a condom that night at your house when we finally got together?"

"Experts claim it's not always perfect or permanent and I'm a creature of habit." He chuckled and added, "Over the years, I heard Old Max' voice inside my head utter scary warnings about what could be passed along and with my history, I worried I'd contaminate you."

Laura concentrated on his words, pauses, and tone of voice. When he moved back to furniture and dishes, she imagined she heard regret. "I'm sorry this conversation is over the phone but that night at your house, um, everything felt new and I didn't want to ruin the mood by asking questions or bringing up my medical history."

"I know what you mean but you don't have to apologize to me, kid—ever—for anything, so please get some rest."

Laura drifted in and out of sleep interrupted by one phone call after another. After the fifth in an hour to ask what to do with something in particular, Laura laughed, "Use your judgment! I only care about my books, CDs, photo, DVDs, and a brass Thai Spirit House my mother gave me. The rest is junk. Oh, make sure to bring the rest of Jack's old LP's, okay? I didn't have them all that night we finally got together."

"Why don't I bring everything for you to check?"

"I want to buy things together, things that are ours."

"I don't want you to be upset; I saw some nice curtains."

Laura laughed at an image of faded drapes. "I give you permission to toss things. I don't mean to be rude, but this medication leaves me sluggish. Do you think I can have some time without the phone ringing? I'd like to rest up for when you come home."

"That excites me, kid."

"What does?"

"Hearing you say *when you come home* like we're already married. This may sound kinky, but going through your things excites me, too. I could get used to it pretty quick. Guess what I'm looking at now—a photograph of you, me, and Ralph eating corn on the cob."

"Granger's BBQ when you couldn't get up on water skis."

Steve described another taken at Ned's daughter's wedding. "We're ignoring each other at the table, probably right before that embarrassing dance. Of all the photographs Ned gave you, why put these two in a frame kept by your bed no less?"

"Those two days were important to me."

"Excuse me?"

"I did more than stare; you let me touch."

After a noticeable pause, Steve cleared his throat. "I also found a bag of unopened CDs—Mark Knopfler, Van Morrison, and Patsy Cline for starters. Doing research into my tastes, kid?"

She laughed, "You caught me. I don't have many secrets and try not to leave clues for people to come across accidentally."

Steve sighed, "We got through an awkward conversation about my vasectomy but I have a few others; it's time we talk."

"Whenever you feel like it."

"Do you know how much I love you, Laura?"

"Yeah, I feel it over the phone."

"I do, too, especially when your voice is husky like now."

Laura chewed her bottom lip. "I read your note, Steve. We're forever. I promise."

Laura headed to the kitchen with breakfast dishes and considered her current situation. How odd to be tired and helpless while at the same time, wonderful to see how quickly everything progressed. Only six weeks earlier, a late winter storm raged as she struggled with a desire to approach the man she loved, with a need to move beyond terror. An amazing night of love interrupted by Stephanie Orsini's furious attack and arrest, then seasons recovered quickly, as did she. Laura returned to the bedroom, opened her suitcase, and returned to the kitchen. She placed Granger's file on the table and ran fingertips along the label: *C. Melvin Marsethe*. She opened it and read Granger's note: *You were investigated before you were hired, Delorange, so don't get paranoid on me. Read the contents with objectivity intact. Ed.*

Laura spread everything around: page after page of interview transcripts—the first set dated 20 years earlier, the second ten years earlier, the third a year earlier. She emptied an envelope labeled *Marsethe* containing 11 photographs of the doctor from his 30s into his early 60s. He hadn't changed much in the 20 years since she left; he looked affluent, intelligent, handsome, distinguished, and physically fit. The blue eyes that enchanted her so much as a child still seemed warm and kind. Laura emptied the envelope labeled *Victim LMD*. In the first, dated the fall she was ten, she stood on the steps of Fallsbridge Academy next to her brother Jack as he posed with his saxophone following a concert. He wore a suit and tie while she wore a pale yellow dress with half-sleeves, a white jacket, dress shoes, and white tights that couldn't mask bruised shins. Laura checked the second photo——January 11, months before she turned 13: her family at a community gathering, perhaps a birthday party; again, tomboyish bruises, innocence. She checked the date on a third photograph and swallowed hard: she stood naked in front of a white hospital wall, hand marks covering thighs and hips, finger marks on her face, neck, and chest. The fourth photograph brought a painful lump to her throat: close-ups of her prepubescent body—tiny breasts, no underarm hair, mere traces of pubic hair. And more: scabbed-over lips, red-raw knife wounds, chest, thigh and pelvic bruises, swollen labia, and two black eyes—one swollen shut.

Laura stuffed the photographs into the envelope and choked on saliva. Despite memories of Marsethe's attacks, his tortures, whispered threats, and painful probes, despite a vision of her younger self ravaged, she felt most embarrassed a man like Granger knew. She imagined he pored over every detail in the transcripts from interviews and hearings, studied photographs, and saw her shameful secret in stark black and white—or worse—in vivid color. Laura wandered into the living room and stared out at the dinginess left behind after snow melted—last fall's leaves, dead grass, branches, and twigs. Underneath the mess, she saw grass sprigs poke through. *How like life*, she thought; *how like spring to grab hold; how amazing to revisit disgusting details and allow my adult self to experience more than pain; how wonderful to have a man like Steve to love.* She watched a robin bounce along in search of worms and smiled at a realization she moved beyond that monster Marsethe.

Laura emptied the contents of the second envelope, identified as *Victim FTS*: an astoundingly beautiful young girl with long, dark hair, huge brown eyes, round pink cheeks, and freckles across her nose. As with Laura's set, FTS photos progressed from everyday events to bruises to the results of one man's need to torture victims into submission. In the last photograph, Laura's heart skipped a beat at an unrecognizable child. When she lifted the third labeled *Victim ARL*, her hands trembled. In the first photo, a bride and groom with another dark-haired girl in a pale pink dress, a smiling face and shining eyes. In another suggesting tomboyish preadolescence, she wore a softball uniform and cap. The final captured arm bruises and a black eye in the glare of overhead lighting. Laura gasped, "Dear God in Heaven, where were you?"

Laura read the transcripts of the other girls' interviews, stunned at how similar their descriptions matched hers: the years the kindly doctor took to set things up; his interest in their education; his inclusion of parents in plans for college, medical school, and a return home to serve the community; the loan of his beautiful leather-bound books; the excitement of successful experiments in his lab; his patience, mentorship, attention and obvious affection; the confusion about what was happening when he sat them on his lap, kissed their cheeks, caressed their arms, and whispered his confession of love; and with her and Victim FTS, his retaliation when rebuffed.

Laura limped back to the bedroom, stuffed the folder into the elasticized section of her suitcase, and shoved it deep into the closet. She grabbed the phone to call Granger. "You can't ask me to get involved now! I intend to marry Steve in a month. Sir, I deserve this."

"You're needed undercover, Delorange."

"You can't ask me to change my plans, sir. It isn't fair."

He snorted, "Fair? Is it fair to send someone else in, someone who doesn't know what the son of a bitch is capable of? You're a war hero, Delorange; you survived him."

"Did I? Then why does this hurt so much?"

"Everyone says you're one compassionate soul."

"Sir, it would be better for everyone if…"

"You're also a smart lawyer and that's how you should approach this, okay? We need rock-solid evidence to nail this bastard before he takes the next step with ARL. Surely you of all people know based on past patterns, there's not much time left before he…"

"I'm trying to make sense of this, sir, really I am but…"

"You're also one ballsy investigator; only you recognized that Orsini broad for the murderer she…"

"Brief someone else, sir. It doesn't have to be me."

"I could pass your resignation letter along to Middlesex today but that's not my preference. I spoke to Marschek and the offer remains in effect. He's appalled at what happened and will go along with the deal. Since the shooting and arrest are a matter of public record, that's great cover with those freaks in Fallsbridge. We'd reimburse Marschek for your salary, so technically you're on their payroll not ours, and could relocate up there no questions asked."

"Sounds like you gave this a lot of thought, sir."

Granger chuckled, "I may have been a shitty investigator but I'm one hell of a case manager. The only loose end in this is your relationship with a certain other cop about to come off suspension."

"You don't need me, sir. This ARL seems strong."

"Pay attention! Marsethe's one convincing subhuman who surrounds himself with others of his ilk who provide airtight alibis. Help the VSP compile a case that'll take care of that village of idiots for good. Face the facts—you're the perfect bait."

Laura gasped, "Bait? That's how you see me?"

"Don't get hung up on a poor choice of words. Think about this overnight and call me tomorrow. Reread the notes from Angela and imagine meeting her in person. Everything will fall into place if you put yourself under my guidance and protection. Trust me."

"I don't trust you for a second, Lieutenant."

He snorted, "Oh, really? I never told anyone what turned up in your background check two years ago, did I?"

"What?"

"Did I say anything to anyone? Huh? Even when you got weird a few months back, did I violate your privacy?"

"Not that I know of, sir."

"Well, I didn't. Think about it and call me in the morning."

"But I... damn!" she groaned when he hung up. She collapsed on the bed, shocked that Granger put a name to the animal's latest victim: Angela—a perfect name for an innocent little girl.

Laura yanked covers over her head, drifted off, and opened her eyes to darkness. When she recognized the voices in Steve's kitchen, she grabbed crutches and hopped to the bathroom to splash cold water against hot, clammy skin. She stared into bloodshot eyes and groaned, "Damn, you look like hell."

From behind, Steve whispered, "Hey, hi."

She hopped in a half-circle. "Hi yourself, mister."

He pulled her close. "You're trembling. Are you okay?"

"I feel sick to my stomach."

"Did they release you too soon?"

"Maybe but I needed to be with you."

"It feels like you have a fever. Go back to bed."

"Okay; will you lie down with me?"

"Later; your mother's in the kitchen and your father and Rick will arrive soon to help unload the truck. I'm sorry we woke you. Go back to sleep; we'll be quiet."

Laura choked, "I have something to tell you and…"

"We have loads of time to talk, kid. Tell me later."

6

Steve leaned against the counter, watched Lynette chop tomatoes for tacos. "I hope they didn't release Laura too soon. I was shot once and know the recovery is slow." He paused then groaned, "I'm an idiot! I forgot to fill her prescription and they only gave her enough painkillers for 24 hours." He grabbed his jacket and searched the pockets. "If she calls for me while I'm gone, tell her I love her."

"If you wait a little longer, John or Rick could go."

"Don't take this wrong but I need time alone: windows open, radio blasting, unlit cigarette dangling. I'm nuts from frustration."

At the shopping plaza, Steve paced until the pharmacist glanced over to suggest he consider other shopping. Steve headed outside, paced between the entrance and his car, and considered he hadn't had a cigarette in ages; surely under the circumstances one wouldn't hurt. But he promised Mickey and a promise was a promise. He yanked his cell phone out and tapped. "Gloria, Steve; did you get the gift I sent?"

"I did. I'm in the process of writing thank you notes. Did Ralph tell you Mark and I ran into him and Joyce last week?"

"No; I haven't talked to him in a while."

"I understand you'll be tying the knot pretty soon yourself. Wonderful—you and Laura are so good together."

"We think so, too."

"Isn't *we* a fantastic word?"

"Excuse me?"

"To describe Mark and me, you and Laura."

"Laura's recovering at my house. It's funny to see her clothes in my closet."

"I thought your house was off limits to women."

Steve rubbed his forehead. "I spent the last six weeks in Laura's hospital room watching her sleep, at the house trying to fall asleep, and in the car driving back and forth. All that alone-time is scary for someone like me; for chrissake, it's why I gave up fishing!"

"If you apologize one more time, I'll scream!"

"I was shitty to you, Gloria."

"It doesn't matter; you're where you are today because of where you were before. Me, too."

"Excuse me?"

"You wouldn't have appreciated her if you met at another time. When I recall the Sigler girl's wedding, I remember how you looked at Laura, how she looked at you, and how you hung on every word. I remember, too, on the dance floor you said you loved her without making a sound. Steve, you and I were good for each other, weren't we? We're better for having cared for one another, aren't we?"

"Gloria, don't feel embarrassed but I love you."

"I know; I feel the same about you."

"I think there's no one I could love more than Laura but..."

"Are you scared?"

"Sure; I can't afford mistakes this time."

"You'll make mistakes; so will Laura. You know, the evening before the shooting I saw Laura at the mall researching classic rock and country, trying to figure out your taste in music."

Steve sighed, "Be honest, does an asshole like me deserve her?"

"You do."

"Thanks, Gloria."

"Be happy. I know I will be."

Steve snapped the phone shut, picked up the prescription, and rushed home. He stopped at the truck where John and Rick lined boxes along the tailgate. "I'll be right back to help."

John shrugged, "Don't bother; we're managing fine."

Rick glanced sideways. "It's good to see you again."

Inside Steve sighed, "I thought John got past his anger."

Lynette shrugged, "John's not angry, just protective."

Steve apologized if the current living arrangement upset her family. "I hope you believe my intentions are honorable."

Lynette crossed the space and promised in no time at all, John would see him as clearly as Laura and she did. She hugged him hard. "Welcome to our dysfunctional family."

From behind, Laura giggled, "Right off a Norman Rockwell print, I swear."

Lynette rushed to help Laura to a chair. "Are you hungry?"

"I feel sick to my stomach; what I'd like is tea and toast."

At the table, Steve read the instructions, reported she should take two pills every six hours until they were gone, and apologized for not filling it earlier. "It's my fault you're in pain."

Laura mumbled, "You worry too much," and swayed.

When her eyes lost focus, Steve grabbed her before she hit the floor. "Lynette, call the hospital and see if fainting's normal." He headed to the bedroom and lowered her gently. "Please be okay, kid."

Laura bounced upright. "Help me to the bathroom!"

Lynette returned. "If she fainted, she needs to go back."

"I didn't faint!" Laura shouted and leaned over the toilet. "I'm sorry; this can't be attractive."

Steve helped her back to bed. "Who worries too much?"

"Toast and tea will help," Lynette said and left.

When Laura asked for help changing out of her now-soiled nightgown, Steve stood and said he'd get her mother, Laura argued but he said, "I intend to show respect for your father's discomfort, kid."

Laura giggled, "How Rockwellian of you; okay, get Mom."

7

Marsethe pulled an album off a shelf and thumbed through pages of his beloved as an infant, toddler, girl, pre-teen, and young woman. He lifted an edge of a plastic sleeve, slid in three additions, and admired Gilbert's skill with a new camera as he zoomed in on Laura's beatific face as she left the hospital, an expression of adoration for mangy Scolarzski. Marsethe studied her lover's face and sneered, "Enjoy her for now."

8

The shape floated along the ceiling. Hovered and swayed above. Undulated like a seahorse. Lifted the edge of the blanket and slithered underneath. Crept beneath silken nightwear and pressed full weight against her. Seared her skin with heat. Tore out tufts of hair by the roots. Rubbed her body with stinky... Laura shoved the beast off and opened her eyes to her mother's shocked expression.

"Do you want to talk about that nightmare?"

"No." Laura noticed tea and toast on the bedside table. "Ooh, raisin bread." She broke off chunks, slurped chamomile tea, and whispered an apology for being such a pig. "All of a sudden, I feel hungry." She pointed to a nightgown on a chair, lifted her dirty one, and watched her mother's reaction to bandages, bruises, and old scars. "Grotesque, aren't I?"

"Honey, no; I don't mean to stare and..."

Laura mumbled, "It doesn't matter. Help me stay awake. There's something I'd like to discuss while we're alone."

17

"What happened earlier? Could you be pregnant?"

Laura muttered, "That's unlikely and you know why. I'd like to dream I can but…um I'd like to discuss something else. Do you remember Lieutenant Granger?"

"Sure; he attended our dreadful party in March and came to the hospital a few times—cold, distant man, rude, too."

"He asked me to go undercover." When Lynette gasped, Laura shrugged, "I'll go ahead with my position with the law firm and can work out of their office in Fallsbridge for a while."

"What? Where?"

"This investigation's important to protect other unsuspecting children who come into contact with Marsethe or the CFEL."

Lynette gasped, "After everything that happened, why go back?"

"Working out of Fallsbridge would be temporary and in no time at all, I'd be back in Burlington."

Lynette's eyes filled with tears. "Honey, rethink this decision, please. Remember how it was to live there and…"

"I'm going to do this."

Lynette stood and paced. "If my feelings aren't important to you, consider how this affects Steve."

"It'll delay things; what I need is advice on how to tell him."

"Laura, he's so excited about the wedding and…"

"No; he's bored because of the suspension. Once he's back at work, he'll have other things to fill his time."

"You can't believe that! What kind of investigation's so important you risk hurting him this way?"

Laura looked away. "If you won't offer advice on how to discuss this with him, there's no reason for us to discuss it at all."

Lynette forced her to look back. "I deserve an answer."

"Mom, you can't know details." When her mother paced again, Laura closed her eyes and curled into the blankets. Lynette asked questions Laura pretended not to hear until she added, "Don't say anything to Dad or Steve. I'll tell them myself."

"This makes absolutely no sense and…"

Laura sneered, "I'm not 13 anymore! No one can tell me what to do this time! No one!"

"Honey, I'm frightened this will end things between…"

When Steve stuck his head around the door, Laura forced a shaky smile. "Please come here; I want to talk to you. Um Mom, don't you think Dad and Rick are hungry by now?"

After her mother left, Steve asked, "What's going on? You're both flushed and there's tension in the room."

"She still treats me like a kid."

Steve sat on the edge of the bed and chuckled, "You act like one sometimes. What did you want to say?"

She swallowed hard. "I want to postpone our wedding."

"Excuse me?"

"Um, only for a while until I…"

Steve stood. "Fuckin' Granger couldn't wait to give you his file!"

"You know what's in it?"

"Of course; when Granger heard we set a date, he made a point of saying you needed to hear what you're getting into. The son of a bitch didn't give me a chance to tell you myself."

"Um, I don't understand. He brought a sexual assault file and asked me to go undercover."

Steve snorted, "You're in no condition to go anywhere, kid. I'm not even working for him but that prick still mind-fucks me! I can't believe you let him waltz in and screw things up!"

Laura answered, "I can complete an investigation in three months—four tops and we can marry in September." When he kept his back to her, she stood and hopped over. When he reached out, she felt his ice-cold hands. "Steve, I'm sorry this hurts. I'd like to get married sooner but need to see something to conclusion, something that should've been resolved years ago." When he stayed silent, she offered to explain why the investigation felt critical to her.

"Are you sure it has nothing to do with me?"

"What could be so…?"

Steve interrupted if she went undercover, he couldn't hear details. She started to speak but he sshed her. "If you say we'll be married in the fall, we'll be married in the fall. Fill me in when it's over."

Laura ran her hand along his arm. "Will you come see me in Fallsbridge once in a while?"

He stood. "Need I remind you without consulting me you made a decision to work for Granger again? When you go, you go—period."

Laura climbed into bed. "Please hold me until I fall asleep."

"Nope," he grunted and slapped the light switch off.

Laura regretted her decision but believed in its necessity. Maybe if she showed Steve the contents of the file, he'd understand; maybe if he saw photographs of Angela after the first attack, he'd recognize the need to act soon. Laura imagined that's how their disagreements would always play out. He'd respond with bitter, distancing tactics and she'd slink off to hide. She pulled his pillow close. "I may regret it, but I'll stay."

She jumped at his voice: "Not necessary; I don't like your decision but support it." She noticed his shoulders drooped in the light of the doorway. "I'm sorry for my behavior whenever I feel cornered."

"I'm sorry, too. Come here, please; more than ever, I need your arms around me."

9

The weekend flew by. Ralph and Joyce brought Chinese on Friday night; Sunday evening, Lynette, John and Rick arrived with pizza, beer, soda, and DVDs. Steve watched Laura struggle to stay awake but she dozed off a dozen times. It felt great surrounded by people who viewed them as a couple. Once everyone left, Steve brushed his teeth and settled into bed. Laura touched his arm. "You're wearing pajamas. Don't you want to make love with me ever again?"

"Sure I do, but you've spent so much time in rehab, I..."

Laura moved so close he felt her heartbeat against his elbow. "My recovery isn't complete until we make love."

"We might hurt your back, kid."

Laura murmured "Maybe, maybe not but we won't know 'til we try." She unbuttoned his pajama top, caressed his skin, and laughed, "Do I have permission to take advantage of this body?"

He moved her hand aside carefully and rolled to the edge of the mattress. "Nope; neither one of us is ready, kid."

In the morning, Steve tried not to disturb her as he prepared for his first day back at work. It didn't work; she inched up behind as he shaved and wrapped her arms around his waist. "Excited?"

Steve smiled at her reflection in the mirror. "It's time to go back but I hate the idea of you here alone all day, kid."

Laura insisted she'd be fine and ran fingers along the towel at his waist. "It feels weird I won't be at my messy desk across from your even messier one. I suggest you avoid arguing with Granger; your suspension may be over but charges still stand; Wilkers' beating is on record so if you value your job, Sergeant, keep that temper under control."

"Yeah, I can kiss Granger's ass for the time being."

"That's not..."

He laughed he kidded, turned around, and drew her close. "Let's fly to Vegas and get married before you go; it wouldn't change anything. We could still plan a reception for September."

"Marriage would complicate what I need to do." She breathed deeply and sighed, "I'll miss everything about you—no, most everything."

"What won't you miss?"

"Your lack of faith in us."

"Excuse me?"

"Wanting to rush off means you think this is a passing fancy."

He buried his face in her hair. "You're probably right. We'll get married in September but I need to get going. I can't be late my first day back." Steve resumed shaving and asked how she wanted him to answer if Granger asked about her condition.

Laura shrugged, "Tell him after next week I won't be on crutches. And Steve? Today while you're at work, wherever you are and whatever you do, think of me?"

"As if I have a choice, kid."

Steve felt nervous on the way in; so much time had passed and so much had happened. Would he blend back in? He inched through the door into a familiar workspace and glanced around; how odd not to see Laura's coat, boots, teacup, or tote bag. Ralph grinned and rushed across the room, plopped into what once was Laura's chair and ran through a laundry list about what everyone was up to. "With Laura on medical leave and you suspended, Macrae, Sigler, Rawlings and I are up to our armpits in perversion—lots of the same sorry-assed crap." The others wandered over one by one, made raunchy comments, and poked fun. Steve noticed Macrae looked healthy again, fully recovered from his coronary; Sigler was tan after a recent vacation to the Barbados but he looked drained around the eyes, scared; Rawlings stood all duded up for a date after work. Steve thought despite how drastically his own life changed in seven weeks, nothing around the station had except Laura was missing. When the sky darkened, Steve's attention drifted outside as rain hit the window. He imagined Laura slept curled deep into the blankets, her hair against the pillow in the morning light. He heard the rain and shifted to Laura on the rug in front of the woodstove as she stared into flames. It was too warm for a fire and his thoughts shifted to an image of... He was distracted when Granger pounded on the glass window of his office, glared, and did that twirlagig thing in the air. The other detectives returned to their desks and Steve immersed himself in files: armed robbery, embezzlement, theft of services, kite-checking, fraudulent tax filing, pump-skipping, domestic assault, underage drinking, stalking, false ID trafficking, on and on and on and on. Though he tried to catch up on the current workloads of his colleagues to lighten the load, he couldn't stop thinking how disappointed he was with Ralph. Supposedly, partners and best friends kept in contact with one another. Steve grabbed his phone. "I was glad you and Joyce came over Friday but where were you the other six weeks?"

"With two out, we were crushed into 70-hour work weeks."

"A phone call or ten-minute visit would've been fine."

A sheepish grin across the space: "All right, buddy, here's the truth. One evening early on, Joycie and I stopped by the hospital with Ben 'n Jerry's Cherry Garcia. As we neared her room, I spotted Laura on the bed in a spiffy hot pink nightie while you drooled all over her. I was eager to spy but got scared my wife might catch a glimpse of you in action and not let me near her for months."

Steve smiled across the space. "Okay this time."

Steve hung up and sorted through active cases. At his elbow, Granger threw a file onto the blotter and sneered, "Your orgy with Delorange is over, Sergeant. Dig into the real world."

10

Mel listened to voices float around the restaurant. First, he overheard Vincent say Endress, Marschek & Furst hired an attorney to work full time in the office. Then Reilly reported Marschek asked her to increase secretarial support from 15 to 25 hours a week. Mel found the level of discussion curious and gestured for Glenn. "Since when does everyone care so much about the law office?"

Glenn refilled Mel's coffee and sat. "I'm surprised you didn't hear Bill Marschek hired Laura Delorange to expand his business."

Mel felt an odd, exhilarating sensation in his stomach. "How quickly He answered my prayer, yes?"

"What does this mean? Years ago, you promised."

Mel smiled slowly at Glenn's predictability and thought to remind the fool not many 36-year-old men postponed lives waiting for elusive rewards. Instead, he patted Glenn's hand. "The outcome depends solely upon your cooperation, yes? Now, call your brother. I need Gilbert to attend to the law office before our beloved returns home."

11

Laura grabbed crutches, hobbled out into the warm spring sun, and wandered the yard. In a shed behind the house, she found tools and plopped down among weeds to cultivate the flower bed. It was muddy from a short rain but she loved the smell of moist soil, decaying leaves, and moss. She found clippers and cut back the wild raspberry canes and weeds left from fall. After lunch and a short nap in the hammock, she inched up and down the basement stairs on her rear end, dragging the hose behind her into the garden. She collapsed on the ground and lifted the moist soil to her face. She heard rustling and turned to watch two fat blue-gray squirrels chomp on seeds she planted. Just as well. It was way too early to assume frost season was over in Vermont. She fell asleep surrounded by piles of mulch and woke when she heard a car door slam. Steve ran up. "Did you fall?"

"Hey, hi," Laura whispered, pulled her headphones off, and rubbed her arms. "No, I guess I fell asleep."

"Where the hell have you been? I called all afternoon!"

"Out here," she mumbled.

"This house is in the middle of god-damned nowhere! What you did was dangerous and irresponsible. Didn't you notice the light blinking on the answering machine?"

"No."

"Where's your cell phone?"

"Inside?"

"I worried when you didn't answer and Granger jumped on his high horse and had me review everyone's current case loads. I couldn't break away long enough to check on you."

"I thought it would be nice to get some fresh air."

Steve rubbed dirt off her face and pulled her close. "How in the world will I survive three months if I can't handle a single day?" He looked around. "Wow; everything looks great. I can't believe you did all this in one day. Are you exhausted?"

Laura admitted only a little because she took naps. "Will you drive me to a nursery? There are bare sections needing attention. It might be late to force bulbs but I can plant perennials to bloom all summer. If I mulch well, you won't have much trouble keeping up with the work until I come home."

Steve whispered, "I love your enthusiasm."

Laura admitted she never thought about what they'd eat for dinner and had no idea what was in the refrigerator. "Um, before we're married, you should know I'm a terrible cook and housekeeper. I don't notice things like groceries or bathtub rings. You won't believe how often I run out of toilet paper."

Steve laughed, "I'm not marrying you to cook, clean, or do toilet paper inventory. Want to go out for Chinese?"

"Great! Help me get cleaned up?"

Steve carried her into the house and stood outside the bathroom door while she went in to change. "Steve, what I really want is a shower; bathing at the sink with a face cloth isn't working." When he didn't take the hint, Laura opened the door and faced him naked. "Do you find my new scars repulsive?"

"Honey, nothing about you is repulsive to me."

"You know, I won't fall if you're in here, too."

Steve laughed, "Okay but under one condition: I do all the work and if you feel wobbly, we retire to the bedroom."

"Deal." Everything was perfect until she felt light-headed and gasped, "I'm about to fall." Steve lifted her out to carry her to the bed. As he dried her gently with a towel, Laura whispered, "Please enter me? Hold me so tight I can't breathe."

"Not yet," Steve murmured and knelt over her.

When he kissed her breasts then moved his tongue to her navel, she stiffened and shoved him off. "Don't do that."

"Excuse me?"

"Don't do anything disgusting."

He collapsed beside her. "Making love isn't disgusting."

"What you were about to do is."

"I thought it would give you pleasure. I'm sorry."

Laura felt tears, moved in behind him, and wrapped her arm around. "Please forgive my reaction but he did that to me and..."

"There's nothing to forgive; I understand."

Laura tugged on his shoulder until he rolled to face her. "Steve, when I upset you, talk to me; help me understand."

"I'm not upset but I am starving for affection."

"Mister, I can take care of that."

It was dusk when Laura opened her eyes again and heard him snore. She rolled onto her side and studied his profile; like always, if she concentrated, he woke up and mumbled, "Laura, are you awake?"

"I am. Someday I'll be ready to do what you wanted to do. Steve, I want you to know even when I push you away or cry, deep down I know you'd never do anything to hurt me."

"Honey, it takes time."

"What does?"

"Learning about and pleasing one another; besides, I feel very pleased right now. Laura, in the past I didn't think a woman deserved an orgasm every time."

24

"Oh."

"Does this kind of conversation bother you?"

"I know it's important to talk about but I'm bothered to think you have others to compare me to; am I a repressed prude?"

Against her ear, Steve whispered, "You're no prude. When we make love, your defenses are down and that's a new experience for me. I knew you'd be like this."

"Like what?"

"I told Keller I feared you'd open your soul to me, only to let you down."

"Only one thing could: if you stopped loving me."

"Never happen, kid."

Laura touched his chin. "I'll bet my face is bright pink from beard rash. In the car, I often studied your face as you drove. At the end of a shift, you had noticeable stubble and I wondered how it would feel against bare skin. When we were partners, mister, I felt chemistry."

"I felt it, too."

"Then why did it take so long to get together?"

Steve confessed from the beginning, he felt confused and ignored how he felt. "Something else stood in the way; I figured out why the lieutenant put us together and hated the truth. Granger could've picked Sigler, a peacock who would've put moves on the first day; or Barber, whose wife would've been in the office in five seconds flat once she got a look at Laura; or Macrae, who couldn't fart without Sigler telling him where to point his ass. And last but not least Bobby, a total jerk."

"That doesn't explain why Granger picked you."

Steve shrugged, "Process of elimination? Granger guessed a new detective could learn something from this ugly bag of shit; more to the point? He didn't think I'd appeal to you."

"And all that time I thought you saw me as a kid."

"That was acting. Okay, your turn to explain what took so long to reach the inevitable."

"Your experience."

"Excuse me?"

"I observed a mature man, a police officer with incredible skills, and most of all, a man successful with women."

Steve chuckled, "Yeah, I forget about the hordes who line up in my driveway, rip clothes off, and demand attention."

Laura argued his relationship with Stephanie Orsini developed quickly. "Scary to watch, mister."

Steve confessed he was heavy into denial then. "How could I fall in love with my partner? Such feelings are inappropriate for the reality of our work. Plus I couldn't believe you weren't thinking *Here comes good ole Stevie boy my fat, sloppy, disgusting slug of a partner.* Anyone you set your sights on will come running. There are men out there—better-looking and closer to your age—who can offer more."

Laura sighed, "When I come home, let's visit Arlene Keller and learn how to live together."

"We do fine together, kid."

"Do we? We say we want to be together and take little steps then push each other away when we're scared or confused. Why do we only let the guard down when we make love?"

"I'll visit the lady doc with you any day of our lives."

Laura felt herself drift toward sleep; Steve's breathing changed, too, and she imagined they might forget dinner altogether. Laura felt warm, too warm. She kicked the blanket off and covered her face with the sheet. He was there—the hideous creature, the disgusting monster, the freak, the beast with the eerily familiar odor. Weird, but her mother was there, too, as Lynette calmly explained menstruation to her 12-year-old daughter. It lasted too long—that first time—too heavy, too thick. Her mother insisted they visit the doctor to make sure. With her mother a few feet away, Dr. Marsethe touched everywhere, prodded and poked cold things inside, and finally assured mother and daughter everything developed normally. After polite conversation, Marsethe asked Laura to read to his bedridden wife—not the first time the girl served as a companion to a lonely woman left partially paralyzed after an automobile accident, but it was the last. An hour after her mother left, Marsethe came upstairs, checked on his sleeping wife, and whispered *"Little Miss Laurette Marie, you have become quite the remarkable specimen."* The doctor's blue eyes sparkled as he took her by the hand and led her downstairs to a parlor. Pale late afternoon sunlight sparkled on fresh snow while Classical music played in the background softly. His hushed voice confessed *"I shall select your first lover soon but now you shall learn what to expect."* He closed the curtains and turned off the lamp. He lifted her sweater over her head and unhooked her beginner's bra. Nothing strange: he did those things with her mother there. He edged her slip to her waist and with one hand, touched her breast. Not strange, either: he did those things with her mother there. He slipped his other hand under her skirt and worked her panties off slowly. Not strange at all: he did all those things with her mother right there. He drew her onto his lap, spread her knees apart

26

gently and touched her in ways that felt terrifying yet exciting, very different from when her mother was there. He whispered, *"The Lord directs my work and I accept His truth: this gift of you is not mine to receive."* In the near-dark room, he demanded she stand in front. She did as ordered and watched him unzip and lower his pants; she noticed a glint of silver as coin fell from a pocket and rolled under a curtain. His voice soothed as he knelt in front, guided her onto her back on the couch, and choked, *"Dear God, forgive me for this love I feel."* When he lowered his face between her legs, she flinched and he whispered *"I can feel how much you want this."* She watched his arm move sideways, felt his body sweat, and heard heavy breathing. When she asked what he did, he choked, *"Ssh, my sweet little miss. There's no need to fear my adoration."* In response to an unexpected surge of something unknown, Laura screamed. Marsethe loosened his grasp on her breast, pressed lips to her wet cheek, and promised, *"From this day forward, only the finest shall avail himself of your elegance."* It took hours to find words to describe what happened. Laura felt unprepared for the swift round of questions from people she didn't know, unprepared for the way her brother Jack avoided her, and unprepared for her father's anger and increasing distance whenever she sought his affection.

Months later on her birthday, the ogre visited in the dark of night, snuck into her bedroom, and silenced her—gained acquiescence—with a knife to her throat. She felt fingertips on her face and slashed the air with her fists. "Don't touch me!" Yanked into a sitting position, she choked, "Get your hands off me, you stupid fuck!"

She heard the lamp switch and saw Steve. "It's me."

"I had that nightmare, the one where he..."

"Please tell me you don't mean *he* as in me."

"Never you, no," Laura choked. "Steve, there's something I have to tell you, something shameful, a secret perhaps best kept—a secret I never told a living soul, not even my mother or friend, Maureen."

Steve smiled. "Honey, you don't have to..."

Laura shuddered, "But I do," and confessed the first time, she didn't fight back. "It felt unfamiliar but exciting; I had an orgasm."

"What first time?"

"Months before the rape, we were alone in his parlor. I didn't know about sex and when he touched me, I liked the way it..."

Steve tugged her closer. "Don't do this to yourself."

Laura collapsed on her pillow. "The molestation charge failed for lack of evidence so it's no wonder everyone suspected in retaliation, I lied about who raped me."

Steve's calmly answered, "From the moment of conception, humans are sexual beings. I believe God gave us a gift to share with the one we love. Some people pervert everything that's beautiful about…"

Laura opened her eyes. "What?"

"God made humans curious, too, and you were curious. Laura, he was an adult—the one who should know right from wrong. It's time you forgive yourself for being human like the rest of us."

Laura felt stunned by his response. "Oh."

Steve headed to the closet, took out a guitar, and returned to sit on the edge of the bed. I have my own secrets, Laura. Years ago, I made huge mistakes, got involved with lowlifes, and allowed lapses in judgment to affect my work. I became a person even I didn't recognize. I wanted to create music but the farther I sank, the worse the music sounded."

Laura stared at the guitar. "I know a little bit about that. Roger gave me some stuff about *Rock-It*. You guys weren't bad."

Steve chuckled. "*Rock-It?* What a bunch of tone-deaf losers Mickey found fantastic. I loved to sing to him at bedtime but after Denise died, I shoved the guitar into a closet until a few months ago when I played for Billy Fellowes. Why the hell do I tell you shit like this? In light of what you just told me, I'm sorry I'm too dense to…."

"Sing for me?"

Steve's hands trembled and he started over a few times before he sounded comfortable. Scratchy at the outset, his voice cleared and his body relaxed. She knew within seconds he picked *Shelter Me* and hummed along. At the end, he sounded more confident when he finished, "*Every time I tumble out I wanna pack it up and leave this town but when I finally get the nerve to get the lead out of my shoes, I thank you, I thank you.*" Steve lowered the guitar to his lap. "That was okay, I hope."

"Better than okay and I love the fact you picked that song! Even though I always said I hated it, you knew I didn't."

Laura asked what kind of songs he sang for Mickey and Steve confessed, "For years at bedtime I sang Mickey to sleep. When he started kindergarten, he heard from older boys fathers didn't sing lullabies ever but most definitely not to boys. In any event, I didn't sing Joe Cocker. *Sesame Street* mostly and sometimes John Denver songs, like *Sunshine on My Shoulders,* Mickey's favorite."

"Can you do *It's Not Easy Bein' Green?* That was my favorite!"

"God, I'm such an old man compared to…"

Laura drew his face to hers. "Come on; kiss me and prove how young you are, mister."

Afterward Laura woke in the dark, felt around in the dark, amazed at how customary it felt to share a bed with a man, to encourage and initiate physical contact, to crave his touch. Her vision adjusted and she saw light in the hallway. She heard the soft, familiar music of Sam Cooke, grabbed crutches, and rose to a shaky stand. She figured if she hurried, she'd make it to the living room and ask him to dance before *That's Where It's At* started. Laura pulled her robe on and tugged the belt tight. Halfway down the hallway, she heard him say, "She's sleeping and it's past time to..." When she moved into his line of vision, Steve mumbled he had to go and hung up.

"Were you talking to a woman?"

Steve kissed the top of her head and chuckled, "No but your hair's pretty tangled, kid. Want me to brush it?"

"I don't care about my hair. Who were you talking to with such obvious affection?" Steve grinned maliciously before he explained while she slept he went out for Chinese then invited Mickey to join them. Laura felt the flush. "I'll dress before he gets here."

Steve followed her into the bedroom and offered to fix her hair. She sat in a chair and as he brushed, felt how his touch brought heat to her face. "Um, I won't mind if you messed it up again."

"I'm too old for so much temptation in one day; woman, dress before I collapse from heart failure!"

"Eat hearty, mister; I need you robust later."

12

Mick watched Laura's eyes follow every move his father made: take plates down and load them with flair: Moo shu Pork, General Tso's Chicken, Pepper & Onion Beef, spring rolls, and fried rice. He even served tea steeped in a small white pot. Laura dug in. "Moo Shu's my favorite and I love you used my Mèmère's teapot! You spoil us!"

Mick dug in, too. "Mmm, most days, I survive on macaroni and cheese, hot dogs, or Ramen noodles."

Laura laughed, "Join us more often."

Mick glanced from one to the other. "Do you live together?"

His father nodded. "How do you feel about it?"

"Great! You guys belong together.'"

Laura answered, "We plan a wedding for September even though we'd like it to be sooner. I need to finish an investigation."

Mick frowned. "Something dangerous?"

"No, not at all," Laura insisted.

"Isn't that what everyone thought about Orsini?"

Laura squeezed his father's hand. "Not like that at all."

After dinner, they sat in the living room to talk and Mick studied them side by side on the couch, and as they spoke, frequently touched. When his father leaned close for a kiss, Mick announced, "Time to go." His father followed to ask if he needed money for groceries and Mick grumbled, "You gave me money last week, I work part time, and appreciate being treated like an adult."

"All right, just trying to..."

"How can you allow an investigation to delay things?"

"Laura will be gone for a few months; keep that to yourself."

"Mom got killed by someone you investigated and last month, that crazy Orsini woman shot Laura. Dad, is this okay with you?"

His father glanced at a window. "I have no choice but learn to accept decisions made by someone else, decisions I disagree with, decisions that wake me in the middle of the night in a cold sweat."

"Dad, I want the best for you and Laura now, not in some distant, dim, and blurry future no one has a right to expect!"

His father drew him close. "It hurts to know you went through such hell with your mother's death but Laura said we'd grow old together and I'll hold her to that promise."

Mick pulled back. "Dad, it felt good watching the two of you tonight. I didn't feel uncomfortable at all. I know what it means when a man and woman touch all the time; 19-year-olds aren't the only ones who can't keep their hands off who they desire."

His father smiled. "And that reality's okay with you?"

"Yeah, you're too old to cruise the bars."

His father nodded yet started his customary cop routine. "Tell me what else is on your mind. I know there's more."

"Someone's making moves but I don't know what to do next; watching you and Laura helps me see it's not enough to be horny; there should be genuine feeling. Do you mind me talking like this?"

"Not at all; keep going."

"I want my first experience to be more than sex and wait for something like I witnessed tonight but decades before I'm 43."

"Yeah, well, some idiots take forever; describe your feelings."

"How do I feel? About her or what might happen?"

"Either. Both. Be honest."

Mick shrugged they had fun together but he got distracted by her body. "In her dorm room when her roommate's out, she pushes me onto the couch and climbs all over me. I suspect she enjoys teasing me like that and last night, said I don't have to hold back but...."

His father put his arm around Mick's shoulders. "Two concerns come to mind: first, the world's full of sexually transmitted diseases, so protect yourself; second, I suspect you're a man who prefers to be in love to make love and that kind of sensitivity might mean you make a mistake like marry too young or marry the wrong person."

Mick mumbled, "You loved my mother, right?"

"Very much, but she never loved me."

Mick began to argue but stopped when Laura slid the patio door open. "You guys can talk in here; I won't eavesdrop."

"I'm late getting Rudy's car back but have another question: What's your opinion of sex before marriage?"

His father nodded. "Under the circumstances, it's absurd to say I disapprove but do. I made mistakes over the years, too many to claim to have answers yet feel married to Laura and as soon as possible, will see our relationship has a legal foundation. I won't presume to tell anyone else what's right or wrong since God knows how often I engaged in sex solely for release. I loved Laura for two years before we were intimate. To be honest, this time it doesn't feel tainted; this time, it feels perfect."

Mick jumped into the car and leaned out the window. "Mom loved you. She told me that night she... that night we went to buy the Christmas tree." As his father smiled sadly, Mick pulled away and recalled it snowed the night his mother died—big, fat flakes he loved to catch on his tongue. As she drove, his mother said, "*I love your father and know this will be hard to understand but by summer we'll live in New York with Uncle Michael and you'll have a new brother or sister.*"

He screamed, "*I hate Uncle Michael and I hate you! No one can make me leave my Daddy.*" Twelve years later, Mick recalled the look on her face, rubbed tears away, and felt a stinging shame how within hours she died and never knew he hadn't meant to shock her.

13

Steve slid the patio door shut and found Laura curled up on the couch asleep. He carried her to the bedroom and tucked a blanket under her chin; in the light from the hallway, he studied her face and prayed she'd love him forever. Heaven knew it was easy not to. He settled on the floor, rested against the wall, and recalled what Mickey said—wrong, definitely. Denise never loved her husband. In fact, he never figured out why she married him in the first place. Steve stared at how young Laura looked, how beautiful. As difficult as it was for him to figure out Denise's attachment, what was Laura's? Beautiful, cultured, and educated, why did a sexy young woman with a law degree tie herself to an over-the-hill cop with barely more than a high school education? Steve closed his eyes and thought, *Shit, you were one dumb kid.* After high school, he believed he accomplished something. While others in his class went places and did things, he felt content to spend the summer as bull-man helping drivers deliver cases of beverages to touristy stores in the Lake Champlain Islands. He turned 18, got muscular, registered for the draft, worked on a tan, got drunk most nights, and got laid on occasion. Frankly, not much else seemed to matter. Night after night, even if he straggled in at 2:00 AM, Steve found his father on the porch, beer can in hand, cigarette lit. They talked, laughed, drank, and smoked together but it soon became apparent Old Max expected his third son to aim higher. Slowly but surely between June and August, his father worked him over good so that by the time Amy headed off to college, it seemed fitting that he, too, head off for something new, different, or challenging. He pictured himself that summer he turned 18: not a bad-looking kid, really, but not bright. He spent too much on beer and cigarettes and borrowed his brother's car so often he had to keep it filled with gas and pay half the insurance.

One hot August night, Steve and Amy went to dinner on her last night before leaving for college. He cruised along familiar back roads in Westford in search of pitch darkness to alleviate her fears of getting caught with pants down around their ankles. He drove alongside acres of corn searching for a dirt road he knew was there. He watched Amy struggle to lift her dress over her head and hoped the road appeared soon. For the first time, Amy took everything off—everything—shoes, dress, stockings, bra, and underpants. She knelt on the passenger seat, twisted her necklace between her fingers, and moved her hips seductively in rhythm to her favorite song on the radio: Whitesnake's *Is It Love?* In the light from the dashboard, he watched her gyrations and felt himself respond. The dirt road came up fast and Steve turned into it without braking. Through cornstalks, the car crashed and finally stopped. Amy laughed, jumped out, and ran naked around the vehicle. In front of the headlights, she caressed her body and taunted him mercilessly to get out there fast. That hot August night, they felt like adults: the stimulus of their first encounter totally naked, the intensity of a first unrushed encounter. With bodies locked together, they rolled in cool, damp soil and savored the ripe odor of crops, humidity, and each other. No sleep. Very little conversation except when Amy called it their *nightlong love fest.*

As faint daylight skimmed mountaintops to the east, Steve opened his eyes and studied flattened cornstalks and clothes strewn in every direction. He imagined a farmer coming upon them unexpectedly and thinking he discovered a scene out of a pornographic movie. Steve tried but couldn't look Amy in the eye; he tried but couldn't budge the car, either. He discovered the problem: a flat tire and bent wheel rim and hiked to a nearby farmhouse to call a tow truck. With a tire and rim destroyed and damage to the front axle, the episode proved costly: five weeks' pay for the car repairs, a long, silent taxi ride from Westford to Amy's house in Burlington, face to face humiliation with her parents, and a phone call to his father for a ride home. He still heard Old Max's fury on the phone and tirade in the car as the old man lost all semblance of control when during the course of a heated argument he learned his son never used condoms.

Six hours later, Amy left for Indiana with Steve as an unwelcome guest at the bus station. He tried to blend into the background as Amy kissed her family goodbye. With her father's undisguised anger as a backdrop, Amy approached Steve. *"Christmas isn't that far off. Wait for me?"* He accepted her light kiss, stuffed his hands in his pockets, and nodded. That night, Steve got pulled over for speeding, the car reeking of pot. He failed a sobriety test, too, and because of his confusion over the transition in the legal drinking age that summer, during his arraignment in court the next morning, he actually heard his own voice agree to enlist in exchange for a clean record. By the time Amy returned to Vermont in December, Steve was long gone. He never responded to the letters his mother forwarded, either; in all honesty, he never bothered to read them.

Steve choked, "Scolarzski, you can be one cruel shit."

A gasped, "Can you feel how much I love you?"

Steve turned and saw terror in Laura's eyes. "You okay, kid?"

"I hate to see you sink that far inside and leave me."

Steve reached over. "I'm with you; I always will be."

"I love the sound of that," she muttered and drifted off.

Old Max suggested the Marines but his brother Tony pushed for the Air Force. Steve made the rounds of recruiters, listened to their spiels, and figured one branch equal to another. Besides, the Army put its guarantee in writing: *join up and learn a life-long career.* He took a battery of tests, trained for the military police, and spent the first three of a four-year enlistment in Germany. Not too horrible: he ran servicemen out of bars and brothels, broke up fights, lectured wife beaters, confiscated illegal substances, drove big-shot visitors around, and did favors for his colonel. He controlled his social life, too—the only nod to vice? Two packs a day. On his third anniversary in the military, Steve earned a promotion to buck sergeant. Not bad for a kid who still didn't need to shave every day. As he passed the stripes, his colonel shared a piece of advice: *"When you slip into that uniform, others see you as an authority figure and maintaining that illusion is always within your control."* That particular truth set up a distance between him and the regulars and in a way, helped him keep his own self-destructive tendencies at bay.

It all seemed simple, predictable, until on the first Friday night of each month, little girls disappeared. Month after month for seven months, girls disappeared from the town just off-post. Local police discovered footprints from an Army-issue boot under each girl's bedroom window and Steve found himself on unfamiliar ground participating in a highly-visible investigation on foreign soil, engaged in a public relations nightmare with local police, and with the exception of seven separate but matching plaster casts, came up with one inconclusive piece of evidence after another. During an unrelated search for drugs in a post warehouse, he discovered photographic plates, a printing press, assorted pornographic prints, and pamphlets featuring little girls. For weeks, he spent nights sleeping in his jeep near the warehouse to study patterns.

Steve approached his commanding officer to outline a theory and described a captain's comings and goings, access to warehouse off-hours, frequent visits to dive bars, and one unprosecuted complaint of assault on a town resident. His CO listened politely to additional facts concerning seven unlabeled film masters featuring children who died at the end. Steve finished, "I believe there's too much evidence to be a coincidence and request permission to have an authority on facial recognition compare photographs of the missing girls to terrified faces captured forever on film. I suspect these snuff films are copied and distributed to..."

His colonel interrupted, "Thank you for your thoroughness," and bundled evidence in an envelope. "It's unwise to jump to conclusions so I'll take it from here; don't discuss it until I give the green light." He shook Steve's hand, saluted him, and within 48 hours, signed his sergeant's transfer orders back to the States.

Steve jumped when Laura touched his shoulder. "Scolarzski, even when you're silent I can hear you scream."

"Kid, ever regret not fighting back about something?"
"Sure."

"Ever had an answer and let someone bury a question?"
She sat up. "I don't understand."

"Sorry I woke you; go back to sleep."

"I'm wide awake," she answered and joined him on the floor.

Steve appreciated her tender touches but when she unbuttoned his shirt, he grabbed her wrist. "Don't; I'm in no mood for this right now." As Laura climbed back into bed, Steve whispered, "The truth is the way I feel at this moment, I couldn't finish."

She laughed, "That's macho bullshit, mister. Why can't you understand it's not the sex I crave but your closeness?"

14

Mel cleaned out the secretary's desk and closet shelves. Gil warned when records were kept on paper, high and mighties with search warrants waited in the wings to confiscate them. For weeks, Mel spent four hours a day scanning paper onto rewriteable CD. He hated computers but Gil claimed digital data stored safely, CDs took up less room, with data encrypted. After hours of concentrated effort, Mel started a fire in the woodstove and tossed in crumpled pieces of paper that broke into chunks, floated up the chimney, and drifted into the wind. He watched red detritus shift and sway and noticed a dark sedan parked nearby. Mel chuckled, "Nice to know where you are, Sergeant Wilkers."

15

Steve felt tired, crawled into bed, and smiled when Laura curled in behind to sigh, "Promise you'll always be faithful to what we share."

"Too easy, kid. Ask something hard."

"Promise you won't worry while I'm gone?"

Steve chuckled, "I promise to try," and felt amazed at how it felt with Laura behind him. She called their sleeping pattern *nested together* and in a way, it felt like they held a diseased world at bay to find refuge in each other's arms.

Laura murmured, "Doesn't your mind give you a moment's peace?" and he chuckled at how often she seemed able to read his. Her breathing slowed and Steve's mind raced again. Between assignments in Germany and Lebanon, he returned to Vermont for nine days' leave. On the evening before he flew out again, he and his father relaxed on the porch. Old Max listened patiently to Steve's descriptions of the case, the conversation with the colonel, the hasty transfer. Old Max laughed it wasn't as if his son didn't hear the rules of the game in advance: *Maintain the illusion*. Steve learned the hard way his father was right: sometimes an illusion of honesty, character, love, fidelity, friendship, and competence was better in the long run than truth. The colonel knew it was too risky—in terms of army PR—to have some snot-nosed kid MP ruin the life of a career officer. And Denise knew how to play a role, too—she pulled her stunts year after year, kept a husband by her side and a lover in her bed, and lied about who Mickey's father was to one of them.

Laura shifted gently and he pulled her hand to his lips; he decided no matter how difficult it might be at times, he'd always be honest with her. He stared at the digital clock on the bedside table; in six hours, he had to be at work. The more he worried and the longer he stared at the clock, the less likely he'd fall asleep. The key was to imagine sunrises over the Green Mountains and sunsets over the Adirondacks. The key was to remember the look in her eyes when they made love earlier. The key was to look at Mickey and see a piece of himself, his brother Michael, Denise, his mother, and of course, Old Max. Steve pictured his father's face as he lay in wake at the funeral home. Only the weekend before, they talked like old times on the porch, beer cans in hand, butts dangling. Mickey was little then, barely able to talk, and Old Max grabbed, tickled, hugged, and kissed. Yet as soon as Mickey squirmed free and ran off, Old Max started up about Korea and dysentery and frostbite and shell shock and... When Steve started to interrupt, the old man choked, "Foolish boy! We heal when we talk and listen!"

Laura rolled over and snuggled against his chest. Her hair fell across his arm like a ribbon of black and he smoothed it, curled it around his fingers, breathed in its clean scent. In that position, its straightness, its glossy shine reminded him of women in Lebanon. His tour of duty was supposed to be easy: a United Nations peace-keeping effort which turned out to be fitting punishment for an eager MP who failed to grasp the difference between commanders and commanded. For the first few months, Steve had a fairly easy go with much the same responsibilities as Germany: he ran kids his own age or younger out of bars, tracked black market deals, arrested drug dealers and users. His new commanding officer was a 24-year career MP who demanded and got Steve's respect who felt shocked—devastated, actually—when in a car together one evening, the colonel pointed to a girl on a corner and ordered the sergeant to pick her up and bring her to his quarters. Steve found himself boxed into a corner: *Do the right thing and get smacked. Do the right thing and be replaced by someone who follows orders.* Steve did the right thing, ignored the order and that time, felt no surprise at the speed of his transfer from the relative safety of Beirut to a real toilet out in the middle of nowhere where all kinds of kids got themselves into dirty trouble.

Steve found it ironic that unlike Old Max—with his horror stories from Korea or his older brother Tony's from Vietnam—Steve served in a so-called peacetime army. He pushed his memories to the back of his mind but from time to time, they floated back to the surface like shit in a toilet bowl. When he saw a therapist regularly, the doctor suggested he talk about his years in the military as if talking helped. Steve knew humans didn't forget crap, knew images surfaced in other ways at the worst possible times, knew horrible memories could drive a man crazy slowly, knew anger and pain could push themselves out sideways, and knew he couldn't talk about it without re-experiencing pain. Who consciously set themselves up like that? His experiences became a part of his life. When he recalled his time in the service, the feelings came fast— that overpowering sense of separateness, loss of everything familiar, and loneliness. When he heard about readjustment problems for veterans, he thought: *No shit!* He could've written a textbook about the kinds of problems kids would have; he had them and unlike his brother Tony, he never patrolled the jungle or ran body bags out by helicopter. Compared to so many others, his tours of duty were a tropical paradise.

Laura shifted. "Hawaii's nice for a honeymoon."

Steve laughed, "How can you say you can't read my mind?"

"Can we?"

"I'd walk barefoot through broken glass to visit the town dump with you."

She laughed and flicked the lamp on. Steve watched her pupils dilate in that funny way they did when she felt frightened. "Talk about what's bothering you. Don't keep me at a distance."

Steve told her everything: selfishness with Amy, poor choices and rotten behavior, loveless encounters, memories of the military, shame about his attitude toward his father's need to talk, need to love and be loved, and finally the two toughest of all: fear Mickey was not his son and his gift of his heart and soul to a wife who never loved him.

Laura listened without comment and Steve feared she felt overwhelmed until she asked, "Why is everything your fault?"

"Excuse me?"

"For one thing, Denise lacked something essential: integrity."

"I won't go through life making excuses or blaming others. I pushed her into an affair with my brother."

Laura laughed, "More macho bullshit! A wife leaves a husband before betraying him like that. You have a problem—you think you should fix everything that goes wrong but not that long ago, you gave excellent advice: *forgive yourself for being human like the rest of us.*" Steve whispered his thanks, amazed at how easily sleep came once she turned the light off and assumed the nested position.

16

Ed grabbed the phone. "It's 3:00 AM; this better be urgent!"

"It's Wilkers. Something weird happening. First, the old man sounded excited—not suspicious—about news of Laura's return. I overheard Marsethe tell one of his cronies Laura's return is God's will and now he's burning a shit load of paper in his fireplace. It's May for god's sake! I'm convinced he's destroying evidence about how the CFEL spent its first 40 years. When the hell does Delorange get here?"

"It's time I get a commitment."

"I hope soon because Marsethe's house is lit up like a Christmas tree, chimney's flinging secrets into the wind."

17

When Granger announced he'd meet with Delorange the next morning to discuss a schedule, Ralph felt his stomach jump to the flutters. *Heavens, will she really come back?* He missed the little lady something awful—her junky desk, colorful clothes, flushed face, stinky tea, dedication to work, wide smile, style, and astounding class. Ralph made a point of arriving early to watch the show. Granger rushed in late, tossed a bag of bagels on the table by the coffeemaker, and snarled, "Keep your hands off until Delorange picks hers!"

Ralph hooted, "With company coming, Ma, should I dust?"

"Screw you," Granger said and slammed his office door.

Ralph turned to Steve. "How's the little lady doing?" His best buddy ignored him to straighten clutter and Ralph persisted with, "You okay inside that screamin' mind 'o yours, podna?"

"Yup, peachy keen."

"When'll she be back for good?" At a shrug, Ralph persisted. "Will she really marry a freak like you?"

For the first time, Steve made eye contact. "She says she will and I'll hold her to that promise."

"Am I invited or are you scared I'll snatch her away at the altar?"

Finally a smile: "I'd like you to be my best man."

"I accept your proposal!"

Ralph checked Granger's schedule, noted the little lady due at 9:00, and smiled when Laura arrived a few minutes early to glance around nervously; she shifted into a sweet smile when her sexy brown eyes found Steve. She inched up beside his chair and pinched his elbow. When the other guys noticed and greeted her, Laura laughed, "Wow, I've missed you guys—even you, Bobby."

Ralph barged over and grabbed. "You are one sight for tired eyes." When he felt her stiffen, Ralph pulled back. "Sorry."

"I'll survive but next time, don't squeeze."

Ralph drew her close again but gently. "This loser Polack has no idea how…"

Granger threw his door open. "Gentlemen, is it prom night?" The ass-wipe crossed the room, took Laura's arm, and like always broke fun stuff up and hogged the guest of honor all to himself.

18

Laura followed the lieutenant into his office and once seated, scanned a file he handed her. "It's strange to be here, sir."

"As a civilian?"

"Am I, officially?"

"Yup; off my payroll Friday, on Marschek's Monday."

Laura took a deep breath. "Sir, I don't know if…"

"Call me Ed. Thanks for agreeing to work on the investigation. It says a lot about dedication." Laura listened patiently for ten minutes as he ran through a deluge of details: a secretary worked part time in a two-room office with modern amenities: a FAX, two PCs, a photocopier, and an air conditioner. "It's the Northeast Kingdom so there's only dial-up technology. Bill says it's slow as molasses in other ways, too, with an assortment of ongoing work: real estate closings, wills, guardianships, DWI, and zoning disputes. You're expected Monday."

"So soon?"

"Shit, the sooner it starts, the sooner it finishes! Wilkers says it'll be easy. Marsethe will come to you."

"Why would he do that, sir?"

Granger took the file from her hands, skimmed through, and pointed to a psychologist's report. "Marsethe has an ego the size of Quebec so be yourself and he'll come around."

Laura laughed, "Me—what exactly does that mean?"

Granger shrugged, "What's to understand?"

"A former cop employed by a Burlington law firm expanding across the state, parking her ass in a village of holy rollers and perverts, waiting for some slime ball to hit on her?"

Granger grinned. "Try this: a former cop shot by a murder suspect she investigated illegally, a woman who decided in comparison to law enforcement a small-town law practice felt safe, a former member who returned to the fold. Have you found a place to live?"

Laura explained her parents never sold the house she grew up in and rented it to the academy for its headmaster. "There's a carriage house out back where my brother and I played school. My mother arranged for someone to get it ready."

After a silence, Granger asked, "Where's your mind?"

"Um, wondering where my fiancé fits in, sir."

"For the sake of honest disclosure, it won't hurt to confess two cops rolled around on the mattress, an escapade that split them apart and destroyed a work relationship." Granger leaned forward. "But that piece of shit out there will not go within 50 miles of Fallsbridge or I'll have his shield. The woman who heads up there will not be encumbered by a maniac. What does Scolarzski already know?"

"Steve doesn't know a thing."

Granger lifted her left hand and ran his thumb across her engagement ring. "Break it off before you go."

"Sir, I don't think you have any right to…"

"Look out through the glass."

She turned and saw five curious faces. "So?"

"Why would a woman engaged to be married leave town? Why go more than 130 miles across state into the middle of nowhere? What would they guess?" When Laura remained silent, Granger laughed, "Come on, your wounds didn't leave you suddenly stupid!"

"I honestly don't know, sir."

"Sure you do! The minds of my detectives twirl a mile a minute and they'll figure out you're on assignment unless they think you ran away with a broken heart. Leave clean."

Laura closed her eyes. "I won't do that to Steve."

"Unless I see you here at your desk Monday morning, you head up there unattached. End of discussion."

19

First Bernard then Roland called Mel with news their mother's health declined. For months one after another called to seek professional advice and Mel repeated the same: "She's 84, for heaven's sake. For everyone's peace of mind, move her out of that drafty house." That wasn't enough; those cretins wanted him there to attend to details. He refused to go back; he escaped once, more than enough. They would learn to accept his distance, figuratively and literally. When Yvonne called, Mel felt stunned by his siblings' combined efforts to control the only child with sufficient funds to provide long-term care. "Arrange for a beautiful room in a respected facility, yes? As always, I'll cover expenses." He hung up with a sad realization such efforts made little difference to one who no longer noticed what went on around her.

20

Steve watched Laura struggle silently with her decision. As days passed, she said little about her meeting with Granger and to avoid putting her on the defensive, Steve waited patiently for the inevitable conversation. The following Saturday she brought him breakfast in bed and he chuckled, "You're leaving after this weekend." When he saw her startled look, he shrugged, "It doesn't take decades of police experience to put two and two together: your meeting with Granger, heavy sighs, sleepless nights, verbal silence, and sudden lack of interest in sex."

"I lied to Granger when I said you knew nothing."

"That's true."

"You know I'll be working in a law office in Fallsbridge, a lot for a detective like you to know but I have a favor to ask."

"Depends on what it is, kid."

She avoided eye contact. "Granger insisted I break the engagement." Steve started to argue but Laura pinched his chin. "Wait; there are two predictable Scolarzski reactions to anger or stress. First: you go off the wall for days and pommel anything that moves or breathes; or second: you go silent and snarl at anything that moves or breathes. People figure it out without you saying a word."

Steve considered her scenario. "I like it—an excuse to be the complete asshole they think I am; I can beat the shit out of Granger."

Laura lifted a piece of bacon and stuffed it in his mouth. "Hands off the lieutenant; he'll be my official contact."

Steve grinned and chewed but the seriousness of her decision hit. "Are you really going through with this, kid?"

"I promise I'll be back soon."

Laura left to get the newspaper and he noticed her nightgown in a heap at the foot of the bed. He'd miss her casual sloppiness, easy style, voice, but most of all, soothing presence. Later in the day Steve relaxed on the porch and pretended to read the paper while Laura weeded the garden. When he got caught staring, she smiled and waved. He pulled sunglasses on to mask worried eyes, scanned the automobile section, and studied her car, and decided his soon-to-be wife needed the best even if that meant she used new wheels to put miles between them. He went inside, brought out a glass of iced tea for her and cup of coffee for him. He lifted her glass in the air and she wandered over to join him. Steve lifted the newspaper section. "I've been thinking since I have a truck, you could take the Chevy or think about something new,"

She scanned the ads. "I appreciate the thought but this can wait until I'm back. It seems like a decision a married couple makes when they live together and talk expenses on a regular basis."

"I'd feel better knowing you have reliable transportation."

She grinned. "Isn't the night before I leave on assignment rushing it or is this another hint you don't want me to go?"

Steve chuckled, "You're right; rushing into a sale means overpaying. Besides, I'm good at shopping around."

Laura headed back to the garden and Steve relaxed with his coffee. He decided life with Laura felt perfect—a life he always dreamed could be his. Soon it would be taken from him and he felt powerless to control a thing. *Shit! I can't even make sure she has a safe vehicle!* He felt pressure build behind his eyes as his mind raced. He tried to separate his personal experiences undercover from how Laura would behave in similar situations. She took no shortcuts, never compromised her values, knew where she stood, believed in a finer world than he did, and cared passionately about honor, integrity, character, love, and commitment—fidelity, too. Steve watched Laura shape a forsythia bush and felt panicked if she left, she'd never return. He knew what happened when a cop felt removed from the familiar, knew what happened when a cop functioned off balance for a long period of time. He'd been there and lost sight of himself. For once, idiot Granger might be correct. Laura needed to leave free and clear of any emotional entanglements, to assume an alternate identify. Yet, Laura might discover playing a role to be more difficult than imagined. If she truly lived and breathed the person she presented to the outside world, she could morph into her creation. In truth, she might become a woman without him in her life. When something grazed his chin, Steve grunted, "Huh?"

Laura whispered, "Are you okay?"

"I'm daydreaming."

"Don't go so far away, mister; it scares me." Steve fought an urge to point out she chose to go away but remained silent as she wandered off. His mind pictured the garage he worked at for months, a decrepit place in Highgate Springs near the border, a shop specializing in restoration of pricey imports. His undercover assignment began after a tip from a suspected felon in another case who bartered details in exchange for reduced charges. The low-life claimed his boss—the garage owner—created a system of delivery of finished product via a reinforced tunnel wide and high enough for a luxury sedan to make a run to another garage a quarter-mile away in Quebec woods near the Phillipsburg Bird Sanctuary: an amazing engineering feat to rival drug smuggling operations along the Texas, New Mexico, Arizona, or California borders but even more so if one considered necessary frost-heave repairs following mud season. A fictitious identity included a record for armed robbery and pesky probation officer who phoned the shop daily to verify attendance. Steve stayed in a dreary apartment over a package store and spent nights with a bottle of something vile in his hand and visions of his wife and brother in bed in front of his eyes. Not the worst, though: he rarely saw Mickey but heard things suggesting Michael closed in. To speed the investigation along, Steve put the moves on the scumbag's lonely sister and engaged in a sordid affair to punish Denise—as if in the end, she noticed or cared—as if in the end, he felt better about a successful court conviction—as if in the end, his soul remained unblemished.

Steve volunteered to go undercover since no one else could handle a goddamned thing the year Ralph went through physical therapy following a gunshot wound to the knee; the year of Sigler's suspension after an arrest for smacking his wife; the year Macrae worked temporarily with the DEA; the year Granger joined the department and played politics; the year a respected boss announced an impending retirement; the year Mickey turned six; and the year Steve discovered his wife in bed with Michael. He closed his eyes, counted backwards, and realized that was the year Laura finished her second year of college.

Steve opened his eyes to a miraculous vision: Laura sat on the porch railing, looking so beautiful even with a dirt-smudged chin. Her eyes had that look: the one of unfathomable love and trust and desire that made him shiver. She extended her hand and led him inside with a whispered, "I need you to hold me so tight I can't breathe."

Inside on the bed, Steve smoothed the hair off her forehead. "When you feel lonely, kid, who will you turn to?"

"Only you. By phone, if necessary, but only you."

Steve twisted the ring. "Should we officially disengage?"

Laura's breath tickled his ear: "Leave it right where it is for now, mister, but hold me even closer. I can still breathe."

Afterward, Laura and Steve prepared a dinner of baked chicken, pasta with sauce, and tossed salad. He cleaned the kitchen and loaded the dishwasher while she packed. He heard her move around the bedroom, go outside, and unlock the trunk of her car. When she came back in, she stopped, started to say something, and stared blankly before heading into the corridor. When he heard her suitcase bump the wall, Steve felt a sudden urge to beg her to stay but whispered, "Let me help with that."

"I can manage."

"Of course; all self-sufficient, independent women can manage anything." When she scowled, he laughed, "I'm teasing, kid."

When he heard her in the bathroom, Steve feared she'd erase all signs of her time with him. He ran in as she threw toiletries into a smaller case, grabbed her perfume, and groaned, "You can't take that." He tugged her to the bedroom and insisted she leave her nightgown, too. "It needs to be under your pillow when you come home." Once her car was loaded, Steve made popcorn and slipped a DVD into the player. When she yawned five minutes into the movie, he begged her to stay awake all night but she drifted off and in the end, he stopped the movie and carried her to bed with full awareness he was in for another sleepless night.

Steve listened to her heavy breathing and found it funny how things changed. His mother predicted if he were patient, he'd rebuild his life with some measure of happiness. If he'd known Laura would arrive, he'd have done things differently: the cigarettes and booze, yes, and definitely the women—all the self-destructive stunts he pulled that scared Mickey, his mother, and Ralph to death. He hit rock bottom on the first anniversary of Denise's murder: a year to the day after a piece of him died, too. There had been a major bust and evidence hadn't been cataloged officially yet: too goddamned easy to lift enough heroin to kill a horse. That night as he drove home, he couldn't bear the sight of one home after another lit up for Christmas. When he got to his dark, dreary house, his mother had already taken Mickey to hers for the night. Alone in the dark, Steve opened a new bottle of vodka, guzzled close to half of it, and felt his heart race as he planned how to score and shoot up. When the phone rang, he ignored it but when it rang repeatedly again and again every two minutes, he answered on the seventh ring of the 12th call to hear Mickey: *Daddy, I love you. Please come get me?* He lied he felt sick and couldn't drive but the truth was he felt close to passing out. He wandered to the upstairs bathroom to empty his bladder because in some perverse rationalization, he didn't want Mickey to hear he pissed and shit his pants. As he passed through his bedroom, Steve stopped and lifted something from his pillow: brown felt glued on a clothespin. He guessed with the brown toothpicks along the top, supposed to be a reindeer. Underneath? A card with four elves wearing green felt jackets, black felt pants, and red felt boots; Mickey's neat printing read: *Don't be mad at me all the time, Daddy. For Christmas, I promise I'll be good from now on.* Steve returned to the living room, threw clothes into a satchel, and stumbled two miles to his mother's, enough wind and cold to sober him up. As he lay on her couch that night, he wondered what compelled him to use the upstairs bathroom instead of the half bath off the kitchen. Could it be God sent him up there? Could such an entity exist in a world so contradictory? The following morning, Steve attempted to return the stash without observation but Granger came up quiet as a mouse to watch. As usual, he got it ass-backwards and accused Steve of using or dealing; when Granger's accusation never officially made it to muck-a-mucks in Middlesex, Steve realized Granger liked to know something no one else did, hold onto it, store it inside, and unfold it later, a brilliant strategy that worked. When their respected lieutenant retired, only Granger— the least productive of them all—was deemed suitable to fill the vacancy.

When Steve heard the alarm at 5:00 AM, he lay still and listened to Laura climb out of bed and tiptoe into the bathroom to shower. He ached to join her but didn't move. By 5:30, she stood by the bed and stared; he figured he got spared the agony of goodbye but she knelt, rested her head on his chest, and murmured, "I'll miss you."

Steve headed to the bathroom, returned, and collapsed in bed. "I expected you to be gone already, Delorange."

Laura kicked the mattress. "Are you kidding me?"

Steve felt the god-awful pressure behind his eyes. "I hate how I behave when I feel cornered so let me pretend you're not leaving."

Laura yanked him to his feet. "You don't know how to let go for even a few months, do you? You don't believe I'm coming back, do you? My God, why don't you trust me?"

"It hurts to see you without our engagement ring and I'm afraid you'll meet someone else or wake one morning, relieved I'm not there."

Laura sat on the bed, tugged until he lay beside her, and whispered, "I can no longer imagine my life without you in it." He suspected she'd stay until he slept so he rolled over and pretended to drift off. Time passed—time he knew she didn't have before a long drive until she sighed, "I'll be back before you know it." He heard her reset the alarm, shut the back door, and slam the car door. He heard brakes squeak on the curve of the driveway and gears grind as she pulled onto the road.

A sense of heaviness began to build at St. Johnsbury, fully in place by Lyndonville. Laura drove northeast through villages familiar from her childhood, and the closer she came to Fallsbridge, the more she felt she made a mistake. At the final intersection before turning east, she pulled into a general store lot to use her cell phone. At no coverage, she ran onto the porch to a pay phone. "Steve?"

"Hey, so soon? Are you there?"

"Almost; um, the way we left things this morning?"

"I'm sorry I was a jerk but I can't seem to…"

"There were other things I wanted to say but didn't."

"I'm listening."

"You said once I left, I wouldn't miss you. I never loved anyone like this until now and…"

"Slow down, kid. I know you love me."

"I hate the way we left things this morning, Steve."

"We left them fine; we'll be together when this is done."

"Um, one other thing but don't take it wrong. You have lots of experience with women and I worry… Um, if I thought you were screwing around, I'd be gone so fast, your head would spin."

"I like knowing what we have is important to you, too."

"Did that sound possessive?"

"No, the way I lived my life before feels empty. I wish we'd gotten together sooner because by now I'd have reversed that dreadful procedure and we'd put our best efforts toward making a baby."

Laura felt the heat on her cheeks. "Steve, I told you I…"

"Kid, I know but I'm feeling Mother Nature's tug."

"I don't understand."

"Mother Nature has a way of making humans crave a little one just like the big one they love. In my case, I feel a huge tug toward a little girl with dark hair and big brown eyes. I'm sorry if my baby craving gives you something else to worry about. Maybe I'm grasping at straws, hoping a baby is something I can give you."

"What you give me is a place I'm loved for me, a place of comfort and shelter. Does that make sense?"

Steve whispered, "Perfect sense," then laughed, "Gotta go; Ralph's making obscene gestures."

"Did you tell anyone about the broken engagement?"

"Nope; not yet; understand?"

"I do. Think of me, Steve? Miss me?"

"Kid, as if I had a choice."

During the last two miles, Laura felt overwhelmed by memories triggered by a familiar curvy road and distinctive spring scent of moist and shadowy pine forests. As she came over the crest of a hill, she took a deep breath as the village came into view. In early sunlight, Fallsbridge was picture-postcard perfect, an advertising executive's dream. She passed under the maples lining Main Street, crossed the wooden bridge, and turned onto Elm Street—no longer home to centuries-old elms but to oaks, birches, ashes, and maples. She parked at the carriage house and turned in a circle. She knelt to unhook her bicycle from the rack, checked tires, and stood when someone approached. She stood, faced a thin, pale woman, and extended her hand. "Hello, I'm Laura Delorange."

"I'm Violet Lemphier. The carriage house isn't quite ready. I hired a carpenter, painter, and cleaning crew but it's in worse shape than Lynette thought. There's a problem in need of a plumber and..."

Laura laughed, "Sorry we didn't give you more notice," unlocked her trunk and lifted her suitcases onto the gravel.

Violet dug into a pocket for a key. "I went in, took the screens off, washed and opened the windows. It smelled stuffy."

Laura thanked her and checked her watch. "I don't mean to be rude but I start a new job in 20 minutes."

"Okay; if you need help with anything, let me know."

Laura dragged her suitcases and boxes inside and took a quick inventory: everything clean. She opened the refrigerator, felt cold air, and noticed orange juice, milk, and eggs. "Oh, Violet," she sighed and shook her head. She noticed furniture but no curtains at the windows, no books, nothing decorative. Laura looked at her watch and recalled it took ten minutes to ride a bicycle to town even across school grounds; she rushed to the car wearing what she wore for the drive.

Minutes later Laura rushed into the law office and found a young woman behind the desk, "Is Mr. Marschek in?"

"He is. Do you have an appointment?"

"I'm Laura Delorange. I was supposed to meet..."

From behind: "You made it. Wonderful!"

Laura tugged at hair clumps. "When I got here to unload my things, I didn't have time to shower. I must look a mess, Bill."

He laughed, "Nonsense," grabbed her hand in a firm shake, and turned. "Reilly? Meet Laura Delorange."

The younger woman stood and extended her right hand. "You sure don't look like a lawyer."

"I didn't have time to change. Do you have a first name?"

"Mom got creative: I'm Reilly Kathleen McGuinn."

Marschek indicated another room and as soon as they sat said, "I heard you were born here during the hippie years."

"I was born at home, too, when my parents believed it was essential to complete the cycle in the same bed in which conception occurred. Now they're ultraconservative Republicans!" When she noticed Reilly eavesdropped, Laura suggested they close the door.

Marschek leaned in to whisper, "Surely you remember there are few secrets in small towns," then raised his voice. "What I have in mind is to familiarize you with existing clients."

Marschek guided her through two file cabinets and took extra time with files to indicate anything unusual or interesting. Laura reminded him while in New York, she prosecuted criminal cases, and since returning to Vermont investigative police work. "I have no defense or litigation experience."

He predicted she'd make a transition in no time. "I called one of your New York references and I'm convinced it was a stroke of genius to hire you; the firm tends to be incestuous in its hiring."

"What?"

Marschek explained there wasn't much diversity: seven partners, all male, Caucasian, late 40's to early 60's; among the associates: nine male and one female Caucasian mid-30's to late 40's. "You'll add a whole new dimension to the staff. You've been out in the real world, so to speak. Of everything, what satisfied the most?"

"Definitely police work—research and investigation."

"You'll help us be creative in our approach to investigations yet remain true to the law. I look forward to your input." At 11:45, Marschek closed a drawer. "Is there enough to keep you busy?"

Laura insisted there was and ran her fingertips along a label: *V. S. Mottolla: Last Will & Testament.* "Mr. Marschek, I think I recognize the name from when I was a kid—village pharmacist?"

He insisted she call him Bill and described Mottolla as an active mid-70's who still managed his business successfully. He had two grown daughters with children of their own but his wife died of cancer a year or so earlier. "Mottolla's a Korean War vet from the Boston area, only one of two surviving elders from the five originals who purchased the acreage and started the farm in 1958. He's an impressive, interesting man."

"I believe the CFEL was founded in the early 70's."

"You know about it?"

Laura glanced up from the file. "I grew up here and we were members but I was young when we left."

Bill checked his watch and announced lunchtime. On the way out, he stopped at Reilly's desk. "We'll have a bite to eat then tour the village. Lock up when you go?" He turned to Laura and explained Ms. McGuinn worked part time.

Reilly stood to shake hands again. "It's nice to meet you; tomorrow I'd like to hear what you expect of a secretary."

Laura turned to Marschek then back. "Um, sure—I'm happy to outline expectations."

On the sidewalk, Marschek laughed he liked what he saw. "You're inquisitive and quick on your feet, too."

Laura admitted she never supervised before. "In New York, the district attorney's office had a clerical pool; I turned in tapes and handwritten notes and got them back neatly typed. I never gave any thought to how that happened. With the state police, so much was electronic we did our own support."

Bill murmured she needn't worry; Reilly was a gem. He led her across to the green. "Has Fallsbridge changed much?"

Laura shrugged, "From what I see, not much except the diner; odd because it looks like it stood in the same spot since the 1920's. The Elm Street Park looks wonderful! In 5th grade, I joined the Arbor Club and planted replacements for dying elms. At the time, the new trees were waist high but some look fully grown. I notice a lot of dirt roads got paved. Fallsbridge feels very affluent and modern. I wonder if it really is or if the CFEL..." Laura stopped and laughed, "Sorry for rattling."

Bill admitted except for Reilly, no one in Fallsbridge spoke to him. "This is one odd little town—lots of unwed mothers who put babies up for adoption but no divorces; do CFEL members hear a distorted version of what Catholic priests preach?"

Laura laughed, "Distorted is the perfect word for the CFEL," and stopped as they neared the snack bar and the ivy-covered brick academy in the distance. The school played an important role in her life for years yet seemed smaller and less intimidating somehow. Laura turned to listen to the river splash over the falls beyond the academy, felt Bill's eyes study her, and concentrated on the menu board. "What do you recommend?"

Bill oohed and ahhed over a Michigan Hot platter. Once the food arrived, they carried boxes to a bench underneath a maple in the center of the green. He bit into his Michigan and rolled his eyes. "Marion would strangle me if she saw what I eat when she's not around." He munched on a French fry and admitted he figured Laura hadn't come to town to process property deeds or guardianship papers. "You're too talented for that and I can't help but wonder how Ed Granger got you to return to a place you obviously dislike."

"I intend to stay with your firm a very long time."

"That wasn't my question."

Laura nodded. "Okay, I'm not certain how long my current assignment will take but I couldn't continue police work."

"Earlier you said you felt satisfied by it."

Laura nodded. "Since you see through evasiveness, here it is: I felt satisfied by research, not field work. Typical garbage included drugs, robbery, smuggling, arson, stalking, domestic dispute, child neglect or abuse, sexual abuse, spousal abduction, missing children, rape, attempted murder, and murder. It's a conscious choice to become involved in work which might make a difference in someone's life before something happens, not after."

"Why here?"

"I left something undone."

"Oh. Do you feel comfortable telling me?"

"No; I hate police work but miss the other detectives.

"Granger?"

"No, Granger doesn't care about..." She stopped and laughed, "Sorry; I know you're friends."

"I met Ed through a professional organization but we aren't friends though he did say you had an affair with another detective."

Laura felt the heat. "He didn't!"

Bill confessed he couldn't believe a capable young attorney wasn't better off in Burlington and pried. "I'd be blind not to see little goes on here though I heard your name at the diner this morning; it appears Reilly told someone I hired a new lawyer and that someone told someone else and so on. Yours is a familiar name, I take it?"

Laura chewed her lip. "I guess; what did you hear?"

"Something about how obstinate you are?"

"Really? I prefer the word determined."

Bill crumpled his napkin. "Good trait in my opinion." He stood and reported he needed to leave by 2:30 to make it home by dinner. As they walked again, he mentioned in the morning, Reilly expected her new boss to set standards and detail how she liked letters and envelopes to look. On the other hand, he wasn't that type of supervisor; he expected people to produce on a regular basis without excuses or hand-holding.

"Your reference at the Queens district attorney's office claimed you bite into projects like a rabid dog and Granger said you focus so hard, nothing distracts you. I like that. The firm could use that kind of enthusiasm again." They headed back to the office and Bill pointed to businesses and homes as he tied locations to files they reviewed earlier. As they crossed the street, Bill added, "I hope your presence expands our client base."

"That's reasonable; may I reject a client?"

"Who might that be?"

"It's a hypothetical question."

Bill studied her. "Unless a South American drug lord asks you to launder money in questionable real estate transactions, my answer's no. Check with me first. I'll probably go along but expect to be included in the decision." As they walked, he jumped from one client to another, and when they reached the office again, stopped his summary, handed her a key, and shook her hand briskly. "Good luck."

Laura watched how in a heartbeat, his car disappeared from sight. In the distance, she distinctly heard the falls and looked around at the one place in the world she never expected to see again except in nightmares. She entered the office, locked the door, and sat at her desk for the foreseeable future. She pulled the Maidstone file and lifted the phone. "Mr. Munier, please. This is Laura Delorange of..."

"Hello! This is Glenn."

"I reviewed your situation and suggest we talk before..."

She heard a friendly laugh. "Laura don't you remember me? My brother and I helped your father and Jack paint your house the summer you were 11 or 12 and I a goofy 15-year-old with a mouthful of braces."

"I remember that summer; wow, it's funny being back."

"I never quite left. I went to Johnson State for a year but transferred to Lyndon, commuted, and saved the family a bundle. I heard you went to UVM then Harvard Law."

"UVM first, yes, but not Harvard—Columbia."

"You're the only one I know who survived a big city."

Laura felt uncomfortable with the banter and suggested they schedule an appointment. "I'm happy to meet at your office; managing a restaurant and inn must take a lot of time."

"It does but since I don't have an actual office, I'll walk over there in the morning. Are you free at 9:00?"

"Free completely. You're the first client I called."

"How about this? Come here for breakfast."

"Um, okay, I'll be there at 9:00." Laura tapped a pencil on the file, shoved it into a drawer, and grunted, "I hate this shitty little town." She detected a shadow and turned to a face at the window.

Violet pointed and shouted, "It's locked!"

Laura opened it. "Sorry but it's spooky here alone."

Violet pulled fabric from a bag and explained they were curtains she never used. When Laura argued that wasn't necessary, Violet insisted she take them unless she hated the pattern. Laura noticed Violet's hands trembled as she held them up. "Sorry they're so wrinkled. I'll iron them and come over later to hang them."

Laura stared into Violet's pale eyes and detected shyness mixed with fear. "Violet, thank you for thinking of me but I don't know if there are rods at the windows."

"There are and they'll work fine. A plumber stopped by, and then a truck pumped the septic tank. He told me something to tell your parents but I forgot. Maybe he'll enclose a note when he mails a bill."

Laura shrugged, "Septic details would go in one ear and out the other with me, too."

Laura felt how deeply Violet concentrated before she answered, "I knew you'd be nice like Lynette." Violet headed to the door. "Brian says I bother people so tell me when I bother you."

"You're no bother," Laura gasped as her throat tightened in response to Violet's timid *I'm-a-useless-unworthy-female* voice, the same fear-filled self-deprecation that as a child, she heard in women—not her mother, thank God, or at least not often. It hurt to be reminded of how CFEL women believed in the truth of words directed at them during sermons and against them by the very men who claimed to love them.

After Violet left, Laura locked the door and pushed familiar numbers on the phone. Before the final digit, she recalled Granger's warning about phone bugs, wall bugs, furniture bugs, and what-all bugs. She flipped open her cell phone but as expected? No service. She glanced at her watch, grabbed her purse, and ran to her car. Within minutes, she felt the weightiness lift as she headed toward the bridge to New Hampshire—windows open, hair flying, bugs smashing, and music blasting. In Littleton, Laura searched for cell service again and found a weak signal in the general store lot. She dialed Steve's cell but it went directly to voice mail; she dialed his desk and waited impatiently until prompted to leave a message. She tried his home number and when the machine picked up, groaned, "Steve, I will **not** be able to pull this off."

Laura returned to the carriage house and at 6:00, Violet knocked. She struggled to get inside with a casserole dish in one hand and curtains in the other. She smoothed them flat on the kitchen table and confessed, "Though you said not to, I washed, dried, and ran a quick iron. If you need me to, I could…"

"Enough!" When Violet reacted by stepping back Laura added, "I won't be waited on. What's in the casserole dish?"

Violet shrugged, "Extra lasagna; I'm sorry if I…"

Laura laughed, "Don't apologize all the time."

"But I…" Violet stopped and smiled. "Okay." Once the curtains were hung, she threw a rounded section of fabric on the table. "If you don't like this as a tablecloth, I'll…"

"I like it! Thank you."

Laura led her guest into the living room and asked Violet to talk about herself. Laura listened to Violet describe herself as wife, mother, daughter, and friend. At the mention of her husband, Laura pictured Mr. Lemphier as the French teacher, a soft-spoken, polite man with soft blonde hair and thin moustache. As impeccably as he dressed and as orderly as he taught, Laura also remembered him as a moody, distracted man while all the high school girls saw him as an unbearably dreamy, romantic soul in need of rescue. Violet spoke affectionately about their children: Ben, Joanna, and Paul. "Paul was an accident. When Brian was named headmaster nine years ago, I drove to Groveton for a bottle of champagne. When people are drunk, it's easy to forget the master plan."

"Master plan?"

"I meant family plan."

"Talk about you as a person, not as a member of a family."

Violet shrugged, "My family is who I am."

"Okay, then tell me how you spend your free time." She expected to hear Violet loved to read but heard her say she loved to turn the stereo on loud, find a rock station, and dance. Laura sighed, "You must be quite the dancer. You look so lithe."

Violet laughed, "I take shoes off, pull Brian's socks on, and slide along the hardwood floor—infinitely more fun than dusting." Violet leaned forward to whisper, "One time Brian came in, announced I looked infantile, and put the stereo on the right station."

"Call me radical but I listen to any station I like."

Violet leaned even closer. "When your mother called about the carriage house, Brian hated the idea of you here. He's convinced any daughter of Lynette Marceau would be a feminist."

Laura shrugged, "I have an incredible fondness for the English language and I believe my mother and I are humanists."

Every inch of Violet's face brightened. "Brian doesn't want me to be friends with you, but I suspect I'll enjoy it."

"I imagine we could if you don't act like a housekeeper."

Violet shrugged, "That could be a problem. I love to cook and bake and often bring gifts to friends."

Laura sighed, "On occasion is fine but what I want to hear is what you dream about or wish would happen."

"Easy one; I fell in love at 17. I'm still in love with him."

"Wonderful! My friends Ralph and Joyce have been married a long time, too, and still feel connected. It's rare to…"

Violet interrupted, "I fell in love but married Brian instead. I think about this man when I'm awake and dream of him at night. Sometimes in the middle of the night, I dream of him and reach out to my husband for all the wrong reasons."

Laura squinted, "Um, that's…"

Violet pushed herself to a stand and headed to the door. "I need to finish dinner; so, can I stop again tomorrow?"

Laura smiled. "Of course but please come empty-handed." Laura watched Violet cross the yard to the back door of the main house; a moment later, music started—clear, fast, and loud. Laura swept the kitchen floor and stopped when she heard tires on gravel. She peered out and heard music stop mere moments before the car did. In the distance, a man stepped out of a minivan, followed by three children. Laura smiled at the sight of the attractive young people with Violet's distinctive slenderness and height blended with Brian's straight, pale blonde hair—in a light breeze, the fineness of that hair apparent as it swirled around four heads like haloes. Laura walked over and watched the two younger children lift musical instrument cases. She extended her right hand. "Hello, Brian, I'm Laura Delorange; I'm not sure you remember me."

With a thin smile, he responded, "I remember you well. Children, this is Miss Delorange, who'll live out back. Miss Delorange, this is Ben, Joanna, and Paul."

She smiled and said, "Please call me Laura."

Brian slammed the door. "Not appropriate; you children are to call her Miss Delorange."

Laura studied the case the younger boy held. "When I was your age, I played the clarinet, too."

Paul asked, "Do you still play?"

"I haven't taken it out of the case in years, too busy to practice."

The daughter asked, "Busy with what? Are you married? Do you have children?"

"I went to law school but I'm not married and have no…"

"Joanna," Brian interrupted as he put his arm around his daughter's shoulder to lead her off, "help your mother with dinner." On their way in, Brian glanced over his shoulder to finish, "Under no circumstances will anyone bother Miss Delorange."

"Yes, sir," three voices answered in unison.

Inside the carriage house, Laura laughed, "She-e-e-it," grabbed her purse and car keys, and left as quickly as she could without spraying gravel. She rolled all four windows down, cranked the sunroof, and blasted the radio as she sped through rolling countryside to the bridge. As she bounced over the crests of hills, she laughed at the feeling in her stomach and squealed around a curve. She slowed down to the speed limit but obviously not soon enough—in the rear view mirror, she watched blue flashing lights fall in behind.

The uniformed officer stopped alongside her open window. "Do you have any idea how fast you were going?"

"Um, I guess maybe 50?"

"Try 58 in a 35 mph zone." He scanned the interior of her vehicle. "Have you been drinking?"

"No and I'll submit to a sobriety test."

"Not necessary at this time—license, registration, and proof of insurance." She dug through her purse and the glove compartment, and in her side mirror, watched him walk to his own vehicle to use a radio. When he returned and handed everything back, she heard a hint of exasperation: "You could have saved us both a lot of time."

"What?"

"You're a trooper with the Vermont State Police."

"Not anymore but doesn't exceeding posted limits by 23 miles per hour warrant at least a written warning?"

"You don't want the points on your license, Laura."

Uncomfortable with the sudden change in demeanor, Laura answered, "And I don't expect any favors, either, Officer."

He smiled and touched the brim of his hat. "The next time I see you floating above the road, I won't do you any."

Laura squinted. "Should I know you?"

He lifted sunglasses. "I'm Gil Munier, Jack's friend."

As the cruiser pulled away, Laura sighed, "Great." Minutes later, she crossed into New Hampshire and stopped when she found a weak signal. When it faded in strength, she drove to a pay phone near a general store, wrapped the cord around her fingers, and muttered, "Come on, come on, come on!" until Steve answered. "I'll go crazy here! People are plastic, too good to be true, artificially sweetened."

A chuckled, "You've only been there hours; it'll get easier."

She took a deep breath. "Hey, I've been thinking maybe your idea wasn't so nuts after all."

"Which one?"

"That we fly off and get married before I came up here."

"What changed?"

"You'd be an anchor to keep me from floating away. I feel like I'm in a Stephen King novel—something lurks beneath a calm surface but not a prehistoric lake monster—more like mind shit."

"You're pretty wired, kid. What's going on?"

"I just got stopped for speeding by Mr. Robot-o-copper."

"Excuse me?"

"Mr. Set-Jaw-Looks-Perfect-in-Uniform-and-Hat-Guy could be on recruiting posters. Did you look that great in uniform?"

"Nah, the doctor always said *Lose weight, Scolarzski.* I had serious belt overhang."

"I couldn't pinch an inch on this guy in a million years."

Steve chuckled, "Boy, you are wired. I've never heard you talk about a man like that."

"He knew Jack and it was stupid to be caught scurrying across state lines because cell phones are useless in the Northeast Kingdom. I appreciate anyone who sets a nice standard for cops; besides, you're the one who awakened me to the beauty of a man's body."

"I'm nowhere close to passable and it seems to me…"

She interrupted, "I've been thinking, too, about what you said earlier about a baby."

"And you agree it would be wonderful?"

"I'm sorry if you're disappointed, but I don't think I can get pregnant and even if I could, I don't think I'd be a good parent."

Steve chuckled, "Unless I seek reversal, I shoot dead bullets anyway, kid. Besides, I won't force the issue."

"Why would you want to? Mick's almost 20 and in a few years, you could become a grandfather."

"Whoa! That's a scary thought! I think I'd be a better father this time; the way I feel about you makes all the difference in the world."

"Why are you so critical of your history with Mick? You love him, he knows it, and everyone around you both sees it, too."

"I detect you wear rose-colored glasses, kid."

"No, I see you as you are but wonder what kind of parent I'd be. How'd you do it? Control and encourage Mick yet let him be himself? Did you cross your fingers and pray things turned out okay? Maybe I'll change my mind; God knows until you I never imagined myself as a..."

"Incredibly gorgeous, sensual sex goddess?"

She rubbed her fingers along her neck. "This is weird."

"Excuse me?"

"I respond to your voice physically."

"I know what you mean; yours increases my pulse rate, too."

"So when's a good time to call tomorrow night?"

"Laura, no; for your safety, I recommend we keep phone calls to once a week. Next Monday evening, same time. I'll wait right here or my cell charged and with me."

"I love you, Steve. Think of me?"

"Yup, I will, kid, as if I have a choice."

On the drive back, Laura kept an eye out for Gil Munier—no sign. Back at the carriage house, she unlocked the door and heard a noise from the bushes. Violet approached and pushed her inside. "Piece of advice: be careful what you do and say around here—very careful."

Laura smiled hesitantly. "Brian, right? I understand."

"All of them. I wouldn't want anything to happen to you."

"What?"

"Just be careful." Violet repeated and left.

Inside, Laura's mind raced in a million directions. Why the hell was she there? She had a man who loved her, made her heart jump and blood boil, asked her to consider a baby together, and saw her at her worst yet chose to be with her. Laura tugged her ugly yellow nightgown on, turned off lights, lay down, and stared at a dark sky. She tugged her pillow close and whispered, "Goodnight, Steve; soon we'll be together."

In the morning, Laura started the day out of sorts. She felt awkward, distracted, not at all capable of representing the firm well. She left her cane at the carriage house and arrived at the Maidstone in a pair of shoes that matched her outfit but put unnecessary stress on her knee, hip, and back. She walked cautiously and jumped when someone laughed, "I'm glad to see I'm not the only one running late."

Laura extended her right hand. "You must be Glenn."

"Yup; you haven't changed much: still the same warm brown eyes and flushed skin I remember." As they walked up the steps, he mentioned the summer he helped paint her house again. "You sat outside, read library books all day, and got so sun-burnt your mother said without a hat, you'd wrinkle like a prune before you were 30."

Laura nodded. "I can smell the cream I rubbed on at bedtime!"

"Obviously you took her advice; your skin's perfect."

Laura chuckled, "I forgot everyone here is a graduate of the seminar: *How to Influence Others through Falsehoods & Flatteries.*"

Glenn muttered, "I hate how my compliment came off as insincere," and pushed a heavy door open. Laura inched inside and thought it looked very different from the dreary, old-boys-club she remembered. Glenn led her on a tour through the restaurant, kitchen, banquet area, and upstairs to vacant guest rooms. He opened the door to a magnificent room with a bay window facing the green. "This is my personal space. On the phone, you asked if the restaurant keeps me busy. That's not the half of it. In winter, there are weeks I don't go outdoors and only come up here to sleep."

She looked at a gorgeous view. "You're okay with that?"

Glenn sighed, "I love my work but what would make my life perfect is someone like you to marry."

Laura headed back to the staircase. "I'm hungry for one of those omelets you promised."

On the stairs, Glenn stopped to confess, "When I was 15, I fell in love with a girl who read books I couldn't understand. That girl may have forgotten me but I never forgot her."

Laura cleared her throat, "Glenn, I think it's important to…"

"Don't worry; I'm no longer that love-struck boy in the bushes."

"That was you? For heaven's sake, I watched them shake!"

"I hadn't figured out the subtle art of drawing your attention; obviously, I still haven't. Come on; let's eat." Once they ordered, Laura reviewed Marschek's notes, jotted new ones of her own, and made little eye contact with her host. She sipped her coffee and fingered the napkin as she asked questions about what he hoped to do to the structure or interpreted current zoning regulations. When the omelets finally arrived, she put everything into the file and picked at the food on her plate. She felt how intensely Glenn watched her until finally he said, "I regret I didn't keep my thoughts to myself but you know the expression: *Nothing ventured, nothing gained.* I wish for you to see me socially."

"Um, I'll be your lawyer but…"

When Laura heard a familiar voice behind say, "Good morning," her heart skipped a beat as she turned to stare into the pale eyes she trusted years earlier. "Little Miss Laurette Marie, you look exactly as I dreamed: perfect teeth, bright and clear eyes, wonderful complexion, excellent posture, good height, and shiny hair."

"Hello, Dr. Marsethe." Laura willed herself to smile and engage in small talk but when he touched her hand, she stood to excuse herself. "I must get back to the office."

Marsethe applied gentle pressure to her shoulders and as she plopped back into the seat, said, "You have no other appointments today and you barely touched your omelet. Carl's feelings will be shattered and avoiding the most important meal of the day will not do for one so beautifully within prime child-bearing years, yes?"

Laura felt the heat and glanced at Glenn, who said, "Mel, sorry but we're in the process of discussing my zoning appeal."

Marsethe studied them both. "I'll see you soon, Laura; Reilly scheduled an appointment for next week."

He headed to an empty table as Laura rushed to the restroom, splashed cold water on her face, and ran a brush through her hair. She studied her face in the mirror. "You look like hell." She returned to the table. "I shouldn't be shocked to run into him but thank you for helping in an awkward situation. I may overreact but that encounter felt…"

"Insulting?"

"Yes."

"Demeaning?"

"Yes!"

"He talked like you were livestock up for auction."

"Yes! For a moment, I doubted my reaction."

"Don't ever doubt yourself. You're very special."

Laura willed away a sudden fear Glenn patronized but when she studied his eyes, thought he seemed sincere, concerned, a friend. She picked at the omelet and uncovered cheddar cheese, maple ham, green peppers, and sweet onions. "Oh, this is fantastic." She bit into the thick-sliced raisin toast, too, and asked if it were baked on the premises.

Glenn nodded. "Besides a chef and another cook, my staff includes a baker known for exceptional pies, cookies, and artisan breads. People come across the bridge to place orders. I'm glad you enjoy the food. We should do this often." Laura thanked Glenn for breakfast, promised to keep in touch, and hurried along pavement to the office; her knee ached as she passed Reilly, slammed the door, and plopped in a chair. She held back tears and thought *any normal woman who came to encounter a monster wouldn't crumble when she ran into him; any normal woman in a hurry to resolve things and go home to the man she loves might stay and fight, not run away like a terrified child.*

Laura heard a knock and Reilly stuck her head around. "I see you're upset, and I'm sorry I told Mel where you were."

"It's fine."

Laura watched Reilly stand at attention and heard an odd confession: "I argued with him once; he yelled for an hour."

"What in the world provoked him?"

"I believed I knew myself better than he did." She started to add something but stopped. "I shouldn't speak frankly to a stranger."

Laura touched Reilly's arm. "You can trust me."

Reilly harrumphed, "The elders warned me you'd work hard to be kind and caring. Maybe manipulative skills will disarm Glenn Munier but they're wasted on me." Reilly pressed her hands together. "I am a member of the Community for Expansive Love and I need only to..."

"...reach out to other members for guidance and support," Laura finished and felt a chill at how readily the words came back.

Reilly studied her carefully. "I guess what I heard is true: you and your family were members once?"

Laura nodded. "I believed that statement until I learned to think for myself. I highly recommend it."

Reilly admitted she heard stories about Laura as a child. "In fact, I could be immoral, too, and deserved censure."

Laura felt the heat on her face. "I admit as a child I could be strong-willed at times but reject the word immoral."

"I'm sorry if I misinterpreted ..."

Laura interrupted, "I can't control what others believe about what happened but am curious. What did you do to earn condemnation?"

Laura found it startling to observe what the elders called *acceptance of God's will into an individual soul* as Reilly's face shifted from confusion to clarity: "Sometimes we need to be reminded of God's presence, earn His acceptance, and adjust our behavior."

"What if surrendering is an easy way out, turning-over thoughts, desires, and love to the control of others who may not have answers?"

Reilly laughed, "They warned me all non-believers talk like this!" She stared vacantly outside and confided, "The elders taught me personal restraint and helped me understand a greater purpose to life than self-indulgence. If not for their guidance, I might never have seen my contribution is greatest when it serves the Community."

"I recognize many benefits to affiliation. My father taught at the academy and my grandfather served as village pharmacist for years; both owed a lot to CFEL support. My brother Jack insists science preparation at the academy made college and vet school effortless and..." Laura studied Reilly's glazed expression and stopped. "Sorry to go on like that; I love language, debate, and research so much it spurred me to law." At no response, Laura cleared her throat. "Earlier you said something about contribution. I knew the elders expected me to study medicine but has anyone explained what your contribution will be?"

"I made my covenant, Miss Delorange. I have begun."

"Do you mind telling me what that is?"

"Yes, I do. The elders warned me lawyers use words to trick and confuse. They warned me as a non-believer, you would denounce them at every opportunity." Reilly walked away before Laura had a chance to respond and the office fell silent. For the remainder of the week, Laura heard the constant click of the computer keyboard and Reilly's voice only when she answered the phone. As Reilly prepared to leave Friday, she suggested they discuss expectations Monday.

"We haven't talked because one of us pouted since Tuesday."

"Yeah, I know but the elders don't want me to get close to you."

Laura remembered what Reilly said earlier in the week about manipulative skills and decided not to beat around the bush. "The CFEL is clear about expectations of members: kindness, decency, honesty, friendship, patience, respect, trust, and love for all God's creations. Over the weekend, think about that because I hope we'll behave like that with each other." Laura saw fear and asked, "Did that sound presumptuous?"

Reilly shrugged, "I'm accustomed to being told what to do, how to think, who to like, and how to behave."

"That's not what I meant, Reilly. With office policies, I'll be clear about what I want but beyond that, I prefer you come to your own decisions not mine, and definitely not those of the elders."

"Will we see you at services Sunday, Miss Delorange?"

Laura hesitated. "No, I imagine it's too soon."

"It's never too soon to return to the Lord."

22

When Monday rolled around, Ralph watched Steve arrive late, collapse in a chair, and hurl keys across the desk so hard, they skidded off and hit a wall. Ralph noticed others watched, too, as Steve lit a cigarette and tapped his fingers over 'n over, faster 'n faster, louder 'n louder. Rawlings glanced at Ralph: "Looks like you're in for one hell of a day." That clown never could let anything drop and shouted, "Rough night, Igor? Hung over? Constipated? Impotent?"

"Fuck off, Bobby."

Rawlings chuckled, "Granger's looking for you."

"Where is he? I've got something to say to the prick!"

Rawlings pointed to the men's room and Steve jumped up. As his buddy stormed by Ralph grabbed, "Don't go looking for trouble."

Steve broke free and kept moving. "Granger, wipe your ass!"

An echoed: "For chrissake, gimme a minute."

"You slimy son of a bitch, you couldn't keep your mouth shut, could you? Just what the hell did you tell her?"

"Tell who what?"

"Laura!"

"I don't know what you're talking about."

"Some asshole told her something and I think that's you!"

Granger edged out of the stall to wash his hands. "Scolarzski, you don't need anyone else's help losing women." Steve grabbed Granger neck, forced his head into the sink, and Granger stomped Steve's instep.

As Steve limped by to grab keys off the floor, Ralph jumped back. "My turn to drive, buddy."

Steve grunted, "I'm going home."

Ralph felt pissed at how often the same stunt replayed itself during 14 years as partners and grabbed Steve's arm. "Yes, you will work today and yes, you will allow me to drive, and yes, for once in your friggin' life, you'll get crap into the open before it eats you up alive."

Steve broke free. "Laura dumped me!"

Ralph followed outside. "No way; the little lady adores you."

Steve jumped into the passenger seat grinning. "Laura's undercover and for her safety she's gotta look free and clear."

Ralph stared at the building. "None of the guys..."

"Obviously you overlook Rawlings."

Ralph climbed in, started the ignition, eased into traffic, and glanced sideways. "What's her assignment?"

"Nope; drive."

"Will she actually come back to marry a freak like you?"

Finally, Ralph saw a smile. "She promised she would."

Ralph cleared his throat and figured any time felt as good as another with a stick-o-dynamite like Scolarzski and broached a tricky subject. "While Laura's away, will you sniff around?"

Steve stared out at traffic. "I have no desire to cheat."

"Excellent; your lifestyle got worrisome but between you and Laura, I see scorching heat, the kind to leave burn marks on the sheets. I know you won't believe this but Joycie and I look into each other's eyes and swear we're still on our honeymoon."

"Babar, how do you keep that passion alive?"

"Easy, budster; flirt all day when a gal's got clothes on if you hope to coax 'em off later."

Summary

23

Laura put in nine-hour days at the office, another two in a garden, another two reading, another on housework that didn't need so much attention, and another driving nowhere in particular. When the humidity felt low, Laura rode her bike into town and stopped at the snack bar for a Creemee. At a yard sale, she bought paddles and a used kayak and secured them to roof racks on her car. At the lake on weekends, she struggled to load and unload, relishing the exhaustion she felt in her almost-healed knee, hip, and back because when she pushed hard, she slept better. Every evening, Violet stopped by to talk for a few minutes and sadly, often brought food. The level of comfort deepened and once when Brian was away for the day, Violet brought Joanna with her. In the office, Laura immersed her mind in work. One morning she felt startled by a noise in the outer office before Reilly arrived, peered around the door to see if someone snuck in—only to see the FAX spew a message from Bill Marschek to expect a call from new client: *Wilkers, Alan Joseph*. Laura grabbed the phone, dialed Burlington, and once the receptionist put her through, gasped, "You sent me Wilkers? What's his presenting issue?"

"Felony sexual assault; do you know him?"

"Vermont's a small state where police know one another. Do you understand? I know what he did."

A chuckled, "You sound surprisingly judgmental in light of the fact Wilkers is a suspect, not a convicted felon. What happened to your belief in equal and fair representation?"

Laura sighed, "My former partner beat the hell out of Wilkers after his arrest. Though Wilkers asked the charges be dropped, they're open pending an internal affairs investigation. Why'd he wait so long to hire an attorney?"

"He didn't. Up until today, he had representation but isn't pleased. Enough said?"

Laura fingered additional pages as they dropped from the FAX. "I'll represent every client to the best of my ability and let the court do its job; thank you for reminding me why I chose law in the first place."

24

In the middle of the night, Steve dreamed his alarm went off and sunlight brightened the room; in his dream, Laura arrived unexpectedly, crawled into bed, and reported she was home forever. When he opened his eyes to a dark room and noted 1:17 AM, he climbed out, knelt in front of the closet, and touched one box after another of possessions Laura left behind. He wondered if his curiosity about what she saved proved he was no better than a snoop. If he looked through them, would that be untrustworthy and superficial? He imagined the LP's were different since she gave permission that night she brought them over and shared them willingly. He felt his throat tighten at the sight of her neat writing and sifted through one album cover after another, read one plastic-covered article after another, until he felt shocked by daylight.

25

When Reilly announced a call from Sergeant Scolarzski of the Vermont State Police, Laura's heart raced as she lifted the phone only to hear a snarled, "Delorange, you left personal crap all over the friggin' place." Laura felt a flush but considered the fact he called her at work instead of waiting for Monday night; she knew she emptied her desk in the office and imagined like Granger, he worried the phone was tapped.

"Scolarzski, feel free to go through anything I left behind."

An instant change in voice. "Thanks, kid."

Laura heard him hang up, twisted the cord and realized whenever he touched something of hers it's as if he touched her. She visualized the file from Granger and imagined when he saw it, Steve would be embarrassed but that was a risk she felt willing to... Reilly interrupted another call from the Vermont State Police, this time from Sergeant Wilkers. Laura picked up and heard, "Grab a pencil. We'll meet in an hour. Head southwest to Lyndon and turn right toward Stannard and Greensboro. I'll wait at the intersection to Caspian Lake in a navy blue four-door sedan."

"You can come here."

"I won't step foot there and Marschek said you'd cooperate."

"Okay; I'll be there."

"It'll take you about 45 minutes to get here." For the second time in less than five minutes, Laura heard someone hang up on her, grabbed a pad and tape recorder, and told Reilly she'd be back. Within minutes, Laura felt her whole body relax as she headed southwest, rolled the windows down, and relaxed. An hour later, she reached the intersection, saw the car in the shade, and pulled up alongside. A tall blonde man walked over and thrust his right hand through the open window. "Hello, Laura."

"This is pretty weird, Wilkers."

"Uh huh; follow me." Another mile down dirt roads, they pulled into a driveway. When they reached the house, she counted five bicycles leaning against a fence and heard squeals of laughter from the back. Wilkers explained the kids were his daughters and their friends. "Do you feel better now about being alone with an accused sex fiend?"

Laura ignored his sarcasm, followed him in, and sat where he pointed. When he joined her at the kitchen table, Wilkers suggested they not pretend they didn't know each other by name and reputation. Laura cleared her throat. "What do you think you know about me?"

"I first saw you with Scolarzski at a retirement party in Middlesex a year ago and again when that little girl from Starksboro went missing. You resigned after that Orsini bitch shot you after—as Barber might say—you and her boyfriend scorched the sheets."

"A little diplomacy might help; you might say you heard I...."

"Let's get right to it. You were a cop for a year and..."

"Almost two," she interrupted.

"Whatever, no matter how you slice it, you're still white bread: no depth or substance—still a virgin, so to speak."

"I may not have 14 years but I saw..."

He interrupted, "I have 15 years and don't expect you to like me or like what they say I did but I expect the best in court."

"You'll get it but why me?"

Wilkers shrugged, "Though you stayed a recruit for all intents and purposes, you saw filth and perversion."

Laura admitted she had but what she couldn't fathom was the idea that after 15 years, she might sink so low as to scar a kid for life. "I know how that sounds, sir, but learned with sexual assault against minors, it's rare when an adult's charged erroneously. There are too many layers of investigation first that..."

"Lady, that's horse shit. In fact, I..."

Laura held her hand up. "Let's not waste time; I don't want to hear you admit or deny it. I don't have to know to do my job."

Wilkers laughed it was always that way at first—the feelings of disgust, the holier-than-thou attitude of those who didn't know what it felt like to work shit cases. "After you're around it a while, lady, shit smells eerily familiar."

"Don't insult me with...."

Wilkers interrupted, "After a while, cops begin to believe the whole world's populated by freaks and wrap themselves up in some stupid little case like... Shit; never mind." Wilkers stood, headed to the refrigerator, returned with two glasses of iced tea, and slid one forward. "Here's your beverage of choice."

Laura laughed, "You can't possibly know that."

Wilkers claimed he saw her a third time at a restaurant with Scolarzski. "Are you two still an item?"

Laura ran her fingers along the rim. "That's done."

Wilkers leaned close and dropped his sarcastic tone. "The State took my girls and now all I get is supervised visits. Rather than risk suspension, I took an unpaid leave of absence and you may be my only hope." Wilkers drifted off to ramble he believed there were three varieties of humans: ones who numbed out early, ones who saw only the worst, and ones who saw only the best. "I include Scolarzski, Rawlings, Sigler, and Granger in a group that sees the worst. Count me in that group, too, but not Barber, Macrae, or you—not yet, anyway. There's an idealistic twist, a naiveté about you. Even though you were a cop long enough to see it, you weren't corrupted by it."

Laura sighed, "*It* as in?"

"The evil in our world."

Laura suggested he listen to his daughters, feel sunshine, smell fresh air, and enjoy the view. "The world isn't evil but some of its people are." For the rest of the morning, Laura scanned files and listened to him describe events from his perspective. She had questions but let her mind absorb details about his wife, her death, their three daughters, move to a new town, reassignment to a new troop, and the witness he fell in love with. In the end, Laura suspected though much sounded self-serving, she had more than enough to start.

26

After a few hours, Al suggested Laura take his accordion file with her. "Let's take a break and walk my property." Al found her intriguing: young, well-educated, and beautiful; incongruously, he also saw her as shy, hesitant, and quiet and imagined that's what charmed Scolarzski. "Laura, I'd like to ask a personal question."

"Ask then I'll decide if I'll answer."

He stopped walking and faced her. "What hurts you the most about being human?"

She licked her lips. "Fear of rejection by people I love."

"And that includes sexuality, does it not?"

"Yup, the most difficult thing I ever did was tell a man I loved him. I felt terrified waiting for his response."

"Was that man Steve?"

"Where's this going?"

Al described a theory of humans presented with moments that offered choices or options. "Like Frost's poem about a road not taken, how we react to or deal with moments become our defining characteristics. We make the same choices over and over and eventually display a predictable pattern of behavior. Laura, have you ever behaved totally out of character?"

"On occasion, I behaved a little out of character because acting in didn't get me where I wanted to go; always, though, choices were slow, deliberate, and cautious—small acting-out-of's you might say."

"You've never done anything that left you regretful?"

"Not deliberately."

"Come on, counselor. Ever get laid in a car at the drive-in or give some guy a hand job underwater at the lake?"

"No."

"Ever cheat on a law exam? Exaggerate? Lie? Mislead?"

"No."

"Did you and Steve have your affair on taxpayers' time?"

"No but once I investigated illegally."

He smiled; if she hadn't behaved abominably at least once, he would have felt impressed yet disappointed—how could she possibly represent him? He pointed to a bench beneath a thicket of sumac trees. "My theory about moments and choices comes from years of observation. I thought I had it down cold. I believed nothing could surprise me again."

"About others or you?"

"About anyone but mostly myself. During the time you investigated illegally, were you surprised at your own behavior?"

Laura shrugged, "I got into some heavy self-justification head."

"I believe humans can convince themselves of anything. I thought I knew myself and what I was capable of doing until I woke one morning, surprised at my behavior but not shocked enough to stop." Al watched Laura's eyes cloud over as if she feared he were about to confess to pedophilia and stood up. "I promise everything you need is in the file. Call if you have questions, Detective."

"Need I remind you I'm no longer with the state police?"

"Yeah, just like I'm not being punished by the CFEL for sticking my nose3 in their business."

27

Laura returned to an empty office and spread the contents of the accordion file around on her desk; she re-organized, typed labels, and stored each category in its own large envelope: notebooks, state police investigative reports, a psychiatric profile of the victim identified only as nine-year-old female *TCS*, transcripts of dozens of interviews, a social worker's findings, an unflattering profile of Marsethe, an almost equally unflattering one of Wilkers, transcripts of dozens of interviews, and a social worker's findings. Laura sifted through everything again and thought it odd how Wilkers provided information not only about himself but also Marsethe. She sat back to read Wilkers' recollection of events preceding his arrest.

Peg said she wouldn't marry me but I wasn't content to live together because our five girls deserved a better arrangement. The week before Thanksgiving, another daughter showed up, a daughter Peg never mentioned. Francesca—Frannie—was soft-spoken, beautiful, and incredibly sensual in her movements. Within hours of her arrival, I felt bothered. I thought I knew myself, my tastes, and how I'd react in certain situations, but I couldn't stop looking at her. Peg asked if Frannie could stay with us, and inside my head I screamed No but I didn't mean it.

A few days later, Peg grilled hamburgers and the younger girls played outside. Frannie joined me in the cellar to sand a bureau for painting. I thought it was good to spend time on chores together so I'd get used to her presence. But she had other ideas and undressed slowly. It took me all of two seconds to get those pants off. I'm ashamed to admit I never once thought about Peg. I heard her footsteps in the kitchen but it didn't matter. With the girls outside and Peg upstairs, that was the most sexually intense experience of my life: the danger of the girls coming down, the betrayal of Peg. After that, Frannie came to me in the yard, my car, the shower, even in our bed after Peg left for work. It got so bad I couldn't be in the same room with her without envisioning our next time.

Laura skipped ahead and discovered his confessions continued for 11 more pages. She flipped back to the beginning and realized Al never identified Frannie's age or described her, for that matter, beyond beautiful or sensual. Was she under-aged? Might she be nine-year-old *TCS*? But that wouldn't fit with Wilkers' description of Frannie as initiator. The victim's psychiatric profile clearly described the victim as *unaware of human male anatomy prior to the alleged assault of March 29.* Laura grabbed the envelope containing police reports and read the section about the alleged two years of molestation prior to the incident leading to Wilkers' arrest. According to the victim's interviews by state police, the child stated *Uncle Al liked me to sit in his lap so he could touch me in my underwear. I didn't like it but then yesterday, he made me touch him in a very ugly place.*

Laura returned everything to her briefcase, locked up, and drove toward the carriage house but changed her mind and headed to a pay phone to call Wilkers. "How old is Frannie?"

"Twenty."

"Al, why give me something so personal to read?"

"Did you finish?"

"No. I didn't think it..."

"Do me a favor, counselor, and read every word."

Laura swallowed hard. "Okay. Al, I'm at a pay phone and should get back before someone notices I'm gone again."

Wilkers laughed, "You're a hell of a lot smarter than I was. It took too long to distrust each and every one of those fucking liars."

Laura returned to the carriage house and after supper wandered the academy grounds—everything well-manicured and spectacular: sprigs of pale green grass, newly-sprouted wildflowers, ferns and mosses, and fruit trees—a veritable Garden of Eden, just what the CFEL ordered. "No weeds allowed in this paradise," she chuckled and imagined Steve's yard looked beautiful, too, bathed in early evening glow. She headed down a well-worn path and stared across the river at fishermen on the New Hampshire side. To sounds of children and lawnmowers in the distance, she sat on a boulder and recalled how she once spent hours alone in the same woods. She ran her fingers along a sumac branch, marveled at how velvety it was to the touch, and studied pine cones, bark, twigs, shrubs, rocks, stones, grass, moss, and wild raspberry canes. She watched spiders spin webs, ants trail one another to a sandy mound, a squirrel...

A male voice said, "I find it peaceful here, too."

Laura turned to Glenn. "I didn't hear you coming!"

He sat beside her. "I stopped by to invite you to dinner and Brian said you headed in this direction."

Laura felt a flush at proof creepy Brian watched her every move but forced a smile. "Thanks, but I already ate."

"And may I ask what you call dinner?"

Laura shrugged, "I had a Cobb salad and iced tea. "

He chuckled, "If I promised you'd eat properly every day, would you marry me?"

Laura sighed, "Glenn, I need breathing room."

"Then how about strawberry-rhubarb pie?"

Laura studied his eyes and imagined he might yield information. "I can stop by later for dessert. Is 8:30 okay?"

"Sounds great. I'll count the minutes."

Laura returned to the carriage house and settled down to concentrate on Wilkers' log as it moved into January.

All that attention made me feel young and sexy again but as good as Frannie was for me physically, she drained me mentally. I walked a thin line at work and got little done. My partner was disgusted and didn't understand I couldn't think straight! I decided to put an end to the charade of honorable father and family man and approached Peg with my suspicion she brought Frannie into the house to test my commitment. Peg refused to answer; she didn't even bother to deny my suspicions. What I investigated blurred into my affair with Frannie, who floated in and out of the house like a ghost. Daytime, nighttime, it didn't matter. It was always the same: if Peg and the younger girls were home, she became big sister and brushed their hair, helped with homework or chores; if they were outside or asleep, Frannie started up with me. I felt disgusted and told myself I could control my response. It didn't always have to end up the same but I couldn't stop. Then Peg left with the girls.

Days, I interviewed people in Fallsbridge and researched the CFEL. Nights, I rattled around that big house and missed Peg. I tried to keep it straight, tried to keep it legal. A social worker from child protection services came around every week and started her shit. While she screamed we had to go into Fallsbridge and protect the kids, the captain screamed just as loud: 'No more mistakes.' 'Get the goods.' 'Remember Island Pond.' 'Find your witnesses.' 'Nail the bastards clean.' Everyone eventually retracted their statements until I had nothing. My mind wouldn't give me a moment's peace so I looked for someone to talk to, distract me, and help me forget. Frannie always seemed to know when I was my neediest, showed up, and let me talk, especially about Angela. Oh, lord, that little girl is such a purist— she believes when something goes wrong a cop is powerful enough to fight to the end.

Laura lowered the notebook—stunned Wilkers discussed an ongoing investigation. Laura glanced at her watch; she had exactly 45 minutes to deal with Wilkers before she met Glenn at the restaurant. She rushed out to her car and headed east with a growing certainty of a connection between Wilkers' arrest and the investigation of Marsethe. Would the CFEL counterattack with the same issue? Wilkers investigated the doctor on an alleged sexual assault on a minor—how apropos if that same state police detective stood accused of a similar crime. The CFEL could confuse the issue by showing everyone who cared about kids and justice that what Marsethe was accused of paled in comparison to what one of the state's own did. The betrayal: a crime against a kid by a so-called public protector.

Laura knew that wasn't too far-fetched a theory and recalled an incident when she was nine or ten when state social workers visited the academy, every child interviewed as part of an investigation after a husband, his wife, and their three children fled the community and lodged a complaint of widespread abuse. The tables turned when the headmaster and the three children's teachers provided conflicting interpretations of the same incidents and situations. In the end, no one looked good. Were the parents too lenient? Were the educators too harsh? In the end, there was too little evidence. For months afterwards, Sunday services included sermons that detailed police harassment, dissected the state's subversion of a community's right to maintain a private school, and listed the violations to the rights of worshipers, citizens, and most importantly, parents. In the end, the members of the community withdrew a little further from outside influences.

Laura crossed the bridge, pulled into a grocery store lot, and called Wilkers. "How could the CFEL get this little girl to lie?"

"Come on, counselor. I know you were one of them."

Laura sighed, "Once upon a time I lived among them and believed their crap wholeheartedly but no more. I read the transcript and listened to the tape; the girl's convincing, not confused."

"Yup, Tina's too well-rehearsed to crack. The kid I worry about is Angela. The longer it takes the state to build its case, the less likely she'll hold on. That's where you come in, counselor. I got kicked off the investigation, so it's up to you to protect Angela."

"I'm not sure I should meet her. It might…"

A harsh response: "Angela and kids like her are why you're here! Call Granger if you think otherwise."

"I know why I'm here!" she muttered.

Laura returned to Fallsbridge to join Glenn at the Maidstone. She desperately wanted inside information about the CFEL but listened to him chat about changes in the town, an addition to the library, academic and sports achievements at the academy, and a sizable gift to build the community center—nothing particularly interesting to a woman who hated that shitty little town. On occasion, she asked questions about his family or business but all in all, what she went there for, she didn't get. When she felt the need to stifle a yawn, Laura glanced at her watch, surprised to see 10:00 p. m. When she stood and thanked Glenn for the wonderful pie and conversation. Glenn insisted he escort her across the dark lot and waited while she unlocked the door. When her knee buckled, Laura grasped the handle as Glenn grabbed. "Are you all right?"

"I'm fine but that wobble's why I still need a cane." Glenn seemed overly concerned about a stumble, as if she fell and split her skull open or knocked out every tooth. As he helped her into the driver's seat, Laura imagined Glenn might mention her condition to Marsethe and a contact occur without a request from her. Laura rubbed her knee. "I hope I didn't do any permanent damage."

"You should see Mel."

"Um, I don't know. I don't trust him."

Glenn knelt alongside the open door. "Driving a standard must aggravate things so can I drive you home? I could keep your car overnight and pick you up early in the morning."

"I'm fine, Glenn, really." Laura pulled away with a wave but felt guilty at how glad she felt to escape his company. She headed toward the carriage house but at the last second, sped out of town. At a pay phone, she pulled out a fistful of change and dialed Steve. At no answer, she left a message: "When you lie in bed tonight, imagine we're in each other's arms; Lord knows that's the only way I'll get through another night."

28

Gil followed at a safe distance, continued past, stopped, and turned back. Her frequent, brief calls seemed odd. Who the hell did she call and why travel so many different directions to find pay phones when there was a phone in her law office and two pay phones in town? He pulled into a driveway, cut the lights, and in the rear view mirror, watched her jump back into her car. He waited for her to pass, gave her a lead, and followed with his lights off until she pulled in and parked next to the carriage house. He waited until windows were dark, headed to the village center, and pounded on the doctor's door. A light came on and

Marsethe answered in his robe. "Laura's back but spent some time tonight at the Maidstone. Have you and the elders decided Glenn should be encouraged to put the moves on her?"

Marsethe laughed, "I find it odd this exasperates you, Gilbert, when in the past, your brother's disdain for participation vexed you; a little competition between brothers is healthy, yes?"

"I don't wish to compete and you know why. What do I have to do to get that hearing before the elders?"

"Patience, Gilbert, all you need is patience."

29

Laura settled into bed, flicked the reading lamp on, and read Wilkers' log as it moved into February: *Cops get so involved with work they become unrecognizable to the people who love them. The job robs them of our dreams, illusions, and in the end, too often the ones they love.* As his musings about his career choice seemed to go on for pages, Laura thought to skip ahead until he mentioned Steve:

> *Today is the fourth anniversary of Beth's death. If four years ago, anyone predicted I'd become involved in a sordid affair with a woman young enough to be my daughter, I'd have argued I was too mature for such undignified behavior. I loved Beth but hated to see her suffer— first the double mastectomy then chemotherapy. I remember the night she begged to be released from the hold the girls and I supposedly exerted over her spirit. All night long, I held her tight but refused to give her permission to leave us. In the end, she waited until the girls were at school and I was at work before she took care of it on her own with pills she hoarded. I screamed for hours **how selfish of you!** but how selfish of me to deny her the freedom to time her own departure.*
>
> *I was surprised when Scolarzski showed up at the funeral. We hadn't seen each other in years, ever since some stupid argument I can't recall. He wore a bad suit and sunglasses that couldn't hide the fact he was crying, too. Afterwards, the girls and I couldn't move, stuck to those stupid folding chairs until he came up and one after another, dragged us to our feet for backbreaking hugs. He even let me bawl all over that pathetic suit. God damn him! A week later, I escorted a prisoner to Chittenden County and stopped, thinking we could talk one widower to another. He reverted to silent fury over a stupid argument that meant nothing to anyone in the universe but him. Right in front of his peers, he let me stand there and make a fool of myself, pretending I*

wasn't in front of him, fucking begging him to talk to me. He had no right to come to Beth's funeral if he was going to be such an ass!

Laura wondered how things got so confused between them; she barely knew Wilkers but suspected like most cops, he was impatient, stubborn, judgmental, and never wrong. From first-hand experience she knew Steve had a way of distancing himself from issues he couldn't control, as if ignoring or turning away accomplished anything. On occasion, he treated her like that and she suspected if she didn't fight her own instincts to hide, she'd be a willing party to a doomed marriage.

When a light came on in the kitchen of the main house, Laura turned the reading lamp off and watched Brian Lemphier drop an ice cube into a glass. He was bare-chested, his fine hair tousled from sleep. She thought it odd how a man so intelligent, well-educated, and with such a great family, could be so antagonistic. Maybe it was as simple as Brian was a consummate CFEL husband: demanding, unapproachable, and unaffectionate. Why not? It worked well on women like Violet or girls like Joanna, raised to feel grateful for any morsel of attention. Laura watched Brian sip from his glass and read a magazine until he turned to stare in her direction. She cowered in the dark until she realized he couldn't possibly see her, sat up, and watched him rummage through a laundry basket. Brian removed a towel, shook it out, moved out from behind the table, and faced her. At the sight of his pale nakedness, Laura imagined it was an accident—surely he didn't know she was there. She returned to bed feeling shamed. Good lord, she spied.

Laura drifted to sleep and dreamed she relaxed in bed with Steve, the room so hot and still, he dripped melting ice onto her flat abdomen to cool her. Hours later, she dreamed she begged him to forgive an earlier rejection and bring her to pleasure a more intimate way. An hour before sunrise, she dreamed she stood naked in front of a full-length mirror, caressed a swollen abdomen, and worked vitamin-rich ointment into stretched and scarred skin. She awakened grateful for dreams of a man she loved and prayed dreams might come true.

30

In the morning, Ralph stopped to pick Steve up and leaned on the horn. He waited, jumped out, and pounded on the back door. His buddy opened the door in skivvies and said he just barely got to sleep. "Why? Did the little lady pop by in the middle of the night and occupy you in the paramount recreational activity known to man?"

Steve yawned, "No such luck; I couldn't sleep."

While his best buddy dressed, Ralph helped himself to coffee and a stale donut then wandered into the living room. Here and there were a few things he imagined might be Laura's but wondered if Steve hid the truth. *Where are all the pretty little feminine touches? Women like Laura bring the light of life to the dank hellholes men call home.* When Steve came in dressed but still looking like a pile of dog shit, Ralph chuckled, "Laura's coming back to marry a freak like you, right?"

Steve grinned. "She promised she would."

During the drive, Ralph waited for chatter but silence remained his podna's customary domain. "I gotta know where the little lady is, what she's doing, who she's doing it to, and why."

Steve mumbled, "Nope," and stared outside.

At his desk, Ralph thought *Quality detectives do their own detecting* and snuck into the file room; he glanced over his shoulder, opened the drawer holding the lieutenant's records; and peered at labels on files near the front—nothing new. He opened further and saw messy printing on a label: *Wilkers / Marsethe / Delorange.* Ralph had no clue about the middle name but thought Al and Laura made a weird combo. Ralph glanced over his shoulder again, turned his back to the room, lifted the file, mashed it under his shirt, and wandered to the men's room for what Granger would assume was another leisurely, world-renowned Babar-crap.

31

At the table, Laura enjoyed scrambled eggs with green pepper and onions as she continued Wilkers' log:

> *After Beth's death, I went years without feeling I missed anything. Then I met Peg. Our life together was good but I didn't need sex; it was her companionship I wanted. Then Frannie arrived and a man with a dignified sex life became insatiable. Why didn't I hear my internal bells go off? Why did I talk about work night after night? If I believed nothing could surprise me again, why didn't I see the blankness in her eyes whenever she whispered she loved me? If I knew anyone in the CFEL was capable of anything, why couldn't I see Peg was part of it? One morning in early March, I watched Frannie sleep—terrified at the fact I knew so little about her. The night before, she pressed for details about Angela and though I knew she asked too many questions, I shared more than I should. At breakfast, I asked what she was up to and for the first time, recognized that*

blankness for what it was: apathy, maybe even disdain for my physical needs. Finally, I became the man I should have been all along: I ordered Frannie to leave and never return.

In the distance, Laura heard what sounded like nine, not eight, bongs from the church bell tower. She checked her watch and gasped at the sight she'd lost two hours. At the office, Laura heard Reilly settle in, again with no greeting and minutes later, announce a call from Sergeant Wilkers. He issued an invitation to lunch at an inn north of Lyndonville. She agreed then spent the rest of the morning trying to work. Laura stared outside at the green and watched two preschool-aged boys fill a wheelbarrow with stones and twigs then push it around only to dump it again. She thought they were still so innocent, pure, creative, eager, and idealistic. How many more years would it take the elders to mold them into the next generation of Brian? Laura studied her briefcase—opened an inch —and figured she should finish the log.

Peg called and arranged to meet at the stable. The two of us, her sister, and our five girls would enjoy a horse ride, homemade pizza, and fun. I thought Peg wanted to start over, forget about Frannie, or agree to marry me after all. Tina was there, fell in the barn and bruised her chest, which later was determined might be a mark made by a man's arm holding a frail child down. Frannie arrived while I cleaned the barn and despite every promise I made Peg, within minutes we went at it like animals. Tina watched and later provided state police and social workers with descriptions that substituted her as my partner in one deviant display.

Laura blinked slowly and thought Wilkers' behavior in the barn seemed particularly inappropriate with children around. He was a grown man and the father of three daughters. Didn't men reach a level of sexual maturity as they aged? Couldn't men be in the presence of a sexy woman and maintain self-control? "If I thought Steve…"

Reilly peeked around the corner. "Did you call me?" Laura shook her head no and watched Reilly disappear.

It's amazing what happens to fools who drop their pants at the sight of a willing woman. Frannie watched her little sister watch and didn't care. She willingly played her sordid part in some perverse script but it wasn't over. Two hours after my arrest for sexual assault,

I heard Frannie's pregnant. I cannot believe how I behaved whenever Frannie came around but what surprised me even more was how I feel nothing for that baby. My girls mean everything to me; I loved them before they were born. Until that moment I heard about Frannie's pregnancy, I never understood how my love for Sandra, Sheila, and Sharon started with my love for my wife.

Laura ran her fingertips along the cover of Wilkers' log and sensed little remorse on his part except he got caught. Yes, he had regrets: his arrest was a matter of public record; yes, he felt shame: his daughters, parents, friends, and co-workers would soon learn his only defense was instead of an engagement sexually with Tina, it was with her older sister. She left the office early enough to take the scenic route north along the Connecticut River then southwest toward Burke Mountain. The blue sky, white clouds, and green mountainside were perfect, the slow drive soothing until details from Wilkers' log intruded. Images floated in her mind, especially those of bestial sex as witnessed by a child too young to understand the concept of willing partners. Laura could not figure out the elusive Peg. How was it possible she might bring her daughter into the house to seduce a man? There was information in the state police reports which portrayed her in an unflattering light, especially the fact Peg took nine-year-old Tina not to the hospital for treatment but to family physician Dr. C. Melvin Marsethe. Why? The shame of publicity or was Peg a willing party to an examination which allowed the doctor to plant evidence?

Laura wondered if Tina started off describing what she actually saw but in words purposefully vague to protect her sister. The tapes and transcripts from the interviews were clear. Over and over, Tina described herself and Frannie in solid roles as victims: *"Uncle Al hurt Frannie first. Uncle Al saw me watching and did bad things to me, too. What Uncle Al did to me wasn't nice."* Laura imagined when Marsethe saw Tina's bruises he suggested something different and an impressionable child found his version made more sense than her recollection. Tina saw something she understood intellectually but not emotionally. She clearly described how horses mated at her aunt's stable and reported she was present at the births of four colts. Perhaps by the time she got to the hospital, what she thought she remembered was very different from what she actually saw. Laura's throat tightened as she recalled the photographs of Tina's chest. Marsethe's report said the bruises were consistent with the type of marks a 230-pound-male would make if he restrained a struggling child. On the other hand, the emergency room doctor noted there was no conclusive way to state what caused such extensive bruising.

Laura wondered how Al got such detailed information about an ongoing investigation: copies of state police and child protective service reports, and transcripts of interviews. If one of the detectives she worked with were arrested, would the others enable access? She decided yes—until that moment in court when the verdict rendered was *Guilty*, cops tended to help and protect one another.

32

When Laura arrived and entered the restaurant, Al assessed her mood as politely embarrassed. After they ordered, he decided to approach the topic head-on and labeled his behavior with Frannie as depraved. When Laura nodded but remained silent, Al said, "When I was 13 my mother warned me only stupid boys thought what they did in the dark couldn't be seen." When Laura squinted in confusion, Al described what his mother had in mind: a boy scratched his ass behind a closed door, picked his nose behind the couch, or farted in a crowded theater. "She beat around the bush but got to masturbation. I doubt she foresaw how degenerate her son could become someday."

Laura leaned across the table. "Don't reduce a serious issue to lame comments. How can you claim you loved Peg? You screwed her daughter anywhere you found a flat surface."

When Laura stood, Al grabbed her wrist. "If you walk out, I don't have a prayer of bringing my girls home." He noticed curious glances from other diners and released her. "The day after the barn, two detectives from another troop arrived with a warrant for my arrest. They dragged me past my peers and one of those assholes said, *'Come on, lover-boy. Let's see if we can get you to dry hump a cup like you do little girls'* —so much for innocent until proven guilty, huh?"

Laura sat back down slowly. "I spent hours going over the details and unless you didn't use one or took the condom with you to dispose of, it seems obvious Frannie provided seminal fluid."

Al leaned back and chuckled, "It also seems obvious former cops are brilliant defense attorneys; I didn't think to take it with me."

Laura looked at her watch and said she needed to get back for an appointment. "First, though, I have a question. Why would the CFEL, Marsethe, Peg, or Frannie set something like this in motion? What advantage could they hope to gain?"

"They needed me gone; I got closer than anyone anticipated." He slid an envelope across the table and recommended she go through notes never entered into evidence because his witness retracted her statement. Al watched Laura finger the contents before she nodded. He stared into her eyes. "You've made it clear this is strictly business but I'd like to make an observation: you look tired, probably work too hard, and never have fun. From one lonely human to another, if you love Scolarzski, do whatever's necessary to make it happen."

Laura stood up. "Yes, let's keep this professional, okay? What happened between me and Steve is in the past."

"Life's too short for foolish pride," Al managed to say before Laura exited. He watched her cross the parking lot, observed a slight limp, and knew she'd spend the rest of her life dealing with her choice of law enforcement as a career: banged-up bones and scarred tissue at least, diseased mind and troubled soul more likely. He suspected Laura said one thing but her eyes showed another. Steve was a lucky man to earn her love—an even luckier one to actually hold on to it.

33

Laura rushed into the office seven minutes late for an appointment. "Reilly, I'm sorry if you stayed late on my account."

"I wanted to be here; they're my maternal grandparents."

Laura reviewed Edgar and Mary Broussange's financial summary with liquid assets in excess of $1,115,000, not including a mortgage-free home assessed at $275,000 for taxation purposes. They described their history of generous gift-giving and stated their intentions clearly: whoever outlived the other would live on interest from investments, individual retirement accounts, and variable annuities. After the death of the second spouse, remaining assets were to be liquidated with half the profits distributed equally among their three children or the beneficiaries of that child if he or she predeceased them, adamant about the proportion since they foresaw competition. Laura provided various options to avoid future tax burdens, which they agreed to consider. At the conclusion of the meeting, Laura asked their intentions for the other half of the estate and wasn't surprised by Edgar's answer: "The CFEL. It was agreed upon the day we were inducted as life members in 1966." Laura prepared a draft will, filed the contents, and figured the generosity of members explained the CFEL's financial health. If she revisited some of the files Marschek shared with her earlier, she imagined she'd discover little changed since her family left—the village was prosperous because so much of its daily life was intertwined with the church. Good or bad, for better or not, Fallsbridge and the CFEL survived side by side; she knew her parents had willingly tithed and intended to be generous upon death. Something else remained intact: the doctor was an integral part of leadership—not an elder, but accepted at its core.

At the carriage house after work, Laura changed for a brisk bike ride to the river. She found the humidity unusual for the Northeast Kingdom but figured that's what she needed: a muscle-numbing ride with healthy sweat as an added bonus. As a small group of boys sped by on bicycles, Laura looked around and realized she reached the green across from the academy. She hopped off the bike, leaned against a maple, and closed her eyes to painful memories; she demanded she stop punishing herself for another's debauchery. If she were forgiving of a child's ignorance, she'd accept Marsethe set up a seduction painstakingly: years of positive attention, years of encouragement from parents to take advantage of the doctor's generosity, years of unthreatening touches and gentle kisses, years of tender concern and when it happened, actions that felt natural. The same night of his first attempt, Laura lay in bed and touched herself in the same place and understood it was wrong for a grownup to touch her like that. She overheard enough conversations between her mother and 16-year-old Jack to know that kind of touching was called sex and sex was for adults. She woke her mother and within hours, told one person after another and overheard a state trooper call it *the doctor-patient molestation incident*. After his arrest, Dr. Marsethe spent seven hours in jail. Charges never made it to court because of a lack of evidence: no vaginal injuries, no retrieval of a semen sample, an intact hymen, and no semen stains on her clothing. The state police obtained a warrant to search his house but found no semen stains on the parlor couch or rug; a quarter under a curtain ruled inconclusive because by her own mother's admission, the child often spent time there and could have noticed it on any number of occasions. The case got thrown out and following the next Sunday's service, Marsethe inched up behind her in the basement of the church and whispered, *I understand your shame and forgive your lie.* In the middle of the night, her attacker entered her home and climbed the stairs to her bedroom. When she smelled mercurochrome and heard keys jingle, she opened her eyes to a hand about to cover her eyes. For what felt like an eternity, his phallus thrust and tore. In the end, she felt something cold and sharp press her skin and was left to bleed to death in her own bed. Laura heard a shout and jumped to her feet but in the distance, it was only children on park swings. She swallowed hard at the thought yes, she survived the freak but if her own experience and that of FTS indicated a pattern, there little time remained to spare Angela the second, worse, and potentially fatal attack.

Laura pedaled to the parking lot behind the post office and scanned the general area for Gil or any other nut from that shitty little town. She dug her pockets for coins and from a pay phone, dialed the station first. At Macrae's voice, she hung up; at the house number, she got the machine and hung up; finally she called his cell and left a message: "Steve, please meet me tomorrow night at 9:00, Cold Hollow Cider Mill. I'm stalled and need to talk this investigation through with the best." Laura pedaled back to the village green, collapsed on the grass under a tree, and pressed her back against its rough bark. As her eyes glistened, she insisted she could find the strength to face the idiots, fools, and perverts in one shitty little town. "I have to find the strength."

A sweet voice asked, "Are you hurt?"

Laura turned to a face familiar from file photos. "I'm fine."

Angela harrumphed, "Strong people don't talk to themselves and don't let themselves get hurt." In an instant, she left before Laura could debate such an erroneous philosophy.

34

As Mel walked leisurely from his house to the snack bar, Gil pulled over in the cruiser. "I saw Laura talk to Angela."

."Do you know where Little Miss Laura is now?"

Gil pointed west. "That's her bike in front of the store. Mel, I've been meaning to tell you or the elders Reilly got tickets to a concert at the Bell Centre and invited me to..."

In exasperation, Mel waved his hand. "Yes, yes, go, go, but use protection." He crossed the green to the store, found Laura in an aisle reading labels on cereal boxes, and chuckled, "A woman in prime child-bearing years needs a low-fat, high fiber diet but be certain to add adequate protein, yes?" When Laura turned, he saw the flush, wide eyes, and lack of confidence that affected him still.

As Laura headed to the register, Mel felt an odd exhilaration when she came face to face with Caroline and made polite conversation. Of course they wouldn't recognize each other—Caroline four years older and a graduate of the business curriculum, never focused enough to be college-bound. Then Caroline did the unthinkable and said, "You must be Jack's sister. You have those magnificent Delorange eyes."

Laura smiled. "I'm his sister Laura. And you are?"

"Caroline Beaudon but Jack won't remember me."

Laura reached to shake Caroline's hand, "I'll bet he will."

Mel watched Laura head out to secure her parcel and pedal away as Caroline fumbled with another customer; when they were alone in the store, she stammered, "I often think about Jack and wonder if..."

"You never meant a damn thing to that fine young man," Mel said and placed his groceries on the counter. "All it takes is one word to the elders. You need our business, young lady. Remember that."

35

Ralph listened to Joyce rummage in the cellar for gardening tools. When she trudged up and offered to take him out for pizza, Ralph lowered a file. "Isn't Meggie coming to cut your hair?"

Joyce laughed she forgot, suggested they invite Meg along, and noted the open file. "Will you have to work tonight?"

Ralph considered confiding his discomfort but sighed, "Nope; I'll finish before you do." Like always when he dealt with awkward, embarrassing, or horrifying cases, he procrastinated. First he prepared a half-pot of coffee; second he turned on the television and checked the weather; third, he rummaged for cookies, candy, or chips; and finally, he plopped at the table and spread photocopies of Granger's secret file in an arc. He imagined a second look wouldn't shock. Wrong; it had been a long time since he felt so stunned at what men did in the name of love or religion to cover sins. He suspected something funny in Laura's past. How dumb—a seasoned professional or so he claimed—not to recognize the obvious. For two years, he studied the little lady and guessed her hesitant approach to Steve proved she was a victim of a hurtful love affair. Ralph discovered she was a victim all right, but of a vengeful man.

Ralph thanked God for small gifts: photos didn't copy well so he was spared that repeat agony. He reread the transcript from victim ARL, felt a knot the size of a bowling ball in his stomach, and closed his eyes to poignant words from one damaged little girl. He put everything back into the file, certain their asshole lieutenant manipulated the little lady into working undercover because of similarities between herself and ARL. Despite her love for Steve and the fine life they planned together, Laura returned to a shit-pit to take on a monster. Ralph heard Joyce fill a bucket outside and imagined he should help with yard work. He watched a streak of pale yellow shift along the wall as sunlight poked through trees. June: best month of the year, perfect for weddings and anniversaries. He thought if Steve and Laura had gotten married as originally planned,

84

they'd celebrate one week the same week as Ralph and Joyce's 25 years. He imagined they'd jump onto the path toward a long, happy, loving marriage and maybe on their honeymoon—just like he and Joycie did—start a perfect little baby to fill their lives with joy.

Ralph jumped at: "It started to rain."

Ralph stood, massaged Joyce's tight shoulders, and decided to ask for advice. "Joycie, I need a woman's perspective on…"

He never got a chance because their darlin' daughter burst in laughing. "Why do I always get the feeling I'm interrupting?" Joyce hugged Meggie and the two gals retired to the kitchen to clip 'n style. Ralph listened to the voices of the two women he loved most of all: sweet, fantastic, caring, loving, forgiving women, a marvel to any man smart enough to love them. He visualized Laura—a miracle his best buddy ached for all his life and finally found.

Ralph heard Meggie pry about their upcoming anniversary and found it incredible Joyce hadn't figured it out, too. For weeks, Ralph knew Meg, his mother Grace, and his mother-in-law Betty hatched plans for the weekend after his and Joyce's 25th anniversary. Not much of a stretch to guess a party yet tacky to inquire exactly what those gals had in mind. An opportune moment occurred as Ralph read the paper and Meg wandered in to rattle on about how few people stayed married or how those who did got bored and other chitchat. She finally got around to it and asked if they made plans for the last weekend in June. Ralph winked. "You mean something G-rated I can tell you about?"

Meg glanced toward the kitchen. "Mom will have a fit but there's a party and you'll need to drag her inside."

"Darlin,' there's one absolutely-has-to-be-there-guest." He grabbed paper, jotted the law firm's name, and pressed it into Meg's hand. "Call and get an address for Laura Delorange at her new place so a special lady can plan a weekend trip home."

36

Laura watched lightning flash, imagined Steve saw the same miles away, and thought *he'll show up at the cider mill; surely he feels the same dull ache I do.* When she couldn't fall asleep, she grabbed Wilkers' notes:

> *I went to Fallsbridge to talk to Vince Mottolla. I got zero cooperation as usual. I left his store and headed over to the diner for lunch where a woman tripped and almost fell into my lap. After she's gone, I noticed she slipped a note into my shirt pocket. She did it so*

badly, if someone watched, they saw. As instructed, I waited at the entrance to Darling State Park at 2:00. She climbed into my car and for the next two hours, rode around while she rambled about things that made no sense. When it started to snow, she became hysterical— something about if she got home late, her husband would notice the garage floor was wet and check the mileage on the odometer. Women in Fallsbridge are so fragile. That one sure was. Later, at her request, I destroyed every note about her. She seemed on the verge of cracking and wouldn't have made a credible witness, anyway. Angela was more composed than that one. She was flaky, emotional, incoherent, and too influenced by Marsethe to be of any long term value.

Why did I trust anyone there? Why couldn't I give just enough information to satisfy Frannie I didn't keep secrets? Why wasn't I cautious about her motives? I will learn to live with what I've done to my life but not the fact my girls will hear how depraved I could be If Frannie testifies in court, my family will reject me.

Laura thought his notes were useless without a name and refolded the pages. She willed herself to fall asleep; extra hours that night might make up for—if she were lucky—a lack the next.

In the morning, Laura dragged herself to the office, stumped about how to proceed. She supposed she had options. If she made overtures to Glenn, he might mention Marsethe again or suggest she follow up with the doctor about her knee. But what would that accomplish? Brief visits to the doctor's office wouldn't lead him to confess to crimes against children or open confidential records. Since the organization's doctor didn't operate in a vacuum, Laura imagined she could research the CFEL itself; others did. She recalled a book published earlier about cults. The Burlington *Free Press* reviewed it since the focus of a section was the Community for Expansive Love, described as *an organization tucked away and folded neatly into the privacy of the rural Northeast Kingdom of Vermont.* True—the CFEL tucked itself away in a shitty little town with freaky people and filthy secrets; it folded itself neatly into and tied its success to the survival of a town with no discernible methods of survival—no industry to speak of once foresters and furniture manufacturers departed. The irony was townspeople saw the CFEL organization and its growing membership as a godsend.

Laura attended the academy and knew by heart the version of local history preached by the CFEL. During the late 1940's and through the 50's, Fallsbridge started a slow descent through a series of events.

First, World War II veterans decided to raise their children elsewhere; second, severe weather disrupted the harvest in the fall and sugaring in the spring three years in a row; third, the lumber mill closed when it became cost effective to transfer harvesting to old forests of the northwest; fourth, without the lumber mill, the furniture factory folded a year later; and fifth, the real estate market bottomed out. Lucky ones with skills to market elsewhere escaped and scattered. In 1965, five friends from Boston fished for trout on the New Hampshire side of the Connecticut River, heard the falls, and discovered an idle mill and silent factory in the midst of the most beautiful country ever fashioned by the hand of God. They called it paradise, pooled their resources, invested in a dying village, and secured its future. The five returned to Boston to extol the virtues of hard work, autonomy, and seclusion—values not at all incompatible with their new neighbors, locals who lived in places unreachable months each year and instinctively turned their backs to any government interference. The five professionals brought their families, money, and vision of the future into the backwoods of Vermont and like their predecessors, made no attempt to widen, improve, or pave potholed dirt roads to or from Montpelier. Laura recalled while a student at UVM, she heard a political science professor compare the culture of that area as a *back-to-the-earth survivalists' nirvana.*

Laura felt exhausted by her thoughts, disgusted by her messy desk, and the repetition inherent within legal work. She felt tired of that shitty little town, stared outside, and wondered how discouraged she'd feel after months instead of weeks. The only action that made sense was forward movement but in what form? If she behaved in ways consistent with her personality, she might never accomplish a thing. "Dear lord, give me some ideas. I want to go home."

She hated how whenever she mumbled, Reilly peeked around the corner. "Did you call me?"

Laura held the Broussange file up. "The rest of today's for research. I'm rusty with Vermont probate law and want to do right by your grandparents." Laura headed out and estimated travel time to Dartmouth; book, periodicals, or newspaper review time; and travel back time. If all went well, she'd work in time to wash her hair and soak in the tub—preparations sure to make her irresistible.

37

On his desk, Steve found a trooper report about a peeper in the woods. When Granger crooked his finger, Steve headed in expecting to discuss possible developments in an old, unresolved case. "Didn't I predict Sivalette would resurface someday?"

"Just do the necessary follow-up, Sergeant. I called you in to say I talked to Wilkers; seems he finds Delorange attractive and asked if you and she are still an item."

"I'm sure you were pleased to report we're over."

"So you say, Sergeant."

"So I do, Lieutenant."

Granger leaned across half his desk to hiss, "Someone in this room is so full of shit, he stinks up the State of Vermont! Don't go anywhere near her while she's on assignment or I'll have your shield."

Steve leaned across the other half. "I agree someone in this room is full of shit; Sivalette isn't someone to ignore, sir, and..."

"Sivalette's on the VSP radar screen so let it play out. If you love that woman, keep away to keep her safe."

"Give me a break. You have no right to..."

"Wilkers says local talent tails her every time she puts miles between herself and that crazy burg. Those friggin' cultists do their damnedest to keep cable companies and cell providers out of their kingdom but kept land lines. I cannot imagine what compels her to find pay phones in out of the way places or who she feels the urge to call. Care to enlighten me?"

Steve blinked slowly. "No, sir; message understood."

38

Laura loved the ivy-covered brick at Dartmouth and its beautiful, well-landscaped campus. She found the library and breathed in the musty scent of old books. With most students gone, it was unusually quiet. She used the computerized system and quickly found the book. She remembered the title as something like cults in the United States but since the author included Canada and Mexico, discovered the title to be: *Classic Cults: Alive and Well in Modern America*. Laura noted the author's name, publisher, publication date, and ISBN number and decided to order a print copy. She wandered through stacks and found the book and similar titles. During the computerized search, she discovered other current resources in periodicals and newspapers and realized to do it right, she could spend a month or more on research. She grabbed an armful of books and planted herself in a carrel next to a window with a magnificent view. As she settled in, she felt as if she traveled back in time to years at the University of Vermont or Columbia, where research for papers always seemed last-minute, rushed, and less than what she hoped to invest. For the rest of the morning, past lunch, and well into afternoon, Laura took notes and made photocopies until her stomach rumbled and neck ached. When she packed up and headed to the main desk, a librarian asked if she found everything she needed and Laura sighed, "This is a wonderful library. I could spend the rest of my life here."

"Obviously you aren't a student with access to the internet."

Laura indicated one book had a handwritten dedication inside. "How'd that get there?"

The librarian scanned the copyright page. "Ms. Adams is an alumnus and faculty member who teaches in the History Department under her maiden name Theriault. She lives in Vermont and I'd like to offer an address or phone number but that's privileged information."

Laura answered, "I understand. Thanks."

Laura headed west across the bridge and stopped in White River Junction to call Granger. "Sir, it's Laura Delorange. I need an address and phone number for a Claudette Adams or Theriault, Vermont resident, writer, Dartmouth faculty member. From her photo, I estimate her at mid-40. I'll hold."

"For chrissake, Delorange. Gimme a number and I'll call back." While she waited, Laura watched traffic in and out of the mini-mart and felt an odd sensation the Caprice Classic across the road was one she noticed in the library lot. She shaded her eyes, squinted, clearly made out three of five characters on the green plate, and scribbled them down. When Granger called with the information, she asked him to run a check on a partial plate. Another chuckled, "For chrissake, call back tomorrow."

Laura dialed Claudette Theriault's number in Thetford Center but reached a machine. At the beep, she started her message about the book and the CFEL then requested Ms. Theriault call collect that evening. Laura groaned, "Shit! My cell is dead up there and the only number I have in Fallsbridge is at the office and well, I can't let Reilly... Um, sorry; forget this dumb message. I'll try again later."

The drive back was glorious and even pulling back into the driveway at the carriage house couldn't dampen her spirits. After she finished her bath and dressed in an outfit she hoped he'd like, Laura headed off—windows and sunroof wide open—to take advantage of a temperature in the 70's. When she noticed how fast she drove, she slowed to 35 but never noticed the distinctive cruiser. By 8:15, she reached Waterbury Center and parked toward the back of the cider mill. She grabbed a hairbrush from her purse and forced it through her tangled mess. She glanced at her watch: 8:26—still way too early. Laura sat, watched, and waited. Every few minutes, she checked her watch and new cars in the parking lot. At 8:45, she left her car and wandered the food area past the cider press to the gift area. She kept her eye on the parking lot doors, returned to the food area, bought two cups of cold cider, two cider donuts, and on the connecting deck, relaxed in a cedar Adirondack chair. By 8:55, she headed back to her car with snacks to wait. Long after the sun set and cider mill closed, Laura watched vehicles pass. At 9:45, she called his cell and heard the standard message, tried his house, and when the machine picked up, gasped, "I wouldn't ask to meet unless it felt important! Pay attention because this is the last time I'll humiliate myself like this. Al Wilkers is my client. Yes, your former asshole buddy and punching bag came to stupid me for help. I wanted to explain in person but..." She swallowed hard and choked, "Baby, I'm sorry I'm yelling but I cannot believe you stood me up!"

39

From the archway, Steve fought against answering. He wanted to explain, warn, or suggest another place and time but Granger was right; he needed to keep his distance. When he heard the call end, he wandered into the bedroom, knelt in front of the closet, and pulled a box forward. Night after night, he allowed himself to look through the contents of one and only one. Sometimes, it contained folded jackets and sweaters; other times, photo albums, postcards, letters, paperbacks, school notes, trinkets, birthday cards, and mementoes. With the quantity of boxes there, he figured he had a few more days before he started over. When the phone rang, Steve listened to the machine pick up: "Steve, this is Lynette Delorange. John and I know the truth about what's going on, so there's no need to pretend. Come for dinner tomorrow and help us feel like we're still a family."

Steve grabbed. "Know what truth?"

"Laura will marry you the first chance she gets."

Steve closed his eyes. "Do you know where she is?"

A long, long pause, then: "Yes. Do you?"

"Yes. I worry all the time. Should I?"

Another long pause then: "I came from Fallsbridge and convinced John to settle there to raise a family and insisted he join the CFEL. I'm terrified this is punishment for so many bad choices."

"Laura's a skilled investigator, smart observer, and quick thinker. Lynette, she'll be fine."

A soft sigh then, "It's good to talk to you. Please come to dinner tomorrow around 6:30?"

"I'll be there." Steve returned to the bedroom and considered Lynette's statement she felt punished for bad choices: how easy to recognize self-paralyzing head crap in others; how difficult in oneself. He lifted the pillow beside his and pulled Laura's nightgown to his face; he breathed deeply and shuddered at a scent fainter than the night before.

40

Mel accepted an invitation from the Lemphier's to join them and Gil for dinner. After an amazing lamb stew, they relaxed on the patio in twilight. When he admired an impressive vegetable garden, Joanna acknowledged it as Laura's effort. He wandered over, doubly impressed by its orderly layout and soon-to-be abundant yield. He felt cautious yet excited as he observed Laura step back into the community as if she never left. He felt acutely aware of the years she stayed away, though during a 20-year gap he followed her accomplishments and overlooked how she ripped herself from him violently and succeeded despite him. *Law school? Really? Such a mind was destined to follow him in his practice of family medicine.*

A car pulled in, parked beside his, and Laura jumped out. "Move along!"

Mel found her reaction extreme though he felt a need to grin at how Brian stood with a flashlight and pointed like an old-dowager critic at a flower show. Mel smoothed things over with, "Your garden is lovely, Little Miss; forgive our natural curiosity, yes?"

Brian laughed, "What's with a hummingbird feeder? You don't think you'll attract any this far north, do you?"

Laura thought *My mother always did* but answered, "Never mind why I do anything. Just go away and leave me alone, all of you!"

Marsethe touched her arm. "Relax; we mean no harm."

Laura sneered, "Don't touch me!"

Gil snickered, "Must've been rancid cider."

Laura gasped, "What?"

"Or stale donuts," Gil added.

Violet drew Laura away in consolation, demanded others leave, and guided Laura inside. Mel bade everyone good night and at home lay in bed, replayed the events, and imagined Laura might not be to blame for her independent spirit. He recalled numerous incidents and verbal exchanges over the years. *Surely a sensitive daughter feels the influence of a free-thinking mother. Yet Laura remains young enough to receive additional*

91

instruction. Her sudden return to the community is fortuitous to say the least; if I attend to her natural intellect, I might witness her full return to the fold and thus, to me. Two potential problems: first is a sweet girl's shame of her past, as if passions is a sin not a miracle; and second, the man in Gil's photographs might be a lover still. Someone is the fortunate recipient of her late-night calls and it seems unlikely my angel escapes to private locations to phone Mama and Poppa.

The phone rang and Mel grabbed. "What!"

It proved unwise to answer since Yvonne sobbed, "Christopher, mother had a heart attack today."

"And?"

"Bernard, Roland, and I thought..."

"What—that I—who insists upon Mel—might take a heavy burden off your hearts and hands?"

A deafening silence until: "Mother called for you last night,; no, she begged for a chance to tell you something important."

"I'll look into arrangements but don't hold your collective breaths awaiting my arrival; I have responsibilities."

A clearer tone—in fact, a laugh. "Never fear, Christopher, we know our place is behind everything else but she is your mother."

Yes, she was his mother—a rare certainty in his life. Mel closed his eyes and whispered, "Yvonne, I will at all times avoid family residences. Provide me with a phone number for the hotel in town." When she finished with the details, he hung up.

41

Laura left early and headed to a pay phone. She reached Claudette Theriault Adams, identified herself, and asked if they could meet. Laura felt no surprise at the instant, "Why?"

"I'm interested in your research of the CFEL."

"Why?"

"I live in Fallsbridge."

"So?"

"Just like you don't know if you should trust me, I don't know if I should trust you."

"If you read my book, you know my position."

"I read most of it but still feel curious about your interest."

"My interest? My younger sister is in and out of a group in Idaho, populated by vicious, hostile men, their abused, passive women, and a tribe of filthy, neglected kids whose fathers are known only to God Himself. It's called *The Heavenly Assembly,* a survivalist camp complete with underground bunkers filled with weapons, ammunition, and dried or canned goods. Only desperate or destroyed people get hooked into these groups. I know which my sister is but I don't know which defines you."

"I grew up in the CFEL but my family left when I was 13. Now I investigate the CFEL's doctor on behalf of the Vermont State Police. If you were to divulge that, I'd fear for my wellbeing."

Laura heard a long silence. "If you're free this evening, I'll see you. I need to see you say those same words to my face."

Laura spent the rest of the day reading the book and drove Route 5 along the western side of the Connecticut River. She had no sense of being followed but made a few unnecessary stops or backtracked to make it difficult. When she realized she'd arrive late, she jumped onto I-91 and sped south. Laura found the isolated farmhouse quickly and Claudette Theriault Adams turned out to be a friendly, soft-spoken woman in her early 40's. Laura accepted a cup of tea, relaxed at her kitchen, and listened to a well-presented summary of an investigation detailed and thorough enough to have been conducted by a seasoned detective. The author claimed she reached a level of understanding and saw the CFEL clearly: undertones, control mechanisms, and insincerity masking deeper intentions, personality breakdowns, rebuilding along some plan she could only imagine had some future goal. "Yet whenever I thought about the people, I wasn't certain: individually, they're intelligent, successful, well-educated, attractive, healthy, affluent people. I saw them not as dregs of the earth with nowhere else to go or nothing better to do with their lives, but as people who'd be successful anywhere."

Laura nodded. "I agree they're impressive."

Claudette stood and paced. "I had the most difficulty with Marsethe. He's brilliant and creative, not as in artistic but certainly as in inventive or cunning. And he most definitely is charming."

Laura licked her lips. "Tell me everything you learned."

She insisted Laura call her Claudette, slid a notebook across, and stated she spent a year on the sidelines, an English teacher at the academy. "Whenever I live in cults, I blend in completely. After the first few months, I did as instructed: compiled a record of female functions and reported everything to the doctor." She pointed to a section on basal temperature and cycle length. "Reduce a woman to her menstrual cycle and you reduce her to the act of copulation; reduce a woman to her cycle and you reduce her to a decade or two of reproduction."

Laura pointed at Marsethe's writing. "And this?"

Claudette laughed, "Marsethe believed me when I claimed to be 33 instead of 39 and saw potential. Those are his instructions for one of the trysts he arranged to facilitate conception. At opportune moments within my cycle, he arranged for one of his hand-selected studs to pay an overnight visit. I said no until I risked detection."

Laura stared outside at a dark sky. "I can't imagine that kind of subjugation of passion or depth of regulation."

Claudette snorted, "If you tell the truth about growing up in the CFEL, of course you can!"

Laura shrugged, "I escaped at 13."

"Or so you claim," Claudette chuckled, studied Laura's eyes, and slid a stack of notebooks forward. "I'll let you borrow these."

"No, no, I can't afford to have them in my possession." She tapped her temple. "I have a good memory especially when material is presented in such an organized way. You proceed like a detective."

Claudette admitted she developed good skills as a news reporter. "My passion for my work cost me dearly in the end. I had difficulty infiltrating the CFEL and didn't get home much; those 20 months cost me a marriage, custody of my daughter, and self-respect. I engaged in a three-month involvement with Brian Lemphier that resulted in an unexpected pregnancy. About to turn 40, lord I felt shocked. In light of my deep love for a seven-year-daughter waiting at home, I struggled for months with my final decision. First I escaped, then I aborted."

42

Al felt surprised to get a call so late at night and even more so when it turned out to be Scolarzski. Within seconds, it became clear he called because of concern for his former partner. They made small talk before Al heard someone at the door. He ran over, stunned a second time to find Laura on the porch. "Odd thing is Scolarzski's on the phone."

Laura ran in and grabbed. "Steve, it's me!"

Al headed into the den to give her privacy, surprised when she finished quickly. "You could have talked longer."

"Thanks, but Steve's worried the phone line's tapped." Al insisted he checked outside lines and pole connections regularly, detailed his process, and asked if that sounded paranoid. She sighed, "Not at all. Could you check mine sometime?"

Al nodded and suggested she make herself at home; he looked through cupboards for something decaffeinated and found herbal tea.

When he rejoined her, Al asked, "Do you still expect me to believe you and Scolarzski are done? The man obviously is…"

"I hope we'll be together someday; enough said?"

Al nodded and listened to her summary of the meeting that afternoon. "Surely you know the woman told the truth."

"I believe the CFEL capable of many things but what she suggested seems too bizarre even for those perverts and freaks."

"From the way you talk, on the surface it seems you got away."

Laura stammered, "What do you mean? I got away."

Al knew to select words carefully, leaned forward, and took her hands in his. "I recognize timidity about you, a response typical of females in the CFEL. If you have brothers, I imagine they're not timid."

"You're right about that. Who's the woman you called flaky?"

"Violet."

"No, she hasn't the strength to take them on."

Al shrugged, "Violet wrestles with the truth but she has a strong center. Ask her about Claudette Theriault Adams."

"Brian would never allow such a conversation to take place." Laura stood suddenly. "Speaking of Brian Lemphier, I need to get back. He spies and pries and it's late."

Al followed to the door. "Piece of advice, Laura: don't let them see, hear, or know; hide everything important, especially your feelings for Steve. Like they did with me, they'll hone in if you let them. They'll see who you are, how you feel, and what you desire. They'll use their knowledge to confuse, intimidate, and control. They'll eavesdrop, watch, and assemble a profile as accurate as any developed by the Vermont State Police."

"I can hide from…."

"No! You can't keep it up! Sooner or later, we make mistakes. I thought I could beat them at their game and you see what happened."

43

Laura returned to Fallsbridge in darkness. As much as she loved Vermont's rural beauty, there was something to be said for the distraction of oncoming cars and headlights, not the fear of deer leaping onto the hood of her car. She slowed down, turned the volume up on the radio, and recalled the words *hone in on you*. Al was correct: the CFEL honed in on him, identified his neediness, fears about aging, and paralysis about involvement with another woman. With their insights, the CFEL sent a distraction to speed him along a path to self-destruction and thwart an investigation into their doctor's own sexual deviance. Laura recalled the tape of Angela's interview: a young voice spoke slowly and clearly, without any of the hesitation which usually accompanied such statements. Angela described a family visit to Marsethe's summer house on Maidstone Lake for an end-of-season cookout. Late in the day with a volleyball game underway, she wandered off to investigate. Marsethe cornered her inside the boathouse, tied her to a wooden beam with nylon boat rope, and thrust himself into her mouth. When she gagged, he withdrew, stuffed a towel in her mouth, and brought himself to ejaculation while she watched; whenever she closed her eyes, he slapped her face until she opened them again.

Laura struggled to keep her attention on the yellow and white lines and recognized the ring of truth to Angela's description of the boat house, how Marsethe talked and acted, how she felt about what happened, about what she saw. The words weren't what an adult might say, but a child's understanding, a child's perception. Angela used unclear words when she described the moment the doctor dropped his shorts to his ankles. *The hair at the top of his legs is gray but darker than the hair on his head.* She named what he thrust into her mouth as *his man-thing* and never identified pubic hair. Laura realized Angela knew the terminology now, after all the cops, therapists, and social workers hovered, questioned, interviewed, and interrogated. Laura wondered how in hell she survived two years with the state police. She came across filth and perversion every day but survived because every time she investigated assault, incest, or rape, she labeled it an aberration, not the way people really were or how she could ever be or Steve or anyone else she cared about; she survived because she believed most people led honorable lives.

Laura bumped over the train tracks before the final curve and watched blue flashing lights move into position. As Gil approached, she rolled her window down and stated, "I was not speeding."

"Step out of your vehicle."

Gil leaned to smell her breath when Laura climbed out and said, "That's mint tea, by the way." Gil smiled slowly, saluted, and left. As he pulled away, Laura shivered at a realization he might be aware of her visit to Thetford, turned the radio loud, and groaned, "Laura, you dumb shit!"

44

Though annoyed Gil called so late with details, Mel answered, "You did well. Now find out who she visited in Thetford Center."

The fool blew any advantage when he added, "Since I put in a long day, make someone else keep an eye on her tomorrow."

Mel sneered, "You do as directed or expect months without certain privileges, yes?" and slammed the phone down.

45

After a night more restless than usual, Laura woke exhausted and started to dress when she heard a knock. She grabbed a robe and opened the door to Brian's pathetic leer. "Your mother called last night. She couldn't reach your cell and asked for a number here."

Laura watched his eyes settle on her chest, tugged the robe tight, and glanced at the clock: 8:37—late again! "I use the phone at the office but should get one installed here."

"Violet would be happy to let a phone technician in."

"I'll keep that in mind." Laura closed the door, rushed through breakfast, left for work, parked at the office, and walked to the Laundromat to call Wilkers. "We should meet soon."

"That's not going to be easy. I started a part time job but meet Thursday with my former lieutenant so how about this? Meet me at the entrance to Darling State Park around noon; I'll bring lunch."

"Okay, see you then."

Laura turned and bumped into Gil, who laughed, "First by car, then on foot? Next I expect you'll use a helicopter to reach a pay phone." As she shoved by, Gil shouted, "If your office line is out of order, report it to the phone company!"

Laura rushed along the sidewalk but slowed when her knee ached. In the office she stopped at Reilly's desk. "Am I paranoid or do people float around like ghosts, getting in everybody's way?"

Reilly laughed, "What happened?"

"Sorry I'm so distracted." When she saw Reilly consult the Wilkers file, Laura felt guilty about giving her fake work, but since Reilly knew about the meeting, expected work as a result.

Reilly pointed to the file. "Some people think he's innocent."

"Everyone says I'm a real Pollyanna about certain things but I was a cop once and prefer to ... Forget what I think. Cops are human beings with all the same problems and deficiencies as the rest of us."

Reilly nodded then mentioned she saw Laura talking to Gil earlier. "I wonder if ... oh, never mind; outsiders never understand."

"Reilly, I think you're blushing. Are you interested in Gil?"

"Outsiders never understand," she repeated.

Laura collapsed at her desk and rubbed her knee. "Shit, shit, shit. Reilly, come here, please?" An instant later, she saw the perennial; head-around-the-door-jamb. "I did something to my knee. Will you call Marsethe? I don't want to but if he has time, will you go with me?" Reilly nodded and in a minute, returned to announce the time.

46

In the examination room, Mel determined her knee swelled but not critically; despite the fact the request must have come from Laura and Reilly kept a safe distance, Laura shrank from his touch. He applied gentle pressure until a tender touch and soothing voice encouraged relaxation. He suggested a cortisone injection but felt no surprise she preferred oral medication and instructions on how to safely exercise a healing joint. He thrust a pair of crutches forward. "No kayaks or bicycles appear on that list and a cane is insufficient at this point, too."

Laura stammered, "Did I do anything serious?"

"Under my care, you'll be fine. In the meantime, allow Glenn to live a fantasy: stay at the inn and let him care for you."

Laura grabbed the crutches. "I can take care of myself."

Mel stood at the window, watched them leave, and felt admiration for Reilly's unthreatening style which brought his angel to him sooner than expected. He called Gil. "You have my permission to take Reilly to Montreal this weekend. As usual, use protection."

"I thought you were mad at me."

Mel tsked, "The reward is for Reilly, who accomplished something remarkable on my behalf. Update your earlier phone call: what was the reason for Laura to be in Thetford Center?"

"I haven't had time to pursue that."

Mel hissed, "You might learn a lesson from your beloved."

47

Glenn hoped when Laura came for a follow-up, he'd make headway but after a cursory greeting, she explained Jake's willingness to sell a 40-foot-wide strip the shared length of their properties; the offer hinged on access to parking for his customers. Glenn said, "If Jake wants spaces, I'll sell for half his offer price. We're not talking acres and I'll take my chances with the zoning board."

"Rather than relying on connections on the board, as your lawyer I recommend you negotiate but sell to satisfy existing regulations."

"I can live with that if Jake cuts his asking price."

Laura stood to leave. "I'll talk to Jake again."

Glenn grabbed her hand. "Stay for breakfast?"

Laura pulled free gently. "Thanks, but I ate at home."

"How about dinner? Tonight's special is Smoked Salmon with Wild Rice and Lemon Asparagus."

"Thanks but I prefer we keep this strictly business."

Glenn chuckled at how easy she made it to finish, , "So once the transaction's complete and title clears, you'll dine with me?"

"We'll see." Laura smiled but stared at the door and mumbled something about rain. He heard a sad tone in her voice and recalled Brian said she had frequent nightmares; she did look tired.

Glenn asked if she was okay and noticed an odd look in her eyes then anger when he added she seemed distracted. Glenn went to his office, recalled the look in her eyes, and called Mel. "I hope you know what you're doing. I don't like to see Laura so..."

"Like a wounded songbird?"

"You can be so unkind."

"That angel is too much her childhood-self, yet I look ahead to the day she rejoins our community and when she does, she will be yours to do with as you wish. To that fine end, be cooperative, yes?"

Glenn winced at the thought of how that might be accomplished but answered, "It's what I pray for but Mel, I'd like it to be her choice."

"Of course it will be her choice, always her choice:"

48

Laura checked as soon as she returned to the office; still there: Marsethe's appointment at 4:00. Though the office visit went well, she dreaded the idea Reilly would leave at 1:00 but what could be done? The doctor didn't preannounce assaults and it wasn't as if he were still a robust young man or she a naïve 12-year-old, either. Laura stewed about the appointment and at 10:00, grabbed the crutches to head to the Laundromat to use the phone. She checked the area for Gil, grabbed the phone, and called Bill Marschek collect. "This is Laura. I'd like to pass a client on to you for representation."

"Nice to talk to you, too, Laura. How've you been?"

She felt the heat on her cheeks. "I'm fine; how are you?"

"Great. Marion and I look forward to a trip to Cape Cod this weekend. Now fill me in."

Laura presented the basics and ended with, "I shouldn't represent him at all since Marsethe is why I came here."

"I'm not aware of an arrest."

"They let him go but it's not over."

Bill muttered, "Without knowing details about why you're there—and this is no way implies I want to know because I don't—I also don't like how sticky the situation could become. Plus this is awfully late to ask me to shift things around in light of the fact it's a three-hour drive."

Laura stammered, "You're right; I'm sorry. I'll do the initial intake then decide if…"

He interrupted, "This can't have been an easy call to make so plan for my arrival around 3:30."

"Are you sure? I wouldn't want…"

"I can do it. I need to remember Granger predicted there'd be times you'd need to rely on me or another in the firm."

"Thanks; stay after and I'll make dinner for you."

"Sorry, can't. Marion has a fit whenever I stay over."

"Okay. See you later." Laura crossed the green and relaxed in the shade. She heard soft music from a nearby radio and found it odd how teenagers everywhere else listened to god-awful junk but not Fallsbridge, where approved music included big bands and classical. The community had its own radio station in the basement of the academy and slowly but surely, she noticed easy-listening soft rock made its presence known. She watched a half dozen teen boys play volleyball while an equal proportion of girls giggled on the sidelines. *How typical: females exist to be decorative but never jump, grunt, or sweat. It's smart to call Bill; held to attorney / client privilege, my representation of Marsethe could prove disastrous.*

49

When he arrived to find Marschek, Mel practiced obligatory formalities: greetings, small talk, weather, and exchanges of vacation plans. Quickly tired of the charade Mel explained, "My preference is for Miss Delorange's representation in a matter I suspect may soon take me into judge's chambers or a court of law."

"What matter might that be, Doctor?"

"A child is confused; on occasion one fails to distinguish between reality and fantasy. Surely you understand that of which I speak, yes?"

"Please provide details."

"I seek reality, not fantasy; I seek justice, not partiality."

"Could you be specific? Were charges filed?"

Mel admitted one had. "I find it incomprehensible the state's attorney pursues a charge already deemed merit-less by a medical ethics review board. I suggest you keep in mind the concept of reality versus fantasy in your discussions with Miss Delorange, too."

Marschek stated his confusion at how the doctor continually brought his associate's name into the conversation. "We divide new incoming clients equally so let's talk about your situation."

Mel repeated his request Ms. Delorange join them, sat calmly, and waited. When Marschek failed to respond, Marsethe added, "Gynecological exams often feel invasive."

"So the matter involves a child who had a gynecological exam. And this child has no grounds for the complaint?"

"The child has none."

"Please begin with a description of the examination in question."

Mel provided an abbreviated report, placing himself and the child in his office during work hours. He found it obnoxious the way the attorney nodded and took copious notes and particularly distasteful how that fool—even after a polite reminder Marschek owed the CFEL a return favor—ignored repeated requests Miss Delorange join the conversation.

50

Laura relaxed in the shade, read the newspaper, and looked up when a shadow altered light. "I find your tactics abominable."

Laura glanced up at Marsethe. "What tactics?"

The doctor smiled slowly. "In light of your chosen profession, I suggest you keep in mind the difference between fantasy and reality. It's absurd to suspect a man of my advanced years of sexual misconduct. I sought your assistance in an important issue and hope I never discover you mislead purposefully." As he walked away; Laura followed his slow movements and recognized he aged but to accept his notion of absurdities, she'd also need to reject experience during two years with the state police. During one particular investigation, she interviewed therapists and social workers, dismayed to learn the perpetrator's age had little to do with sexual abuse of children. The forbidden nature of some acts could be unusually stimulating. One psychiatrist stated that as abuse escalated over time, many pedophiles discovered in order to be adequately aroused, they needed victims to be younger and younger and younger.

51

Steve arrived early for dinner, embarrassed by the idea of a night with his fiancée's parents, as if he were a 19-year-old seeking approval. Steve felt surprised by how much he enjoyed the company and conversation, especially when they offered to show home movies. Wasn't that everyone's worst nightmare of an evening? but he loved every glimpse of Laura with her family and often found himself laughing. During one, Laura as a three-year-old beauty in a baggy dress—her brown eyes huge, her black hair curled halfway down her back—stood with Jack at a snack bar and waited impatiently for a girl to hand an ice cream cone over the counter. Laura jumped up and down until she hit the top of her head on the underside of the counter. From outside the camera's range, Lynette ran to console but Laura turned with a scowl. Steve chuckled, "How prophetic. Laura was an independent lady even then." When he saw how they studied him, he chuckled, "It's selfish to say this but it's too early in our relationship for her to be 130 miles away."

Lynette sighed, "This is my fault. I came from Fallsbridge and convinced John to settle down and raise a family there. Growing up there felt easy and peaceful, our contributions valued. My father earned a good living as the town pharmacist and I learned from an early age how to earn rewards for being well-behaved in church or school, and earning good grades. I mean, the CFEL elders awarded me a full scholarship to Lyndon State. It felt subtle at first but in an approval-based culture like that, it doesn't take kids long to seek more of what's offered."

"Sure, I get it," Steve said with a nod. "I understood which buttons not to push with parents, teachers, or parish priest and conversely, how to get my own way."

John chuckled, "That's a benign take on what Lynette means. The CFEL offers financial benefits; for example, we bought a house we couldn't afford without support and the community had its own broker for large purchases. Every item had to be designed and produced in the United States or Quebec, but costs were too good to complain."

"Excuse me?"

John shrugged, "GM, Ford, or Chrysler automobiles or Boston Whalers are available and priced to move. Think about individuals, too. The CFEL is a master at manipulation—knowing your place in the community and living up to expectations has its rewards." At Steve's confused look, John sighed, "Think about Jack and Rick versus Laura."

Steve shrugged, "I don't know your sons that well yet but your daughter? Laura can be reserved at times, sure, but she has her strengths and any fears she has, she works hard to overcome."

John chuckled again. "With all the strengths the rest of us see, wouldn't you think Laura would be more confident?"

"But she's done that, right?"

"With you, yes," Lynette answered.

"So you think my concerns are valid; I should worry??"

Lynette nodded. "For those who don't fit the mold, the reaction can be difficult. Many leave eventually like we did but most stick around to reap the benefits of adaptation."

On his way home, Steve stopped by Ralph's. When Joyce answered the door, Steve apologized for the late hour. "If Ralph's free, I promise I'll only take a minute to ask a favor."

"Take all the time you need. Come on in."

Ralph came in laughing, "Budster, nice surprise. Joycie says you need to ask a favor. Lay it on me."

Steve took a deep breath and said, "Later this week I'll need someone to drive me to and from outpatient surgery at Fletcher Allen then run other errands, too. I could ask Mickey but..."

Ralph smiled. I'll do it."

"Thanks. Don't you want to know why?"

"I admit some days I'm a half-witted detective but I think I know why. It's kinda hard not to eavesdrop when a loud-mouthed cop keeps his voice down on phone calls or snoop to see what he shoves into a drawer when someone comes too close."

"Excuse me?"

"Others don't know you like I do, Scolarzski. When I cautioned you against a scary procedure because the right woman looked for you, too, you said, 'Fuck that crap,' and barged ahead." Ralph grinned, "Am I right? You putting the family jewels back under the knife?"

Steve nodded. "Thanks for not poking fun and if the reversal works, Laura may thank you someday, too."

""Good thing she's out of town, huh? I'm thinking part of recovery is down time; kinda hard to keep away from a woman so fine."

At home, Steve studied a calendar and—taking in mind recovery instructions to take it easy—scrubbed both bathrooms and the kitchen, washed and waxed floors, vacuumed and dusted, took every set of sheets off, and washed and hung them outside so Laura could smell summer while she relaxed in bed. He gathered newspapers, magazines, cans, and plastic containers for the recycle enter. After days of focused effort, he felt exhausted yet satisfied the house was ready to become their home.

52

Marie preferred to wake first in the Sigler household. It helped to have a clock radio six inches from her ear with annoying little chirps that didn't bother Ned. She opened her eyes to blinding light, blinked slowly so her head wouldn't throb, and listened to Ned snore—*the son of a bitch actually made it home last night.* In the kitchen, Marie prepared coffee. Her stomach churned at the smell and she dropped to her knees in front of the cupboard, searched behind bottles of juice and found one labeled *Natural Apple Juice - No Preservatives.* Marie swished the colorless liquid, filled a glass, swallowed quickly, and felt warmth soothe. As she bent to hide the bottle again, she popped a peanut butter cookie into her mouth.

After her shower, Marie dressed for work, heard Ned toss and turn, and figured he fell between affairs to explain why he seemed to be home a lot. *How annoying to be stuck in a botched marriage with the bastard underfoot: a self-righteous inquisitor who put Spanish Catholics to shame, snoop who searches dirty clothes hampers and trash cans for proof of weakness, and cheat who on too many occasions comes home in the middle of the night to shower to erase the stench of another woman.* Marie studied her husband's profile. *On another man, his pointed nose, prominent chin, and wide forehead might be ugly but Ned in his 50's is more handsome than his 20's; strikingly handsome, in fact.* Marie slipped her wedding ring, watch, and earrings on and at the last moment, shook his shoulder. "Rise and shine, asshole."

Ned muttered, "For god's sake, Marie, it's Saturday."

"Not Friday?" she laughed and fell on the bed fully clothed.

Ned turned. "You smell good; how about it?" Marie shrugged, stood to undress, tossed clothes aside, and thought, *They'll wrinkle. Who cares? Ironing again seems minor in comparison to waiting for another woman to enter and exit his life before he'll screw his wife. At the current rate, we might hit four times this year. Four!* Marie climbed back into bed and watched him grin as he moved the sheet aside. *Their best sex occurred when he felt—for a moment, anyway—she was better than a hand job alone in the shower, better than waiting, better than nothing.* Ned performed a few perfunctory moves before he positioned himself and groaned, "I can't wait another second."

Marie shoved him off, grabbed a condom from the bedside table, and tore the package. "I won't accept another woman's disease."

Ned rolled away. She knew he'd get past the insult and waited. It took mere seconds before he renewed a declaration of undying love. In a way, it sounded hilarious to hear generalized words. *No name. No label beyond woman since all he needs is the body beneath to be female.* He kept fake love words coming as he rolled the condom on and moved back into strike position. As he closed his eyes, she whispered, "I want you but need something else first." With a smirk, she closed her eyes to his look of dismay, undisguised annoyance, and less than exuberant attention.

When she cried out, Ned leaned close with a perverted grin. "I like that better than your usual fallen log approach."

"And I like what you did better than slash and burn."

Ned chuckled, "Shit, I forgot how cynical you can be." His voice changed, turned husky, as he lifted her chin and drew her mouth to his. He bounced up and hopped off the bed. "For Christ's sake, you've already had a drink!" She watched him storm out, ready, willing, and able to go the distance and smiled at a thought *coffee might have disguised things better*.

53

Laura awakened as the sun crept across the hardwood floor. Even though Saturday, she decided to kill a few hours of another lonely weekend without Steve, headed into the office, and sifted through a pile of unopened mail. Most of it appeared to be junk until she noticed something promising: a small envelope with a hand-written address and decorative stamp. She tore it open and read an invitation to a 25th anniversary party for Ralph and Joyce Barber. She dialed the RSVP number and after introductions, added, "Meg, I need help with a gift. Is there anything in particular your parents hinted they'd like?"

"I'm sure anything will be fine since it's you they want to see. You were partners once with Steve Scolarzski, right?"

"I was, yeah; um, I imagine he'll be there, too."

"Sure; Steve's going to help plan the party. Dad'll be ecstatic to hear you're coming. He's hell-bent on patching things up."

"Um, waste of time. Thanks for thinking of me!"

Back at the carriage house, Laura rummaged through a box, pulled out CDs, and lined them up. She plopped down on the floor to read the directions for connecting the speakers and peripherals to the receiver. She went through her collection, selected favorites, and copied them onto a cassette for Steve. Hours later, she finished with the first side but stopped when she heard a knock. "Violet, come see what I accomplished even without help with technology." Laura loaded in a cassette and flipped the switch. "This tape is for... um, in the car."

As rich sound reverberated to fill the small room, Violet laughed, "I never figured you for the show tune type."

"Oh, not just show tunes—Andrew Lloyd Webber show tunes!" The two women stood in the middle of the room and swayed to *Think of Me* from *Phantom of the Opera*.

Violet added, "You could've asked Brian for help."

"I'd set the house on fire before I'd..." Laura stopped when she noticed Joanna at the screen door. "Come in!"

As 15-year-old Joanna sidled in, she said, "Mrs. Lezzarro asked me to baby-sit. Will you be around, too?"

Violet glanced at Laura. "There's a girl with some difficulties and at times says things Joanna can't handle. Angela reminds me of how I remember you at the same age: bookworm, verbally precocious child, deep thinker." Laura licked her lips and considered how to answer but her dilemma ended when Violet finished, "Brian and the boys are at an all-day golf tournament. Oh, Lynette called to say the family would be at the cabin until about 4:00 tomorrow."

Laura laughed, "Great! I'll go in the morning."

"What cabin?"

"Mom's parents have a camp on the New Hampshire side of the river. The spot's quiet, secluded, with great fishing."

"That sounds nice. If you have a chance, stop by and meet Angela. She's wonderful."

Laura spent the rest of the morning reading and cleaning. When she heard tires on gravel, she watched from behind a curtain as Angela jumped out of a sedan and dropped a book bag to the ground. She fumbled to unhook a bike from a rack as Laura walked up. "Let me help; I have the same problem with mine."

Angela squinted, "Are you that crybaby from the park?"

"I'm Laura Delorange; I live here in the carriage house."

A woman climbed out, said she'd be back in a few hours, and extended her right hand. "Hi, Laura, I'm Rita Thompson Lezzarro; I went to school with Jack. How is he?"

Laura filled her in on the basics: "Jack runs a veterinary clinic in Texas, been married for 11 years, and he and his wife Sarah have three children between two and ten."

"I hear you're a lawyer and recall a younger brother, too."

Laura nodded. "Rick's 20 and recently finished his second year at UVM. He's thinking of veterinary medicine, too."

"Wow; John and Lynette sure raised one smart brood." Rita turned to her daughter to suggest if Laura were free, Angela might ask what they discussed in the car. When Angela picked at threads on her book bag, Rita sighed, "Honey, did you hear me?"

"I'm not deaf, Mom!"

Rita glanced at Laura, Violet, and Joanna. "This is not okay; you know how I feel about inappropriate communication."

Angela shrugged but lowered her voice, "I'm still not deaf."

After a moment of awkward silence, Rita left and Violet invited Laura to join them. In the kitchen, Joanna poured four glasses of lemonade, added ice cubes, and carried them to the table; she sat and watched Angela doodle on a paper napkin. "So Ang, what do you want to do? We have all the Disney movies on DVD and could..."

"Only babies watch cartoons."

"Okay; we could ride our bikes to the academy, use the pool, then pick flowers for our mothers and Miss Delorange."

Angela swung her feet under the table like a little kid even as she insisted Joanna's ideas were for babies. "I don't need a babysitter. I can stay alone for three stupid hours."

Joanna shrugged, "Sure, but we always have fun together."

Angela looked from one face to another. "Don't look at me; just leave me alone." When Laura leaned forward to touch her hand, Angela jumped up. "I hate it when people think because I'm a kid, they can..."

"I understand; I felt that way, too, but learned not all people..."

"I especially hate people like you!" Angela groaned and grabbed her book bag to escape to the living room.

Laura followed. "I'm sorry if I upset you."

"Why does it matter? I'm just some dumb kid."

Laura glanced at Joanna and Violet, who seemed to have blended into the woodwork. "I'll bet you feel lonely and...."

Angela's response gushed in torrents. "People like you make me sick! Do you think I can't figure this out? Mrs. Lemphier told you about me and now you think you should be nice for a couple of minutes. I don't know you and even if I did, I'll bet I wouldn't like you one bit." Angela took a deep breath and continued on in a rush of rage. "There are too many weird people in this world like you so why don't you go spread your happy chatter in some other direction?"

"Um, I'll go back to the carriage house and listen to show tunes." When Violet laughed nervously, Laura shrugged, "They relax me and anyone's invited to join me."

Angela growled, "Show tunes? That's almost as stupid as Joanna's cartoons!"

On her way out, Laura said, "I'll read, too; if you change your mind, you know where to find me."

It took a while before Laura heard a knock on the screen door and Angela's harrumphed, "Don't ask why I changed my mind or I'll leave, just like that!" She snapped her fingers and wandered inside. "Mrs. Lemphier said you just put your stereo together."

"I sure did. Get comfortable while I get a snack."

As Laura grabbed glasses and ice cubes, Angela plopped on the floor. "It looks weird the way you put popcorn on a plate."

"I do stuff like that. Want something to drink?"

"What do you like?"

"Iced tea."

Angela answered she'd have that, too, checked the bathroom and bedroom and said the place looked comfortable. As she headed back toward Laura, Angela stopped suddenly. "I would never sit like that."

Laura looked at how she pressed the bottoms of her feet together, legs bent at the knees. "It isn't ladylike but comfortable."

"If a man were here, he'd think you wanted to do sex."

"He would? Why?"

Angela tugged on her hair and twisted it. "That's how men are." She dropped onto a pillow and leaned against the couch. "I sat like that and Dr. Marsethe thought I wanted to do sex things."

"Not every man's like that."

Angela laughed, "Yes they are! Boys, too; the last time Joanna babysat me, she told me about how this boy put his hands on her butt and squeezed while they danced."

"It takes time to learn the difference between..."

"And my cousin told me a boy snuck up behind her at the lake and pulled her hand between his legs when no one looked."

"Boys expect you to say no when they do things like that."

Angela pushed herself to a stand. "I can't talk to someone who won't listen! I don't know why I came so I'm leaving."

"After Dr. Marsethe hurt me, I hated everyone, too."

Angela stared from the door. "He did things to you, too?"

"Yes."

"Mom took me to a doctor and no one said what she is but I saw a list at her building and looked up psychotherapist. Am I crazy now?"

"Honey, no. It helps to talk."

Angela returned and sat. "Dr. Follette says someday I'll want a man to touch me but not like that! Touch me kindly."

Laura relaxed at a realization she could handle the conversation. "Someday you'll love someone and touching will feel beautiful."

Angela picked at a scab on her knee. "What's the difference between what Dr. Marsethe did and when someone I like makes me do sex things?"

"There's the first difference. You said *make me* and with a man you love, you'll want to and you'll say yes."

"Or I'll say no?"

"You won't want to; you'll never want that feeling to end."

Angela kicked her legs out and scratched a scab off. "Tell me about the first time you did sex things and wanted to." Laura worried how Rita might feel and hesitated, but Angela continued, "Mom gets mad when I talk about this; she thinks I could've tried harder to get away."

"You're not to blame for what happened, Angela. He is."

"He said because of how I sat in my bathing suit, I invited him to love me like that."

"How you dressed or how you sat makes no difference to someone with his problem."

Angela rubbed her eyes roughly. "What's his problem?"

"He's a pedophile, a man who prefers little girls to women."

"Oh; did you ever do sex things and really want to?"

Laura sighed, "Yes, we were friends and I enjoyed his company. I imagined he'd be a gentle lover, felt terrified but wanted to be with him enough to take a chance so one night I asked him to make love together." Angela winced and Laura squeezed her hand. "I won't go into details, but there's a difference between having sex and making love."

"I want to know about the man."

"Details aren't important."

"They are to me!"

"Okay, his name is Steve and he turned out to be one of those people who are different once you get to know them."

"I don't understand."

"He's like you; if someone believed you're the way you present yourself—hostile and smart-alecky—they'd give up."

Angela grinned and nodded. "The way you talk reminds me of someone I knew but I said something that made him ashamed of me."

"Al Wilkers?"

"How'd you know that?"

"Al and I are friends."

"Why didn't he come back like he promised?"

"It's a long story but Al never felt ashamed of what you told him." When Angela stared at her hands, Laura lifted Angela's chin until their eyes met. "You know he cares about you and so do I."

"Are you a cop like him?"

"I used to be. I'm a lawyer now."

"Can I visit again?"

"Whenever you like, stop by here or the office."

Angela chewed her lower lip. "Your music stopped and when I read, I like music."

Laura went to change CDs and listed composers: Sibelius, Khachaturian, Bizet, and Mozart. Angela selected Khachaturian, took a book out of a bag, and grabbed popcorn. Laura asked, "What's the title?"

"It's called *Atlantis: The Lost Continent Finally Found* by a professor from Brazil. Before this, I read H. G. Wells' *The Invisible Man* and Ray Bradbury's *Martian Chronicles*. What's yours?"

"It's a novel about lawyers written by a lawyer."

"Is it hard to become a lawyer?"

"Sort of; there wasn't much time for fun if I wanted to get good grades and pass the bar exam."

Angela shrugged, "I have no trouble getting good grades or passing tests. If I don't become a psychotherapist like Dr. Follette or a detective like Mr. Wilkers, I might become a lawyer." Laura sat a foot away, watched the girl read, and jumped when Angela poked her arm. "It isn't polite to stare." Laura started to apologize but Angela asked, "Do you believe in mermaids?"

"I do."

"Do you think mermaid people live in Atlantis now?"

"Could be."

"Do you believe in the Loch Ness monster or Champ?"

"Yes; I think they live deep in the lakes to hide from people."

"Me, too; do you believe in extra-terrestrials?"

"I'm not sure but it would be exciting."

Angela licked her lips. "Joanna said because of what happened, no one will want to marry me. Is that true?"

"No; the right man will come along someday like Steve."

Angela fooled with the hem of her shorts. "When I told Detective Wilkers, he couldn't talk. He was ashamed of me."

"No, he..."

Angela interrupted she had another question. "I wake up at night and remember. Um, will I forget?"

"I'll be honest. You'll wake up less often and meet wonderful people. You'll fall in love with someone kind and gentle but no, you'll probably never forget. At least I haven't."

"Too bad, but still you want to get married to a man?"

"Not to any man: to Steve."

"Does he hurt you?"

"No."

"Did you ever cry in front of him?"

"Sure."

"Did he yell at you when you cried?"

"No."

"Did he slap your face when you cried?"

"No."

"Did he shut you up by shoving his penis in your mouth?"

"No."

"Did he ever?"

"No."

"What would you do if he tried?"

"He wouldn't but I'd tell him why that frightens me."

"Would he think you were dirty if he knew?"

"He knows what happened and it didn't matter. You'll meet a man like Steve and he'll know what happened wasn't your fault."

"I believe you." As Angela returned her attention to her book, Laura leaned back and watched Angela's sneakered foot move to the brisk tempo of Khachaturian's *Saber Dance*.

Later in the day Rita arrived for her daughter and Laura felt no surprise when Violet knocked on the door minutes after. "Brian cannot hear how we spent our day."

"I won't discuss it; besides, I had the impression today was a private gathering for women."

"Thanks; Angela really likes you."

"I like her, too." When Brian's car pulled in, Violet rushed off.

Laura collapsed in bed, tossed and turned, floating in and out of fogginess. She refused to go so deep hideous creatures tiptoed in to watch or go so deep she felt fingers against her bare skin, smelled sweat, or tasted what got smeared on her tongue. Instead she pictured: *Steve wrapped arms around, touched her gently, and with intensifying speed and passion, asked permission. As always, she cradled, caressed, guided him inside, and fell asleep in the shelter of his arms.*

54

Gil checked recording equipment, surprised Laura used the law firm phone for anything other than business. He jotted the name, skimmed a file, and studied a photo of Steve Scolarzski—from newspaper reports a former partner linked to the psycho who shot Laura. Gil thought he looked old for Laura but hell, whose business was it? Gil was 12 years older than Reilly.

Gil felt annoyed Reilly wouldn't go to Montreal because David got sick and decided they'd go the following weekend—with or without the old man's consent. Since Mel became irrational at times, it seemed wise to head him off. Gil decided to follow up on the Thetford woman and considered how to proceed: go down and take a look, or call a friend at the phone company for the name at that address? Too easy: Claudette Theriault Adams. He called another colleague in the Department of Taxation: previous year's W2's issued by Dartmouth College— occupation: associate professor. Gil phoned Mel, presented facts, and let the old fool believe he rescheduled a weekend getaway for research.

Gil heard papers rustle in the background as Mel said, "Fine job, Gilbert; now I remember why the name rang familiar. Lynette Delorange's sister married a cretin down the valley. My records list the sister as Claire Therault but Claudette Theriault is close, yes? Lynette, Claire, Claudette: quite a sisterly-sounding grouplette, yes?"

"Mel, those records are useless. Now that you're computerizing everything, have someone research and fix them once and for all. By the way, Laura used the law office phone today to let someone know she'll head to Chittenden County soon for a party."

"So as I predicted, all she needed was time to settle in, yes? Good, good. Now about those records you mention."

"Another call, Mel; gotta go." Gil hung up before that task could be assigned and leaned back to daydream. *In another week, Reilly and I will be in Montreal. No David, no Mary, best of all, no Mel.*

55

Ralph found it odd how his best buddy showed up on the doorstep offering to help with yard work. They stacked wood, pulled weeds, trimmed bushes, and worked up a dandy of a sweat in the sun in silence. Hours later, Ralph offered lemonade or soda and his buddy proved vocal chords still worked. "No, thanks; as much as I needed company, it's time to head home for another restless night alone."

As Joyce wandered in, she overheard Steve and her beautiful eyes got sappy with sentiment. Ralph picked at his fingernails, considered what he might say to keep her from skipping town, and decided to risk her vengeful wrath. "Our darlin' Meggie sent the little lady an invite to some doin's and I hear this very day, she accepted." Joyce's color faded but before she had a chance to pry, he finished, "Darlin,' don't you think Laura's been gone long enough to actually miss this loser?"

Joyce snorted, "You said they broke up."

Ralph shrugged, "That's an official line spouted by two cops but two civilians know otherwise."

Steve played the game correctly. "Laura regrets we aren't married so what if we tie into your festivities? We need witnesses."

"I could help with wedding plans," Joycie offered and Ralph grinned. *Do I know my amazing wife or what?* Joyce and Steve sat to plot how—since the little lady worked undercover and all—there might be a small, private, secret ceremony out of the way of snoops. Joycie finished with, "It'll take covert maneuverings to break a few away from the main event but cops can pull that off."

Ralph poked Steve's arm. "Will Laura keep her own or saddle herself with a loser name like Scolarzski?"

"Who cares?" Steve shrugged.

Ralph noticed color return to Joycie's beautiful face as she offered a kazillion ideas for a ceremony stuffed inside a celebration. He leaned close to Steve. "Don't forget you promised I'd be best man."

56

When a courier delivered airline tickets, Mel checked for accuracy—nothing more vexing than the CFEL business manager making inefficient arrangements. He studied details carefully: from Monday to Wednesday, he breezed in and out of hell in 54 hours: from Montreal to Houston by air, 150 miles from Houston to Lake Charles by rental car via I-10, check-in at the tourist hotel, then a cursed excursion into familial environs. In truth, he hoped to avoid Grand Chenier entirely.

The trip felt like madness. Why in the good Lord's name hadn't he refused to accept the burden passed through Yvonne? Though custom dictated as parents aged, the eldest assume a leadership position, he left decades earlier with no intent of return. Until that pathetic phone call, he remained steadfast in a resolve to dissociate himself from idiots who through no fault of his own were blood kin. Only his mother could fill in the gaps and unless those fools purposely misled with exaggerations of medical distress, a conversation needed to take place immediately.

Mel found it a questionable time to leave Fallsbridge: a nuisance field representative for child protective services hovered in the background; after years of collaboration, Gil behaved in a peculiar manner; Vincent and Matthew withdrew into their businesses, leaving him with daily details on behalf of their community of souls; frequently Violet conspired in the garden with Little Miss Laura; Mary verified a daughter increasingly consumed by daydreams; Brian became distracted by a need to hire four new certified though values-compatible teachers before the start of classes; Glenn became outspoken at times and downright nosy about his beloved Laurette Marie; Wilkers continued to appear at odd times and invade other's privacy; Caroline spoke without permission to a customer never formally introduced; Peg wasted valuable time not on a medical need but on a personal one as she sought permission to keep and raise her first as-yet-unborn grandchild; and Laura traipsed through four Vermont and two New Hampshire counties in search of pay phones.. No, even for 54 hours, not the soundest time to travel.

Mel phoned Gilbert. "Compelled to leave for a few days, I insist upon knowing what Laura does. Tonight you must approach her to…"

"I no longer pursue women on command."

"And since the elders and I have not yet decided who among you shall earn that privilege, I'm not interested in you doing so! Listen to me carefully: offer friendship in a familiar setting, casual conversation, good music, and a strong drink or two to loosen a young woman's tongue."

"I'm not interested in a late night out, either."

Mel tapped airline tickets along the wall. "Consider your generous salary, living arrangements, and respected career within our community. The elders have been known in the past to rescind offers."

A heavy sigh, "I hear you."

57

Laura escaped the carriage house, drove in circles for an hour, and bounced across the bridge. At a pay phone, she paced until he answered. "I love you and want to spend the rest of my life loving you. If it can happen, I'd like to work hard on making a baby." When he started to speak, she laughed, "One last thing then I'll shut up. I beg you to meet me tomorrow night at the cider mill. We can both be careful and…"

"Laura, come home. No one has the right to ask…"

"I'm not done with my assignment. I spoke to Angela today and that man is a filthy excuse for a human being and deserves to get killed in prison for what he's done to her, me, and only God knows how many other unsuspecting children!"

"You can't mean that."

"Oh, really? What makes you so sure, Scolarzski?"

"You're too virtuous, Delorange."

Laura let her breath out slowly. "I miss you."

"I'm sorry but I won't be there. Wilkers claims you have a regular tail. Is it possible that local's there now?"

Laura looked around. "I maneuvered back and forth and only once noticed headlights on a mini-van with Maine tags."

"Okay, but be careful. I heard you'll be home for the party and I won't pressure you to stay past Monday at dawn but while you're home, I thought we could get married."

"Yes!"

"I promise Joyce, Lynette, my mother, and I will handle all the details but I'm worried about your tail, so don't call Monday. Save every thought for our wedding night."

"I love the sound of that."

"Where would you like to go, Laura? The party's in Middlebury and there's a great inn we...."

"Let's spend our wedding night at your house in your bed."

"Our house in our bed sounds perfect. Laura, when you left your message about the cider mill, did you call me baby?"

"Yeah, it sorta snuck out."

"I like it... makes me feel warm, cuddly, and lovable."

"You are, mister. I better hang up but think of me?"

"Much to this old fart's chagrin, that's every minute."

During the return drive, Laura rounded the final curve into Fallsbridge, watched blue flashing lights move in behind, and checked the speedometer: 42 mph. Gil came alongside and she passed paperwork in what began to feel like a regular drill. When Gil pointed to an empty bottle on the passenger seat, she laughed, "Something wrong with soda?"

"Step out of the vehicle."

As soon as she did, Laura extended both arms sideways parallel to the ground and brought her hands slowly and smoothly to the tip of her nose. "Want me to hop along this yellow line on one foot?"

Gil chuckled, "Laura, you were doing 50 in a 35 zone."

"Actually the speedometer read 42, Officer." As a vehicle squealed past, she laughed, "Now there goes a live one."

Gil leaned close. "I've got other things on my mind; care to join me for a drink?"

Laura felt a knot in her stomach. "Why would I do that?"

"We could catch up on Jack."

Laura imagined after drinks Gil might feel chatty. "I'll meet you at the Maidstone." Minutes later, Laura entered, headed toward live music, and saw Gil at a table with a woman, and turned away in relief.

Gil ran up alongside. "Hey, hey, don't disappear."

"You're with someone."

Gil snorted, "Her? No way; just polite conversation." He took her elbow and steered her to a corner table. "What would you like?"

"I'll get my own, thanks."

Gil grinned. "Not tonight, Laura. What'll it be?"

"I said I'll buy my own."

Gil leaned so close she saw tiny dark specks in blue irises. "What's the problem here?"

"This is a mistake; I'm uncomfortable with your type."

His eyes crinkled with laughter. "And my type is...?"

"You strut like you think every woman here checks you out."

Gil seemed serious when he said, "They do I don't like it."

"Um, I'll take a white wine spritzer."

Alone at the table, Laura glanced around a crowded dance floor and waved to Glenn who approached quickly. "I don't like to interfere but Gil has quite the reputation."

"I'll have one drink and leave. It's harmless."

"You may think that but don't get drunk or you'll wake up alone with no idea where you are or how you got there."

Laura sighed, "One wine spritzer won't leave me drunk," and studied Gil at the bar. With incredible skill and genuine ease, he lifted two glasses into the air to snake his way back to the table in tempo to a song the band played. Laura stared at an odd-looking, colorful concoction and muttered, "This isn't a white wine spritzer." She grabbed her purse, headed to the bar, and ordered. As the bartender slid the glass toward her, Gil came up and offered to pay. She slapped money down and on the way back, stated over her shoulder, "We can do battle if you want."

"Or we can play nice?" They returned to the table to sip drinks. Gil tugged her to her feet and on a crowded dance floor, whispered, "I saw Glenn a minute ago; don't pay attention to harmless sibling rivalry."

Out of the corner of her eye, Laura watched Marsethe gesture and head upstairs. A moment later, Gil said, "Sorry but I need to use a restroom," and headed up the same staircase.

Laura grabbed her purse and on her way out, passed Glenn. "Deliver a message? Gil's too old to play games by someone else's rules."

58

Glenn watched Gil hang out by the ladies room. When they made eye contact, Gil crossed the room. "Why the smirk?"

"Be more discreet; Laura saw Mel's signals."

"Impossible."

"Believe what you want but Laura left a message. *Gil's too old to play games by someone else's rules*—verbatim, big bro."

Gil stared across the room at Marsethe. "I warned the old man she's not like the others—she's too smart for his shit."

Glenn chuckled, "Yup."

59

At 1:00 AM Laura gave up on sleep. She spread CD's on the floor, made notes on a pad, grabbed a cassette, stuck a microphone in, and whispered, "Steve, I'm alone in the middle of the night and can't sleep because you're not here. On Side 2 is another batch of songs with special meaning to me." By 2:30, she filled the tape with many soft, whispered messages between favorites; toward the end, finished, "I'm almost out of room so here's the song you know is my favorite of all time: Sam Cooke's *That's Where It's At.*. Even as a kid, I knew love would feel like this."

At 7:30, Laura woke on the floor surrounded by CDs. After a quick shower and breakfast, she rushed out to a bright, sunny Sunday morning to head off. She entered the dark law office and sat at Reilly's computer to type her list. She noticed activity outside and watched people cross the village green from every direction toward the church; dressed in their best, worshipers looked prosperous, content, and kind. She dropped the blind when a face appeared and opened the door to Glenn. "Care to join me at services?"

"Um, that's not a good idea."

"Okay but think about joining me or rather—us—next week." With a warm smile, he headed to church.

Laura heard organ music, grabbed her cane, headed across the green, and entered a side door of the church. Fond memories flooded her mind as morning sunlight filtered through stained glass windows and cast bright color onto rich mahogany pews. As the congregation rose to sing, organ music blasted out of pipes and bounced off ceilings like a revival meeting. Near the aisle a few rows from the front, Glenn stood beside Marsethe; behind them the Lemphier's; and behind them, Reilly and a woman with a baby. Laura faded into the shadows, studied rows of faces, and recognized two waitresses and Carl the cook from the Maidstone, Caroline from the store, Betsy from the post office, Leroy from the gas station, and others she didn't know by name yet. The song finished and Marsethe climbed over Glenn on his way to the pulpit. The doctor looked remarkably young and healthy with his striking height, slim build, and full head of almost-white hair. He wore a well-tailored charcoal gray suit, a crisp white shirt, and a reddish-maroon tie. Laura snickered, "He immersed himself in a power outfit."

From behind, a man answered, "I agree." When Laura turned, Gil added, "I'm late, too. Let's go in together."

"I heard music but I'm in sandals and...."

Gil nodded at a rear pew. "I'm always late and stay in back."

"No; I'm no longer a member and have no plan to..." but stopped when from across a distance of 500 feet, his blue eyes focused on her and his deep voice, with its unusual cadence and style, oozed from the speakers to soothe in a melodic tone. "Friends in God, let us greet this wondrous morning with a kiss for our neighbor, yes?"

Gil leaned and Laura laughed, "Don't even consider it."

Marsethe's voice bellowed, "On such a wondrous morning, in the warmth of His sunshine and overwhelming love, we give thanks to the Lord our Father for His return of one of our most beloved lambs." When the congregation turned to look where he did, Laura felt the heat as a few members applauded. Marsethe extended his hand into open air and Laura heard a tremble in his voice. "Come to us, child, and accept our welcome back into our community of souls."

Gil leaned in. "You belong here, Laura; you always did."

"Um, no, I should go."

"In this light, with that enticing flush on your face, you look like the angel Mel believes you to be."

"You're crazy; you all are," Laura laughed and shoved past.

Outside, Marsethe's powerful voice followed: "The lamb sought our companionship today and shall return again for love, understanding, and acceptance. Let us pray Laura opens her heart, mind, and soul to accept our gift of love and devotion."

Laura drove north to the bridge to New Hampshire and along the east side of the river to the cabin. When Rick opened the door, Laura laughed, "Finally! Normal people!" The four caught up on news and out of a well-stocked cooler, ate cheese, fruit, and crackers. By mid-afternoon, each fanned out to his or her favorite fishing spot and Laura joined her father where he sat along the shoreline. "Did you accept the invitation to the party next weekend?"

John nodded. "Steve stopped by, too, to tell us the plans."

"Does Rick know to keep it quiet?"

"We haven't told him a thing."

"I will. Um, do you accept my marriage to Steve?"

"I admit I was against it at first but he's a good man."

"Thanks, Dad. Um, can I ask another question?"

"Sure, ask anything and I'll try to answer."

Laura explained she had confusing dreams but couldn't fit things together chronologically. "Do you remember when Rick fell into the tunnel and you got someone to backfill it?"

"That couldn't have been Rick, honey. That happened long before Rick was born, even before we left for Essex."

"Are you sure? I thought…"

John cast his line and shrugged, "I'm not good with stuff like this. You'd better ask your mother."

Laura hugged him and said, "Okay, I'll see you next weekend." She headed upstream to Rick. "Do me a favor and deliver something to Steve? I made a tape but don't listen."

"Talk tape or music tape?"

"Both actually."

"Any sexy stuff?"

"Who, me?" Laura went to her car, grabbed a ribbon-tied package from beneath the driver's seat, and returned.

Rick breathed deeply. "It smells like you; he'll like that."

"I could wait until Friday but I want him to have it."

"About Friday; what's the deal? Mom and Dad are secretive."

"During the party, Steve and I plan to marry."

"What? Don't you want a ceremony all your own?"

Laura shrugged, "We'll have a reception in the fall but this needs to stay small; at the moment, I'm undercover and in my assignment, unattached. Please keep this quiet."

"Sure."

Laura noticed though he smiled, Rick's eyes seemed lifeless— unusual for someone who in the past, always laughed and joked. "How are things with you and Gina?"

Rick shrugged, "She returned my ring after she asked a question I couldn't answer: *If you love me, how could you betray me?* She called it off."

Laura listened to her brother offer insights into his behavior that reminded her of Al Wilkers' comments about what people did in the dark or were capable of if they believed they'd never face exposure. She whispered, "What do you wish would happen now?"

"I'd find a time machine to go back seven months?"

Laura hugged him hard. "You can't go back but you can take this opportunity to reassess your life, where you hope to be someday, and work hard to become the man you want to be."

"Sis, it won't mean anything without Gina."

"You should talk to Steve; he made mistakes, too."

"Yet you forgave him?"

"I love and respect the man Steve struggled to become."

Laura watched him settle down to fish in the warm sun: a handsome young man with all the energy and passion he should have at 20. Yet for women like her and Gina, sexual contact was an expression of love, not something offered or accepted lightly, definitely not to be wasted on sordid affairs. Laura added, "It isn't enough to love Gina. Decide if you can abstain until your wedding night, and if yes, promise Gina and wait however long it takes her to see you keep it."

Rick shaded his eyes and squinted up. "She won't listen long enough for me to make such a promise."

Laura winked. "Try harder; Gina loves you."

Behind the cabin, Laura found her mother cleaning fish. As Laura sat beside her on a wooden bench, Lynette threw stinky hands in the air to wrap arms around. "I'm so glad you came! We've missed you and I know Steve does too. He came for dinner not that long ago."

"How is he? How'd he look? What did he say?"

"We talked about all kinds of things and enjoyed his company. His hair looks lighter from the sun."

"That happened last summer, too."

"And he's lost weight."

"A lot?"

"Just a little. He looks good. Honey, come back with us and spend the week planning your wedding."

"I can't but not because I don't want to. The investigation's slow but I'm not concerned; it's only been a few weeks. Mom, do you remember anyone named Lezzarro, Thompson, or Beaudon?"

"Jack dated Caroline Beaudon for a year and went to school with Rita Thompson, but the name Lezzarro's unfamiliar."

Laura cleared her throat. "The girl Marsethe is accused of molesting last fall is Angela Lezzarro, Rita's daughter."

Lynette gasped, "How old?"

"She's 11 now, 10 when it happened."

"Lord, that man is despicable."

"Everywhere I go, he's there: restaurants, park bench, general store, Creemee stand. There's no privacy and Brian's a terrible snoop; I suspect he sneaks into the carriage house at night and…."

Lynette choked, "He does what?"

"Let's not waste a second on him. This morning, I peeked into services and those people are nuts! I can't believe I agreed to go back."

"Don't you dare say you weren't warned?"

"I won't; it's a surprise how much a part of me Steve became."

Lynette smoothed damp hair off Laura's forehead. "During the past year, I watched a remarkable transformation. Honey, you were always a hard-working student, capable young attorney, and eager state trooper, successful on whatever terms you selected yet separate from others. About a year ago, Steve dropped you off at the house after work when Jack, Sarah, and the kids were home and you brought him in to meet us. That was before I knew he was the trooper at the rest area and thought: *What's Laura doing? This isn't like her at all.* You were giggly and flushed and honey, so sweet to see."

Laura grasped her mother's hand. "Angela reminds me of how angry I felt and want to apologize for how often I…"

"Honey, you don't need to…"

"But I do! I said I'd never have children because I might be as horrible a mother as you. You never punished me or…."

"You were in pain."

"Thanks for sticking it out. I hope Steve will; too."

"That man is so in love with you, he'll stick around forever."

Laura noticed Rick. "Mom, I have strange dreams lately about all kinds of things and need to ask a question. Did you breast-feed Rick?"

"I breast-fed all my children, honey. It fell in and out of fashion over the years but I believe mother's milk is a perfect food. Why?"

Laura shrugged, "Like I said, I have strange dreams that seem so real. It's like I'm in a fog. Lately I think a lot about having a baby with Steve so maybe it's my mind engaged in wishful thinking. Um, another dream I have is when Rick fell into the tunnel from the kitchen and..."

Lynette shook her head. "Let's not talk about Fallsbridge, Laura. Let's look forward to you marrying the man you love."

When it started to rain, mosquitoes invaded, and Laura sighed, "This seems like a good time to head back to one shitty little town."

Laura headed north along the river and at a pay phone in Lancaster, called her brother collect. "Sorry I don't have my customary pocketful of change and most of these phones don't take credit cards."

Jack laughed, "No problem. So what's up? What's new?"

"I'm feeling nostalgic. I spent the afternoon with Mom, Dad, and Rick and leaving was tough. This morning I snuck into services and left wondering why I went back."

"I'd never return, not even for a million bucks."

"It's strange being back; there must be something in the air because I dream stuff that can't possibly have happened the way I see it."

"Like what?"

"I don't know—stuff that happened when we still lived there but in my dream, I'm younger or older than when it really happened."

"Like what?"

"Do you remember when Rick fell into the tunnel and needed stitches? Dad had a guy with a backhoe fill it in. I must've been 12 or 13 but in my dream I look 7 or 8."

"Laura, I'm the one who fell in."

"Really? Are you sure?"

"Yeah, I needed stitches."

"Well, you know how funny dreams can be, Jack. Um, I met your friend Gil Munier, now the village cop."

"Now that's a surprise! Among our group, he was the loose cannon, unlike a younger, serious brother Glenn."

"Jack, I called with important news I'd rather give in person but can't. Um, Steve and I will get married next Friday."

"That doesn't give me time to plan how to get there!"

"There'll be a reception in the fall. This is to make us official."

A chuckled, "Any reason for a rush?"

Laura sighed, "I'm not pregnant if that's what you wonder. Not that I wouldn't want to be but you know my history."

"I envy you for how happy you sound. Don't say anything to Mom or Dad but ever since their party, things with Sarah are strained—the fact that happened during high school doesn't make a difference, just resurrected a mistake I made a few years ago."

"Oh, um…"

"Sorry to burden you with my soap opera; just trying to prepare you for the fact Sarah and the kids might not make it in the fall. So what dates should I research to book a flight?"

60

In preparation for his house becoming Laura's and his home, Steve organized the bedroom closet shelves and racks, dropped to his knees, and pushed shoes to the back. Inside a box labeled *Law Books*, he noticed the loose envelope he avoided for months, the one with Granger's familiar scrawl; inside, copies of police or social service reports, and photographs of a badly bruised and bloodied young girl with swollen yet familiar dark eyes, then other photographs with injuries far, far worse. Steve checked the label on back: *Victim LMD*. He read pages of notes and interview transcripts, studied photographs. He opened an envelope marked *Victim FTS* and cringed. *Dear God, more of the same.* By the time he opened the envelope marked *Victim ARL*, he held proof a freak attacked at least three beautiful little dark-haired girls, three innocent children with lives forever stained by a pervert's handiwork. Steve stared at clouds floating in a bright blue sky and saw why painters chose them to represent heaven. *Clouds renew the spirit and create an impression of massive power, overwhelming goodness, and unending possibility. Once we're married, maybe Laura will stand naked in front of me in daylight. Certainly in the hospital, she showed me scars and I see others in the photographs now. Whenever I feel hidden ones in unusual places—at the base of her spine, between her thumb and index finger, under her arms—Laura stiffens and guides my hand to smoother spots*

Steve returned the envelope to the box and thought *If you neglect to get a marriage license, you provide her with an escape route.* He drove to the Delorange house in Essex for Laura's birth certificate. Lynette left the room and Steve glanced at John. "You're okay with this, right? It's important for me to know if…"

"I'm better than okay."

Steve leaned against the door. "Surely it occurs to you there are younger, better-educated, more successful men who'd…"

"That hasn't crossed my mind lately."

"Okay, well, it seems to me if my daugh…"

"Nonsense," John laughed and opened the door wide.

Steve sat in their living room, surprised at how comfortable he felt because he believed the wedding might happen. When Lynette returned with the document, Steve's hands trembled as he read Laura's date of birth. "My god, she's such a kid compared to me and I worry..."

"Nonsense," John laughed again.

Steve scanned it. "Marsethe was the attending physician?"

Lynette sighed, "Yes and what he does is even more depraved considering he delivered every baby there for the past 40 years."

61

Monday, Laura worked at her desk. When Reilly prepared to leave, she stuck her head around. "I see the Wilkers' hearing on the calendar but nothing before."

"Thanks for the reminder; I'm embarrassed to say I've done little since the last time Al and I met."

"I'm sure you do your best."

Laura chuckled, "That's debatable. You worked for Bill for a long time. How do I compare?"

Reilly shrugged, "Bill would have gotten overly involved in Mr. Wilkers' theory someone set him up but it seems to me cops can be just as bad as anyone else—maybe worse."

"I've known a few who go off on their own power trip,"

The phone rang. Laura answered to hear Glenn. "Come for lunch. Carl offered to whip up a cheese soufflé just for you."

"I am hungry; okay, I'll see you in ten minutes."

During the walk to the restaurant, Laura forced herself to smile as she passed one familiar face after another. Each person's greeting looked friendly enough but she found it difficult to keep a smile in place. She entered the restaurant and Glenn rushed over, took her arm, and confessed temperamental Carl fussed over his ready soufflé. Glenn pulled out a chair. "Sit, sit. I'll let Carl know his curtain rises."

Laura asked, "Is it always this quiet in the afternoon?"

"The lunch crowd's gone and the dinner crowd's hours away. It'd be perfect if we could do this every day—my treat."

"That's no way to run a business," Laura laughed and watched Marsethe take a seat. "Does he eat here a lot?"

"Sometimes Mel goes to the diner or snack bar, but for the most part, he eats here since his wife died."

Laura wondered how any woman—even one confined to bed—could stay married to a monster and whispered, "I remember Mrs. Marsethe; I liked spending time with her."

A waitress approached with two plates and Glenn said, "Carl will watch your reaction; humor his employer, please."

Laura took a bite and gasped, "Amazing!"

Glenn sampled his, too. "Would you like to go to a movie tonight? We'd have to go all the way to Newport but..."

Laura sighed, "I'm sorry but no."

"I hope you're not interested in Gil because ..."

"It has nothing to do with Gil."

Glenn's eyes showed pain but his voice sounded casual. "Okay, another time; thanks for your help with my zoning issue."

Laura finished the excellent meal, thanked him again, and stood to leave. "Sorry to have to run but I have a deadline."

When Laura reached the door, Marsethe grabbed her elbow from behind and pushed her forward. He closed the restaurant door and faced her on the steps. "I observed a painful encounter, yes?"

"I need to go," she mumbled, yanked free, and kept going.

Marsethe laughed, "Why run from a harmless old man?"

Laura lowered her hand into her purse, felt for the recorder, and walked back. "I'm someone who knows you aren't harmless."

"No, you are a female with unmet desires." Marsethe leaned close. "I remember Little Miss Laurette Marie Delorange all too well. In response to my tongue, her skinny legs trembled, a remarkably honest reaction to sensual pleasure. I suspect, though, she taught herself denial which if left untreated becomes a lifelong emotional illness, a condition unsuitable for lovely young women in prime childbearing years."

"Does this stuff turn you on, Doctor? Do you talk like this as you jerk off in front of little girls?"

Marsethe smiled. "Autoeroticism is not necessary with certain little misses. Many years ago, one finished me off with orgasmic cries."

Laura choked, "You don't care how you hurt others."

Marsethe lifted her chin until their eyes met. "How deeply I care. It is with pleasure I know I burn on in memory as the first sensual encounter for many a fine young woman like you—immense pleasure and satisfaction for which there is no adequate description."

Laura caught everyone's attention as she raced along the sidewalk all the way back. She slammed the office door, locked it, and collapsed on the couch. After deep breaths to slow her heart rate, she removed the recorder, rewound the micro-cassette, and printed information on a label: date, time, place, and names—a wasted effort. By not informing him, their conversation would be ruled inadmissible in any court of law.

62

Mel returned to finish, summoned Glenn, and demanded a ride to the airport in 15 minutes. "We'll take the Cadillac."

"I have a business to run here. Ask Gil or Brian."

Mel threw his arm across to grab Glenn's wrist. "Must I remind you business success is the result of benevolence, not necessarily merit?"

Mel watched Glenn squint in an unusual manner. "My gratitude isn't eternal, old man. I'll be there in 30 minutes, not a second sooner." Mel's eyes followed Glenn into the kitchen, where for a split second the younger man glanced back. Yes, Glenn had reason to fear retaliation; still, Mel found the exchange amusing—as if successfully negotiating a window of 15 minutes became a manly achievement.

During the drive, Glenn remained petulant but Mel ignored the behavior to consider more important truths: wrong for weaklings to cling to the strong, for family to insist upon contact based upon blood, for a man to be dragged from home: a breach of all things honorable that despite statements to the contrary, those fools knew to appeal on the only level that would work: his need to hear the truth from a shared mother.

At the airport in Houston, Mel stood on the sidewalk, struck in the face by heat and dry air, struck in the heart by a flat landscape: no green mountains, no shimmery lakes, not Vermont. Five miles down the road, he felt offended by a rental car with air conditioning in need of maintenance; he turned around to head back, but a request for another became a complaint then irate demand. The name tag on the man behind the counter read *Service Manager*. Indeed. Idiots survived everywhere, bred like rabbits, and populated the planet with other unfortunates like themselves. At the rate the country journeyed, within two—at most three—generations, the gene pool would be so diluted most everyone would look and think the same. No competition equaled no struggle, no struggle equaled no success, no success equaled no excellence, no excellence equaled no growth, and no growth equaled no positive change. Surely, those few who exceeded the norm would shine like gods.

At sundown, Mel crossed the state line into Louisiana, left the classical selection, and tuned into a local station. Nothing prepared the mind and soul for home quite like the trash his family enjoyed. At the hotel in Lake Charles, he showered off Texas dust and Louisiana salt-mist before heading down to the restaurant for crawfish simmered in fragrant gumbo with okra, seasoned with sassafras. Even as he savored an exceptional meal, it was a meager bonus for his excursion back in time into the bowels of his past. Small pleasures were to be appreciated for what they were until his reverie was disrupted by the painful visage of a man at the doorway: his brother, Bernard—stoop-shouldered, overweight, with a nonexistent hairline. He had a ruddy, spotted complexion and as he neared the table, gave off a familiar odor of cooking grease, the man a replica of despicable Louie Marsethe.

Bernard approached. "You made it, Christopher."

"I go by Mel and it's apparent I made it, yes?"

As Bernard scanned the room, Mel imagined the others lurked nearby in search of a gratis dinner. He buried his anger, barraged his brother with questions about their mother, and listened with two ears: those of a son and of a physician. It became apparent that although Bernard failed to understand the minutiae of their mother's condition, he understood she would never return home. "Her doctors think she's holding on long enough to see you again."

Mel felt exhausted from the flight and drive and dreaded, too, a detour to the hospital. To say that might prompt an invitation to accompany Bernard in some motor vehicle which surely reeked of bass, moldy moss, muskrat pelts, and cigarettes; worse might be an invitation to spend the night with the man's family. Since he had a rental car, Mel insisted he'd follow. Despite his chosen profession, Mel hated to step inside hospitals except to attend to the birth of new life—a joyful occasion which swept him too briefly into the very arms of the Lord. Birth forms were so unlike the decrepit form before him. He listened dispassionately to the staff coronary specialist explain the permanent damage to heart tissue: one more episode—even minor for others—would be her final. Mel was impressed by a night nurse: her skills, professionalism, and interest in his mother's care. A spirited conversation about flaws in the health care industry was interrupted when his mother opened her eyes. Mel caressed her hand gently and leaned close. "It's Christopher. I'm here, Mama, and I love you."

Mel studied her, obviously drugged into a relaxing stupor. As she smiled like a young woman experiencing a long-ago, merry escapade, he recalled pictures of her as a young woman, bride, and new mother, but his musings gave way to reality when spittle leaked from her mouth. After he spoke to her doctor and the efficient night nurse, Mel gained permission to spend the night in a chair beside her bed. Certainly his plan was a waste of one night's charge for a hotel but a necessity. If he were to leave, her final breath might occur and he'd never know the truth he desperately sought and she so desperately concealed. When he detected a sickeningly-sweet perfume, Mel opened his eyes to a woman's smile. He studied her face and decided his sister Yvonne looked healthy with bright eyes and mousy-brown hair showing a mere hint of gray. She was dressed professionally and he recalled she taught at a local high school; over the years, his mother sent letters, cards, and photographs and if Mel recalled correctly, Yvonne's husband wasn't much to look at—overweight, swarthy, and short. Somehow, though, the Neanderthal managed to provide her with a house and two sons. Mel studied the recent photographs she displayed and saw young men in their 20's.

Mel rubbed his neck, sore from a restless sleep. He heard his mother's breathing change and heard her close to awakening, none too soon if he were to escape Yvonne's smile or the faces of two of his three brothers who peered from a doorway. Bernard waved and Roland nodded with no sign of Norman. When their mother's eyes opened, she studied faces and when her eyes found Mel, she took his hand. At his repeated insistence, his siblings left to allow privacy. Mel expected a disclosure of momentous proportions but instead heard, "What do you think of Yvonne? Just a toddler when you left for Baton Rouge."

"She's beautiful with fine sons."

"And what of Bernard, Roland, and Norman—were you surprised to see such old men?"

"No more than when I look in a mirror, yes?"

She laughed in agreement. "And me? I'm a little old lady now, inches shorter, and no red hair."

Mel kissed her cheek. "To me you'll always be a tall, elegant redhead turning heads up and down the streets of Grand Chenier."

She talked of Louisiana politics, lack of rain, changes in the Catholic Mass, and last year's hurricanes—four in all, one right after another. Mel waited patiently but she rambled on about grandchildren and surprisingly, news of a great-grandchild born to Bernard's second daughter. Mel encouraged her to talk yet felt eager to reach the heart of his visit. Finally, she did: "None of this is why you came, Christopher, but I have a question: why did you never give me more grandchildren?"

He considered the truth: *I have beloved progeny of my own, exemplary models of fine breeding upon whom to build a future* but responded with a different form of truth: "Ellen failed to conceive."

"What a tragedy for someone with gifts from God to bestow."

"Mama, you asked me to come for a reason."

"I beg for forgiveness in advance. If I'd told you years ago, maybe you wouldn't have run away after high school."

Mel tsked, "I earned a full scholarship to the state university—a better future for me, Mama; at the time, you agreed."

"I never wanted my firstborn to leave but that hard-headed Louie Marsethe made life impossible for the child of mine who wasn't his." Mel felt the warmth pass through his body and smiled at a truth he always knew. His birth certificate said one thing but his education told him another. There was no way he—a young man who excelled academically, a blue-eyed blonde with red highlights, a boy who reached 6'1" by 14— could be the offspring of that cold, stunted lout with an IQ of perhaps 90.

Mel listened as she described a wretched time in the nation's history. "After the second world war, there was so much poverty here in Louisiana. I worked hard and…"

"My father is Daniel Melvin, yes?" Mel interrupted. At her frown, he added, "Daniel Melvin singled me out my freshman year from thousands of other bright students; a tall, fair-skinned, blonde general practitioner in Baton Rouge who became my mentor; who generously supplemented my scholarship so I wouldn't need to work part time; and helped me gain acceptance to medical school to carry on family tradition. Mama, I knew the truth then! You picked Melvin as my middle name because you loved him and he chose me because he loved us."

"I never knew a Daniel Melvin."

Mel leaned back and listened to a glossed-over telling of a typically sad story of a young girl who fell in love during a rigid decade; worked too hard too young; responsible for younger siblings; so desperate for affection she became involved with an older man with a wife who denied him physical pleasures. "He had a little girl who…"

"Deserved him more than his whore and bastard son?"

"I was only 16 and didn't know…"

Mel thought to hiss *You didn't know if you snuck into woodsheds to fuck a married man, he'd disappear when you got knocked up?* but felt his face flush at the realization she was after all, his beloved mother. He controlled his voice. "Tell me everything you remember; spare no details, Mama, no matter how reckless you may appear as a result."

For 45 minutes, Mel listened to glean four critical details. During their involvement, his father went home on weekends to a wife and daughter in Lufkin, Texas; at the time of Mel's conception, his father was 28; his daughter Lynnandra was born seven years to the day before

Mel; and he squeezed out an existence as a salesman of products to repair roofing. "One night, I told him I suspected a miracle occurred."

Mel snorted, "Let me guess—you never saw him again."

"I saw Gerald for months until I made a Holy Confession and Father Billodeaux took me aside to discuss my sinful situation. Without the church's blessing my life would have been tragic but since it was early, Father Billodeaux spoke to Louie Marsethe, the handyman. Louie had no education but sense enough to ask for the cottage on rectory grounds, a permanent position as gardener and handyman, and a wife who promised before God never to leave him."

"And you got a moron for a..."

"No! I got a good man's name for your birth certificate."

When his mother started crying, Mel asked for his real father's name and felt stunned at: "His first name was Gerald, his parents were from England, but I never knew his last name."

Mel choked, "All my life I painted a sweet picture of my beginning: a beautiful young woman succumbed to the affections of the man she loved only once before their planned marriage. A loving man wished for a future together but disappeared mysteriously at sea or war or another unknown calamity. When a romantic fool imagines his own conception, he is incapable of envisioning sordidness."

His mother answered with a cold stare. "Christopher, why can't it be enough to know Gerald and I loved each other?"

"Perhaps it's always been enough to not be from the seed of a Louie Marsethe, but it isn't, Mama. I believed I came from quality and now find I'm the sort I disparaged my entire life." Mel stared outside and thought, *And my progeny is trash one generation farther along.*

His mother insisted, "You were conceived in love and through an unfortunate set of circumstances, born to me alone. No misinformation on a birth certificate changes that in the eyes of God."

"But I..."

She choked, "No, you listen—your hard work and achievements speak volumes about what constitutes quality but I have one more thing to say. Seed? From Gerald, you came from the very best."

Despite voices behind, Mel escaped outdoors. When Bernard, Roland, and Yvonne caught up, Mel noticed Norman steps behind—Mel's favorite little brother until the day he showed up unannounced in Vermont. Yvonne asked, "Did you get what you came for?"

"That's my business."

They invited him to breakfast but Mel declined and returned to his hotel to make calls: first to the airline to reschedule his return; second to Glenn to report a changed itinerary; third to Gil to seek an update on beloved Laurette Marie—no answer; and fourth to Matthew to arrange a guest sermon Sunday. "It's time to remind our community it is their devotion to one another which saves us from destruction." When Matthew agreed it was a fine topic for Founders' Weekend, Mel sighed, "With how busy I've been, I forgot." Mel contacted a private investigator to find a long-lost sister. When the man insisted he was busy, Mel asked his customary fee and heard $250 a day plus expenses. "I offer $500 a day for immediate attention." As expected, greed led to acquiescence. How difficult would it be to find a woman with a horrible name Lynnandra, born on August 10 in or near Lufkin, Texas, 74 years earlier?

63

Laura put a CD on and hummed as she chopped vegetables. Violet knocked on the screen door, plopped on the stool to chat, and reported Brian would be away for the evening since the elders invited him to their monthly meeting to discuss applicants for vacant teaching positions. "I have company for dinner, people I want you to meet. Join us at 7:00." An hour later, Laura knocked and heard someone shout her in. She crossed the kitchen and overheard Violet say, "She's become a close friend and I know you'll like her, too. Here she is! Laura, meet Brian's sister Peg and my nieces, Maria and Tina."

Laura wondered how to escape an awkward situation and mumbled, "I didn't know Brian had a sister."

Peg said, "He has two. Um, why is your name familiar?"

"I'm the attorney who took over for Bill Marschek."

As the five stood awkwardly, Joanna rushed in. "Sorry I'm late; did Frannie come, too?"

Peg glanced at Laura. "Frannie's my oldest daughter who's seven months pregnant and in this humidity, out of sorts." Peg asked if Laura were staying for dinner and at Violet's nod, tsked, "Because of what I said, you hook me up with a lawyer?"

Laura laughed, "Why don't I just go?" and left.

Minutes later, Peg and Tina stood on the other side of the screen and Peg mumbled, "You must think I'm rude."

"Not at all. I don't like surprises, either."

"Violet only did what she thinks I can't do myself. I have a legal question. If someone files a false report and someone else is arrested, what happens to the first person?"

Laura rubbed her hands together. "That might depend upon the circumstances, in particular whether or not a false report was filed intentionally. That answer's vague because I cannot put your question into context. Perhaps you could provide an example."

"Lawyers are big on ethics, right?"

"We like to think we are."

Peg knelt in front of her daughter, whispered in her ear, and after a moment, stood up. "Tina has something to say."

Laura cleared her throat. "You should consider this first: I represent a cop suspended over a pending sexual assault case. If I were a state's attorney or judge, I might question if a defense attorney exerted undue influence on behalf of her client."

Peg hesitated. "The only thing your client did was trust the wrong woman." Peg knelt eye level with Tina. "If I stay, can you tell Miss Delorange about Uncle Al?" When the little girl nodded, Peg led her inside and sat beside her on the couch.

Laura studied the little girl as she swung her legs—as young as Angela looked, Tina seemed younger—took the recorder out of her purse, dropped in a new micro-cassette, and placed it on the table. She described everything she would do, stated the date, time, and place and asked each to identify herself by name. After Peg and Tina finished, Laura stated, "Laura M. Delorange, attorney representing Allen J. Wilkers. This conversation was initiated by Peg Stenzola and is recorded with permission. Tina, please tell me about Uncle Al."

Tina stared at the tape recorder until her mother reminded her it was there so Miss Delorange could remember everything later. After a lengthy silence, Tina stated, "I loved Uncle Al and wanted him to be my daddy. Mommy loved him, too, but then I saw my sister and Uncle Al in the barn. His butt was ugly." From that point forward, Tina's voice sounded less shaky as she reported facts: they all lived together at Uncle Al's house until one time Uncle Al made her mother cry. Tina didn't see him, Sandra, Sharon, or Sheila for a long time. As the child spoke, Laura recognized the similarity to what Al himself described: a horse ride and pizza at Melanie's farm, right down to the trip to the barn with Tina to rub the horse down.

At a pause, Laura smiled. "You're doing great."

Tina looked from one to another; her voice changed, became firm and sure. She fingered her mother's watchband and said, "Like always, Uncle Al forgot I was there when Frannie came. Like he told me to, I waited with Folly at the end of the barn where the oats are."

Peg interrupted, "Folly's a horse."

Tina giggled, "Folly is Auntie's favorite mare and so very gentle I can ride her alone. Folly had to be so very careful because Uncle Al and Frannie were there and she coulda stomped them. Frannie got naked and Uncle Al almost did, too, but he kept his pants around his feet. It was ugly what I saw."

After a minute of silence, Peg said, "Go on, honey."

Tina rubbed her knuckles. "Most of all I saw Uncle Al's butt as he did things to my sister! Frannie made noises like it hurt and I yelled at him to stop but he didn't. Frannie looked at me but didn't make him stop. He stayed on top of her while they made a baby."

Peg choked, "Tell us how you know about making babies."

Tina giggled, "I watched with Auntie when High Spirits put his penis in Folly and when Folly's belly got big, I got to rub it and feel the colt before it got born. I watched and there was a lot of blood but Auntie said it was okay and Folly didn't die. She wasn't hurt at all, stood up, and let her colt drink milk. I watched Uncle Al and Frannie and now her belly sticks out. I know how babies are made, don't I?"

Laura whispered, "Yes, you do. What happened next?"

"After a long time, they stopped making noise and got dressed. Uncle Al saw me and tried to make me laugh."

Laura asked, "What did Uncle Al do to you, Tina?"

"Uncle Al did bad things to Frannie."

Laura repeated, "What did Uncle Al do to you, Tina?"

The child thrust her chin forward. "Nothing."

"Why did you say he did?" Laura whispered.

Tina looked to her mother. "I couldn't think of the right words and Dr. Marsethe said that was because I'm so little. He said I couldn't remember because Uncle Al gave me a bad bruise."

"How did you get bruised?"

"I ran too fast to get to Folly and tripped on the oat pail." Tina scrunched up her nose. "When Dr. Marsethe found sticky stuff on my belly, I didn't know what it was so I said yes Uncle Al probably laid on me like that and yes maybe he did bad things to me, too."

"Did he?" Laura whispered.

Tina giggled, "No but Uncle Al has hair on his butt."

Laura repeated, "Did Uncle Al do anything to hurt you?"

"No but he makes me so very mad! He can't be my daddy if he does mean things to my mother and sister."

Laura glanced at Peg and promised to see about scheduling Tina to speak to a woman judge. "Tina, thank you very much."

Peg kissed the top of Tina's head and suggested she run back to the house. "Help Auntie Vi put dinner on the table, okay?" As soon as her daughter left, Peg sighed, "Al doesn't belong in prison."

Laura touched Peg's arm gently. "Al loves you."

Peg snorted. "Don't be ridiculous! Before Frannie showed up that day, I gave him an opportunity to choose me. Violet can be a go-between if Tina needs to make a statement but that's it. I've done my bit for justice and he's history!" Peg left and Laura recalled the look on Peg's face as Tina spoke. *How sad for Peg and Al, too: his indiscretion cost him dearly in the end: no Peg, no Frannie, no new infant in his life.*

64

Ralph spent the better part of the evening staring at branches moving in a light breeze and a hazy orange sunset. He recalled details from the file and felt a painful lump in his throat. He had a cop's awareness of the effects of rape. All state police personnel received training to assist victims after a trauma: how to talk, how to reassure, who to contact, and how to gather information and evidence in a non-threatening manner. He had experience, sure, but neutral, removed, theoretical, and objective experience didn't prepare a cop to deal with a friend as victim. He stared at a dark sky and felt amazed Laura found the courage to offer love to his best buddy of all time. He grabbed the phone and dialed Steve. "Since I'm only the best man, do I havta get a haircut?"

"Do everyone a favor and take a shower, too."

Ralph cleared his throat. "Now that the big day's nigh, how are you doing with the family jewels, every man's greatest pleasure tool."

A chuckled, "Better every day and glad it's done."

Another throat-clearing and: "So... does the little lady know why you stopped liftin' weights 'n lounge around on cushy pillows?"

"I haven't said a word; it's a long-shot because after 14 years there's only a 40% chance I'll ever shoot a live bullet again."

"Keep the faith you get armed 'n dangerous again, podna; I'd bet serious coin on it." Ralph swallowed a chunk of vile saliva. "I gotta confess I lifted Granger's file and read about this monster Marsethe."

"Excuse me?"

"Um, what kinda judicial system…"

"Shit! Laura will be devastated you know."

"Nothing can change how I adore that girl but that's not why I called. I'm petrified 'cause a note says some local talent follows her every move. What if that asshole tails her here?"

"I have ideas but let's put our heads together and fine-tune."

"Yeah, okay, we'll plot tomorrow at work."

Ralph hung up, spread file contents across the table, and lifted information about the CFEL gathered by the attorney general's office and department of social services. He sifted through dry, fact-based reports, the sort of thing town clerks stuck into promotional brochures to lure tourists, investors, and retirees: population and economic growth, building permits, birth to death ratios, and academy information. Every teacher had at least a master's degree in their field, a few even more. The curriculum was primarily college-prep yet provided business coursework for the non-college bound. He figured all private schools were heavy into preparation yet still found it interesting 100% of Fallsbridge Academy students graduated, Of those, 94% went on to earn at least a bachelors and another 23% continued on through post-baccalaureates, including doctorates. Ralph sighed, "Perfecto-kids?" He continued to flip through until he saw a note from a social worker: *Since 1969, there have been 0 recipients of welfare, food stamp, ADC, Medicaid, or unemployment benefits within the zip code assigned to the town of Fallsbridge.* He reread the statement and muttered, "What the hell do they put in the town well?"

Ralph found a booklet with colorful photographs—a child's eye view of life on a farm except the one he read seemed different. The photographs were of real people on a real farm in Fallsbridge, Vermont. He checked copyright information and discovered the author and printer based in the town. *What a surprise.* He read from cover to cover: a family of four, newly arrived in town; interesting how the family consisted of father, mother, oldest child son and youngest child daughter. All were fresh-faced blondes with blue eyes. Invited to attend Sunday services, afterwards the family climbed aboard a school bus to join members at the farm. The physically-able worked dairy, beef cattle, chickens, and assorted crops. The CFEL Co-op grew, produced, or packaged milk, meat, cheese, maple syrup, and produce. Less able members performed clerical tasks or staffed a day care center for children younger than four. He focused on an incredible statement *Every Saturday between May and October, bright-eyed and eager teens assemble at 7:00 AM to help with chores until a community barbecue.* Ralph laughed, "Is this shit for real?" as he headed into the real meat of the propaganda: money. Adult members were encouraged to donate 20% of their earnings. Many members were professionals such as teachers, accountants, realtors, and builders; others were entrepreneurs with far-ranging distribution of clothing, maple syrup, cheddar cheese, and dried produce. From their success and generosity a community evolved with its own farm, general store, law enforcement, radio station, planning board, gas station, real estate office, post office, building supply and hardware store, general practitioner, dentist, legal firm, and veterinarian. Ralph studied a photograph of one of the barbecues: a sea of people ate, talked, laughed, played horseshoes or softball, and listened to the radio. *In fact, everything about the booklet suggests peace, love, and goodness. How ironic these clods haveta be instructed ad-nausea how to be good and have fun.* Ralph closed the pretty little booklet and removed the one piece of evidence he most dreaded to read again: a transcript of Laura's interview by a state psychologist on behalf of the medical ethics review board. At repeated prompting, Laura finally identified herself by name, that day's date, and her date of birth. Ralph braced himself to read intimate details about a former colleague, a loyal friend, and amazing woman about to marry his best buddy of all time.

LMD—*Mom took me that day because I had a problem.*

TF—*Please describe your problem.*

LMD—*I started my period and it was awful. I was scared when my mother told me what would happen in the exam but she promised she'd be there the whole time so I said it was okay.*

TF—*This will end sooner if you don't stop so often.*

LMD—*I know, I know, but my throat hurts when I talk. I can do this. I can. He asked me to lie down on a dumb table with holders for my feet and...*

TF—*Please identify he by name.*

LMD—*Dr. Marsethe. My mother was nearby in a chair and explained things. It was okay at first but those things were cold and they hurt and I started crying. The next thing I remember is Dr. Marsethe touched me funny.*

TF—*Describe how his touch was funny.*

LMD—*I never touched myself there like that. I didn't know what he was doing but he whispered it was okay because he was my doctor.*

TF—*And your mother was still there.*

LMD—*Yes, so I knew it was okay.*

TF—*It will end sooner if you don't stop so often.*

LMD—*I know, I know. I'm sorry. Dr. Marsethe told my mother everything was perfect. Then he said his wife got a letter from her sister in Boston in the mail.*

*Could I stay and read it to her? Mom said okay because I did that a lot and
sometimes Mrs. Marsethe lets me borrow books. She's very nice.*

TF—Did you read the letter?

*LMD—Only about half before she fell asleep. Dr. Marsethe came upstairs and
kissed his wife. Then he held my hand and we went down to his parlor. That's
where her piano is and I was only in that room once before.*

TF—It will be over sooner if you don't stop so often.

*LMD—I know, I know but… Um, Dr. Marsethe told me to sit in his lap so he
could finish his exam. He took my sweater off and pulled my panties down around
my knees. He rubbed me between my legs and stuck a finger inside where it hurt.
Then he said I had to take off all my clothes.*

TF—Tell me what happened next.

*LMD—He spread this thing on the couch like a tablecloth and said I had to lie
down on top of it. It was cold and then he unzipped his pants. I watched a coin
fall out of his pocket and roll under the curtain and…*

TF—Tell me what he looked like when his pants were down.

LMD—It was dark in his parlor and I couldn't see. I didn't want to see.

TF—Earlier you said you watched a coin roll.

LMD—I did. It rolled under the curtain where light was.

TF—Tell me what happened next.

*LMD—He knelt down on the rug, put his face between my legs, and licked me.
He was breathing loud and moving his arm back and forth.*

TF—Describe what he did with his arm.

LMD—I couldn't see except it moved. He was probably touching his penis.

TF—You saw him touch his penis.

*LMD—No, it was dark. Then he finished moving his arm and kissed my cheek.
He cried and said he was sorry to love me like that.*

Ralph read a report from the medical ethics review board—no
surprises there: no physical evidence and no witnesses. It boiled down to
a child's word against that of a respected physician. The most damning
part? the mention of testimony that following the incident, Lynette
Delorange discussed the incident on a few occasions with her daughter.
Lynette, not Laura, interpreted the movement of the arm as sexual in
nature; Lynette, not Laura, initially named a penis. Ralph lowered pages,
felt tears, and thought *too many young females are victims of perverse freaks 'n
monsters and lately, it seems our culture deteriorates further, faster.*

He jumped when Joyce asked, "Still working? I thought we…"
She stopped, dragged him to his feet, and hugged hard. "What's wrong?"

"Will Laura find happiness with Steve?"

"Yeah, he's almost as good a man as you are."

Ralph waited until Joyce headed up to bed before he settled back to read a report from an investigator in the attorney general's office. It boiled down to a lot of speculation with little hard evidence—a whole slew of uncorroborated shit about elders, confidential sessions, subtle and emotional control, personality development through reward and punishment, and meddling in the state-mandated curriculum. *Despite how ludicrous it seems, something real weird goes on there or the little lady would never have been sucked back into action by our loser lieutenant. From her own experience, Laura knows truth isn't enough. Hard evidence—difficult to come by legally sometimes—is required to bring it all to a standstill.*

65

Steve felt drawn to the boxes in his closet, pulled one out, and sifted through until he found a file he intentionally avoided: Laura's personal log the weeks following the initial assault.

> *I made a big mistake when I talked about it because after the people from Montpelier and St. Johnsbury left, it was just me. I told the truth to the lady that I didn't fight back right away because it felt different. And I knew I made a mistake saying that because the look on her face said I was bad. The elders told Dad I made a big stink so other people came and poked around private CFEL business. The elders called a confidential session and it was awful because no one believed me. There were seven men and two women around a table and Elder Matthew said they already knew I was a little liar because once I said we weren't doing anything when Aaron already admitted we kissed in the dugout.*
>
> *They said I was proud, boastful, conceited, and arrogant. Maybe I am but I don't think any girl's supposed to shut her mouth and do what she's told all the time. So they tried to teach me a lesson: I'm not special. They said I was a liar who maybe enjoyed what happened to me—if it happened at all. The elders gave Dr. Marsethe a turn to talk and he said it was all a mistake because he would never hurt a child on purpose, especially not one he loved as much as me. He looked right at me and said he could never hurt me in a million years.*
>
> *After I sat in the hallway by myself a long time, the elders called me in to say Dr. Marsethe could go back to work but I got penance: ten hours a week for a year cleaning the stable. I said they could punish me for lying about kissing Aaron Preveau in the dugout, but not for something I didn't do. Mom warned me not to say insulting things but I*

forgot. When Elder Robert said I should leave the room, I asked if he would tell me what expansive means. He forgot I'm a good reader and speller with a real good vocabulary and thought I meant it. He said words like growing, enlarging, spreading, unfolding, and opening. When he finished, I said it was really the Community for Expensive Love, like high-priced, extravagant, and extreme. They were mad before but then they got real mad. Elder Robert said I was spoiled, undisciplined, and vain. When I left, I said I was glad the people in Montpelier came because someone else would take care of Dr. Marsethe.

Steve turned a page and felt his throat tighten at the next entry: the night before an event that would haunt Laura forever.

Tomorrow is my birthday and I'll officially be a teenager. I should look forward to cake and ice cream but Dad is mad and Jack leaves whenever I enter a room. I didn't mean for this to happen; all I wanted was to tell the truth. At night, I can't fall asleep. I wonder if I'm like Dr. Marsethe said. He said he knew I wanted him to do things. He said he could feel how much I wanted him to love me like that.

Steve fell into bed and stared at headlights dance across the ceiling. *Laura refused to be punished unfairly by the elders yet in the end, punished herself far worse. Even if she didn't fight back or felt a natural curiosity about her body, it doesn't change an important fact: under the law, adults can't prey upon defenseless children; physicians can't prey upon trusting patients.* Steve pulled her pillow to his face and breathed her scent in deeply. "Thank you, God, for giving me another chance."

At work the following day, Steve spent a productive day organizing files, entering data, and allowing feelings of excitement about the weekend to creep in. The evening, too, was fantastic: he picked his mother up at the airport, Mickey joined them for dinner, and later at the house gabbed about the anniversary party and wedding plans until his mother dozed off. When he heard a knock on the back door and saw it was 10:51, Steve flipped the outside light on, surprised to see Meg Barber on the porch. She waved and held up a piece of paper. Steve opened the door partway. "Hi, Meg."

"When I hired the disc jockey, he asked for a playlist and I'm stumped. If we have special things to announce, he'll do that, too. You know—anecdotes or special song dedications."

Steve scanned her notes. "You have good ideas here."

Meg waited a moment. "I'm sorry. I didn't think about how late it is. Should I leave?"

Steve shrugged they didn't have much time left and opened the door. "Besides, I haven't been sleeping well lately."

"I understand. Dad said Laura broke it off."

"Did he now? What else did that old gossip say?"

"He wants to pair you up again this weekend."

"Impossible."

"That's what Laura said when she RSVP'd."

Steve chuckled, "Did she now?" scanned Meg's short list, and suggested they look at some of his CDs since what they needed was old-fashioned, romantic music. As they wandered into the living room, Steve imagined Ralph and Joyce would be fine if some of the songs on the playlist reflected his and Laura's tastes, too. He spotted Mickey's CDs and realized he could come up with one beaut. He inserted the Crash Test Dummies, skipped ahead, and as *Swimming in Your Ocean* started, howled, "Does that describe your father or what?"

"Oh yeah, the man is known to be easily distracted."

Steve remembered Laura's CDs in one of her boxes and retrieved them. He admitted he didn't know much about Sarah McLachlan or Beth Neilson Chapman's music, but they could keep them in mind. For hours, Steve and Meg rifled through one CD after another until he disconnected the player and connected the turntable. He explained he couldn't loan out the LP's but she needed to hear a particular Sam Cooke song. Steve counted the tracks and carefully lowered the needle. As *That's Where It's At* began, he visualized the night Laura came to him, the first night they expressed their love, the night she was shot, and the night he almost lost her forever. He felt his eyes water, turned to see Meg's look of curiosity, and shrugged, "What can I say? It takes me back to a happier time."

Meg nodded. "It must be tough to go through this again, Steve, and I risk a lot here but need to say something. You deserve more than what Denise or Laura could..."

Steve held his hand up. "Please don't start this conversation again; I have no desire to be anything but friends."

"I know you always say it isn't about my father, but..."

Steve put his hands on her arms, turned her around, and steered her to the door. "Leave before you embarrass us both."

When the phone rang, Steve grabbed and heard Ralph. "Are you free to surveill with me tonight?"

"Yup."

"Pick ya up in ten, fine budster."

Steve hung up and said, "There's a call I need to..."

"I know your job's demanding but you look like you could use comforting. Let me stay or I can come back later."

"The answer's no, Meg; it'll always be no."

When Meg finally left, Steve knocked on the door to Mickey's bedroom and peeked in. When he saw his mother slept soundly, he wrote a quick note and taped it to the door.

66

All day at work, Laura struggled to concentrate as she imagined she'd find a perfect combination wedding-anniversary party dress in Montreal. When Reilly left, Laura locked up, headed out, and stopped by the carriage house to grab a credit card. On her way to the border, Laura stopped at the general store for something to eat. When other customers left and only she and Caroline Beaudon were left inside, Laura approached the deli section to order. As Caroline wiped the counter, she looked over and Laura saw pupils dilate in that funny way cops often observed. "My mother says hello."

"I always liked Lynette," Caroline said, switched the meat slicer off, and built a sandwich way too big for one. Laura pictured Jack at 16 and a junior when night after night, he argued with their father—the name shouted back and forth was Caroline.

"You and Jack dated in high school, right?"

Caroline nodded. "Jack was a junior and I a sophomore but when you moved, I never heard from him again."

Laura clearly saw pain. "What happened? Why did I hear your name when my father and Jack argued?"

Caroline whispered, "My mother was frail and needed medical care. I was warned never to discuss it."

"Discuss what?" Laura watched Caroline wrap the sandwich, lower it to a cardboard container, and add pretzels. Laura tried to continue a conversation but in the end, paid and rushed north to what she prayed would be a far more rewarding and successful endeavor.

In Montreal Laura headed toward Parc du Mont-Royal and The Plateau downtown shopping district to stop into one boutique after another in search of the perfect dress—something beige but not boring, something with a dip neckline but not so low to show scars, something above the knee but not short—in other words, something subtle enough to escape most men's attention but sexy enough to drive Steve wild. At the sixth store, she found it jammed among a host of others: cream-colored and shimmery with a feel of silk to fingertips. She tried it on: an inch above the knee, a low but not plunging neckline, a clinging effect at the bust and hips. She noticed the perfect shoes and stockings, too, and off in a corner, the sort of underwear racy catalogs promised drove men wild. She added up the cost of her purchases, computed the Canadian to US dollar exchange and at her estimate, flushed at the thought if she figured correctly, the excursion equaled half a normal week's salary. "What the hell," she laughed and handed the salesclerk her card.

Laura enjoyed the trip back along the dark, winding roads of southeastern Quebec and northeastern Vermont and crossed the border at Derby Line. When she neared Fallsbridge and noticed the cruiser, she smiled and waved as she passed. Inside the carriage house, she left everything dark and changed into her new outfit. She started a Van Morrison cd, raised the volume, and swayed back and forth to *I Forgot that Love Existed*. The dress felt heavenly as did the imaginary arms that held her so close, she couldn't breathe. When the song finished, Laura chuckled, "I hate this shitty little town." She showered quickly, dressed again, and raced to her car. She felt her body relax the more miles she covered heading west. Although she sped all the way, Laura didn't arrive until 1:15. She fished through her purse for the house key, and groaned when she couldn't find it. She ran to the back door and pounded until a light came on. When a woman inched forward but didn't open the door, Laura asked, "Is Steve home?"

"No."

"Is he working?" At the woman's look of fear, Laura pressed her hand against the glass. "Are you Lea?"

"Who's asking?"

"Laura!"

Lea opened the door, tugged Laura inside, and held her close. "He left a note he's working. Can you wait?"

Laura stared at his plants lined up along the counter like little soldiers and felt the tightness in her throat. "I have an appointment first thing in the morning; I should head back."

"Are you okay?"

"I needed to see him. I've been so..."

"Lonely? As lonely as he is, I bet; how many hours away?"

"It's almost three."

"You're too tired to get back on the road. Get some rest and I'll let him know you're here."

"No, not if he's working."

"I'll set the clock for 5:00. Get some rest and if the two of you are lucky, he'll be home before you go."

Laura thanked her and after the door closed, studied the room. Steve made changes that seemed feminine somehow; she grinned when she figured out what they were: throw pillows on the chair and four average photographs from a summer class she took at UVM framed—each transformed from ordinary to almost professional. She searched for her nightgown in drawers, came across a pamphlet from a urology group, and read about a procedure to reverse a vasectomy with detailed instructions on healthy recovery. With a sudden flush, she appreciated he considered such a move, studied a diagram and wondered, *Does tampering with the equipment affect performance?*

Laura replaced the pamphlet, found her nightgown under her pillow, changed and called into the hallway. "Lea, are you still up?"

Lea came to sit on a chair beside the bed and whispered the sweetest things about Steve as a baby with a round face and big blue eyes, incredibly silky skin with soft peach fuzz on his chubby pink cheeks, a good eater. "Neighbors stopped me on the sidewalk to peek into the carriage because if he were awake, he gurgled, cooed, and smiled—a joy. Stop me if this is prying, but do you want children?"

"Right away if I can get pregnant."

"Piece of advice: avoid children too close together. Steve wasn't the baby for long because Michael was born 14 months after. By the time I was seven months, I couldn't pick Steve up, the delivery was rough, and when I got home, still couldn't pick him up for weeks. He got around on fat little legs all by himself unless his father or big brothers were home. I regret it and wonder if that's why Steve has trouble connecting."

"I don't understand."

"I think nowadays magazines call it bonding."

"Believe me; he has no trouble bonding. Just look at Mickey, Ralph, you, and me. And I've seen how he is during investigations. It doesn't always show but he has a huge heart."

Lea sighed, "Do you know about his first marriage?"

"We won't fall apart like that because we won't allow it."

Lea squeezed Laura's hand. "You're good for him." She described a 4th of July when Steve was almost three. "Michael stayed

143

behind but Max, Paul, Anthony, Steve and I watched fireworks over Lake Champlain. Steve wailed and pressed his hands against his ears."

"I did that, too, until I was about ten."

Lea described a day Anthony took Steve without permission. "I left Steve in the back in the sandbox and when I came back out with a basket of laundry, he was gone. I scoured the neighborhood, stood in the street, and called his name. When a neighbor reported she saw a strange woman talk to him, I felt convinced she kidnapped my beautiful boy!"

Laura curled up into a ball. "Were they gone long?"

"Long enough to humiliate myself in front of the neighbors and police—when Anthony pulled up on his bike, Steve hung on for dear life and displayed a prize bag of penny candy: squirrel nuts, mint juleps, jujubes, spicettes, red dollars, and atomic fireballs. My little angel's face was filthy as he displayed the bag as if it held treasure."

Laura chuckled, "Steve still loves candy. Our first day as partners, I opened the glove compartment and a bag fell out. He claimed he needed it so he wouldn't light a cigarette."

Lea huffed, "Anthony knew better than to load his little brother up with sugar. I swear to God, Anthony got him started on sugar that day and 12 years later, cigarettes."

Laura murmured, "He quit and better stay quit if he expects me to have his child. He needs to be around for decades."

"Yup, you're good for him. Denise was afraid of him."

Laura laughed, "Of Steve? I can't imagine."

"Scared of losing him."

"Oh. I do worry about that, actually."

Laura felt herself drift but listened to Lea describe how difficult it was for Steve as the third of four boys, between super-achievers like Paul and Anthony and a heartbreaker like Michael. "I believe it made a difference in the life of one special little boy."

Laura nodded. "As a middle child, I know what you mean: my older brother Jack is handsome, smart, and successful; my younger brother Rick is gorgeous, smart, and on his way to successful."

Lea offered again to call Steve or the station dispatcher. "He'll be upset if he misses you."

"No, he's working."

"Okay, but first one more story then you can sleep." Lea described a little boy who loaded the bathtub with toys—not only the usual boats and ducks but people made from Popsicle sticks and a three-corner hat of aluminum foil. "He loved honeysuckle bubble bath and shampoo because they made mounds of suds. When he climbed out, he smelled so good I had to hug my little angel. "

"I love him like that, too. I love everything he does," Laura sighed and buried her face in the pillow. When she opened her eyes again, it was to Steve's smile as he lifted her off the bed and carried her to the bathroom. As the tub filled with warm water, honeysuckle bubbles floated in the air. They faced each other naked and Steve's husky voice whispered, "Your hair's longer."

"And yours is lighter."

"You have a tan line, kid."

"And your legs are still as white as snow."

"You have more freckles."

"And you have less flab." Laura climbed into the tub, sat down in the warm fragrant water, and reached for his hand. "It isn't fair what you did to me, Scolarzski."

"Excuse me?"

"You left me addicted to you."

Steve climbed in, sat down, and drew her forward. "Healthier in the long run, woman, and cheaper than drugs."

When the alarm went off at 5:00, Laura stretched contentedly and extended her arm sideways. She bolted upright and snapped on the lamp. No one was beside her; no one had slept there. She ran into the bathroom. No water on the floor, no wet towels, no empty plastic bottle, no scent of honeysuckle. She dressed quickly and headed into the kitchen. "Last night I dreamed Steve and I made the best love ev...I'm sorry. That wasn't dignified."

Lea carried teacups over. "You think I'm too old to remember?"

"I didn't mean that."

"Such desires can last a lifetime; Max and I had a wonderful relationship." Lea went to the stove and served French Toast. "I regret not calling Steve; he'll be upset when he gets home."

Laura dug in. "Do you know the plans for the weekend?"

Lea nodded. "That's why I'm here. Honey, I'm so excited because finally, my boy has the woman he deserves."

"Sleeping here was enough."

"Enough for what, honey?"

"To dream sweet dreams—to renew this sad soul."

Laura sped east along the interstate through foggy mountains as the sun became visible above the pines, its haziness signaling another hot, humid day. When blue flashing lights moved in behind, Laura pulled over, smiled at Gil, and laughed, "You're out and about early."

Gil reminded her village speed limit was 25 and leaned in. "Isn't that the same thing you wore yesterday?"

"So are you planning to ticket me for being unfashionable, officer? Maybe I should ticket you for spying." She looked at her watch, saw she had enough time to shower and dress before work, and when he made no motions to write a ticket, pulled away.

67

In his office, Gil dialed the number Mel left for a hotel only to discover the old man checked out the night before; no answer at the house, either. When he tried the cell, the old man grunted, "This better be urgent! I sit in this deplorable Newark airport only to be…"

"I just stopped Laura, gone overnight again."

A chuckled, "If that bothers you, I find…."

"I don't give a shit who she sleeps with."

"Who is your best guess?"

"I figure Wilkers; with him, Laura's not a smart-ass like with me. If anything bothers me, it's the waste of time and energy, Mel. I'm only in this for the reward."

"Are you positive Laura was with Wilkers overnight?"

"Not 100%; I lost her outside St. Johnsbury but before that when she stopped for gas, I overheard her ask how far it was to Walden. That sounded like she headed toward Caspian Lake."

The doctor hissed, "How in hell could you lose her, Gilbert? We are talking Vermont, not New York, the Northeast Kingdom, not Manhattan! We're not talking multiple road choices! She was on 2 or 5, yes? Obviously, it has become too difficult for you to do the things the elders and I require from our law enforcer!"

"Be fair; she's a trained cop and may have seen me."

Mel groaned, "First pay phones and then overnight trips—she begins to annoy." A long sigh then, "All is not lost so early in the game; the presence of Wilkers is but a temporary vexation. His own sexual proclivity will remove him from the picture exceedingly soon."

68

Steve brought in the daily *Free Press*, sat at the kitchen table to read, and thought he detected her perfume. "Laura?"

His mother called from Mickey's bedroom. "How'd you know? She arrived around 1:00 but left at 5:00."

"Why didn't you call me?"

"She said not to if you were on assignment."

Steve wandered back to his bedroom. "I understand."

Lea followed to recommend he get rest and added, "I hope it's okay if I told her stories about when you were little."

He groaned, "Not the one about Tony and the bridge?"

"No, I forgot that one."

"Thank heavens; Mom, I have to be in court at 2:00. I'll set the clock for noon but wake me if I oversleep."

"Will that be enough?"

"Sure; I don't need much sleep." Steve heard the door close softly and wrapped his arms around Laura's pillow. He pulled it to his face and breathed in her refreshed scent. He rolled over and noticed a note. *Scolarzski, I insisted your mother not bother you but now I wish you were here. I had the sexiest dream. Help me fulfill it this weekend as husband and wife?*

69

Ralph figured he should put in some organize-his-desk time since he'd be gone a week—a second honeymoon and all, a chance for him and his gal to scorch sheets like newlyweds. When Steve wandered by, Ralph said, "I thought you were gonna get some shut-eye before court."

Steve admitted he caught five hours and lifted his file in the air. "I'm ready to testify; this idiot asshole roped himself up good. The state's attorney doesn't need my testimony with this loser."

Ralph fingered the cord on what used to be Laura's phone and thought if true, the grumpy face across from him made no sense. "Usually you wear a shit-eatin' grin when a freak's...."

"It's not a case that's got me down," Steve interrupted. "Laura showed up in the middle of the night but left early."

Ralph groaned, "Lordy, you missed her because I couldn't surveill alone. Buddy, I'm sorry."

Steve shrugged, "Not a problem."

Ralph settled on the corner of the desk. "In a few short days, the little lady becomes the little missus. If you can't wait, go find her tonight. I'll do surveillance alone. Besides, I can stay awake all night if I know you and Laura scorch sheets in another county."

Steve stared outside and stated he wouldn't step foot in that wacko village. "My presence could put her in jeopardy; besides, the internet has different opinions about length of time for abstinence and I'm not about to risk meager performance on my wedding night."

"I get it; the family jewels are still under wrap?"

Steve nodded and grabbed his car keys. "I'm off to get a falafel and diet cola at *Ahli Baba's* before court. My treat. Care to join me?"

Ralph hooted, "A falafel? Are you avoiding red meat, saturated fats and sugar, trying to carve lard-body into hard-body?"

Steve eyed the area for big ears. "Yup, just like trying to get faulty equipment back into working order, there isn't much I can do between now and my wedding night."

70

Al double-checked with Reilly if her boss recalled lunch plans, heard she did, and headed off. He parked in the shade and watched cars enter and leave the state park. Laura arrived, looked around, then leaned her head back to close her eyes. When his approach startled her, she squinted in the bright sunlight. "I guess I needed a nap after last night."

"Sounds like fun. Scolarzski?"

"No; did you bring lunch like you promised?"

"Sure did." The air felt instantly cooler as Al grabbed the picnic basket and blanket from the trunk before heading up a path beside a rocky stream, shrunk from its springtime rush to a slower flow; in another month, it would be a mere trickle. When they found a picnic site Laura liked, Al spread the blanket on the ground. "Counselor, want to hear what happened with my ex-boss?"

"Yes, then I have something to tell you, too."

Al decided she shouldn't play poker—her flush probably meant bad news and he had enough for one day. Al stabbed a blade of grass into the dirt and laughed, "Today my boss asked for my resignation; he thinks if the case drags on much longer, I won't be back but in jail or drummed out of law enforcement. My supervising lieutenant is a first-class jerk who had a hell of a time getting to the point but I figured out where the conversation headed and promised to make it easy: no ugly scenes or wrongful termination suits; I'd go quietly like a lamb to slaughter."

"Would he hold you to that if your situation changed?"

"What? If it's possible I might go to trial soon, I have to prepare my daughters and parents. They shouldn't read details in the paper or hear them in court before I have a chance to..."

"That might not be necessary," Laura interrupted, rummaged through her canvas bag, and placed a tape recorder on the blanket. After a few seconds of static, the first voice came out loud and clear, then the second: Peg, Tina. Al closed his eyes and felt how Laura studied him for a reaction. He avoided eye contact and felt his eyes moisten at the sound of Tina's sobs. When Peg's voice shouted, Laura switched the recorder off.

Al insisted she play it all and concentrated on every tone. "My God, did you hear the hatred in their voices?"

"I not only heard it but saw it, too."

"Did Tina mean it when she said she loved me?"

"Yes; she adored you."

Al studied Laura and observed definite contradictions: innocence alongside brutal realism, idealism with pragmatism, and naiveté with cynicism—a confusing set of characteristics he found intriguing. Al asked if he could pose a personal question and at her nod, said, "I understand you had a sexual abuse incident in your teens." When she winced, he added, "Granger told me."

Laura laughed, "Why doesn't he draw maps so tourists can locate the place I returned to be tortured again?"

"I'm sorry; will Tina forget that disturbing image of me?"

Laura stared off at nothing and confessed certain images floated in and out of consciousness, especially memories of something unfamiliar prior to the incident; a man's sexual anatomy a perfect example. "Tina used the correct terminology when she spoke about Folly's impregnation. Her Aunt Melanie may have treated it like a zoology lesson but Tina— even at her young age—made the appropriate connection to what she saw between two humans. A girl can't control her thoughts and fears. She might be in the middle of a conversation about the weather and all of a sudden, recall what happened. At a dance, a boy might accidentally brush his hand against her breast and she'll lose it in front of their friends."

"I'm sorry I..."

"Tina's recovery depends on the support she receives. Then there's the other problem: with Frannie due to deliver in September, you'll be a nagging presence in their lives forever, especially if the baby's a boy who looks like his father."

"What's your impression of Peg? Was I set up?"

Al noticed once Laura was focused, she seemed attentive. "From your version, I thought yes but from Tina's, I couldn't tell but even when she screamed in anger, Peg cared enough to act decently. This is gut instinct, Al, but I think Peg came forward because she loves you. There was something she said that didn't get onto tape."

Al sat up straight. "What? Please tell me."

"Peg said *The only thing that man did was trust the wrong woman.* Direct quote."

"Shit."

Laura announced she scheduled a meeting with the state's attorney assigned to prosecute, who contacted the social worker, psychotherapist, and judge. "All agreed to give me half of a 20-minute recess in an ongoing trial. I figure that's short but once the tape starts, no one will insist upon a time frame."

Al opened the picnic basket and recited its contents. Laura selected chicken salad on whole wheat, cheddar, and iced tea, but passed on wine. "Laura, please; the wine's fantastic. Try it."

"I have to go back to work."

"Reilly's gone by now. Who'll know or notice?"

There was a hint of a smile. "Gil Munier or Mel Marsethe?"

After lunch, Al cleaned up the trash, rolled up the blanket, and locked it and the basket in the trunk. He pointed to a well-worn path and headed into the woods. As the slope of the land inclined gradually, Laura asked him to wait, opened her canvas bag, and leaned against a boulder to yank socks and sneakers on. "I'm a woman who often rides a bike." For the next hour, they hiked the foothills of Burke Mountain. From time to time, he stopped and caught his breath; he felt stupid as he made jokes about his age or low level of fitness. He watched her wander on ahead and wondered how Steve kept up with a woman that young and fit, a remarkable fact considering months earlier she was in the hospital. As they finished their descent, Al considered an interesting fact he picked up along the state police grapevine: it took Scolarzski two years to move the woman from *Hello* to *Let's hop in the sack.* That seemed like an amazing contradiction in an age where first dates often ended in bed. And then he knew, too, through that same grapevine, since Denise's death Scolarzski was successful with more than a few women. Instantly, Al felt shamed by how readily he assigned two people to a quickie in the back seat of a cruiser when in fact, a relationship with a woman like Laura must mean more. He tugged on her arm and when she turned, saw that horrible look of fear again. "Steve's a fortunate man."

"We're no longer involved," Laura insisted and reminded him of their conversation when he mentioned the most difficult thing about being human. "I always accepted myself as the type who loved to ride a bike, kayak on the lake, read, or listen to music. It rarely occurred to me it was odd to be alone. One Saturday I woke and felt an unusual ache when I realized I wouldn't see Steve for two days. So the most difficult part of being human for me is learning to deal all over again with loneliness."

Al studied her eyes. "As I said, Steve's a fortunate man."

"And as I said, we're no longer together."

Al opened the passenger door. "My lawyer knows I can be foolish but may overlook I'm also one hell of a detective. I hear things in people's voices—yours in person, Scolarzski's on the phone—and my gut tells me this separation isn't permanent."

Al jumped into the driver's seat as Laura chuckled, "I need to keep feelings hidden in one shitty little town."

71

Compared to the rest of Texas, Mel found Austin different—a clean, prosperous, attractive college town on the Colorado River. He found Miss Lynnandra Florence Scott's home where it stood on the northeastern bank of the river within walking distance of campus. It was a perfectly lovely spot, though not Vermont. When he rang the bell, Mel decided to be completely honest right from the start but how did one tell a 74-year-old spinster she wasn't an only child? The white-haired, elegant woman who opened the door took control when she studied him and laughed, "Which one are you?"

"Explain that please?"

"You've got Father's eyes. For god's sake, we all do."

What a revelation the next three hours were—over a 15-year span, Gerald Peter Scott's sales route took him from Lufkin, Texas to Tyler, Beaumont, Leesville, Grand Chenier, Sulphur, Lake Charles, and Lafayette. It appeared, too, that at some point during those years in each locale, his father left behind a woman carrying his unborn child. Mel sighed, "It appears our father was a promiscuous man."

A sly smile: "Libidinous maybe, but always monogamous."

Mel laughed, "Explain that statement, yes?"

Lynnandra insisted it was easier to show him and retrieved four photo albums from a bookcase. She placed them on the coffee table and returned for three more. Mel skimmed the first few and saw each contained photographs of a lovely young woman and her beautiful infant who, according to carefully printed labels beneath each photo, grew into healthy young children, adults, and parents. The albums were neat, orderly and thorough with their newspaper clippings of birth announcements, school activities, athletics, military service, wedding announcements, and career achievements. Not a single birth date overlapped a calendar year.

Mel turned pages slowly. "He might have been serially monogamous but what of your mother's feelings?"

Lynnandra shrugged, "She contracted tuberculosis and lived away from us; she died when I was 11."

Mel murmured his sorrow for her loss and lifted a fourth album which chronicled the life of a female named Cheryl, born to a Shirley Windower in Tyler, Texas. The photographs and news clippings concluded abruptly with a 1998 death notice.

Lynnandra sighed, "Father was upset he outlived her."

Mel glanced up. "Gerald Peter Scott still lives?"

Lynnandra answered he died two years earlier, a month shy of 95. "He lived long enough for five of you to find him."

Mel lifted another album and skimmed: more of the same academic and athletic achievements, more of the same successes, more of the marriages and births of a new generation. In the next, Mel studied his own mother's smiling face in a black and white photo—her beauty far less brilliant than what Gerald himself knew existed. Mel whispered, "Color would have captured Mama's flaming red hair and sharp blue eyes. It is apparent our father had exquisite taste in the selection of each specimen."

"What an unusual choice of word!" Lynnandra laughed. Mel skimmed the four remaining albums before she returned them all to their rightful places on the bookshelf.

Lynnandra insisted Mel join her for lunch, summoned a young woman, and issued detailed instructions on how the fresh bass was to be prepared. Over an exquisite meal featuring a wide variety of fresh-picked vegetables, Mel complimented her on her apparent knowledge of nutrition. At her smirk, he apologized. "As a medical doctor, sometimes I assume others are less informed. I confess on occasion, I am a patronizing man."

Lynnandra admitted she patronized, too. "Father was an insufferable snob about his acquired knowledge and status in life."

"Forgive this next assumption, yes, but my mother described Gerald as a door-to-door salesman who scraped out a meager living."

"Nonsense," Lynnandra laughed and insisted during the war years, while others lived day to day and hand to mouth, their father provided inexpensive but sturdy materials to fix sagging roofs. "It was one thing to skip meals, or skip replacing worn shoes or torn clothes but a roof over a family's head yet another." By the time he returned to Lufkin permanently, Gerald Peter Scott saved enough to design and manufacture a specialized instrument for use on derricks in southeastern oilfields. "Father's route took him all over eastern Texas and western Louisiana. In restaurants and bars, he listened to men complain about their work and heard suggestions for improvement. He collected a multitude of ideas, synthesized them into an original design, and capitalized on the fact he was first to obtain a patent."

Mel confessed he pursued a similar goal and hoped to bring an idea to fruition soon. "At a future meeting, I'd like to bring data from 12 years of research to share with a person I suspect would understand my work cognitively and respect the ambition behind it."

"Yes, I'd love to hear more."

Mel confided he pondered submitting a patent application for medical test he designed. "I have an attorney I'd like to ask to aid me in the process but she will no doubt debate the ethics of an individual seeking to improve the future of the human race. It is a matter of education, is it not? How can one not desire the birth of each child to be wanted, to be planned, to have a chance at excellence?"

Lynnandra agreed with a nod and characterized their father as a self-taught man who despite his pride in his accomplishments, believed strongly in advanced education. "Father was generous in his support of the mothers and eight children who survived. He was fiercely proud of the fact one became a medical doctor, one an attorney, one a certified public accountant with her own firm, one a classical pianist with the Philadelphia Philharmonic, one a registered dietician at a large hospital, one a college professor, one a registered nurse, and one an elected politician."

"Which describes you? The nurse?"

Lynnandra laughed heartily. "By age 30, I earned a doctorate in nutritional science, oversaw clinical rotations at a hospital in Dallas for 33 years, and taught at the university here. I retired from both and currently do private consultations."

Mel lowered his fork. "I deserve that. As I said, I am a patronizing man. Old-fashioned, too."

Following lunch, Lynnandra sat beside him on the couch as they went through his album page by page. He felt stunned by how much was there: the birth announcement in the parish news, the photographs of him with his mother, his Eucharist at age seven, the concert solo on French horn at age 13, the four other children of his mother with that moron Louie Marsethe, his Confirmation at age 14, the academic awards in high school, the awarding of a full scholarship to LSU, the admissions to medical school, his marriage to Ellen, her automobile accident and paralysis, his personal embarrassments and failures. He stopped at a clipping about criminal charges filed for performing illegal abortions. Mel cleared his throat. "It pains me our father learned of this. Although the state dropped charges for lack of evidence, I was forced to leave Johns Hopkins for the unauthorized use of lab facilities. What must our father have thought of this?"

Lynnandra pointed to a clipping about his expulsion from Temple following a year of residency. "On more than one occasion, Father said *Christopher's genius may often be mislabeled as aberration.*"

"Thank you." When he noticed the time, he explained he needed to make visiting hours at a hospital in Lake Charles. "Mama is on her death bed and for that reason alone, I learned the truth. All my life, I knew I was not the offspring of Louie Marsethe and now, despite my joy in learning my heritage , I feel ill-equipped to manage the depth of loss. I missed meeting our father by a mere two years!"

At the door, Mel and his magnificent half-sister hugged and she whispered, "Promise you'll come back to discuss your research."

"A promise is made."

As Mel drove east to Lake Charles, he recalled his father's words over and over: *Christopher's genius may often be mislabeled as aberration.* He felt an odd discomfort in his heart: his mother waited too long and denied him an opportunity to know his father. At the same time, Mel felt an odd exhilaration at the realization he was right all along: he was who he was because a brilliant man selected a magnificent specimen to carry his seed. Despite his mother's failing condition, Mel decided it was time to return to Vermont and continue his life's work. He felt a renewed resolve that his benevolent intervention into the procreation habits of those less fortunate than he was a worthy endeavor for a son of Gerald Peter Scott.

Though he returned exhausted, Mel felt renewed by his new sense of direction. At the hospital while he waited for his mother to awaken, he relegated himself to a visit with Yvonne and Norman. Thank the good Lord for small gifts—nuisances Bernard and Roland were nowhere in sight. The youngest of the brothers, Norman was a distinguished-looking 54-year-old with the least amount of traces of Louie Marsethe's prehistoric traits. Mel made polite inquiries about his health, personal life, and business endeavors and felt disturbed at Norman's prediction the expansion of his business would take him to New England in the near future. Mel determined his mother slept and Yvonne's attentions elsewhere before he said, "Do not visit Fallsbridge again, Norman. My home is no longer your way station."

"I didn't hear Vermont had storm troopers at its state line."

"You mock me?"

Norman smiled. "Last I heard, Vermont's still part of a free nation. I can visit without staying with you."

"I repeat: do not visit again." When he heard his mother stir, Mel shooed his siblings from the room and knew he sounded like a babbling fool but confided, "Lynnandra was amazing, intelligent, successful, and graceful. It's true I come from the best seed."

She squeezed his hand. "Then you forgive me?"

Mel considered his true feelings: *Your lifelong silence cost me something dear* but understood nothing productive would come of it and squeezed back. "I forgive you." She smiled and dozed off.

Mel consulted with the shift supervisor and discovered a piece of exciting news: the impressive night nurse left a note: *If you're interested in continuing our conversation, call me at home. I know of a fantastic tavern near the hospital where we can have a drink.* He called and she provided an address where they would meet in 15 minutes.

Mel bid his pesky siblings goodbye and watched Yvonne's eyes moisten. "You're going back to Vermont already?"

Mel snickered, "I am a busy physician with babies to deliver, illnesses to check, and aging patients to oversee."

Norman shrugged, "When she dies, you'll have to come back."

Without bothering to answer he may decide to skip funeral services, Mel exited, walked the dark street, and found the tavern a block from the hospital. He waited in a booth from where he could watch the comings and goings of a well-dressed clientele. It was not a pick-up joint but a place where a gentleman could escort a lady: dim lighting but not dark, dark wood of pecan or cherry, clean, acceptable establishment. The music was softly subdued: easy-listening he believed it was called. Sometimes, he discerned a touch of country but not the barbarous *since-you-cheated-I-must-maim-you* garbage a band played at the Maidstone. Incredibly, Glenn paid for such hogwash.

The young lady arrived, waved from the door, and hurried over. "Like it, Doctor?"

"It's wonderful. Call me Mel and what shall I call you?"

"I'm Elisabeth—with an s, not a z—Grunwald; call me Ells."

A waitress approached, left a bowl of spicy snacks, and took drink orders. Mel described the beauty of Vermont, quaintness of

Fallsbridge, and warmth and generosity of its townspeople. "Not to mention the opportunities you will find for a career in health care."

She studied him warily. "I have a great job here; why leave?"

"What do you earn?"

Ells hesitated as the waitress lowered drinks. "My base is low 50's; when I'm on nights, there's a shift differential. I do well."

Mel settled in to present his offer. "I oversee your training as a physician's assistant, with responsibility for a full range of medical services. In exchange for a contract stating you remain at least five years, the community pays for an advanced degree of your choosing at Dartmouth, and transportation as well." When she didn't respond, he added, "You're young enough to consider a medical degree and as a reward for hard work, you would inherit my practice."

"What if I never aspired to be a doctor?"

Mel chuckled, "Oh, probe your mind, Little Miss. I'll bet such an urge exists." At her continued silence, he explained the community would provide a furnished house at no rent and subsidize one vacation trip home a year. In response to her look of confusion, he finished her salary would begin at $65,000 with excellent annual increases and full benefits.

She laughed, "What is this? You don't know me. I could be the worst nurse at the hospital for all you know."

Mel admitted he had exceptional instincts. In her eyes, he saw integrity and genuine concern for the elderly and frail; in her voice, he heard honesty and character; in the reactions of her colleagues, he saw respect; and in her demeanor, he saw strength and quality breeding. "I confess in addition to my need for a skilled successor, I think of a fine young man who is a perfect match."

Ells smirked. "I've met my fair share of duds."

Mel opened his wallet and displayed a photo. "Glenn is physically, emotionally, and intellectually perfect for you. However, his brother may be more to your liking. Both are single."

Ells shook her head. "And what if I'm not to theirs?"

Mel laughed, "Since you are to my liking that is unlikely. However, if my instincts prove faulty, Fallsbridge has other suitable men, professionals with homes of their own to share with wives and children. Be honest. I pique your interest, yes?"

Ells shrugged, "Maybe—Louisiana hasn't been the same since Katrina." From her tone, he heard even if she hedged on the package, she neared acceptance of his original offer: round trip airfare to visit. If all went according to his wishes, he'd arrange for late September and allow her to be dazzled by Vermont's breathtaking autumn, the reality of winter in the Northeast Kingdom far in the future.

Mel was surprised at her suggestion they go to her apartment to talk in private. In her voice, he heard a different tone. How was it possible she might be lonely? How was it possible such a magnificent creature could be susceptible to the attention of a stranger 30 years older? He wondered if she were one of those women—like Rita Thompson Lezzarro or Francesca Theresa Stenzola—who found older men more attractive than a Gil or Glenn.

An hour later, Mel stormed out of her apartment revolted by his failure and disheartened for trying. He presented his package, saw his trophy in plain sight, and did irreparable damage by focusing on unmet desires. She did everything requested: removed all traces of lipstick, perfume, nail polish, and makeup; scrubbed her face until her skin glistened; and brushed her hair up and held it with Bobbi pins. Her pubic hair was pale and breasts nicely small. He enjoyed the game but in the end, none of her playfulness worked.

Mel arrived at the airport five hours early for his flight, called Glenn with the time of his arrival, and complained of a long layover in Newark. Mel settled into an uncomfortable scoop chair and forced himself to read to avoid interaction with 360° of human detritus. During takeoff, the lights of Texas then Louisiana disappeared from his window and Mel breathed a sigh of relief Little Miss Elisabeth Grunwald ultimately declined his invitation to visit.

From his seat, Mel studied horribly plain faces surrounding him. It was certainly true the citizens of the United States of America—once the envy of the world—no longer looked healthy, educated, or prosperous—its melting pot theory a mislabeling of a blend to nothingness. By the multitude of filthy brats on the flight, it was apparent low quality individuals managed to perform something of which he was no longer capable. Despite his wishes to the contrary—recalling his shameful failure in Little Miss Elisabeth Grunwald's bed—he knew at his age, it was unlikely he could alter his preferences. The only bright spot was the fact his sin was not that of homosexuality. When Mel felt something bounce off his head, a red plastic plane fell into his lap. He turned to stare at the monster behind him, annoyed so many fools felt the need to tote their brats when they flew places for a weekend. Mel focused his eyes on the child, issued a deep growl, and observed it—in all likelihood a girl—jump onto its mother's lap like the creature it truly was: yet another persuasive argument for the use of birth control and abortion.

72

As soon as she realized it was Friday, Laura bounced out of bed. On her bike ride to work, she watched workers on ladders remove red, white and blue ribbons from the tree branches, the last remnants from the Memorial Day celebration, and replace them with the forest green and lemon yellow theme the CFEL used on all its literature, signs, service handouts, and choral robes. Farther on, another group tied green and yellow ribbons to lamp posts. At the library and school, children tied green and yellow balloons to park benches, hand rails, and signs. The front of the Maidstone looked festive, too; on the steps, a wooden easel stood with a painted *Schedule of Events*. The weekend marked the 40th anniversary of the official founding of the Community for Expansive Love, a date noteworthy for its formal shift from ragtag group of businessmen with big ideas to recognized religious organization and its valuable tax-exempt status.

In the office, Laura greeted the 9:00 AM appointment: the Choiniere brothers owned and operated a sheep-shearing, woolen yarn-production operation and sought representation during re-application for a Vermont Seal of Quality from the State Department of Agriculture. As with other small businesses, the standards for earning a label were stringent but the pay-off with consumers priceless. Marvin Choiniere explained, "We were denied the first go-round and want every t crossed and i dotted this time."

When the phone rang, Laura apologized and grabbed. "Reilly, please don't interrupt when…"

"I'm sorry, but Dr. Marsethe insisted."

"Then you insist he call back."

Laura hung up and smiled. "Sorry about that." She reviewed the original application, pointed out inconsistencies, examined their assets and liabilities statement, and appraised their product samples. At 10:00, she escorted them out and asked Reilly to schedule a second appointment in a week. "That gives me time to finish my research."

Reilly pointed at the phone. "You know who is on hold; he calls every ten minutes."

Laura answered at her desk to hear, "I'm displeased with…"

"If you wish to hire a different attorney, I can recommend a firm in Newport or St. Johnsbury." There was a long pause before she added, "Because of our past you need someone committed to…"

"Yes, perhaps it is imprudent to start over at this time."

"I have to go."

"Another moment, please! I returned from a rewarding visit south and seek counsel in a different matter entirely: an application to the U. S. Patent and Trademark Office for..."

"I'm sorry; I have all I can handle at the moment."

"I hear you are not too busy for the Choiniere Brothers and their fleecing operation."

Laura chuckled, "I'm sorry; I need to go," hung up and wanted to enjoy his obvious annoyance but instead, thought about Steve and the weekend. She watched Reilly daydream, too, and stare outside from her perch by the window. Laura walked over and squeezed Reilly's shoulder. "Why don't you go help set up?"

"I need to save vacation time."

"No vacation time's needed for something like this. Go on; it's fine with me." Reilly rushed off to join Gil and Glenn as they draped the dark green bandstand with yellow bunting.

Alone in the quiet office, Laura performed routine tasks, stared at her watch or the clock, and noted time crept forward like a snail. At 11:30, she couldn't bear another minute, changed into biking garb, and locked up. On her way by, she waved to Reilly who raced across the grass. "Aren't you joining us for the celebration?"

Laura checked her watch. "Within the hour, I'm off to my parents' house. This evening is a 25th wedding anniversary party. Someday, I hope to find what Ralph and Joyce Barber have together."

Reilly shrugged, "The CFEL teaches members to build what is necessary. The good Lord gives us life and opportunity but it's up to each of us to make a success of those gifts."

Laura nodded. "True, but not every woman who works on building a strong marriage gets one in return."

"Do you plan on having a family someday?"

Laura recognized the subtle probe could lead to a report to Marsethe and decided to give the girl a tasty nugget. Laura sighed, "I often think with or without a husband, I'd love to have a baby someday. A woman in her mid-30's feels the biological clock wind tight. With my police background and law degree, most men get turned off quickly."

Reilly smiled. "Glenn may be the one man God created for the purpose of loving you for the gifts you bring."

Laura visualized Steve's face and murmured, "Lofty aspirations that beautiful are worth pursuing." When she glanced at her watch, she saw their conversation moved time forward a quarter hour. She waved to

Reilly, Gil, and Glenn and shouted, "See everyone Monday!" as she pedaled away from one shitty little town.

At the carriage house, Laura entered the kitchen and noticed a phone on the wall by the refrigerator. She thought *that was unbelievably fast* and as if through a psychic connection, it rang. She lifted, cleared her throat, and whispered, "Hello?"

"Laura, it's Ed!"

"Ed?"

"Granger? We worked together for a while?"

"Okay but how'd you get this number?"

"There's this thing called directory assistance. Listen; are you coming to the party tonight?"

"I wouldn't miss it!"

"How about we grab a drink beforehand and catch up?"

"I don't drink."

"For chrissake, Delorange, a drink can be a soda or that friggin' crap you kept in your desk."

"Where and when?"

"How about 3:00? The wife and kids want to go on the tour so let's meet in the Ben & Jerry's lot in Waterbury Center."

"Then 3:00 it is." Laura hung up and thought *He's divorced with no children as far as I know. Doesn't matter; I have more important things to think about than an attempt to disguise official contact as chitchat.*

Laura checked every seam on the dress and slid the silky stockings onto her forearm to check for runs. She opened her weekend bag, packed it full of sexy underwear and nighties then normal clothes, too, in case Steve expected her to leave the house at some point. Finally she grabbed her razor to shave her legs and underarms in the shower later. She noticed her carefully-planned schedule in disarray and groaned at a knock. She opened the door to Brian. "What?"

"It's business, so let me in." When she locked the screen door to block entrance, he chuckled, "I have a job for you this fall."

"What kind of job?"

"The academy sponsors an evening adult education program. In addition to a small group from other parts of the county preparing for high school equivalency tests, we offer pottery, swimming, archery, photography, and hunter safety. We've never done much with legal issues and when Marschek staffed the law office didn't think to..."

"Don't exaggerate, Brian; everyone in Fallsbridge has at least a high school diploma; many have college degrees. It's what the elders self-righteously call a *lifestyle success story*."

Brian corrected her. "Since 1977, the academy holds a 100% graduation rate but people out in the hills from before the CFEL..."

"And this bunch of losers sure as hell need to be brought up to snuff." When Brian nodded in all seriousness, Laura suggested he get back to her when he felt clearer about expectations. "I'd like to hear what the elders and you consider suitable topics."

Brian shrugged, "I'm sure the elders will approve anything except feminist, abortion, or political-secular issues."

Laura thought *that certainly squashes creative debate* but smiled. "I'll think about it." She grabbed her things and ran out into glorious sunshine.

Two hours later Laura pulled into the Ben & Jerry's lot and checked for Gil—no sign. All around car motors idled, voices laughed, children shouted, a wasp flew in one window and out the other, a woman's sandals flapped against her soles, an 18-wheeler whined up the hill, a young man struggled with a crying toddler, two women ate ice cream out of cups, cameras clicked, and a flag whipped in a soft, warm breeze. From outside, a voice chuckled, "Who's a million miles away?"

Laura turned to Granger. "I wish I were, then I'd be a million and some odd miles away from one shitty little town."

He opened her door. "Scolarzski's been a pain in the ass about the shitty way you treated him."

"What?"

"I know I ordered you to break it off but can't understand why you did it in such a way, everyone but Barber pays the price."

Laura laughed, "Are you kidding me? You put up with Steve's foul mood then go home at the end of the day to a place you call home, spend time with friends or family, and do what you feel like doing??"

Granger reached for her hand. "I didn't mean..."

She shoved him off. "I never meant to inconvenience you! God knows I sit around having the time of my life with people I love." She dug in her purse and tossed two micro-cassettes. "Enjoy these, you self-centered son of a bitch!" Laura stared at a group of tourists. "Why didn't you prepare me for Wilkers? He's nothing like what I expected."

Granger nodded and suggested they take a walk. He asked, "Do you think acting on impulses is wrong?"

"Wrong as in evil, immoral, or illicit—or wrong as in improper, misguided or inappropriate?"

He laughed, "I take it you don't like the word wrong."

Laura admitted wrong sounded ambiguous to a lawyer. "At first, Al's behavior seemed immoral but the more I thought, the more I leaned toward inappropriate. It's clearly one of the ethical dilemmas we debated in law school. Am I easy on Al because I like him or he was a cop? Am I soft because his wife died and he felt lonely? Would I be unsympathetic if you were in a similar situation or severe if it were Steve?"

"Sure you would; you tend to run black and white."

When he patted his pocket and asked about the tapes, Laura said, "You can't do anything with the first. For my own peace of mind, I wanted to hear the bastard admit he assaulted me. The second is a copy of an original offered to the state's attorney with a voluntary statement from Peg and Tina Stenzola. I meet next week with the judge and prosecutor."

"Good progress."

Laura laughed, "Progress? Are you nuts? All I do is sit around that shitty little town and spin my wheels."

"It takes time; keep going." Granger cleared his throat in a way she knew meant trouble. "There's something you need to know before you see tomorrow's *Free Press*. "In court this morning, Stephanie Orsini's psychiatrist testified she doesn't pose a threat."

Laura groaned, "She killed Mac and she tried to kill me!"

"Let me finish; the gun used to shoot you was not the 9-mm that killed MacClure. Her lawyer's talking temporary insanity."

Laura snorted, "The woman wore a wig and gloves, drove a different car, and loaded bullets—premeditated in my book. She left me to bleed to death in the snow and drove home to make breakfast for her son. How can anyone buy temporary insanity? She's lucid enough to load a gun and get herself there, then insane long enough to pull the trigger?"

"Let me finish! Her attorney claims her delusions converged upon a woman who just happened to be a cop. She remains in custody at the state mental hospital but returns to court in September; in the meantime her attorney petitions for private treatment and a closely-monitored, drug-controlled release." Laura rubbed her forehead and thought *God, I'm naïve to think anything makes sense or happens the way it should, stupid to think anyone cares about justice. In the past, I always believed if I live an honorable life, things would go my way.* Laura half-listened to Granger add something about the DSA calling to schedule another meeting to discuss the case. She thought of where she headed and thought *Why question anything now, you idiot? In hours, you marry Steve.* She turned to laugh, "I don't care how this turns out, sir, as long as that bitch stays away from me and the people I love. See you at the party."

For the rest of the drive, Laura recalled moments with Steve: *conversations; debates about cases; the rest area birth; the day Granger introduced them; the Sigler daughter's wedding reception; their amazing dance; disagreements about music, sports, restaurants, or movies; and the joy she felt when they held each other close.* As she pulled into her parents' driveway, she flushed with pride at the commitment they were about to make: *fidelity, honesty, love and if they were so blessed, a child who captured the best of them both.*

After a shower, Laura brushed her hair at her old vanity and noticed posters and plaques her parents never removed as if someday they expected her to return. Not too far a stretch, really: for too long, she let a monster rule her existence, leave her fearful and untrusting. She spent four years at UVM, returned home for a while, then headed off to Columbia for three years of law school. She had vague recollections of favorite classes or professors, research for papers, library carrels that felt as comfortable as her bed in her dorm room. How sad her memories included few friends, parties, sporting events, or broken curfews. She pulled her navy blue high school yearbook off a bookshelf and thumbed through; it was painful to realize she sleep-walked through a portion of life many others held dear. There were few signatures of other students— in fact most were from teachers who complimented her as a serious student sure to go places. Unlike what she imagined her brothers' would be filled with: signatures from friends and girlfriends, with clever tales of noted parties, picnics, detentions, and beer blasts. Out of curiosity, she headed into Jack's old bedroom—still intact to some degree but not like hers—and noticed a similar bookcase. She searched for his yearbook but didn't see one the same navy blue. She noticed another similar-sized lighter blue book with white. pulled it out, and scanned Jack's yearbook from the Cummings School of Veterinary Medicine at Tufts. She found her brother's photo and noted his personal info listed him as Class Salutatorian from Fallsbridge Academy and holder of a Bachelors of Science in Animal Sciences from the University of Vermont. Farther down the row was a forest green similar-sized book with gold lettering.

From behind, her mother said, "There you are."

"I'm feeling reminiscent, I guess, after dreaming Dad and Jack argued in the kitchen at night after I went to bed and it seemed like…"

Her mother touched her gently on the shoulder. "Laura, I worry you spend too much time reliving the past."

Laura stood. "Yeah, I do, but tonight I marry the man I love so it's time to let go of the past, right?"

Her mother hugged her. "Yes, so let's go to your room. I'd like to see if I can work wonders on those beautiful curls while they're damp enough to style."

73

Ralph felt aflutter and watched Joyce pace with a full blown attack of her own. As a couple, they were seen as smart-assed jokers and foul-mouthed pranksters. They loved to focus on everybody else's private dreams and hidden intimacies and the truth was he and Joyce liked their victims—not them—to be the centers of attention. Meg called and offered to pick them up for the drive to Middlebury. The girl had no idea her mother knew and proceeded to talk about dinner reservations, parking, and the restaurant's dress code. Sweet Joycie played along nicely and reported she had a new dress perfect for the occasion. Joyce glanced over and finished with, "We'll be ready when you get here at 6:30." Joyce hung up and crossed the room wearing an utterly delicious grin. "Let's start our celebration in the shower."

74

Mel exited Trudeau L'aéroport International in Dorval, stood on the sidewalk, and studied passing cars. After an hour, he called the Maidstone to hear Glenn left hours earlier. During the drive to Vermont, Glenn apologized many times over and blamed his late arrival on an unusually long border crossing at Derby Line. Despite multiple attempts at conversation on Glenn's part, Mel felt determined to remain silent and at the house, unlocked the door to a stench of musty locked-up-tightness. He turned and growled, "I ask you to oversee the house and you can't manage one open window!"

Glenn—usually one to stammer—stared back defiantly. "I came as often as I could and won't apologize once more today."

Mel noticed a light blinking on his machine and headed over as the phone rang. He grabbed on the second ring and heard Gil report: "Laura stopped to change at her parents' house and left her car there. She went with them, not a date, to a 25th anniversary party for a sergeant named Ralph Barber."

"Do you mean my Little Miss is out of town again?"

"Am I wasting my time again? I left messages for you at home and the hotel."

"Yes, yes, sorry, sorry; stick with her. Without guidance, a young lady finds opportunities to divulge from His path, yes?"

A pause then, "I want to be home for the celebration."

"You wish to be with Reilly, yes?"

"Don't assume less than honorable intentions."

Mel chuckled, "I swear you are still that seven-year-old who visited one Thanksgiving and dropped peas under my wife's table."

"Huh? What does that have to do with anything?"

"Be patient; your reward awaits you."

He heard a low laugh, almost a growl. "Old man, I get tired of all the gaps between weekends with Reilly."

"Your decadent urges..."

"Are infinitely more decent than yours! You were there when I petitioned the elders to marry Reilly and adopt David."

When he heard the dial tone, Mel hung up and smiled. For a young man who still hated vegetables, Reilly was the proverbial carrot dangling on a stick—to control the woman was to control the man who loved her passionately. He lifted the phone and dialed Mottolla. "In the morning, speak to Mary McGuinn. Tell her the elders are aware her daughter enjoys the company of Gilbert without their approval. If this continues, I as village physician shall file a report to guarantee the nosy State of Vermont takes David."

"The State? Are you sure this is wise?"

"It is a threat to remind members who presume to know how to live a life without benevolent guidance."

Vincent sighed, "I'll talk to Mary in the morning."

Mel hung up and turned, surprised to see Glenn behind him. The younger man seemed ornery still and ready to argue like his older brother but there would be no more debates that night. Mel needed to concentrate, reassess where he stood with his project, and reorganize his and the community's plans. How was it possible a man in his late 60's—a doctor who accomplished miracles on a regular basis—still behaved foolishly? How was it possible he for even one moment placed the future of his project on a stranger in Lake Charles simply because she possessed admirable characteristics? The perfect match for Glenn always was and always would be Little Miss Laurette Marie—time to set the future back into motion. Mel studied Glenn, observed a trace of the orneriness, but something else, too: in the younger man's eyes all the kindness and respect displayed in the past. Time to forgive him a need for some measure of independence; time to mend fences. Mel whispered an apology for his anger at the airport and in the car. "When I rearranged my schedule, I failed to take into account hours of layovers in the dreariest of airports. An old fool is forgiven, yes?"

Glenn shrugged, "Yeah, I hear Newark's pretty bad."

Mel wrapped his arm across Glenn's shoulder and guided him to the door. "Gil is incapable but perhaps you understand good things come to he who trusts his elders and waits patiently for a reward."

"I don't understand."

"Do you love a woman?"

"Don't be cruel like this, Mel. You know I do."

"Be patient; I witness a change in Laura, likely due to her evolving relationship with you. She is on her way home to us."

Finally a nod and smile: "I pray for that every day."

75

After his botched meeting with Delorange, Ed headed home to change for the party. He arrived early, nursed a drink, and nibbled celery and carrot sticks. He wandered, checked place cards, and plopped into a chair when he found his. The place looked festive like a wedding reception and figured that's what Meg Barber had in mind: the kind of gathering Ralph and Joyce couldn't afford the first time. Ed found the idea of a marriage lasting 25 years remarkable, but even more amazing? The Barbers put out vibes they still ran red-hot for one another.

Ed watched Scolarzski cruise the room. He looked good all polished up in a dark suit, tie, dark socks and for chrissake, wing tips and a decent haircut for a change. His son Mick followed and an old lady in a pale blue dress. Scolarzski introduced her as his mother, visiting from Florida. Ed found her presence odd when she clearly said she hadn't seen the Barbers in years. He checked the other place cards and showed them to Scolarzski; all the guys were together, their wives or dates, and lo and behold, Delorange, her parents and brother. Ed leaned back and figured the seating arrangements alone were worth the price of the gift.

Delorange arrived a little later in a shimmery wheat-colored dress that hinted at surprisingly decent cleavage. She wore heels, too, with pale stockings that shimmered like her dress. She looked drop-dead gorgeous with her mass of curly black hair off her neck—elegant and flamboyant— unusually sexy for a woman who acted so unsure of herself and only hours earlier crumbled in front of his eyes. She floated around behind the chairs, gave Mick a hug, the old lady a squeeze on the shoulder, and left behind a trace of some great perfume. She smiled at Ed

166

then nodded in Scolarzski's general direction before she sat and scanned the crowd. Ed thought she looked calm, confident, detached. Her parents and brother followed and Ed stifled a groan when Scolarzski ran through introductions again. Ed felt amused when Delorange and the Polack ignored each other as if they thought it was a secret only months earlier, they engaged in recreation that ripped sheets off the bed.

Ed thought Ralph and Joyce weren't all that surprised when they arrived but annoyed at the attention, especially applause. They made the rounds of tables, gave away kisses and hugs, and Joyce bawled in a way women got away with all the time. A disc jockey played fantastic music, food tasted great, but the conversation at their table barely passable. Meg Barber hung around like she always did when Scolarzski was there—cute when she was younger, awkward now—and teased, flirted, and tried to get Scolarzski involved with the disc jockey; the Polack didn't bite.

Ed watched Scolarzski and Delorange avoid eye contact and found their behavior hilarious. If Barber were his usual self instead of a nervous boob, he'd surely run over and abuse them both big time. A huge cake and ice cream later, guests moved en masse from the dining area to the bar, where the disc jockey set up a new camp. Ed found the music a bit too 50's, 60's, and 70's for his tastes, but in the end decided the sweetly romantic stuff sounded appropriate—some Sam Cooke, Elvis, Righteous Brothers, and Supremes. When the DJ announced Marc Cohn's *True Companion,* Ed observed a chink in Scolarzski's armor as the Polack's eyes settled on the back of Delorange's head as if he willed her to turn. Ed saw his chance, grabbed them both by the hands, and tugged them to their feet. "Igor, even you can handle this tempo so give the girl a whirl." He watched them on the dance floor and thought their coolness was all too smooth; by the end of the song, he knew his attempt at public ridicule backfired—they moved together as if that's where they belonged.

76

Laura imagined everyone saw how difficult it was to keep inches between her body and his. Her heart jumped when Steve whispered, "Do you still plan to marry an old fart in 55 minutes?"

"If that fart remembered the license, I'll be there."

Steve patted his pocket. "It's right beside the wedding ring I insist you to wear when we're lucky enough to be together."

Laura choked, "Don't make me bawl."

Steve pulled her closer. "Go right ahead, kid. Granger's staring and will figure I insulted you."

The song finished and another started with a fast tempo. For a second, Steve looked as if he might try to dance but squeezed her hand and rushed off. From his table, Roger hooted, "Igor lives!"

After the song, Laura watched the disc jockey call Meg Barber up to hand the microphone over. Her hands trembled as she shuffled note cards. "I have a partner in crime. Sergeant Steve Scolarzski, get up here."

Her mother leaned close. "Excited about later?"

"You have no idea," Laura answered glanced at Granger who stood nearby and eavesdropped shamelessly. "Mom, with so many cops in close proximity, we need to keep..." but had no opportunity to finish once Meg told not-so-subtle jokes about what kept some marriages alive. Yet among all the raunchy stuff was so much love, Laura's heart ached for Steve and her to find one small piece of what Ralph and Joyce shared.

Steve took the microphone. "Fifteen years ago, I got a new partner. After one day with the guy, I went home in total shock. Picture what happened during that first shift: the man talked about a mule's nonexistent sex life, the destruction of the planet Krypton, blueberry pancake batter, and whether or not Batman wore dresses at home."

Meg grabbed the microphone. "And that's an abbreviated list!" Laura and the guys laughed since each and every one at some point spent time alone in a car with a man who could speak volumes about electric blanket controls, jalapeno peppers, and ant colonies.

Steve took the microphone and described a day his son Mickey left a box of CDs at the house. "Anyone who knows cops know we check everything, stunned by one song that describes Ralph at his most romantic. Here's *Swimming in Your Ocean* by The Crash Test Dummies."

At the lyrics *When I'm sampling from your bosom, sometimes I suffer from distractions,* Joyce shouted, "Who spied?"

After the song, Meg returned the microphone to the disc jockey and suggested he head into her list of romantic oldies. Ralph and Joyce were called to take the floor alone for a favorite song: The Righteous Brothers' *Ebb Tide.* Laura watched how nervous they were; it was unlike Ralph to look uncomfortable but that didn't last. As soon as the song ended, he reverted to form, bounded across the floor, and tugged his wife behind. He grabbed the microphone and laughed. "It's incredible how some fools forgot my bride and I know things about them no one else on earth does." Ralph pointed to Meg and Steve. "Be forewarned, darlin' daughter and bestest buddy: someday you'll be centers of attention at an event like this and **will** regret a dangerous precedent established tonight."

When her mother wandered off to the dessert bar, Laura turned to her father. "Earlier at the house I noticed you kept lots of my stuff and in Jack's bedroom found his old yearbooks and wondered…"

John touched her hand. "Let those memories go, honey, and replace them with new ones with Steve."

77

Marie decided no matter what Ned said or did, she'd never forgive him if she missed the party. The Barbers' daughter called and made the plan clear: to make it before Meg brought her parents in, they had to be gone by 6:00. Ned knew the plan; they discussed it at breakfast; he agreed. Marie twirled the invitation and waited in her new dress, best jewelry, and new pumps. Robbie came in from work and reminded her he had a date and needed her car. Marie nodded and begged her son not to tie up the shower but in the end, it didn't matter. Robbie rushed through his routine, left for his date at 6:30, and his father still wasn't home. Danielle ran in at 6:45, sweaty and breathing hard after her evening jog. She glanced at the clock then at the wrapped gift on the table. "Why haven't you left yet?" When Marie shrugged her answer, Danielle whispered, "Where's Dad?"

"Who knows? I never do."

Danielle excused herself to change and that time, Marie didn't bother saying a word about the shower. When Danielle returned, she offered to drive her mother to Middlebury. "I'm sure he'll show up and even if he doesn't, someone can drive you home. Or you could call me; I'll give you the number where I can be reached."

Marie's heart ached at the sound of Danielle's voice. Ever since Melanie married the year before, Danielle took over as the child who tried to maintain balance, kept her eyes on things, mediated and fixed, but Marie decided there would be no more of that and hated how quickly she made the same tired old excuses. None of the children believed any more their father was called out on so many emergencies. "What I'd like is a ride to the car rental agency."

Once there, it was clear Danielle didn't want to leave but Marie insisted everything was fine and promised in the morning, she'd make pancakes and tell her about the party. The instant her daughter pulled out of the lot, Marie's resolve faded but she forced herself inside to display her driver's license, use her credit card, and sign the agreement, proud she had the automobile insurance policy number just in case. Marie drove off the lot and imagined one drink would toughen her up. It would be difficult to show up at the party without Ned. For god's sake, they were all his friends, not hers, and it would be humiliating to show up and sit alone or worse—watch the bastard arrive with some new young *friend* in tow. In Burlington, she stopped for one drink at Revver's Bar & Grill; in South Burlington, she stopped for one more at Nicky Porter's; in Shelburne, it was yet another at Muddy's Tavern. When she exited, the car clock read 8:50 and Marie had no energy to continue a toughening-up trek through Charlotte, Ferrisburgh and Vergennes. It would be easier to go home and sleep.

Marie watched a red car speed along a side street and pull onto Shelburne Road without stopping. Marie swerved the big, heavy rental vehicle into the left lane and leaned on her horn as she passed the huge red junker. It was a Chrysler or Plymouth from the mid-80's, a lot like the first new car she and Ned ever bought—big and gas-guzzling but unbelievably safe for children. Marie saw the driver of the other car was a kid in a turned-around filthy white painter's cap who laughed, flipped the bird, and accelerated to keep up alongside her. She braked hard. The right lane for the turn onto I-189 was coming up in less than a mile and she needed to get home before she vomited all over the rental car. The scumbag accelerated and braked whenever she did, making it impossible to pull back into the lane. When another car pulled out of a gas station into the right lane, Marie waited for the collision but the scumbag was smart enough to hit his brakes hard. Marie watched headlights fall behind, switched lanes easily, and headed toward the interstate.

It wasn't over—the red junker cruised up alongside in the left lane. Marie scanned the area ahead, turned for a split second, and saw a boy in the passenger seat throw something. As a can sailed over the top of the rental car, Marie stared into the rear view mirror and groaned as a pedestrian stumbled and fell. She felt her eyes water and jumped when the windshield smeared with something dark. She groped for the wiper controls on the unfamiliar car but it was too late. She braked hard, skidded blindly through an intersection, and hit a parked pickup.

Marie stood in a restaurant parking lot and watched the tow truck leave with the rental car. As a patrolman approached, she joked it was a good thing that car had an air bag. He nodded neutrally and asked questions but she apologized and ran off to the side to vomit in the bushes. Marie pulled herself together and described the vehicle, its driver, and the two passengers she saw. She managed to recall three of five digits on the license plate and finally asked, "Is the person who got hit by the can okay?"

"She's fine; the can hit the sidewalk and exploded."

"Thank God!"

The patrolman smiled in agreement and offered her a ride home. Marie accepted gratefully since there was no way she'd call Danielle; most definitely, she wouldn't ask dispatch to try and find Ned. Inside the patrol car, the young man suggested she be more careful in the future. "I suspect if I'd done a breathalyzer back there, your blood alcohol level would've been above legal limits."

Marie choked, "Why didn't you? Your report would've been easy: a little shit for reckless endangerment, his passenger for assault on a pedestrian, and me for DWI."

The patrolman insisted, "Another driver verified those boys harassed you for miles."

Marie finally relaxed. "That's true."

He glanced sideways. "And I prefer not to arrest the wife of another law enforcement officer."

"Shit," Marie sighed and remained silent the rest of the way.

At home, Marie collapsed in bed. She heard Robbie come in right on the dot for his 11:00 and Danielle at 12:10 for her midnight curfew. Ned came home at 1:15 AM, sat on the edge of the bed, and whispered her name; she pretended to be out cold. Marie thought the bastard reeked of another woman but wouldn't ask. There was no way she'd let him see how easily she could be destroyed.

78

Ralph pressed clammy palms together, watched the clock roll toward 9:30, and grinned at the thought of Scolarzski's last half hour as a single guy. Ralph scanned the crowd and at 9:45 made eye contact with the justice of the peace, who disappeared into the corridor. At 9:50, Ralph wandered around, spoke to Steve and Laura's families, and drew them away from the crowd one by one until they assembled in a small room upstairs. The ambience wasn't spectacular like a church or synagogue or magnificent like a garden but the room looked refined with flowers Joycie lifted from the downstairs bash. The effect was complete when everyone formed a semi-circle of loving faces: Lynette, John and Rick behind the bride, Lea and Mick behind the groom, Ralph and Joyce on both sides as best man and matron of honor. Ralph found it difficult to contain himself until the justice of the peace pronounced them husband and wife. Steve kissed his bride and Ralph tried to keep his mouth shut. The newly married man was his best buddy of all time and although thousands of sentiments threatened to scream their way out, it didn't feel right to utter sappy sentiments about the need to make love, share dreams and a bed, or more realistic ones about how to make babies, remain faithful, or enjoy a king-sized bed. One managed to escape his lips when Ralph lunged forward and hugged hard. "Guys, stay in love and your life together will always feel this splendid ."

79

Steve found it difficult to return to the party, mingle, and chat with the guys. He watched Laura do the same on the opposite side of the room and heard his mind whisper *my wife,* a startling thought. He wondered if Ralph was right when he claimed year after year after year: *Love given freely and purely becomes love returned ten-fold.* Steve jumped when his mother squeezed his hand. "Lynette and John insist I go home with them. Three's a crowd on wedding nights."

Steve chuckled, "I forgot you came with me."

Lea kissed his cheek. "It's not as if you have nothing else on your mind tonight, Stefan."

Steve stared across the room when Laura stopped to talk to Joyce, who laughed, threw her arms around, and bawled all in two seconds. Ralph crossed the room to slap a key in his palm. "Joycie's mother rented us a hotel room for the weekend with room service, hot tub, and king-sized water bed. You take it."

"I appreciate the offer but my wife wants to go home."

Ralph nodded. "Ten years ago I would've wagered you'd never turn your life around. I hope you're as proud of you as I am."

80

Bobby didn't care what they said when they drew straws—if Scolarzski drew the short one, Barber would've raised holy stink. Sure, Barber wanted his best friend there but shit, all those other losers? Since when were dispatchers, troopers, or secretaries more important than a fellow detective? Six got stuck there—a dispatcher, four troopers, and Bobby. He and the dispatcher took turns answering one stupid call after another. When a deer got pommeled on the interstate, he notified the game warden. When a sobber called to report a peeper in the woods, he dispatched a trooper. A kid called to report UFO's and Bobby called the airport to hear a blimp hovered over Centennial Field. A guy called about a brawl in a public park and Bobby dispatched a trooper. After seven hours, there were no big news-grabbing calls to offset his sacrifice.

81

Gil observed people leave in pairs and small groups. At midnight, a sea of bodies poured into the . Some staggered, most didn't. Cars started, voices shouted, lots of laughter; a guy carried boxes and speakers; others toted flowers and gifts. A small group hovered in front then hugged and kissed. Two males and two females climbed into the Delorange car and left. Gil waited until the last vehicles left before he pulled out to head east. There'd be repercussions with the old man but why stay where he wasn't needed?

82

Laura suspected Steve and Ralph's concerns were exaggerated but let them coordinate her exit. Groups of people milled around when Ralph pulled his car up by the door to pile flowers and gifts into the back. Laura took advantage of confusion, climbed in, and crouched down. As Ralph pulled away, she heard a vivid description of a room waiting for him and Joyce at a hotel—king-sized bed, satin sheets, hot tub, and heart-shaped soaps. "Joycie, I'm gonna bathe you real nice and real slow."

Laura laughed, "Hey, don't forget I'm back here!"

Ralph flung his arm over the seat, rubbed the top of her head, and laughed, "Tryin' to set a romantic mood." At the Middlebury Inn, he pulled into a space, turned off the ignition, reset the dome light, and grabbed their weekend bags before slamming the door.

Laura peered over the seat and studied cars. When Steve pulled up, she jumped out and settled into the passenger seat. Steve grabbed her in a crushing hug. "Kid, we are so right for one another." As he drove, Laura felt different—subtle at first then awareness their lives changed. It felt comforting to know they were linked, intertwined, connected, and unified. It felt more than a legality of marriage; it felt spiritual as well. Two people met, learned about each other, danced their fancy footwork, and denied the truth as they fell in love. Despite two years of games and distancing tactics, in the end they found themselves where they craved to be. Laura hadn't meant to talk out loud and felt stunned when he chuckled, "Yup, it's as if we bumped up against destiny, kid."

Laura found it amazing how comfortable Steve was as he drove, talked about all sorts of things, parked near the house, escorted her to the steps, and unlocked the door. He lifted her off her feet and insisted it was tradition for a bride to be carried across the threshold. Inside, too, he was comfortable as he turned on lights and selected music for the background. When she giggled at her voice on the tape, he headed into the bedroom, folded bedding back neatly, undressed, and brushed his teeth in only socks. She hung out in the background feeling useless especially when Steve jumped onto the bed and stretched out naked like a cat in the sun.

Laura headed into the bathroom, changed into a new red negligee, and brushed her teeth. She stood in front of the mirror and studied her face, amazed she took such a step. Marriage was alien and unlearnable except through practice. What if Steve stopped loving her? What if he went ahead with that dreadful procedure but she couldn't get pregnant? What if she never learned how to cook well? What if he got disgusted with her haphazard housekeeping and bills-paying? What if she tried hard to be a good wife but failed? Laura heard the music shift into Sam Cooke's *Bring It on Home* and realized since they arrived home, half her tape played which meant she wasted 25 minutes in the bathroom. Laura hoped Steve fell asleep; it seemed preferable their first time as husband and wife occur more naturally in the middle of the night or accidentally first thing in the morning. As she approached the bed, Laura saw he was awake still wearing only a grin. He fingered the hem of the negligee and murmured, "As nice as this feels, it needs to come off."

Laura relaxed, pleasantly surprised it felt natural to initiate moves of her own. Afterwards, it was Laura who stretched out like a cat and murmured he drove her crazy. "Want to make love again?"

Steve collapsed on his pillow. "You married an old fart about to turn 44 so we'll have to take it one day at a time."

She snuggled into his arms and twisted chest hair around her fingers. "What I married is a very sexy guy who's about to discover 44 is the age at which he hits full stride."

Laura heard his breathing change and his heartbeat slow. When he loosened his grip and rolled to his side, she pressed herself against him from behind and felt herself drift, too. They crossed a rolling meadow with a picnic basket, spread a blanket in a field of wildflowers, and relaxed beneath a bright blue sky. They talked, laughed, and caressed until she knelt naked in front of him in sunlight while he touched every inch of her body but never gasped, winced, or looked away at the sight of her. "I could do that with you."

Steve grunted, "Hnnh?"

Laura rolled onto her back and stared at a sky full of stars. "I could be naked in sunlight and allow you to see."

When Steve drew her into his arms, Laura felt surprised to discover his arousal and startled when he apologized. "I don't want you to think this is all we'll ever do together."

"Let's take advantage of the situation and over and over again, drive each other wild."

Afterward, Steve chuckled, "There's something I need to confess. I didn't know what gift to get for this important an event in our lives or if there's..."

Laura nestled in behind. "Being together tonight is better than anything you could ever buy for me, anyway."

Steve pulled her hand to his lips. "I know we haven't talked much about finances but now that we're married, you should know I spent a chunk on something I hope will make you happy."

Laura pulled away and bounced into a sitting position. "I never had a chance to get you anything so this isn't fair, mister!"

"Laura, I had the vasectomy reversed. If we're lucky, I'm shooting live ammo again or may someday soon."

Laura collapsed beside him. "Sorry I was about to accuse you of picking out a new car for me without my opinion but this is wonderful! Thank you!" She pressed herself against him and murmured, "Interested in flushing your system again?"

83

Mel couldn't sleep and headed out, air warm and humid though nothing like Louisiana, the sky black and filled with stars, unlike the reflective umbrella over Lake Charles. No cars on the streets, no other pedestrians, few lights on inside houses, a flickering light of a television, little noise except a hayseed band at the Maidstone. Mel stared across the street where inside Rita slept sitting up on the couch, an open book in her lap, her head tilted at an uncomfortable angle—in the morning, she would be sore. How easy it would be to make his way to the dark back yard, find a door unlocked, climb the stairs to Angela's bedroom. How easy it would be to awaken her with a kiss, prove once and for all his love.

Mel visualized the autumn afternoon months earlier: Angela smiled in his direction—clearly an invitation to follow when she wandered off. He found her alone in the boathouse and observed so much in that wondrous child's eyes: curiosity about his manhood, shame of her sudden desire to learn, and fear of others coming upon them as they made love. Like another he adored, the child felt confused by her sensual self and told self-protecting lies.

Mel examined houses on both sides of the street, studied one window after another, and discerned a fine community of souls slept in preparation for another day of joyous celebration. *It is easy to make my way*

175

now; she wants me; that afternoon in the boathouse, I felt how deeply she desired my touch. In his peripheral vision, Mel caught an out-of-place movement and studied the darkness: *a cat or raccoon?*

Mel stared at the dark window he knew to be the bedroom of his beloved Little Miss Angela Rita Lezzarro. He closed his eyes and savored a sweet recollection of another afternoon, another child's awakening, another love distorted by lies. *It was never Little Miss Laura's fault—others invaded our privacy, twisted the truth, shamed her, and turned her away from me in her moment of need.*

Mel detected light and opened his eyes to a beam as an unfamiliar voice demanded, "What are you doing here?"

Mel shoved a flashlight aside and saw Wilkers. "I returned from a long air trip and walk stiffness out. I do nothing wrong here."

"Then I suggest you move along."

Mel considered arguing. *You're no longer in a positon to demand a thing*, but turned away.

84

Ralph kicked his shoes under the bed and stripped. He climbed into the hot tub and when the bubbles hit, shouted, "Joycie, you won't believe how fantastic this feels!" A moment later, his beautiful bride stood fully dressed by the tub; she looked awkward, as if she forgot how often she joined him in marital pleasure during 25 years of wanton lust. Ralph extended his hand and did his best eyebrow-lift-come-on combo; though she smiled, Joyce stayed back. Ralph studied her eyes and detected her embarrassment; years ago surgery left scars across her breasts but those were pretty much gone. Two weeks earlier, though, a third biopsy on her left breast left a new pinkish-red one. He understood Joyce preferred to hide under covers in as little light as possible and thought to say *If you think YOU have scars, you should see some pictures of Laura* but he wouldn't violate the little lady's privacy or be insensitive to Joyce. He imagined he could dim the lights but hiding in the dark felt unacceptable on a second wedding night. Ralph stood up and proudly displayed his flab, scars, gray pubic hair, and all. He turned around and suggested she check out the brand new but cute dimples on his fat ass. He faced her again and whispered, "Darlin' girl, even if someday you lose that body part, it won't make a bit 'o difference to me."

Joyce's chin trembled but she undressed and joined him in all her full-bodied perfection. "Ralph, I love you more today than ever before."

"I know, darlin.' Thank you for the best 25 years of my life."

85

Laura found the weekend glorious. They worked in the yard together; washed, hung, and folded laundry together; watched old movies together; cooked together; and made love at any old time of the day or night. They left the house only once on Saturday when they drove to Joe's at sunset for chili dogs, fries, and ice cream. It was around 7:00 PM Sunday when Laura felt the tenseness begin; in the morning, she'd be a dutiful cop and head back to a shitty little town and an investigation going nowhere pretty damn fast. She was aware how her behavior turned obnoxious but felt unable to control her emotions. When she was living at home, her father labeled it her *stink-mode,* when nothing could distract her from a decision to be foul.

Steve prepared dinner and insisted upon cleaning up. To make things worse, he presented her with a slice of Lea's homemade raspberry pie with French vanilla ice cream and asked if they could talk about their careers. He settled onto the couch beside her and mentioned since he was eligible to retire in a few years at full benefits, it made sense that as a couple they concentrate on her career. Laura felt surprised at his logical and straightforward tone during the discussion but stunned when he said, "Unless you'd feel embarrassed by my lack of ambition, if and when we're blessed with a child, I'd take the lion's share of responsibility at home."

Laura chuckled, "Aren't men supposed to get the woman pregnant then become relatively passive in the process?"

Steve shrugged, "For most of my life, I admit I never envisioned a house-husband scenario but with you, I guess I experienced a major shift in priorities."

"Remember I might not be able to get pregnant."

Steve lifted her chin and chuckled, "It won't be for lack of trying." He continued Ralph thought they could start a business together. "Not a stereotypical retired-cops-as-security specialists doing background checks, either. I'd want to keep in touch with him, sure, but my first choice would be to return to college and earn a secondary education degree in math. Unless you think that's dumb at my age."

"You'd be a great teacher."

Steve jumped off the couch and dropped to his knees. "I hope you know a life we build together will get better as years go by." Steve pushed himself to a shaky stand and rubbed his knees. "Time for this ancient fart to get some sleep. "

Laura rushed through her bedtime routine, climbed into bed, and whispered, "I can be a good wife for you if you teach me how."

"Love me, Laura. That's it."

"Not a problem," she whispered and snuggled close.

In the morning, Laura left while he slept for a grueling drive with thousands of thoughts to jam her mind; even music couldn't override them. Laura recalled what Steve muttered half asleep in the middle of the night: *This is how it could be all the time, kid.* Not is now as she experienced their weekend together but could be. The drive felt exhausting enough but then she spent an unproductive morning in the office. With each passing hour, everything she felt with Steve drifted further and further away until she thought *time to move forward or give up. As intelligent as he is, though, he'll study every move, listen to every tone; as wary as he is, he'll suspect my motives and question a sudden change of heart. For over a month, I avoided him, shrank from his touch, and ran at the sound of his voice. But I can change that one shaky little-girl step at a time.*

After work, Laura stopped at Beaudon's General Store and saw Marsethe. As she moved along a narrow aisle to study labels, he stopped beside her. "You were missed during our community celebration."

Laura turned. "It was a mistake not to be here."

"Explain that statement."

"I tried to reconnect with someone I should forget."

Marsethe guided her onto the porch. "When young people follow their hearts, they discover passion subsides. Learn to place your trust in a higher order. I know he whom you seek."

Laura muttered, "I doubt anyone will love me as I am."

"I do. Allow an old fool to align your future with he who God allowed to be conceived expressly for you."

Laura inched back. "You can't expect me to forget, Dr. Marsethe. I have trouble with men because of you."

His eyes clouded over. "For that momentary aberration, child, I shall forever beg the good Lord's and your forgiveness."

"I'm not sure I can forgive," Laura gasped and left the porch. Inside again, she checked fresh produce and felt a moment's satisfaction before she prayed she showed enough confusion to intrigue him, or enough weakness to suggest he might move things in a different direction. When Caroline bagged her groceries, Laura failed to engage her in conversation and left more curious than ever.

Laura headed out and hesitated when she saw Marsethe waited. He asked, "You wish to know of Caroline, her history, and her sadness?"

Laura nodded but when he suggested she follow him to his house, she choked, "I'll never be alone with you again."

He chuckled, "Experienced former cops remain in a vehicle parked on the street for all to witness."

"Okay." Laura followed and within minutes, Marsethe threw a rubber-banded manila envelope onto the passenger seat.

At the carriage house, Laura chopped vegetables, tore lettuce for a salad, and diced leftover chicken on top. She ate, stared at the envelope, and headed to the couch to read. Inside she found a cover letter attached to a short story for a fiction contest. Laura studied the front, noticed un-cancelled stamps, and cringed at the invasion of privacy, but settled back to read.

Rainy Seasons

At daybreak, Caroline stood on the porch and watched storm clouds tumble along Camel's Hump. It was almost as if overnight, the heavy snow of March shifted into the gentle rain of April. She decided although autumn was perfect in Vermont, spring came close.

Caroline grabbed the broom and shoved clumps of dirt off the stairs. It was a futile task since within the hour customers would stomp across the wooden floorboards in muddy boots. Although she grew accustomed to the accompanying odor of manure the dairymen dragged in, she prayed if she ever reached her mother's age, memories of spring might also include the scent of lilacs. She grabbed the stack of newspapers off the steps, flipped lights on inside the store and started coffee. Once everything was ready for business, she unlocked the door and checked the melodic bells that announced an arrival. She grabbed croissants unsold the day before and ran upstairs.

Caroline found her mother already waiting patiently at the table. The frail woman smiled at the sight of croissants, reached for the jam, and wheezed, "Sell the store while it's worth something, Caroline. Put me away before I hurt myself. Or you."

"I could never do that," Caroline whispered.

Her mother sighed that was ridiculous, a decision based upon the obstinacy she'd inherited from her father. "The store was a comfortable lifestyle for us but not for a single young woman like you." Caroline studied her mother's pale eyes and almost forgot her lucidity was temporary, elusive at best. It amazed Caroline when it happened out of the blue while they sat and sipped tea, read the daily paper, filled in the crossword, or relaxed in front of the television on Sunday, the only day the store closed before 9. As she studied her mother's alert eyes, for one instant Caroline forgot how only 24 hours earlier, the same woman in a fit of rage broke a window with the telephone and cut her delicate hands trying to pick up the pieces. Her mother blotted raspberry jam off her chin. "I was 43 when you were conceived. My doctor said I couldn't but there you were, born two days before I turned 44." Caroline settled back to listen although she knew the story backwards and forwards: her father awakened early, drew his wife close, whispered unusually romantic words for such a no-nonsense man, and deposited a gift. Months later, morning queasiness left a sickening fear tumors grew inside a place the doctor labeled barren; later, aching nipples when the greedy infant suckled. Caroline started to speak but unexpectedly, her mother pushed herself to a shaky stand and with a delicate flip of her thin wrist excused her only child to go downstairs and tend to whoever stumbled in.

Routine passed time, numbed her mind and soul. Caroline preferred work without thought or passion, predictable days that blurred into weeks, months, years. Her pace was always harried, although better in spring when she didn't need to cater to the demands of summer tourists, suffer the thousandth leaf peeper, or drag out the snow shovel.

Between customers, trucks and sales reps, she raced upstairs to check on her mother at least once an hour. Caroline was unable to bear the image of her frail mother bleeding, with a broken bone or wedged between the tub and toilet after another stumbling slide.

Baked goods arrived daily. Dairy, meat and produce twice a week, groceries once a week, including frozen foods demanding instant attention. Caroline knelt in front of freezers and rotated. Finished, she felt numbness in her fingers: frozen foods, frozen shelves, frozen fingertips. She wiped her hands on her apron, peered down and thought it tragic she'd never felt lips of any age against her breasts. A waste of well-designed equipment, really, since cows nursed calves, dogs their puppies, and cats their kittens. Even mice nursed their pink eyeless offspring, furtive things that matured into fuzzy gray blobs that scurried into dark corners the instant a foot touched a cellar stairs.

That April morning, Caroline stared across the road as her clumsily-pregnant neighbor headed over. Rebecca arrived every morning precisely at 8:00 for the day's groceries. Now there was a girl who understood responsibility: a mother dead for a decade, a father, four brothers, three meals to fix, a huge farmhouse to clean. At 8:02, Rebecca moved cautiously through the small store and clutched her abdomen as if lifting the extra weight brought relief. Caroline recalled how 12 years earlier, a customer asked her name and the little girl answered in her melodic four-year-old voice: "Bec-ca." The girl was lucky, everyone said, to have a father who allowed her to live at home during her disgrace. The boy was lucky, everyone said, to be alive. Rebecca was surrounded by her father, four older brothers and half-dozen farmhands: a surly bunch of men who believed 16-year-olds could control hormones in ways animals could not when pheromones wafted across the barnyard.

As Rebecca waddled down an aisle, Caroline noted the girl's radiance, a soft contentment that had not yet been dimmed by a dark, punishing bedroom with only books or a radio for entertainment. As she watched the girl study a label, Caroline wondered if at 16, Rebecca understood how one single moment might forever define her future.

Sometimes late at night, Caroline watched a gangly boy climb the gnarled apple tree to the second story: how simple for someone desperately in love to find his way. It amazed Caroline how much she could see: the boy on his knees in front of the rocker, his cheek against Rebecca's abdomen, feeling their baby's movements, Rebecca holding him close and later, both on the bed caressing. Because they lacked the sense to dim the light or close the blinds, Caroline dimmed her mind, climbed into bed and envisioned them locked together in passion reserved for reckless romantics.

↔

Every Friday, a woman who wore elegant hats arrived for a roast, a woman who never wasted time on idle conversation as she wandered the aisles. After years of polite indifference, Caroline felt startled when the woman commented she never saw anyone else cut and tie roasts so affectionately. "Where did you learn?"

Caroline shrugged her shoulder toward a rickety metal stool near the dairy cooler. "For years, I watched my father. When he died nine years ago, I sharpened his knives and took over."

"How remarkable," the woman answered.

Caroline gasped, "No, not remarkable at all," and willed the woman to go. Alone, Caroline wished away sudden memories of a quiet man who, even after 90-hour workweeks, prepared elaborate meals on Sundays for his wife and daughter before dozing off in front of the television. He suffered a heart attack in his sleep and the day before he died—which of course, she couldn't possibly have known was about to happen—Caroline perched on her stool and watched him slice perfect center-cut, boneless pork chops. He confessed some days he regretted the time he spent running the business since he never took her to a Red Sox game. Caroline insisted she hated baseball and her father chuckled, "You hate TV baseball, honey. If we were at Fenway Park, you'd love the noise of the crowd, follow the game on the field and even be fine with the stale popcorn, greasy burned fries, and waterlogged hot dogs."

In the end, Caroline disappointed him again. She might have answered yes, she'd certainly love it. Or she might have suggested they close the store for a day and take the bus into Boston. Or she might have whispered how much she loved him. She didn't say any of that, of course, woke during the night to the wail of sirens and lived to regret her silence.

↔

On Sundays, a man shared dinner with Caroline and her mother. Sunday was the only day dinner was prepared with care with the luxury of time demanded for a roast with chunked vegetables and corn bread, or meatballs, spaghetti, salad and soft Italian bread. Sam's presence felt familiar and Caroline knew if he stopped his routine, she'd feel the loss. She ached at his vulnerability when thrice a year—near her birthday in August and on Christmas and New Year's Eves—he asked her to marry him. Caroline said no despite so much about him she found endearing and knew she would miss if he ever gave up trying.

One early May weeknight ten minutes before closing, Sam arrived unannounced. Without a word, he winked his hello, grabbed a spray bottle and rag, and started to clean. He found markers and drew smudge-less sale signs. He dusted cobwebs from corners and neatly piled receipts. He worked as silently as she, which felt comfortable. After she cashed out, Caroline went into the office to lock everything in the safe and found Sam bent over a drawer, alphabetizing files. Even more than such wonderful things, though, she loved the way his hair curled softly onto his collar when he needed a haircut or how patiently he endured her mother's reminiscences even when they strayed toward the bizarre.

After she suggested coffee and dessert, Caroline took his hand and led him upstairs. When they discovered her mother snoring in front of the television, Caroline laughed and tugged him to her third-story bedroom. As she unbuttoned her blouse, Caroline watched him lick his lips and imagined Sam might be the sort of man who'd appreciate her enough to linger afterwards. She unzipped her jeans, watched him rub his shirt collar and understood she needed to make love to him in a way no other man would ever feel.

Caroline watched his lips move and anticipated hearing a declaration of forever but Sam's whisper pierced the silence: "No."

"But I thought you wanted me."

"Lord, you'll never know how much I want you. But not like this. Never like this."

As Sam turned away, Caroline grabbed the waistband of jeans caught at her knees. To the sound of his footsteps on the stairs, she felt the heat of embarrassment replace that of desire.

↔

In late May, Rebecca's baby was born. Caroline thanked God for giving the young mother some female company in that big, drafty farmhouse. Often in the stillness of night, Caroline heard the baby cry and her heart ached for demands other than her mother, air brakes, or the tinkling of the bell as a customer opened the door. The baby was named Rachel after Rebecca's dead mother, a beautiful biblical name for a beautiful child with the same silky blonde hair and pink skin as the boy in the apple tree.

Caroline hired two teenagers for the busy summer: a girl to run the register and a boy who pumped gas and made lifting look painless. Tourists breezed in and out and Caroline behaved as usual: professional, competent, smiling. She preferred the anonymity of tourists who didn't care one way or another who she was or why. Tourists didn't know her history or her present and certainly didn't care enough to ask. Tourists didn't notice she never boated on the lake five minutes away or rode the ski tram on the mountains an hour away. Tourists didn't care if she made conversation as long as the service was prompt and polite.

Long, hot, humid and sunny days arrived with more and more tourists in bold, unflattering prints, tourists who smelled of bug bomb and sun block. Tourists with their strange accents never asked pointed questions about Sam. Tourists didn't care what she thought or how she felt. Other than the fact the general store was quaintly old-fashioned with its creaky wooden floorboards and drafty windows, tourists didn't care it had been owned and operated by her family for five generations. Caroline was so busy she failed to notice summer rushed right through July.

One humid evening after her mother was tucked safely between cool cotton sheets, Caroline turned off the lights and sat on the dark front porch. She loved the sights of summer as airplane lights and stars sparkled overhead. Bats swooped for mosquitoes. Rebecca's cat skulked for mice. When lightning pierced the western sky, she counted 11 seconds until thunder. She loved the sounds of summer, too: insects, dogs, cows, frogs, owls. She heard the whine of a truck miles and miles away then television or real voices from houses in the distance.

At such moments, Caroline felt something heavy and lifeless slide from her body: a weight built upon love for a parent returning gradually to infancy, weariness from long workweeks with no lazy weekends as buffers to renew and soothe. Most of all, though, Caroline missed Sam. It had been months since he stopped by for bread, milk or eggs. It had been so long since he joined them for dinner, even her mother noticed his absence.

On the dark porch, Caroline dozed in the warm summer breeze. Near midnight, she woke with a start as her attention was drawn to voices raised in argument. She focused her vision across the road where two men grabbed, tangled, shouted bitter threats and shoved until one stumbled to the ground. When the apple tree boy jumped to his feet and ran off, Caroline crossed the road to her neighbor and whispered, "Mike, you might not be able to keep them apart."

"What?"

"Even if you succeed, you risk losing your daughter forever."

He turned with a snorted, "What the hell business is this of yours?"

Caroline touched fingertips to her heart. "You'll lose her here, Mike, where everything matters the most."

Mike stared up at his daughter's bright bedroom window and chuckled, "Interesting parental advice from a workaholic old maid shopkeeper." In the morning, Caroline awakened to the sound of a chainsaw, stumbled out of bed, and stared blankly at sections of apple tree littering the grass.

That day, Rebecca arrived late, around 10:30. Two-month-old Rachel slept in her stroller beside the porch while Rob Greene relaxed on the bench and read the paper. Three tourists plopped along the aisles in flip-flops. Maurice Favreau from the farm two miles north took a Danish and cup of coffee onto the porch and sat with Rob. For an instant, the sky turned threateningly dark and it poured then moved off as rain puddles evaporated before their eyes.

Sam ran in, rummaged through the freezer for a creamsicle and glanced over wearing his heartbreakingly-sweet smile. Caroline approached and whispered, "I miss you, Sam, and I..." but stopped at the sound of Rebecca's scream.

The stroller was empty. In the shadows, Caroline watched in numb silence as the county sheriff arrived, then the state police. The many men in Rebecca's life ran over as did the scrawny boy whose name turned out to be Billy. Hostile accusations, a scuffle, some blood.

Rob and Maurice felt confused. From the instant Rebecca covered the baby to when she returned, they sat a mere twenty feet away. Molly the cashier was confused, too, since she stood near the window the whole time and saw no one, nothing. In the background, three tourists lowered their eyes to protect themselves from the mother's agony, defensive because they were the only strangers.

Finally everyone left. From behind the blinds, Caroline peeked at a group of men huddled together in the parking lot and felt stunned to see sparkly sunlight skip across the lake like a sailboat. She locked up early and taped a note to the door: 'Closed for Illness.' Not a lie, technically. Guilt was an illness, as was shame, as were the tears she couldn't stop or the body-crushing sobs so unexpected, she collapsed against the wall for support.

Caroline forgot about lunch then cried right through supper time, too. From time to time, she observed ominous shadows appear behind the blinds as customers tried to force the old wooden door open. Most wandered off. Some grumbled. Others cursed.

Finally the sun set and Caroline climbed the two flights of stairs to her room, lay quietly on the bed and listened to rain against the tin roof. In August, it wasn't supposed to fall softly like a spring soak but rather burst out of thunderclouds and hit the ground hard, forging rivulets in dark soil. She blinked back tears and listened to piano music begin below: beautiful, flowing. It amazed her how one day her mother couldn't find middle C yet on the very next, breeze through Beethoven. When her mother shifted flawlessly to a Chopin polonaise, the familiar melody flooded Caroline's soul with memories of another summer night, another argument, another frightened girl banished to her room. She stared toward the garage roof and almost imagined a boy padded across in his socks. One night, like so many others, he left his sneakers beside the ladder but that night, when her father took out the trash, the music stopped and she and the boy were caught in the blinding beam from the opened door like deer in headlights.

She pushed herself off the bed, ashamed because her mother would be hungry. Caroline permitted herself another moment of solitude and knelt on the floor in front of the window. She stared across the road where six men hovered, one a uniformed state trooper. Billy sat on the bed and held Rebecca in his skinny boy arms. Caroline winced when Rebecca rushed to the empty crib. Had she heard her baby cry? Moments earlier, Caroline herself imagined from somewhere dark and hidden an infant wailed in primal hunger.

↔

Caroline opened her eyes when something touched her wet cheek. Sam knelt while in the background, her mother leaned against her cane, peered timidly into the room, and moaned choking apologies. Caroline gasped, "How did Mom get up here?"

"One step at a time grabbing the banister like earlier, halfway up."

Caroline swallowed hard. "Earlier?"

Sam admitted her mother heard Rachel cry, inched down the side steps, and rescued the baby from the thundershower. "She thought the baby was yours." Sam stroked her arm and whispered Rachel was home, safe in her mother's arms.

Caroline stared at her mother. "Will Mom be arrested for kidnapping? Will I for not watching her better?"

Sam murmured of course not; Rebecca and Billy understood. Even Mike calmed down finally. "But the police said since your mother's more mobile than she appears to be, you need to consider hiring a companion."

Caroline studied her mother's huge, frightened eyes and turned back to Sam's gentle ones. "I suppose she told you everything."

Sam nodded. "Your mother thinks you're still 16. She thinks she let you keep your baby this time."

Caroline struggled to her feet, smoothed the wrinkles from her cotton blouse and confessed sometimes she dreamed Rebecca was her lost daughter, Rachel her first grandchild. "Mathematically that's possible."

Sam squeezed her fingers. "Marry me and you can count on becoming a grandmother someday."

Caroline whispered no man deserved a wife who felt anchorless. A part of her floated somewhere out there. A piece of her heart disappeared with an infant whose face she never saw, who moved inside and touched her in indescribably intimate ways, with hair and skin she could only imagine were like hers or a boy she barely remembered. "How I wish I'd been strong like Rebecca. How I wish I'd fought back."

Sam soothed with, "You shouldn't go through life without leaning on someone for..."

Caroline interrupted she gave birth in that very room. During 19 hours of labor, she listened to piano music below and rain on the tin roof above. When Sam offered to help look for her daughter, Caroline choked, "It might have been a he. No one told me. Let me see. Or touch."

Her mother's voice choked, "I go to my grave knowing I made the wrong decision."

Through the wet glass and across the road, Caroline watched Rebecca settle into the rocker. Billy dropped to his knees and peered at their sleeping daughter. Caroline imagined behind hundreds of other rain-streaked windows *all over the world, other fragile souls struggled to forgive themselves for the crime of being human.*

Laura imagined she knew the rest—all the angry whispers that floated up to her bedroom night after night. She raced out and drove across the bridge to a pay phone. "Jack, I know things are tough with Sarah now and I don't want to add problems, but..."

A chuckled, "Is this you, Laura?"

She stared at her sandals. "Yeah, hi, sorry."

"Congratulations! Mom said the ceremony was beautiful."

"When we left, did you say goodbye to Caroline?"

"What?"

"You never said goodbye to the girl who carried your baby, did you, Jack?"

A long silence then, "The elders said I wasn't intended for Caroline. They said any baby would be genetically inferior."

"You're too smart not to have smelled their bullshit! You have a child who doesn't know his or her real identity."

"Not true; the doctor called Mom after the baby died."

"That's bullshit, too, Jack, and I intend to prove it."

"Please, no."

Laura felt a pang of guilt but answered, "If you prefer to deny this other person exists, I find that tragic, Jack."

"I beg you to leave it alone."

"Okay, Jack. I'll leave it alone—for now." Laura hung up, crossed the bridge into Vermont and parked outside Marsethe's. *How in the world can I find out if another Delorange exists in our world? And why would you start me on a path you surely knew would haunt me?*

86

All weekend, Bobby fought a nagging sense he missed something the other night. Not only the party—still pissed about that insult—no, a vague feeling about a peeper in the woods. The woman described a guy in a flannel shirt, weird for the weather—summer, for god's sake. And more—she said as single woman living alone without a dog, in a house in the woods with no close neighbors, she panicked. Bobby recalled earlier, Scolarzski worked a similar case. What the hell was that suspect's name? Off and on over the weekend, Bobby called Scolarzski at home. No answer. No machine even. The phone just rang and rang and rang. Curious. Bobby reviewed the trooper's report and headed out to a house in West Bolton. Great location, fantastic view, extremely private. Bobby noticed a car in the garage, knocked loudly at the house, but the lady chose not to answer or was off somewhere with alternate transportation. He found it odd, though, that on a hot summer day, all the windows were closed tight. No signs of an air conditioner, either. Bobby ran the tag to see a vehicle registered to a Marsha Buerton of the same address. He walked the perimeter, scanned the woods, and found up the hill 35 feet from the house, weeds and grass stomped down pretty good. Bobby returned to door, pounded again then left a note: *Ms. Buerton, give me a call. I have questions. Sergeant Robert Rawlings, Vermont State Police.*

When she called to explain where she'd been, Bobby stored the file away but something nagged. Bobby studied Scolarzski across the room: odd how the phone rang and rang all weekend. Bobby pulled up a chair, slid the Buerton file across the desk, and watched Scolarzski glance at details before he groaned, "Is she dead?"

"No, the first trooper on the scene conducted a search, found nothing suspicious, and left. Ms. Buerton was too shaky to drive and called her mother to pick her up. This morning she went back to dress for work and found my note." Bobby pointed to the description of the peeper. "Didn't you investigate a turd like this?"

Steve opened his drawer and retrieved a file. "If that turd had been Sivalette, she'd be dead."

Bobby lifted the file and sifted through. "I remember now; this scumbag walked on a technicality last year."

Scolarzski nodded. "Sivalette's been quiet and I suspect he's a walking time bomb."

Bobby noticed Marie Sigler wander in, wave, and deposit a wrapped gift on Barber's desk. Ned crossed the room, leaned close, and tried to keep the conversation private. Marie laughed, "I don't care where you were Friday night," And left.

Sigler faced his colleagues. "She friggin' deserted us!"

Macrae snorted, "With Melanie married, Danielle working, and Robbie in high school, it's not like you wash, hang, and fold diapers." Bobby thought Macrae sounded unusually cruel but had to agree, of them all, Sigler most deserved to have shit piled on.

87

Laura felt how slowly a workweek progressed with nothing to look forward to; on Wednesday she left for work early, drove to a pay phone, and called Maureen in New York. "It's Laura! Is this a bad time?"

"You know I always run late. What's new?"

Laura rushed through a laundry list of the past few months: shooting, resignation from the Vermont State Police, position with a private law firm, and the most important: "Then there's Steve."

"You allowed a man in your life? Tell me more!"

"I love him, Maureen, and can't believe I found the courage to willingly place my heart and soul in someone else's hands."

Maureen chuckled, "Not to mention body. I'm astounded! After everything you said over the years, how'd this happen?"

"He melted away my fears."

"Outrageous! I'm having trouble believing you have a man in your life, never mind got through the dirty deed itself."

Laura stared at her feet. "We thought our marriage could…"

"Whoa, girl! Hey! Because you had sex with a guy doesn't mean you marry him. This isn't the biblical era. Sex doesn't translate to fallen-woman-in-need-of-validation. Even for someone hung up on sex like you, it's okay to play in bed."

Laura sighed, "I'd like you to be a bridesmaid at the formal event but here's my real news: we married already, secretly."

"Wow. Why secret?"

"I'm on an undercover assignment and must appear single."

"That's another whole phone call! So is Steve good looking?"

"I think so."

"Sexy?"

"Incredibly so."

"Good conversationalist?"

"That's how it started. We spent hours just talking."

"Does he love music and love to dance?"

"He has different tastes but is a fantastic slow dancer."

"And when you and your talk-dancer had sex the first time, how did you feel afterward?"

"Glad I picked him."

"Wow, I envy you. When's the formal wedding?"

"Last Saturday in September."

"I'll mark my calendar now."

"Thanks. Anyone in your life?"

"Nah, a bad affair a while back but that's another sorry saga for another call. I work too hard too many hours and you know me—I intimidate everyone eventually. Shit! I'm really going to be late! Give me a number; I'll call later and we can talk dirty all night."

"I can't use the phone where I live because it's bugged."

"What? Tell me more."

"Don't worry about me. I'll write a letter instead!"

Laura headed to the office and managed to put her mind on task for a 9:00 appointment: a new client, one of the few remaining people in town not members of the CFEL. A 35-year-old man with no prior record, Harvey Browne was arrested for cultivating marijuana plants in a back yard garden. He grew it for medicinal purposes because his mother suffered from ovarian cancer. Mr. Browne insisted his mother threw up as soon as she took most medication and heard marijuana was therapeutic. Laura was surprised when he added, "For years my neighbors joked about the existence of the plants. In winter I kept one in the house and one on the porch. Gil overlooked them until the day he informed me I hadn't met the guidelines for the new state law governing medical marijuana."

Laura glanced toward Reilly. "Did you ever sell any?"

"Of course not."

"What do you have the CFEL might wish to control?"

Browne shrugged, "Nothing; the house is in my father's name, my car's nine years old, there are too many little mouths to feed, and my wife and I barely earn above minimum wage at dead-end jobs. I have nothing of any real value, Miss Delorange."

Laura admitted she knew of similar cases. "I'll research allowable limits for your purpose to keep it decriminalized but you need to register with the state as a licensed caregiver. If you want, I can review your application before you submit it."

"Yeah, thanks; I'm not good with government forms."

"In the meantime, request a new prescription from her doctor for an approved dispensary. No more home-grown until this is settled."

"Got it; thank you."

Laura recalled his statement: *nothing of any real value.* To whom? She wondered why the family bugged the elders or Gil. As a family unit, they exhibited values the CFEL promoted: a multigenerational family under one roof who took care of one another, a well-maintained home, and adults who worked rather than accept hand-outs. The only thing she saw missing? Membership in the Community for Expansive Love.

Laura asked Reilly, "What do you know about the Brownes?"

"Not much. They keep to themselves."

"Does it bother the elders to have non-members here?"

"Why would it? The CFEL doesn't want failures as members."

Laura thought to argue *that didn't answer my question* but nodded, returned to her desk, doodled on her blotter, and smiled when she saw she drew her new initials over and over in script, printing and gothic: *LS. Should I call myself Laura Delorange-Scolarzski? That's one hell of a mouthful for a business card! I have time to think it through and keep it simple.* She swiveled in her chair and recalled a passage from Caroline's beautiful short story: *one single moment might forever redefine the future.* True, oh so true. It seemed easy to reduce everything to the sort of cliché about choices the CFEL spouted: *it is within your power to win or lose, to study or fail, to accept or decline, to be healthy or ill.* Yet within such an approach to life, she discovered there was some measure of truth. Marsethe's attack wounded her severely, both emotionally and physically; it came pretty damn close to destroying her. But she persisted, struggled and recovered. In time, Laura took a long, hard look at the people she loved and respected: her parents, Rick and his then-fiancée Gina, Jack and Sarah, Maureen, Ralph and Joyce, Helen and Roger, and of course, Steve. In the end, the only logical decision? Move forward in a full life with Steve, the sooner, the better; time not to push things forward but to shove them over a cliff.

Laura grabbed the phone and called Marsethe. "I can't imagine how you got something so personal from Caroline Beaudon."

"Did you enjoy your reading?"

"It's beautifully written but sad. Um, is it fiction or more like a memoir? I mean, I know in high school, she and Jack..."

He interrupted, "It's Caroline's story."

"But is it...?"

He interrupted again. "I'm pleased you enjoyed your reading." Laura waited—his move, his choice how they moved forward, how easily she slid back into the fold. It took a minute but he bit. "I hoped you'd follow me in my practice and research. It pains me to know you are a lawyer and not a doctor to assist me as I advance toward retirement."

"I have regrets."

"Explain that statement, yes?"

"I often think of the hours we spent in your office and lab and your magnificent library of books you encouraged me to borrow. I never forgot the satisfaction of completing difficult experiments or the challenging discussions afterwards but you defiled that with..."

"Please do not hang up in anger. It occurs to me you are young enough to follow the original design."

"I don't know if I make decisions from strength or weakness but I won't become a doctor to please you or the elders."

A long pause then, "I defiled all the purity of your love for me."

After an awkward silence, Laura said, "I have work to do; as unrewarding as legal work is, I earn what I'm paid."

"Child, if I arrange for a third party to join us, may I show you how my work evolved in the years you were away?"

Laura let his invitation hang as if it were abhorrent and finally said, "I confess I'm curious. Violet is acceptable."

"Not Reilly or Glenn?"

"You heard me! I said Violet."

"Violet is acceptable. Sweet Miss, my heart skipped the day I heard you would return and today, it soars!"

Laura hung up; things would surely begin to happen if she found the courage to push harder, deeper, faster. She glanced at the clock, groaned, "Shit!" grabbed the tape and notes, raced out, and sped all the way to St. Johnsbury, relieved she wasn't stopped. She pulled up at the courthouse, jumped out, and took steps three at a time. Her knee ached as she slid along the floor in dress shoes and ran up to a woman to ask directions to Judge Meehan's office. In the direction the woman pointed, Laura took off again and found the door plate. She knocked softly, pushed her way in, and mumbled an apology to five clearly irritated faces.

Meehan pointed to an empty chair. "Make this fast."

Laura placed the recorder on his desk and hit play. Midway through, Laura watched one woman glance at a clock but no one left. When it finished, Meehan lifted his phone and directed someone to arrange a meeting with Peg Stenzola. He turned to Laura. "I will keep the tape, counselor. If you ever request an appointment with me again, keep to my schedule, not yours." He didn't wait for an answer but summarily dismissed her. At her car, Laura collapsed into the driver's seat, stared at her reflection in the rear view mirror and smiled—one moment of satisfaction before heading back to one shitty little town.

88

Steve watered and weeded Laura's garden, prepared dinner, and invited his mother on a guided tour of renovation plans. As they walked the perimeter, he said, "I wish I'd started this sooner: first, an extension to the deck gives Laura a front porch to take advantage of the view; second, with Ralph and Mickey's help, there'll be a wing with another bedroom and full bath; and third, I'll ask Laura to buy new furniture. I'm thinking a rocking chair would be nice in case we have a new member of our family by this time next year."

Lea sighed, "You deserve that and so much more."

When his mother dozed on the couch later, Steve missed Laura more than ever. If there were a God, her assignment would be over soon and two newlyweds could begin a real life together. He visualized the look on Laura's face—confused, perhaps frightened—when he went off in circles about their careers. In all his excitement, he may have disclosed too much too soon leaving her overwhelmed by his plans, as if in such an over-organized marriage, there would be no opportunity for her own dreams. Steve felt another headache on its way and squeezed the skin between his eyes. It would be another sleepless night without Laura in his arms, another long, lonely night when he wouldn't hear her own accumulation of dreams, desires, and secrets. He smiled at the memory of Laura's voice when she asked him to teach her how to be a good wife. He was no one to ask; he had no frame of reference beyond himself, Denise, a weak marriage, and a child likely fathered by another man. He always found Denise attractive and at first, their sex life fulfilled, but after the first year he felt a deep loss, as if she died years before she did. Between them, there was no love, no foundation, no core, no spirituality, no hopes, and no dreams for the future. They lived an empty, shallow relationship which by its very nature was easy to maintain. Far harder would have been to insist upon something permanent, then nourish it.

A voice startled him. "Sweetheart, are you okay?"

Steve moved to the couch, took his mother's hand, and asked about her marriage to Old Max, raising children, love and honor and commitment, and what she saw between him and Laura. His mother offered practical suggestions on how to hold onto the kind of deep love she saw at their beginning. "Accept when the physical part fades but never the love. That's how I approached marriage with your father and I still miss my husband, lover, and best friend."

"Thank you. I miss Dad, too."

Lea pushed hair off his forehead. "He'd be so proud."

At work the next day, Steve tapped his pencil across an accident report filed overnight: a 24-year-old man DOA at 12:29 AM after his pick-up hit a bridge abutment. No indication of braking, no seat belt, no passenger, no discernible blood alcohol or drugs, no cash, no credit cards, no wallet, no photographs. A quick check with the auto insurance carrier listed his beneficiary as a 22-year-old wife. Something nagged at the back of his mind and a vague recollection solidified; Steve headed to the file room and found Laura's notes from ten months earlier. The dead man was her Orwell guy all right: a pathetic dud she investigated for grand theft auto and breaking and entering; a futureless high school washout who lived in a trailer without a flushing toilet; a loser who became a favorite of Laura's because he was a harmless, romantic soul.

Steve returned to his desk with the file, read every report or statement, and felt his eyes moisten at the sight of Laura's neat writing: *I was saddened to learn five months after their marriage Tara delivered a still-born baby girl.* Steve recalled the debate they had about what could and could not be done to help the failures and flops of their world and enjoyed a memory of Laura's husky voice when she whispered her prayer for their future: *They need to make love over and over again until they conceive a child alive at her birth.* At the time, he laughed at her sappy sentiments but in hindsight knew he fell in love with her for those very traits. Partnered with her, he saw a different world through her eyes and discovered inside a sarcastic, jaded cop, a loving man ached for release.

Steve headed out to the garage where they towed the pick-up and from the damage, knew the driver moved pretty damn fast. The mechanic reported the brakes checked out fine. Like the trooper, Steve thought it likely the driver fell asleep. Steve headed out to the decrepit trailer at the end of a trash-strewn pot-holed dirt driveway Laura noted in her report but which turned out to be far more depressing than she described. He dropped to his knees, studied tire tracks in the grass and loose soil, and at first glance, matched those on the pickup. A woman walked up and watched him. She was young, very young, and should have been a hell of a lot prettier with those blue eyes and strawberry blonde hair but those eyes were bloodshot with dark circles underneath, her hair tangled and dull..

"I'm Tara," she said and squinted in the sunlight to report the evening before, Nicky showed up unannounced and begged to move back. "I kicked him out but I think it was Nicky who pulled into the driveway around midnight when I made out on the couch with Jeff." Steve stood up, brushed dirt off his knees, and moved into the worst part of any cop's job: a summary of details and a request she identify a body.

Steve drove to the station and stared at a fantastic sky: bright blue, no haze, clouds skipping along mountaintops. He recognized the old one-two-three: wife screwed around, husband found out, pain overwhelmed. That scenario made sense to a cop who lived it himself, yet there was a difference: Steve boozed, the kid pointed his pick-up at a bridge; Steve displayed anger and hostility, the kid gave up; Steve survived and met Laura, the kid decided nothing was worth it; the kid was wrong and would never know it.

Steve lifted the phone and to the woman who answered, identified himself as Sergeant Macrae of the Vermont State Police. A moment later, Laura laughed, "Roger, hello! How are you?"

"Doin' okay, kid, but I've been better."

A pause then a gasped, "What's wrong?"

Steve ran through the facts and ended with, "It may have been suicide, kid, but it's listed officially as *fell asleep at the wheel*."

"Oh God, oh God, oh God! Why do people do such horrible things to one another?"

Steve pinched the skin between his eyebrows. "When love is missing from a marriage, it's easy to justify any behavior."

A long pause then a whispered, "Sergeant, I believe you were lucky to find a woman who adores you."

"Yeah, I do feel lucky lately."

Steve heard a catch in her voice. "It hurts to hear but thanks for letting me know. Reading it in the paper would have crushed me."

Steve hung up, glanced across the room, and saw Rawlings interview a woman. As he neared, Steve overheard enough to know it was the woman-with-the-peeper. He knelt alongside Rawlings' chair. "Don't make the same mistake the DSA and I did last year."

"What mistake?"

"If a witness sees a particular photograph, she should also see at least 50 other guys in the same ethnic and age group. Juries despise the idea cops and prosecutors purposely mislead." Steve returned to his desk and watched Rawlings bring the lady a cup of coffee. He and Granger disappeared into the conference room and ten minutes later, Rawlings escorted his potential witness in to view an assortment of four dozen photographs and mug shots. Twenty minutes later, Rawlings came to the door and with a sad smile in Steve's direction, lifted his thumb.

89

Friday morning Laura received three phone calls one right after another: at 9:03, Judge Meehan's clerk reported all charges against Detective Wilkers dropped officially; at 9:06, a social worker stated the Wilkers girls would be returned to their father's custody within 24 hours; and at 9:11, Al promised he owed her a huge favor. Laura stared out her window toward the green where Peg Stenzola sat on a bench. Laura told Reilly she headed to the Maidstone for breakfast. As she crossed the street, Peg headed over to say, "I'll testify against Mel. Even if I'm arrested for taking part in the scheme, I'll testify if you represent me and apologize to Al."

Laura smiled. "Apologize to him yourself."

"I can't; with Frannie in her final trimester, the reality's too close, too chilling. It's difficult because I still love him."

"No woman should be apart from the man she loves."

Peg laughed, "Easy for you to say but I'm about to become a grandmother for the first time which should feel wonderful but doesn't. He and I are done; he made his choice."

In case anyone watched, Laura continued on as if running into Peg were an accident. As soon as Laura pushed the heavy door open, she inched into the dim foyer and worried she'd run into Glenn. And then she did and he was cordial and businesslike. When he asked if she'd like company, she nodded then sighed, "Forget that; I left my purse."

"If you have trouble with breakfast as my treat, pay me another time." Glenn gestured for the waitress and within minutes, Laura oohed and ahhed over yet another perfect omelet.

90

Saturday morning, Steve fiddled with the stereo and wondered how Laura managed to record messages on the same tape as music. He checked the owner's manual then called Sigler, the closest thing to an electronics genius at work. Ned claimed Steve needed one of those old portable CD / cassette units with a microphone; he had one Steve could borrow. Steve thanked him and headed out.

There was no way to describe Ned's appearance except to say he looked like shit. The kitchen was a mess and the living room cluttered; in the mud room three baskets of dirty laundry stood on top of the washer and Ned looked sheepish when he asked for help. Steve showed him how to measure detergent, fill the tub but not stuff it, and set water temperature. As water filled, Steve lowered the lid and joined Ned at the kitchen table. Steve accepted a cup of coffee and braced himself for the coming conversation. Ned's confession wandered all over: lack of interest in the kids as they grew up, focus on work, and lack of involvement in whatever Marie found worthwhile. He even admitted to a few affairs. Steve wanted to argue there were more than a few but kept quiet. Finally Ned finished, "For once I'm not guilty of anything and didn't deliberately miss the party. My father had a stroke and I sat with my mother for hours. Marie won't listen to me long enough to explain."

Steve knew he sounded sanctimonious but a point needed to be made. "Did you call your wife from the hospital?"

Ned shrugged, "In my own defense, let me say it's not easy living with a drunk. She's not always there, if you know what I mean." Steve certainly knew; for years following Denise's death, he wasn't there for anyone: not Mickey, not Ralph, not himself.

On his way out, Steve showed Ned how to set the dryer and added, "It's not difficult to dust, vacuum, or wipe countertops, either. A husband can't give up on a marriage until every ounce of love is gone. Between you and Marie, I see pain and anger at times, but I also see love that goes back to the very beginning. Find that again if you can; find whatever that intangible is that Ralph and Joyce kept alive."

Ned nodded. "I hear you and Laura made quite a scene at the party: close dancing, secretive whispers, and drooling, for starters— Roger thought the two of you looked like people still very much in love."

Steve shrugged, "Well, I still am."

Throughout the weekend, Steve joined Rawlings keeping an eye on the Buerton house. Steve listened to Bobby ream himself up one side and down the other for going out to the appliance store Sivalette managed. "It was a mistake picking him up at work 'cause in the line-up, he looked too mainstream to be pegged as the flannel-shirted, baggy-panted, booted freak in the trees." They parked at the far end of her property, under the trees, and out of sight of the driveway. Not much happened on that road in West Bolton: on Saturday, pick-ups went by on their way to the recycling center, three kids raced by on bikes, a couple of horseback riders went north at noon and came back at 2:30, but no sign of Sivalette. By Sunday afternoon, Steve felt reassured danger passed and when Bobby arrived to relieve him at 6:00 PM, said, "It's likely the line-up scared him off but it's wise to stay overnight. In the morning, I'll tell Granger why you're not there."

At home Steve went through his CDs and found the process difficult with so many favorite songs and artists. To whittle selections down, he picked two criteria: the most appropriate lyrics about love, romance, and forever combined with danceable music. Without copying her too much, he hoped to duplicate what Laura achieved: a mood, tone, and state of mind to share. Steve fiddled with Ned's equipment and when he had what he wanted, pulled the electric typewriter out to type the list. The damn tape was dried up and brittle with no replacement. He ended up at the kitchen table, printing.

In the morning, Steve stopped by the Delorange's and found Rick home. "Are you going to the cabin this week?"

"I am." Rick studied the package. "That looks suspiciously like one I delivered to you not long ago."

"Yeah; tell your sister I count the seconds until she's home."

91

Laura scrubbed the tub when Violet shouted through the screen door, "If you're here, I'd like to finalize plans for our visit to Mel's lab."

Once arrangements were made, Laura accepted an invitation to join the family for supper. Brian served as perfect host and the children continued to astound with their manners, intelligence, maturity, and talent as they performed with Ben on piano, Joanna on flute, and Paul on clarinet. Laura enjoyed their spirited rendition of a familiar piece until Brian said, "You don't need to fake interest."

Laura gasped, "Untrue! This *Scherzo* movement from *Schubert's Symphony No. 9 in C* is beautiful!" She observed an odd look in Brian's eyes—impressed or disgusted?—and returned attention to his far more intriguing children. As the evening dragged on, she chastised herself for accepting a second glass of wine from Brian, who tried hard to charm as he hovered. When Paul went to bed, she thanked them and escaped to a weird sensation: in comparison to the main, the carriage house felt safe.

Laura felt a light buzz from the wine and drifted into a sultry dream about fog and heat. Steve and she lay naked, arms and legs tangled on a checkered blanket atop pure white beach sand as they studied cloud formations. When Steve's breath tickled her ear, Laura detected a stench of cigarette, opened her eyes a slit and as her vision adjusted to the dark, rolled onto her side. In faint illumination from the moon, she noticed a tiny red dot. When the smoker took a drag, she saw Brian's leer. He crossed the room, ground the cigarette out on the floor, and sat on the edge of the bed. "I won't be sent home like a naughty boy."

"Leave before I kick the shit out of you for attempted rape."

"It's not rape with the way you move and the noises you make. You knew I was here, Laura; it's obvious you enjoy what you do to me."

"I'm not interested."

Brian slipped his hand under the sheet. "Let's not waste time playing games."

Her mind ran through possibilities: she could kick and risk serious injury or batter him around in a different way. "Think what might happen to your reputation if I report this."

Brian laughed, "Go right ahead; tell Wilkers, tell Gil, tell the elders, hell, tell Mel. Trust me; my reputation's fine while everyone's aware of *yours* as a liar with a vivid imagination."

Laura assessed how easily she'd startle with a heel to the groin but said, "Mel wants me to consider Glenn."

Brian hooted, "Glenn? That fag's no match for..."

Laura interrupted. "You'd be wise to consider what you can thank Mel and the elders for—you're the youngest headmaster in academy history with a home rent-free."

Brian sighed, "Past experience says if you stay, Mel will approve an alignment with either Gil or me. Why don't we forget this and..."

"Mel and I made our peace."

"What?"

"You're mistaken about my relationship with Mel. If you don't believe me, ask your wife." Brian stood slowly and at the door, reminded her he never touched—he only looked. As soon as he left, Laura relocked and re-bolted the door. She checked every window but couldn't figure out how the little creep got in. She grabbed a flashlight, rubbed as much of the burn mark off her mother's wood floor as she could, and flushed the disgusting butt down the toilet. She returned to bed and spent the rest of the night nodding off in a seated position, knife under her pillow.

Monday at work, Laura felt productive beyond any of her wildest expectations because at the end, she'd make a weekly call to Steve. At 5:00, she rushed to the carriage house to change into something comfortable, and headed off for a light supper at a snack bar she found in Groveton. Finally, the time arrived and she parked near the pay phone. But Lea answered. "I don't know if he still is but most of the weekend, he did surveillance with Bobby Rawlings."

Laura studied passing traffic. "When you see my husband, tell him I think about him way too much."

"Steve left a message for you, too. Your brother Rick is at the cabin and has a gift for you."

Laura giggled, "What is it?"

"A surprise, sweetheart, something he thinks you'll enjoy. When will you be home?"

"I'm not positive but I think soon."

Laura hung up and within the hour, arrived at the cabin and knocked. Rick pulled the door open wide and she saw he and his friends played poker. When he asked if she cared to join them, Laura said, "Thanks for the invitation but I only came for my package from Steve."

Rick disappeared for a moment and returned to slip a wrapped box into her outstretched hand. "Steve said he counts the seconds until you come home. Sis, you guys are so lucky."

"It would be even better if we lived together."

Rick sighed, "You know what I meant. Stay the night. We'll let you have one of the bunks." She thanked him but said goodnight.

Inside her car, Laura removed a cassette tape and note; she scanned Steve's list and noted most were songs and artists she didn't recognize. Steve's voice broke the silence: *Every night as I fall asleep listening to your tape, I pray we'll soon be together so we can dance to all our favorite songs and forget everything that's happened to keep us apart.*

Laura recognized a few songs and artists, like Van Morrison or Joe Cocker but most were unfamiliar. When a romantic country song *The Keeper of the Stars* by Tracy Byrd finished, Steve's voice said, *Laura, I can't describe how I feel any better than that. I miss you.* As she pulled into the driveway, Laura turned the lights off and stared into the main house where in the kitchen, Brian poured a glass of soda. She laughed, "You son of a bitch. How will you entertain yourself if I don't give you anything to listen to?" She ran in and rummaged through her canvas bag for the portable player she used when she kayaked or rode her bike. As soon as she locked the door and secured the deadbolt, she changed into her ugly yellow nightgown, lay down in the dark, and pulled the headphones on. *Laura, I grew up believing marriage meant someone was there to make my meals, raise my child, wash my clothes, and sleep with me. That's an awful lot of my's and me's, don't you think? Since I met you, I've begun to understand marriage means someone will always be there to share a life that's enriched every day by giving in, letting go, and opening up. If we can meet each other halfway and forgive each other when we do something thoughtless, I know we'll finish our lives together, better off for having loved this deeply.* The second side of the tape featured a few more recognizable songs by Van Morrison, Sam Cooke, and Peter Gabriel followed by new country songs or classic oldies. She listened to Steve's soft voice again. *Laura, I promise from this day forward, I will dedicate my life to you. Um, this is getting sappy, so let's move on to another piece of incredible music. As a kid, I loved this song and this voice.*

Laura sighed, "I love this song, too," as Louis Armstrong sang *What a Wonderful World.* She started to drift toward sleep until she heard his voice again. *I didn't know it at the time, but I spent my whole life searching for the love you bring. I decided I could live alone and I thought nothing good would ever happen. Then there you were in front of me smiling, talking, blushing, and making me wish I could take back every selfish act of my life. Laura, now for a reason you know all too well, here's the song that seems appropriate to close this verbal love letter.* The instant *I Forgot That Love Existed* by Van Morrison finished, Laura flipped the cassette and started it from the beginning. Laura felt the sensation, ache, and longing, turned on her side, and dreamed she melded into the nesting position they both loved. Laura dreamed at the very scent of him, her nipples hardened against his back. *Steve laughed, Yeah, I'm awake, too, shifted position, guided her onto her back, knelt above her, and lit a cigarette.* Hnnh?

Laura opened her eyes to an odor on clothing and hair, on breath 20 feet away, and straightened her nightgown. "Brian, this is sinful. How can you covet another woman's body?"

"To be accurate, it's a sin to covet another man's wife."

"Go away; this is an unwanted intrusion."

Brian moved closer. "I doubt that. I saw the way you moved, heard your sounds. Feel how you arouse me, Laura."

She felt terrified but said, "Even rats get erections, Brian. Run home and see if your condition impresses your wife." At no response, she added, "I'll tell Mel you snuck in again."

"Go right ahead; as long as women don't get pregnant off-schedule, Mel doesn't care who fucks them."

Laura felt under the pillow but in her excitement about the tape, forget a knife. She waited until his silhouette moved in front of the window to block moonlight and kicked in the general direction of his crotch. When he flailed wildly, she jumped across the room to the kitchen drawer. "Brian, I have a knife."

"You are one frigid bitch," he groaned and limped across the room. He unlocked the door and slammed it on his way out. Laura relocked, re-bolted, and checked windows—no sign of forced entry. She slept sitting up again in case the little creep came back.

After an unrestful night, Laura woke early and headed to East Haven to use a pay phone. "Your tape is wonderful."

His voice sounded sleepy. "Nowhere near as lusty as yours."

"I woke you?"

"Yeah, Rawlings just barely dropped me off. Boring shit and... Oh, sweetheart, I'm sorry. How are you?"

"I want to come home."

"Are you done?"

"No, but I want to come home."

"Do it right and it moves through court like a tornado; do it sloppy and it hangs around forever like friggin' nuclear waste."

"Yes, Sergeant; I remember your training sessions well."

He insisted if she followed his instructions, the results of her investigation would dazzle everyone. She heard him yawn then add he spoke to Lynette who mentioned John's birthday was July 20th. "Sure seems to me since a certain pair got married secretly, people come up with all kinds of ideas for gatherings that require out of town guests."

"That's not far away at all!"

"Oh, Laura, I miss you so much."

"I know; I miss you, too. Um, Steve, help me here? This little creep Brian manages to sneak in past locks and deadbolts with windows closed and locked; screens aren't stripped. Any ideas?"

"Extra keys to every lock?"

"Nope. I replaced them."

"Skylight?"

"Nope."

"I can call Al and ask him to check things discreetly."

"Okay; then maybe I can sleep."

"Laura, I don't like the sound of this."

"Awareness of the little creep is half the battle."

"I hope. Who do you love, Delorange?"

"You, Scolarzski, only you, always you."

92

As soon as he woke, Mel phoned Violet to confirm the arrangements. He headed to the lab, and though he kept the room spotless and equipment sterile, checked countertops for dust or smudges, floor for marks or dust balls. Others ridiculed him for what they saw as unnecessary precautions but Mel insisted all visitors wear lab jackets, hairnets, face masks, gloves, and paper slippers. He knew Laura would have no problem respecting his request; unlike the many fools who surrounded him, she understood a need to establish order in a far too disorderly world. In the refrigerator, Mel reorganized bottles before he stood in the center of his lab and noted things still to be done: fluorescent fixture to adjust, drawer handle to tighten, black mark on the floor to remove, and cardboard boxes to flatten for recycling. He carried two diskette and one DVD tray upstairs, stored them in an airtight container, taped them shut, and shoved them Last, he peeled three of four posters off the lab wall, rolled them up, slid them inside plastic sleeves, and stored them behind the desk. The day progressed at worse than a snail's pace and Mel wearied of repetition: each workday differed little from the one preceding or following: infant inoculations, enlarged prostates, burning urinary tracts, swollen elbows or ankles, pregnancy consults, high blood pressure, nasty stings, allergy flare-ups, sports or school exams, spider bites, rashes, broken fingers, and stove burns. Mel headed to the Maidstone for dinner. If Glenn joined him, the final 90 minutes surely would fly by like a whispered prayer but Glenn spoke with a woman from Coos County, New Hampshire, hoping to book the facility for a wedding reception. Mel studied the bride-to-be, spectacular in a Celtic way: black hair, fair skin, blue-green eyes; good height and posture, too, and dainty nose, feet, and hands. He imagined she came from exceptional stock and wondered if she'd consider a genetic consult but decided to pass when he saw her beside a galoot whose confidence labeled him the fortunate fiancé. In a straightforward way, the woman successfully negotiated a per-plate price with Glenn fully 10% less than the initial quote. Mel concentrated upon the tone of her voice and imagined a union between her and Glenn, rather than the gorilla that from his behavior and skull shape, might test a full 25 IQ points below his intended. Mel thought *The true tragedy of her choice will appear in the future, exacted upon her as-yet unborn children.*

Brian showed up complaining of painful testicles and Mel insisted he visit the office in the morning. When Brian admitted they were tender because of a kick, Mel laughed, "I'll remind Violet of the fragility of male sexual organs."

Brian shrugged, "It wasn't Violet."

Mel squinted, "It's not decided who earns permission to pursue Laura or visit her n the carriage house. Do not make me repeat that!" He scanned the restaurant to study faces, *most familiar but some not—to lose control in public is pathetically stupid but Brian often brings on such reactions.*

The fool continued, "Everyone expects Gil but good luck with Glenn; everyone's convinced he's a fag."

Mel chuckled, "Glenn is heterosexual—interested only in one his entire life, an admirable commitment to virtue, yes? I foresee within a year, Laura and Glenn produce a magnificent female specimen. Think of it! Our Lord showed me the lineage of she who is intended for David and guided Laura home to enable me to accomplish the task in His name." When Brian began to whine again, Mel insisted he go home so his wife could attend to an appointment. Alone Mel fingered his coffee spoon and twirled it until he noticed the time. Clearly fools moved time forward.

Mel headed home and waited at the window. At 6:30, Violet parked in the driveway and jumped out. On the other side, magnificent

Little Miss Laurette Marie Delorange climbed out, inspected his garden, said, "Everything looks exactly as I remember," and wandered past the rose bushes. In a moment, they stood at his back door and Mel watched his angel's face light up—suggesting her unhealthy fear replaced by curiosity. After everyone agreed to don sterile, protective garb, Mel led them through the office and lab. While true he provided a less than complete description, he needed time to assess her loyalty to the community and his life's work. As in her past life of inquisitive child, Laura listened before asking intelligent questions. He felt pleased when she stopped to study the poster he left on the wall, his genealogical study of Family T, well into a third generation under his guidance. He described the family as native to the area, certain to have been doomed at some future point by in-breeding. He displayed statistics to prove his intervention benevolent: from one generation to the next, measurements of IQ increased among children; general health improved; level of completed education increased; number of offspring per couple decreased; and the coup de grâce: adults of each succeeding generation abandoned menial labor for professions. Though Laura challenged his motivation, in the end it became apparent she respected the quality effort and statistical validity of his findings. When it became obvious Violet felt confounded by the bio-science and statistics, he chuckled, "Enough for this initial gathering; time for a break so head to the kitchen."

Laura straggled to reexamine the chart of Family T. "This is fascinating. Um, do you have similar data on my family?"

"In fact I do, but what you saw is enough for two ladies to absorb in one sitting; allow me to prepare adequately for our next."

Laura continued, "But my mother said you offered to..."

Mel nodded. "Your maternal grandmother Marie Marceau experienced a medical crisis and I offered to access information on Lynette's behalf but that was not for then or this first gathering. It can wait for a future session." Mel encouraged his guests to relax and as they drank lemonade and sampled Glenn's extraordinary maple-spiced pears, he faced Laura. "I need legal assistance in a patent application for a test I perfected after years of study." Laura asked questions and debated him on the ethics of his research but in the end, his deepest dreams came true when she acknowledged he should focus on the medicine of his project, she on legalities. He felt as if 20 lost years were but a merciless dream and her mind still his to sculpt. After they left, he felt stunned to see 7:50, a mere 80 minutes sure to be the most satisfying of his life.

93

Laura collapsed in bed and felt her heartbeat shake the mattress. She took the tape recorder from her pocket and tested to see she got it all. How was it possible a man that brilliant failed to understand the ramifications of his research? Details presented were like a high school biology lesson: dry, factual, memorizable—yet the ethics of it incomprehensible. Marsethe claimed there were more than 50,000 human genes, many not yet mapped, functions unknown. To her argument life shouldn't be patented in any form, Marsethe claimed over 10,000 such patents already existed and provided examples, one a case Laura recalled from a class at Columbia Law. In 1980 the U.S. Supreme Court ruled a genetically engineered organism which ate oil spills was not a new life form but an invention. Laura shivered at a memory of a heated debate during class when she stated, *No one should play God*, only to hear loud and clear the majority of her peers believed genetic engineering should be encouraged for the potential breakthroughs in medicine alone.

Marsethe admitted a lifelong interest into the miracle of human conception led to a tangible result. Although his original interest rested with genetic markers to predict future occurrence, he concluded 12 years of studies suggesting a new technique to work in conjunction with samples taken from women of child-bearing age. She fast-forwarded to hear his description again: *"Non-invasive first-trimester nuchal translucency screening tests exist but are limited in efficacy to women in their 11th to 13th weeks of pregnancy. While amniocentesis cannot be conducted safely until the 18th to 20th week, my test is safe to administer 13 to 18 days following conception."*

Violet asked: *"What difference does that make?"*

Marsethe again: *"One fact alone proves my discovery unique and worthy of patent: debilitating genetic disorders like spina bifida or Downs syndrome can be detected following a woman's first missed menstrual cycle."*

Laura replayed sections and realized she had questions—too many—and considered asking Violet to go back but returned alone. When Marsethe opened the door, Laura insisted he join her in the gazebo. "I have questions but won't be alone with you inside." Once seated, Laura said, "If I agree to assist with a patent application, I need details."

Marsethe explained 12 years earlier he contacted 15 colleagues nationwide who agreed to test women in larger markets. In addition to her help with the application, he wanted her to prepare contracts for each to sign. "I trust their signatures on letters over the years would serve as proof of ownership but I'm a cautious man. There can be no question as to where the procedure originated. You can imagine this could be a profitable venture; even our sweet Violet excited by the idea a woman at risk could find out so early."

Laura took a deep breath. "I get stuck with how easy it would be for a woman to choose abortion, not to mention how spine-chilling I find women and fetuses as test subjects in the first place. You claim intent to identify debilitating conditions but to me it smacks of elitism. In the near future, could people with sufficient funds menu-choose a child."

He chuckled, "As in our many debates in years past, do I detect a moral and spiritual dilemma here?"

Laura nodded. "A few months ago, my partner worked a case involving a young man with Downs Syndrome. If his mother had access to your technique years ago, Billy might not be among us today."

Marsethe sighed, "Yes, I understand your quandary. Be assured it is a humane way to provide options for rational adults to make rational decisions about the quality of life they add to an already-crowded planet."

Laura stiffened at his choice of *quality*. "That's one very biased word! Who are you to decide what constitutes a quality life?"

"Who should if not the educated? Think critically, not emotionally. A Darwinian concept of survival of the fittest applies only to third world countries now. In our developed world, the stupid and weak are protected without any potential payoff for the bright and strong."

Laura recalled how an hour earlier, Violet seemed entranced by the doctor's theories while Laura felt frightened to the core. "Um, I'm not sure I'm the person to help with this application after all."

Marsethe patted her hand. "Do not allow an opinionated old man to frighten you with my beliefs but I beg you to consider this: productive members of our society find themselves trapped into a form of servitude to the needy and weak. Yet that is a situation not beyond remedy for those strong enough to accept the challenge."

Laura stared at leaves in a light breeze. Who could argue against making every effort to bring wanted children into the world and bestow every gift God had to offer? Not her, certainly, and not anyone she knew who enjoyed adequate nutrition, medical care, enviable education, and others to love who loved them. On the other hand, it seemed likely those in agreement with ideas like Marsethe's could move quickly from justifying aborting less than perfect fetuses to euthanasia of seriously ill. How long before trained eyes targeted the frail, elderly, or deformed? Laura said, "I'll give this more thought but have to go." She glanced at her watch and estimated travel time: if she drove like a maniac, she'd arrive around 11:00. It felt essential to spend the night in the arms of a man who could never buy into a philosophy of disposable life.

94

When Ralph and Joyce got home, they unpacked and decided there could be no more Igor-isms at fancy events. Whether or not he wanted to, the budster would learn to boogie. Ralph called Steve, demanded he come over, and settled back with a shitload of mail—too many bills, not enough good stuff. Joyce sifted through CDs and by the time Steve arrived, had everything so organized she put professional DJs to shame. At a cha-cha kind of beat, Joyce grabbed her new partner and dragged him around in time to a seductive beat. The rhythm sped up and she teased and badgered until his buddy loosened up. Joyce suggested Steve pretend to be a male stripper and his best buddy groaned, "My back won't let me bump and grind!" As Joyce coaxed, Ralph's amusement turned to unease. Joyce seemed reckless and Steve not all that innocent, either. Ralph cleared his throat for attention but when none came, headed outdoors to stare at a couple who never noticed he left.

Ralph sulked on a bench under a red maple and turned at: "How odd to find you here alone in the dark."

Ralph leapt to his feet and grabbed Laura for a hug. "How long you been spying, little lady?"

"I just arrived; um, Lea said I'd find my new husband here."

Ralph insisted she be quiet, led her inside, and indicated where to stand and peek in. He watched Laura grin when ten feet away, the Polack said, "My bride is a Moody Blues freak and there's a song I'd like to learn to dance to."

Steve changed CDs and a song with a fantastic beat started. Laura whispered, "That's *Talkin,' Talkin* and why aren't we in there?"

Ready to confess his fear of betrayal, Ralph didn't get a chance. Joycie squealed with excitement, crossed the room, and grabbed Laura. Steve followed and reached for his bride's hand. Ralph knew all was well when a slow song started and Joyce insisted their guests spend the night in the guest room. "You newlyweds won't have to worry about us old-timers, either; we'll be too busy to eavesdrop."

95

Laura ran out to grab her bag, Joyce locked up, and Steve called home. "Mom, I won't be back and didn't want you to worry."

"I'm glad, Stefan. Enjoy this time together."

Steve headed into the guest room, found Laura in a blue almost-covers-nothing one-piece nightie, and came up behind as she brushed her hair. "Please tell me I'm not dreaming."

"If you are, I am, too, so let's make the most of this." Laura turned to face him and he wasted no time doing just that.

Afterwards, Steve confessed, "I wished we lived together so our first major fight would be out of the way."

"What's that got to do with anything?"

"It'll happen eventually and I want it over and done."

"Want what over and done?"

"The first time you say no to sex because you're pissed."

Laura laughed, "As a kid I recognized when my parents' battles moved into the bedroom. I can't imagine that happening to us but I also can't understand how you were so insensitive to Ralph."

"Excuse me?"

"When I arrived, he moped in the dark feeling left out."

"Interesting observation; okay, next lesson Joyce dances with both of us and later the three of us neck on the couch."

Laura punched his arm. "You're supposed to argue so I can prove your theory faulty." She settled in and proceeded to talk about people she met, cases she handled, fears and concerns, and asked for advice on handling a confusing hint of unethical medical research. "I couldn't help but think of Billy Fellowes and how much value his life has."

Steve sighed, "Yeah, he's a wonder. I think he found a new job and I need to stop by and see how he's doing." Steve must have dozed off because the next thing he knew, early morning light filtered in and Laura dressed in yesterday's clothes. She leaned close to whisper, "I love you," and left. He heard the outside door close and glanced at the clock: 5:10 AM. He climbed out of bed to watch her car disappear around the curve and shivered at a fuzzy memory: in the middle of the night, she curled up in his arms and detailed her meeting with Marsethe and asked for advice. Steve felt mortified all he could remember answering was something lame like: "Sounds important so play it slow but play it safe."

Ralph wandered into the living room in his boxers and yawned, "The rooster ain't barely crowed, buddy."

"Yeah, but my wife's already gone." In the kitchen, Ralph prepared coffee, scrambled three eggs, and toasted two bagels as Steve summarized what he could recall of Laura's summary of her investigation. "I'm not sure if I should worry but with a freak like Marsethe, how involved can Laura get before she's too damn close?"

Ralph admitted with the crap he read in Granger's files, Steve had a right to be concerned. "There's a whole buncha cuckoo shit I suspect barely scratches the surface; time we recruit Wilkers."

96

The drive almost felt routine and Laura figured at the rate established, she'd get home once every week to ten days. As a matter of fact, only eight days remained until her father's birthday party—not bad; not nearly enough but it would do. Mount Mansfield looked ringed in fog in pre-dawn light, a sign of another humid day, a genuine bonus after a long, cold, snowy winter. She breathed rich, moist air in deeply and planned her next contact with Marsethe: make a slow approach and look hesitant but display curiosity and respect for his project. If she followed Steve's advice and played it slow and safe, she'd do well. The key? Butter up the doctor's massive ego. Laura slipped Steve's cassette in and smiled at his soft, sexy voice. She thought it odd how a man so wonderful might feel insecure about their relationship. To her, everything felt amazing: the love, marriage, and plans for the future, comfort of sleeping in his arms, desire, and the fact she enjoyed sex. She chewed her lower lip and decided the next time they were together, she'd encourage him in every way imaginable. She recalled a time months earlier when he attempted something different and she shoved him off. In fact, the idea of shoving aside all her inhibitions felt... Laura visualized Angela's face, stunned at how easy it was to forget, or how crass to assume any other victim would find the same acceptance she did. Laura's attitude shifted from an investigation about justice for her or Angela to protection of all future dark-haired, dark-eyed girls who drew a monster's attention.

Laura arrived at the carriage house and hurried through her morning routine. She arrived at work on time, settled in as if nothing were unusual, and breezed through detailed work. At the end of the day, Laura headed out of the cool office into the humid summer afternoon and grabbed her bike. As she pedaled away, she held the scents of summer inside: the heat, humidity, aroma of flowers and grass freshly mowed. She passed under the maples and stopped in the shade near the green where a young woman tossed a Frisbee to her dog and a dozen boys played stickball. In the middle of the green, three women talked on a bench, their babies in a neat circle of carriages. Laura leaned her bicycle against a tree and crossed the street to the library. In the fiction section, she skimmed through new titles and picked up a suspense novel by an author unknown to her. Softly a librarian called, "Would you like a new card, Laura? I believe yours expired a decade ago."

Laura moved closer. "Mrs. Cabrell?"

"Yes; you may be all grown up but you haven't changed much." She patted Laura's hand and slid an application forward. "Just a formality, dear." When Laura finished and slid it back, Mrs. Cabrell suggested while she laminated the card, Laura peek at the Gallery of Stars. She pointed to the stairs leading to the children's section.

Laura looked. "Gallery of what?"

"You'll see."

Laura inched down one step at a time and studied photographs of children beginning in 1968. Every summer at the end of vacation, the library staff awarded an engraved gold ball point pen and blank book to the child who read the most and could prove it by answering specific questions. Laura touched the frames where for three years in a row in the 90's, it was her face staring back. When she got to recent years, it was Angela's beaming face smiling at the camera. Laura gasped and rushed back to the counter. To Mrs. Cabrell's warm smile, Laura whispered, "Thank you for remembering me for an accomplishment." Laura returned to her bicycle and plopped down in the grass under a maple.

When something icky touched her ankle, Laura jumped. It was Angela. "Did I scare you?"

"Yes and I'll bet you hate it when people do that to you!"

Angela giggled, "I do; I visited you but the door's locked."

"I'm glad you did; try again soon. Listen; I'm hungry and thirsty. Would you like something from the snack bar?"

"I'm not supposed to eat between meals; Mom says I'm getting fat." Angela looked around and confided. "Mom took me to a doctor in Newport to make sure no baby grows inside where he ... you know."

Laura squeezed Angela's hand. "I know everything hurts now but I want you to believe it gets better."

Angela rubbed her hands along her arms. "You don't have to answer but if I was your daughter, would you love me?"

"I love you already, sweetheart."

"What about Steve? Do you love me as much as him?"

"My love for you is different from my love for Steve but just as important." Laura squeezed Angela's hand and added, "At the library earlier I saw your photograph."

"I saw yours, too; you were pretty then like now."

"Thanks. Are you competing this year, too?"

209

"No, that stupid contest's for little kids and…" Angela jumped to her feet. "He absolutely cannot stare at me!"

Laura turned. "Dr. Marsethe can't bother you here."

Angela raced across the grass. "I don't want him to catch me somewhere I can't get away!"

Laura hoped he'd cross the green and when shoes stopped in front of her, whispered, "She's in such pain."

When Marsethe lowered himself to the grass, she noticed he seemed wobbly but with a voice as forceful as ever. "That child is high-strung, not self-assured like you."

"If that's true, why am I so frightened all the time? All I've learned to do is hide a little better."

Laura watched beautiful blue eyes soften into a warm smile as he changed the subject abruptly. "Please join us Saturday evening at a party I host to celebrate Glenn's 37th birthday."

"Okay; I'd love to."

Marsethe pushed himself to a shaky stand. "Wonderful; plan for three events: 8:00 PM Saturday at the Maidstone, 9:00 AM Sunday at services, and 6:30 PM Tuesday at my lab for a follow-up."

"I can make the first and third, but…"

He sighed, "I slaved for weeks over a guest sermon and it is imperative you hear my words first hand."

Laura sighed, "All right; this once."

97

Bobby coordinated weekend surveillance with other detectives and troopers so he and Scolarzski weren't doing it alone. When Sigler had the balls to recommend Ms. Buerton simply vacate premises, Bobby tossed Scolarzski's file onto the idiot's desk. "Read it! If that's Sivalette in the woods, he won't go near the place unless she's there. His routine is to work a lady into a real lather before he lays a finger on her."

98

Laura arrived at work early, spread the Burlington *Free Press* open, and studied a photograph on Page 3 with caption: *Is There Another Story Here?* On the courthouse steps, Stephanie Orsini held Steve by the arm and leaned close. The accompanying article offered no surprises about how three respected psychiatrists testified Ms. Orsini posed no threat to the public; one after another described her as a productive member of society, gainfully employed. Laura grumbled, "Ms. Stephanie-the-psychopath-bitch-Orsini is that and so much more." Laura skipped to a paragraph detailing the suspect's return to the state hospital for continued observation, evaluation, and treatment. "Yeah, right," Laura chuckled and imagined Ms. Orsini would be released too soon, gather up her son, and head off into the sunset like some romantic outlaw to bear her second child alone. Maybe she wouldn't go anywhere at all and remain in the area like a festering wound—a constant reminder of how ineffective the law truly was. All morning, Laura stewed about the article and shortly after lunch, changed into shorts and t-shirt for the bike ride home. She stopped beside Reilly's desk. "I can't concentrate and need to cut out early. I need time alone with my thoughts."

Reilly admitted she read the morning paper. "Do you want to talk about it?" When Laura shook her head no, Reilly added, "It said you investigated her in an earlier felony case but..."

Laura held her hand in the air. "I don't want to talk about how... never mind. It's done."

"It mentions a Sergeant Scolarzski. Isn't that the same name who called a while back?"

Laura collapsed on the couch. "Reilly, enough, please; I'm trying to put this behind me and build a new life."

"Um everyone knows Glenn wants to get closer but...."

Laura sighed, "Ah yes, the famous **everyone**."

Reilly twisted a pen. "Do you have a boyfriend in New Hampshire? Everyone says you go there at night."

"I have no boyfriend anywhere."

Reilly pointed to the article. "They mention a shooting. Is that why you limp sometimes?"

"Reilly, I have no desire to talk about this any further."

"If you change your mind and want someone to listen, come for dinner. I'd like you to meet David and my Mom."

"Who's David?"

"My son."

Laura felt the flush. "I didn't know you have a child; if you don't mind, I'd like to hear more."

Reilly shrugged, "There's not much to tell."

"Um, do I know the father?"

Reilly smiled in the peaceful way she often did when she parroted the CFEL. "When the elders said it was time, I wanted it to be Gil but Dr. Marsethe explained why it should be Bill."

Laura gasped, "Bill? Bill Marschek?"

"Yes."

"Why go along with their scheme? What was in it for you?"

"David is perfect, handsome, healthy, and smart. Plus, Bill provides very well for us both."

Laura rubbed her forehead. "I must be missing something important. You're young and unless..."

Reilly interrupted, "After Dad died, the CFEL trained Mom to take over his responsibilities as business manager to keep the house."

Laura squinted in confusion. "Um, I know the elders prefer members in core roles but I don't understand what..."

"It's about cooperation and leverage."

"Oh; what did Bill get out of it?"

"Marsethe said Bill would have memories for a lifetime."

Laura squinted and shook her head. "Why would you confess something so intimate? Did Marsethe tell you to open up?"

Reilly laughed, "I told him you were too smart for this."

Laura asked what Marsethe hoped to set in motion as a result of the conversation but Reilly shrugged and fed stationery into the printer. Laura grabbed her purse. "Okay, fine, clam up now and report I was suitably shocked. I'll see you tomorrow."

Laura pedaled the circumference of the green twice before she pulled up at the Laundromat and checked the area for Gil. He'd been noticeably absent of late and she wasn't certain if she should feel relieved or concerned. She called Granger's direct line and heard what she already knew from the newspaper. In the end, he grudgingly admitted it was only a matter of time before Ms. Orsini was released under supervision. "Her attorney's working on a deal where she takes medication and meets with a psychiatrist three times a week."

Laura interrupted, "If this doctor's male, warn him!"

"It's possible they'll keep her there."

Laura pressed her forehead against a wall. "She's smart enough to play the game. I'll call again soon to fill you in; there's so much going on, I feel adrift and need advice."

Laura hung up and noticed a dark Caprice Classic pull away from the curb across the street. It was the same vehicle she saw after her visit to the library at Dartmouth, the same she suspected followed her after she met with Claudette Theriault at her house in Thetford. She recalled she asked Granger to run a check, squinted until she made out most of the characters on the plate, and called the lieutenant again. When his line stayed busy one try after another, she gave up.

On Saturday, Laura organized boring hours alone into a series of chores: first, garden work before it got hot in the sun; second, install two room-sized air conditioners so windows wouldn't be open overnight; third, iron a dress for Glenn's birthday party that night and another for services in the morning; and fourth, make a grocery list for the coming week. After a shower, Laura pulled stockings on then yanked them off to go bare-legged. Who could argue global warming was a fallacy? As a kid, air conditioning was unheard of in the Northeast Kingdom of Vermont. She brushed her hair, pulled it off her neck, and held it with a comb. She studied her reflection in the mirror and wished her preparations were for her husband. She wondered how to conduct herself at the party; she could find someone she felt comfortable with—Violet, Rita, or Reilly—and stick to them like glue, wander around until someone sought her company, be bold and take initiative with someone new, or hide in a corner and wait for Marsethe to draw her forward.

Laura headed to her car as Brian held the car door for Violet and smiled sheepishly. "Can we offer you a lift?" Laura hesitated but when she saw Paul's smile, jumped into the back with the children. At the Maidstone, Laura listened to a five-piece country-rock band and noticed bar stools removed so tables were free to stand around. She sampled food displayed beautifully and placed throughout the bar: raw vegetables, dips, hot and cold hors d'oeuvres, shrimp cocktail, strawberries, fruit soup, carrot sticks in olive rings, breads and rolls with whipped cream butter, hot broccoli and cheese puffs, and one amazing dessert after another.

When Brian asked what she'd like from the bar, Laura said, "Nothing, thanks."

"I apologize for the other night; when I've had too much to drink, I..."

"You weren't drunk either time. How'd you get in?"

Brian shrugged, "The tunnel," and left to join his wife.

Laura thought: *of course*. As children, she and Jack played in a tunnel connecting the main to carriage house: off to one side a root cellar, off the other, a wine cellar. In summers, it felt cool—dark and scary and slimy with spider webs and mice—the sort of place to spark a child's imagination. One year she wrote a history that featured their tunnel as a stop on the Underground Railroad between Kentucky and Quebec. But the tunnel no longer existed; she clearly remembered an autumn day when Rick fell from the kitchen and needed stitches. Her father arranged a back-hoe to fill it in. Laura imagined if a tunnel still existed, she would have noticed the trap door. Before her parents stored furniture there, it was roughly where the bed stood and the trap door opened down. She grinned at a realization *a better housekeeper would move the bed to mop the hardwood floor all the way under.* "Talk about finding a monster un..."

"Did you say something?"

Laura turned to a smile. "How are you, Caroline?"

"Great! I got to close the store early. How are you?"

"Fine. Um, Jack says hello."

Caroline smiled sadly and suggested they check some orange things across the room. As they sampled delicacies, Caroline indicated an elderly woman seated on one of the few chairs. "I'd like to introduce my mother, Gretchen Beaudon. Mom, this is Laura Delorange."

The woman beamed. "I do remember you, Lynette!"

Caroline handed her mother a plate of assorted finger foods, arranged a napkin, and stood. "Mom, I'll be right here if you need me." She turned to Laura. "Sorry about that; Mom gets lost in time."

Laura jumped when arms wrapped around from behind: Angela. "I didn't know you knew Glenn. He's my godfather and there he is!"

Someone shouted for Glenn to make a speech but he refused. Marsethe stood and stated, "Glenn Munier is the finest young man I'm blessed to know. As he turns 37, he looks across this room of loving smiles and sees the eyes of she whom he has held in his heart for most of his young life. I ask for all of you to join in my prayer this fine young woman sees the wisdom of Glenn as the father of her unborn children." Laura flushed but considered Marsethe never mentioned a name; neither he nor Glenn looked in her direction; and it seemed possible in the bar that night stood other single women who fit the bill,

The din of music, plates, glasses, and conversation filled the air. A man approached Caroline and asked her to dance. Laura decided he was older than Caroline by ten years and attractive in a mature, polished way. Was he Sam from the story? Laura noticed Gil for the first time; he looked different in a suit, dress shirt, and tie—better-looking than usual in a professional way. He waltzed with Reilly in a very intimate we're-the-only-two-people-in-the-room way. Laura thought they were quite brazen in public and scanned the crowd; from his expression, Marsethe was aware, his displeasure obvious. Laura wandered off in his general direction and decided to allow him to take the initiative. As she approached from behind, Marsethe's attention shifted from the dance floor to a man Laura recognized as Elder Matthew. Laura overheard Marsethe say, "The offer is $30,000 plus expenses; I'm inclined to accept.

As productive as her first specimen was, I predict one with Gilbert shall exceed all expectations. It's wise to move now; her fecundity dwindles."

Elder Matthew chuckled, "Do what you want though it may be too late; see how she clings to Sam tonight?"

Laura glanced around, shocked at how freely they spoke in public. Maybe she misunderstood; maybe she expected the worst and created things inside her head. Laura watched the doctor climb the stairs and enter Glenn's apartment. She considered following to eavesdrop but got distracted when Reilly crossed the room with an adorable little boy. Reddish-haired David wore baggy shorts and wobbled between long legs on chubby ones of his own. Reilly introduced her mother, Mary McGuinn, a strikingly-young and attractive grandmother. Both women laughed when as Laura spoke, David grabbed her around her knees and peered up with heartbreaking blue eyes. Laura gasped, "Do you think he'd let me hold him?" Reilly nodded and Laura scooped him up, a bolt of lightning until he relaxed, wrapped his arms around her neck, and pushed his face into hers. When David squirmed, Reilly announced bedtime. In a moment, they left and Laura felt startled by how empty her arms felt.

99

Glenn danced with seven different women, each time staring at Laura as he worked up nerve to approach. The unexpected and official change in status felt exciting yet frightening. Before they made a grand entrance together, Mel promised by the end of the year—if Glenn played his role well—Laura would become Glenn's wife; the grand design went further: a prediction of pregnancy before their first anniversary. He couldn't imagine what happened to a preference for Gil but figured his older brother finally admitted what he said in private: *I'm no longer willing to perform on command*. Laura looked lost as she wandered the room and for a second, appeared to seek a conversation with Mel. When she blended into the crowd, Glenn didn't see her again until she lifted David. The song ended and Glenn thanked Margaret for their dance, crossed the room, pleased to see Laura responded with a smile. They talked, circled the room, and danced. Angela came around and asked him to dance; followed by more dances with Laura, conversations with other guests, a sit-down dinner, and the embarrassing cake and song part. When he noticed the time, Glenn felt shocked Laura spent hours in his company without trying to escape. By midnight, most of the guests left and Glenn asked, "Would you like to share a glass of wine in my apartment?"

Laura shrugged, "That's not a good idea."

"Which? Wine or apartment?"

"I rarely drink and you scare me."

"I do? Ask anyone. I'm harmless."

Laura cleared her throat. "I don't trust men."

"Even one who loves you so much he waits 21 years for a dance?"

Laura glanced at his apartment door and nodded. "I'll have one glass of wine." He watched her grab her purse, climb the stairs and at the top, turn with a smile, open the door, and enter.

Glenn rushed to the bar to grab a bucket of ice and bottle of white zinfandel. Mel followed to whisper, "There is to be no conjugal activity until her consult is conducted, no sexual contact until blood tests are administered and results analyzed." Glenn shrugged him off and Mel snickered, "Recall this fact, my heated young friend: only months ago, another man enjoyed her most wondrous of places."

"Why must you turn everything sordid?"

Mel snickered, "We are but animals in search of exhilaration. Do not get high and mighty or you shall see a decision reversed."

100

Laura removed the tape recorder from her purse, placed it on the table, and checked the phone; as expected, Glenn's had a redial option. She glanced over her shoulder at the door, hit record then redial, and listened to a series of 11 changing tones. She returned the recorder to her purse and relaxed on the couch with a prayer Marsethe came up to call a buyer with the CFEL's counter-offer. She felt stung by her own duplicity. If Glenn loved her, what she did went beyond despicable; if he were as patient as promised, the way she mislead willingly felt abhorrently cruel. Glenn entered and handed her a glass of wine. "I think everything went well tonight. Did you enjoy yourself?"

"Yes, very much; um, thanks for the wine but I should go."

"I thought you came with the Lemphier's; they left."

Laura felt the flush. "How stupid of me to…"

Glenn asked for a minute before taking her home. "I saw the photo in the paper. Were you and Scolarzski involved?"

Laura nodded and confessed when she met Steve she had a problem trusting any man could love her enough to see past her fear and inhibition. "Recently, Steve married someone far more confident about everything she brings into an adult relationship."

During the drive Laura made casual conversation yet felt shamed by how easily she misled. At the door, she fumbled in the dark for keys, turned to say good night, and wrapped her arms around his neck. "Thanks for not pushing; I promise we'll spend time together soon."

He grinned. "Sit with me tomorrow at services?" Laura nodded and escaped quickly.

Wine proved to be an excellent sleeping aid and in no time, she opened her eyes to daylight. She remembered services, showered, and dressed. At the church, Glenn led her to a prominent row in front.

When the adult choir finished a hymn, a youth group took its place on risers behind the pulpit. Elder Vincent waited until organ music faded before announcing, "Our sister in God, Joanna Lemphier, arranged a contemporary songwriter's hymn for voice, clarinet, saxophone, piano, and percussion." He faced the group and chuckled, "I'm assured of light percussion. Joanna indicated this songwriter, Van Morrison, is an Irish artist, a favorite of Laura Delorange who as you know, recently returned to our community. This is in her honor." Joanna sat at an electronic keyboard and nodded to a young woman. Slowly the first soprano, then an alto, then another soprano hummed—when all eight female voices joined in perfect harmony, instrumental accompaniment began, and strong voices sang a melody familiar from Steve's CDs:

> *Whenever God shines His light on me*
> *Open up my eyes so I can see*
> *When I look up in the darkest night*
> *Then I know everything is gonna be alright.*
> *In deep confusion, in great despair,*
> *When I reach out for Him, He is there*
> *When I am lonely as I can be*
> *Then I know that God shines His light on me.*
> *Reach out for Him, He'll be there*
> *With Him, your troubles you can share*
> *If you live the life you love*
> *You get the blessing from above.*
> *Heals the sick and He heals the lame*
> *Says you can do it, too, in Jesus' name*
> *And He lifts you up and He turns you around*
> *And He puts your feet back on higher ground.*

The volume changed from slow spiritual to quick revival. The percussion steadily increased as a saxophonist stood for a brief solo in bluesy mode. Joanna turned away from the keyboard for a moment and glanced at Laura with a hesitant smile. Laura returned it and as the music stopped, applauded loudly. The rest of the congregation joined in far more conservatively until Marsethe stood and headed to the pulpit. Laura decided if the doctor spent weeks in preparation, there was no payoff for his efforts. His thoughts were disjointed and when he focused, it was on a theory women were intended by God to remain subservient to the men who protected them. At the word *protected*, Laura stifled a laugh at an image of saber toothed tigers and wooly mammoths roaming the woods of the Northeast Kingdom of Vermont in search of barefoot, pregnant women. Marsethe provided a few Biblical references in support of his position, all from early in the Old Testament right alongside *an eye for an eye* and references to eye-gouging and hand-chopping as approved methods of discouraging misbehavior. Marsethe's voice softened as he spoke surprisingly gentle words about the natural order as created by God; the separateness of two souls that disappeared in the face of true love; the love a man and woman built together; friendship, honor, fidelity and honesty which led to commitment; and the purity of love which led to a lifetime of spiritual and physical fulfillment.

Laura felt two stares: Marsethe from the pulpit and Glenn inches away and felt awkward. When something pulled her hair, she turned, stared into David's sweet face, and watched him try to climb over. Reilly lifted her brows in a questioning way and at Laura's nod, lifted her giggling toddler over the pew. Laura experienced the same sensation as the night before: *Oh, he feels and smells so good!* Unlike the evening before, David snuggled into her arms and sat quietly. Laura's attention returned to Marsethe as he spoke of the CFEL's achievements in education, health, and life expectancy. "Every community which prides itself on its evolution toward the Godlike controls the fertility of its membership. Rampant reproduction diminishes the quality of all life: mother whose health is put in jeopardy, father whose life's partner is distracted and exhausted, and children who receive less attention than what is necessary and fair. The greatest gift to show our Lord and one another is reproduction based upon science. There are those among us selected by He who knows all to lead the way to our fourth generation." Marsethe's eyes focused on hers as he continued, Marriage is the strongest emotional bond a human being experiences in a lifetime, equally strong as that felt between mother and child. Thus, marriage is far too important a decision to make alone. Oftentimes, a young person's judgment is clouded by physical desire and distorted passion. The community elders and I see through a far clearer lens called genetic science." Laura stifled a sigh as

Marsethe returned to his seat. After a few statements from Elders Matthew, Robert, and Vincent, services ended.

Laura handed David back to Reilly with a smile then headed out into blinding sunshine and incredible heat. As she negotiated the steep steps with her wobbly knee, Glenn ran up alongside and invited her to join him and a few others for breakfast. When she stammered that might be too much for one day, Glenn laughed, "Nonsense," grabbed her hand, led her across the green toward the Maidstone, and explained Mel and the elders approved his courtship of her.

"Did I miss the fact we live in the 1890's?"

Glenn shrugged, "It might sound ridiculous to you but everyone here understands and accepts the need."

Laura stumbled along in uncomfortable shoes and wondered: *understands and accepts the need to what? Limit the population? Report every bodily function to the doctor? Hide passionate love like Reilly and Gil? Go along with everything like Violet and Brian? Give up on personal needs like Glenn?* Laura studied him. "Do you agree with the CFEL's approach?"

Glenn shrugged, "I waited 21 years for a chance to be with you and find no fault with their approach if the result is us."

"But the choice must be mine, too."

Glenn squeezed her hand. "Of course it does but I hope waiting 21 years proves I'm a patient man."

On the steps of the Maidstone, Glenn greeted others and led them inside. He selected a large table away from the kitchen and the group talked, laughed, and sipped coffee or tea in the air-conditioned restaurant. Glenn and Laura sat along one side of the table; Gil with his mother Ada along another; Reilly, David, and Mary along the third; and the doctor alone along the fourth. When David reached his arms out for Laura to lift him from a high chair, Marsethe murmured, "Children possess a God-like talent to see directly into souls. The love of a child is a gift no one can buy, a reward earned through acts of kindness."

Except for Marsethe and how he preached all the time, Laura felt comfortable with the group. Whoever decided who from that shitty little town might ease her into an intimate setting, chose wisely. The only ones missing were Caroline or Violet and her children. Laura fought laughter when Glenn pulled more chairs over for Caroline and Gretchen; an instant later, Violet and Joanna arrived, too. Laura thanked Joanna for the surprising performance at morning services. "That's one amazing group! Do you perform often?"

Joanna smiled. "The elders invite us once every three months."

Marsethe snorted, "If the youth group wishes future invitations, undoubtedly they will have to explain the jazziness toward the end," reached for Joanna's hand, and squeezed it.

After a fantastic meal, Laura excused herself. Reilly followed to extend an invitation to join her and David at the lake for a swim. After agreeing where and when to meet, Laura headed to her car. It sat in the blazing sun, every window closed tight. As she rolled them down and fanned the air, she groaned at the heat from vinyl, and laughed at the fact she once believed summers in Vermont too mild to warrant cloth seats or artificial cooling in anything that moved and created its own breezes.

101

In the shade, Al watched from behind the post office. Laura left alone but Glenn Munier stood on the steps and stared after her. Al lowered the binoculars and imagined Scolarzski and Barber overreacted. Of them all, Glenn was the least scary—an honorable man and from the look on his face, too enraptured to allow her to be harmed in any way.

102

Laura changed into her bathing suit and tugged on the straps until stretched fabric covered scars. She grabbed a brimmed hat, sun block, and sand umbrella; despite her dark hair, she burned and peeled before freckles showed up. Laura met Reilly and David in the Maidstone lot and decided to take Mary's car with David's seat belted in; plus, it had air conditioning. Laura recognized the dark Chevy Caprice Classic and checked the tag. "Does anyone else drive this car but you or Mary?"

Reilly squinted in confusion then answered, "Gil borrowed it once when the cruiser needed transmission work." Laura breathed a sigh of relief. Gil hadn't been so invisible after all, just cloaked a bit.

At Maidstone Lake, they set up two sand umbrellas and David squealed with excitement as a piece of grass floated by, a streak of sunlight crossed the blanket, a neon-green bug landed on his toe. They cooled off in the lake in small doses and ran back to blankets where David played in the sand with a plastic shovel and bucket. He separated tiny toys into groups, pushed one set toward his mother, one toward Laura, and kept one for himself. When he climbed into her lap to offer and receive affection, Laura sighed, "You're so lucky to have him in your life."

"Glenn's eager to give you one of your own, you know."

Laura stared across the lake and thought *I want to become pregnant with Steve, a possibility far-fetched with a male who had a vasectomy reversed and a female with a botched up body beyond repair.* Good lord, she couldn't even remember her last period. Then she recalled it happened before she left for Fallsbridge, probably the last week in April. Before that? During the winter, maybe right before Christmas but not again until March, shortly before she approached Steve that first night. Surely the gaps were too long, spacing too irregular, to conceive easily. She smiled at another thought: *Unless, of course, the couple in question is sexually active every day for months and months or years and years, a scenario to envision only if we live together.* When David sifted sand onto her leg and giggled, her attention returned to Reilly's last statement. "Glenn's been honest about his feelings but after a failed relationship, the thought of another man is strange' if I were searching, it would be for a man like Glenn."

After a few more splashes in the lake, Reilly opened the basket to announce lunch. David had a ravenous appetite for someone so tiny then curled into Laura's arms and stared at her with huge blue eyes and long reddish eyelashes. Reilly laughed, "Be careful not to encourage him. Soon enough, he'll do that to seduce girls."

Laura felt his body change as he fell asleep: all his energy faded away until David stretched out, soft like a Raggedy Andy doll. His little face looked unbearably sweet and he made slurping noises as he slept. Laura felt herself drift, too, from a big breakfast, lunch before she felt hungry, and heat. She curled up on the blanket, held David close, and dreamed she lay on the bed at home; a breeze blew across carrying a scent of lilacs. Hours earlier, she and Steve returned from the hospital with their baby: a girl, a pink-skinned angel with tuft-like black hair. Steve curled on the bed behind, reached around as she nursed their daughter, touched the infant's face, and whispered, *I love you already, little girl.* Laura kissed his hairy arm and jumped when he scratched her breast. Hnnh? She opened her eyes as Reilly grabbed David. Laura sat up and noticed two exposed scars—more noticeable than usual with a slight line of sunburn but not even close to hideous ones crisscrossing her skin. Reilly wouldn't make eye contact and muttered, "Marsethe's wrong to encourage mothers to breast-feed so long because now David tries to access breasts of other women."

Laura choked, "It's okay; he didn't mean to..." but visualized another face. "I wonder if Steve ever closed his eyes not from passion but he found the sight of me so horrifying."

Reilly gasped, "Tell me how this happened."

Laura choked, "I shouldn't have said that out loud." Because the mood changed—even David looked frightened as he scrutinized them both—Laura confessed the whole truth: the first assault in Marsethe's parlor and the destructive rape later.

Reilly choked, "Glenn would keep his eyes open."

Laura shook her head. "You didn't see all the scars, so don't make promises no man could keep."

Laura felt no surprise when the day ended abruptly. Reilly blamed it on a need to prepare Sunday dinner for Mary but Laura understood awkward situations led to awkward little lies of escape. God knew how often Laura did the same maneuver to get away from whatever she couldn't endure. When Reilly dropped her off at her car, Laura thanked her for a wonderful day, squeezed David's chin, and whispered, "You're lucky to have this little person in your life."

Back at the carriage house, Laura rubbed aloe cream on her sunburned shoulders and wished Steve were there to do it for her. She removed an anniversary card from her purse and wrote: *By the time you receive this, almost a month will have gone by on the calendar yet in real time, we've been married nine days. Will you dance with me under the moonlight? Will you lie on your back beside me and count stars? Will you let me kiss you all over? Dear husband, do you love me as much as I love you?* After she sealed the envelope and fixed the stamp, Laura felt relaxed enough to sleep.

In the morning, Laura left early to drive to the post office in Littleton. She thought it paranoid to distrust Betsy at the Fallsbridge branch, *but Marsethe got his hands on Caroline's story somehow, didn't he?* In the office, Laura felt frustrated. Reilly wanted to talk about the lake visit but Laura waved her off; it felt awkward to get close to others; their knowledge of you changed the dynamics of a relationship and gave one person an edge over the other.

After work, Laura worked in the garden until it was time to speed across the bridge to a pay phone. She called collect and when Steve answered, whispered, "I need a breath-stopping hug. I wouldn't mind if it broke my back."

"This won't last forever, kid."

Laura pressed her forehead against siding and jumped as a young woman climbed the steps to the store. "They listen to everything I say and Gil still follows me. He might be watching me now, waiting to see if I meet anyone. I'm sorry. You can't enjoy these calls. I'm sure you prefer conversations with composed adults, not crybabies."

"I love everything about you, Laura."

"Things are starting to change, Steve, and I recognize Marsethe's influence more every day. I don't understand why people are so easy to

222

lead around. Doesn't anyone think for themselves? It seems like strong personalities have a field day in a village where people normally shut up and follow. Oh, I'm rambling again."

"No problem. I get aroused by your voice."

"Is your mother there?"

"In the living room watching TV—she can't hear me. I'm in the bedroom, headphones on, your pillow close. I relaxed, listened to your tape, and got incredibly aroused."

"I wish that pillow was me."

"Me, too, kid. Me, too."

Laura stared at her toes. "Your voice goes right through my skin and curls my toes. Um, I should go; collect calls are expensive."

"Cost will never be an issue, kid, but what **is** an issue is unless you keep your head clear, it'll drag on. I rehashed some of what you said when you were home, and I fear you lost focus. Stick to the assignment."

"Got it, Sergeant; thanks for the refresher course."

Laura found it easy to slide back into the community—scary, actually—to realize all it took was one birthday party, Sunday Service, and group breakfast to become involved. Mary McGuinn asked her to serve on the church landscaping committee; Rita Lezzaro recruited her to brainstorm fundraiser ideas so Angela's class could take a whale watch out of New Bedford; Brian reminded her about teaching an adult class in the fall and she agreed to estate planning and simple wills; Betsy from the post office cajoled her into volunteering time to negotiate contracts with vendors for the annual Harvest Festival; but the most interesting and challenging request came after Violet chaired a committee to craft a branding campaign for CFEL-sponsored business products. The goal was to capitalize on Vermont mystique and incorporate a ragtag Limited Liability Corporation known as *Fallsbridge Community Products* into *Nature's Bounties*, soon to expand to national markets. First task: secure the copyright and trademark protection to the name, since a vitamin manufacturer existed with a similar name. Slowly but surely Laura blended in but with a clear eye on her reasons for being in Fallsbridge. She rarely let her guard down and remained wary of every member of the CFEL; she had good reason to feel that way. Marsethe operated freely within the structure of the community. Hardest to forget, forgive, or overlook was Elder Vincent providing the doctor with an alibi for the night of the rape for injuries so severe, doctors claimed if she hadn't regained consciousness and choked, "Mom?" over and over from her dark bedroom, she'd have bled to death before dawn.

Without an appointment, Marsethe stopped by the office to compliment her on her work for the Choiniere brothers in obtaining a Vermont Seal of Quality from the State Department of Agriculture. "I understand Violet is equally impressed with your contribution to the expansion of *Nature's Bounties*."

"Thanks; I enjoy researching how other successful......"

Marsethe interrupted, "I'm also here to confess my research is stalled; I need evaluation of my work thus far."

Laura recalled his charts. "I'm not comfortable with the science and won't presume to offer insights into unknown territory."

"When might you be available?"

Laura preferred it be immediate but knew she lacked knowledge in the subject matter; she thumbed through her calendar. "I need preparation time. Tomorrow's my father's birthday, there's a party Saturday, and I'll be gone all weekend. How about Monday, same time as before? I'll check with Violet."

Marsethe stood with a smile. "It's good to care for others, so long as one remembers where she belongs, yes?"

103

Steve checked in with Bobby on the Buerton situation to find everything under control. "I'm out of here until Monday." At home, Steve found a note from his mother: *Stefan, I'll spend the weekend with a friend and call later with a number. I know you said it isn't necessary to be alone with Laura but I was a newlywed once and know you need the run of the house.*

Steve took a quick shower, changed into shorts and t-shirt, went onto the deck barefooted, and relaxed. He recalled Lynette said Laura promised to leave by 1:00, drive like a maniac, and show up by 4:00. At 4:26 he heard a driver grind into first, gun the engine, and head up. Steve tiptoed across gravel. "Ouch, ouch, ouch."

Laura hugged and groaned, "You showered? Why didn't you wait? You know how much I..."

"You nag something awful lately," Steve laughed and lifted her off her feet.

104

Ralph felt amused when Sigler asked for help. "I tracked Marie down and talked her into joining me for something social but she made it clear a birthday party is harmless enough. So, can we double date?"

Ralph thought to point out *cheap dates didn't impress wayward wives* but answered, "Sure; we'll pick you up tomorrow around 6:00."

Ralph chuckled when he and Joyce arrived at the Sigler house and found Marie leaning against her car. Seems the lady didn't care to go inside and chatted with her kids in the driveway. Ned hung out in the background and looked positively gleeful when Ralph parked behind Marie's car. She insisted they go in hers and Ralph figured: *Fine; the lady found her own voice and needs practice singing with it.* When they arrived at the Delorange house in Essex, Ralph reminded Joyce of the last time they were there for a party during the winter. She squeezed his hand and whispered, "Of course I remember."

They headed to the porch with a pretty little wrapped-up gift. When John answered and insisted none were expected, Ralph laughed, "Only barbarians show up empty-handed," which got a glare from Joyce. They crossed to the back yard where on a table, a metal bowl filled with ice and cans of beer, soda, iced tea, and lemonade waited invitingly for him to grab a brew for him and soda for Joyce. They wandered to folding chairs under maples and Ralph pointed to citronella candles. "Darlin',' this place looks like a newspaper insert for a lawn and garden center."

Joyce sniffed, "We could have a yard like this if we worked at it."

He sipped. "I like our yard fine—minimum maintenance time equals maximum relaxation time."

Ralph loved sitting in the shady shadows. From a safe distance with bomber sunglasses on, he observed doin's. Lynette and John were nervousy-hostessy types—they fussed over every detail, rearranged, reorganized, stood back, studied, and rearranged again. Rick, the good-looking baby of the family, showed up in casual chic: cut-off jeans with well-placed worn spots, an a-shirt which nicely displayed his chiseled chest and muscles, and sandals. That great-looking kid wore a thin chain around his neck, which when studied closely, indicated under the a-shirt rested an engagement ring returned by pretty little Gina. Joyce stared at Rick then sighed, "Stephanie Orsini screwed up so many lives."

"Does that mean you changed your mind about fidelity? Men no longer need to store peckers'n their pants?"

Joyce muttered, "Of course not."

Mick Scolarzski showed up with his grandmother, Lea. Ralph studied the kid and thought he definitely matured: no longer little Mickey but Mick The Man: good-looking in a different way from poster-pretty Rick. Mick looked rugged, durable, chunky in an athletic way, not fat. There were even a whole buncha baby chest hairs peeking out of his shirt.

Off by the gazebo—prettily surrounded by rose bushes—the Siglers were in the midst of an argument. No, it looked like Ned told his wife what to do and she crossed her arms over her chest to pout. Ralph leaned closer to Joyce and whispered, "Looks like we won't be parking later with our double-datees." When Joyce didn't answer, Ralph figured she reached that point when she ignored him. Roger and Helen Macrae arrived and made a bee-line for Ned and Marie. Ralph found it odd how after untold work hours together, they chose to socialize. But hey, he and Scolarzski were like that. Scolarzski. Damn. Nice of Lynette to invite the other detectives, but could the budster keep the secret? Roger and Helen were cuddly, playful, flirtatious and all that nice stuff that happened after a big scare like a major coronary. They fussed around the food and drinks in a way that suggested she cared what he put into his body and he liked the fact she did. Ned and Marie were a different story. Ned was a lyin' womanizer who—until Marie took off—pretended their marriage was fine. He denied he used his position to pick up all sortsa dizzy dames who found the concept of *a cop* erotic. Marie pretended she didn't have a problem with booze. At every social event, she sat by herself for hours 'n hours, a can or glass of soda clenched in her hands to prove she didn't need stronger fluid. Ralph suspected the instant she got home Marie poured a stiff one as a reward for getting through another day.

The budster and his bride were late, very late. When they finally showed, they got hugged 'n mauled. Ralph noticed a dainty flush covered every inch of the little lady's skin. Even his budster sported a warm glow. Ralph leaned close to Joyce and whispered, "Absolutely nothing renews a human spirit like 26 hours of uninterrupted sex."

He watched Laura pull Roger, Helen, Ned, and Marie aside. "Can the four of you keep our secret?"

Nice party: small, intimate, fun; the group chomped hot dogs, hamburgers, barbecued ribs, chicken, potato salad, corn on the cob, tossed salad, potato chips, pickles, olives—great stuff for lip smacking. Ralph took a plate back to his perch to watch the show: his budster's body never more than an inch from the little lady; John and Lynette fussed over something that fell off the side of the table; Helen removed half of the potato chips and all of the ribs from Roger's plate, substituting skinless chicken; and Ned gouged himself on everything while Marie picked at nothing. Ralph saw a mop of red hair run by and as Joyce sat down, pointed, "Pretty little Gina's here after all." Ralph watched her kiss Lynette, John, and Laura but not Rick; he barely got a nod. Ralph saw a sweetie, an angel—like expensive bookends, she and Rick a perfect pair.

Gina filled a plate and with a timid smile, headed over to an empty seat. "Hello, I'm Gina Farrusco. I don't think we've met." Joyce introduced them both and confessed they met in March at another party. Ralph saw her blush and decided one way or another, Rick's torture would end when Gina said, "I can't forget the betrayal."

Joycie answered, "Infidelity's a tough sin to forget but a woman in love gives her man one last chance before goodbye."

Ralph decided it boiled down to the girl loved the guy and vice versa. He wandered through groups of chatterers and gossipers, barged in as the budster planted a sloppy one on his bride, and squeezed the Mick Man's biceps. Ralph found Rick hiding inside. "It's none of my business but there's a redhead out there who looks like she's looking for you."

A slight difference in color but the eyes that smiled had the same beauty as his big sister's: sad, dark, soulful, and oddly enough, sparkling, too. Rick whispered, "Really?"

Ralph picked at his cuticles and offered a piece of advice. "That one's the serious type. A man should never make a move with a woman that fine unless he's prepared to give her everything." The rest went off like a hitch. Sure, Ralph saw awkward shyness, a blush or two, a tied-up tongue, but a lot of love screamin' to be set free. He noticed Laura's eyes scanned the crowd and settled on his as if to say *I know what you did and I love you for it.* He let his breath out slowly. "Yeah, well, I love you, too."

"Thanks," Joycie answered with a quick squeeze of his hand. Ralph settled back and watched the evening progress. In the end, romance floated in the air alongside fireflies for everyone except miserable Marie and nasty Ned.

105

On Monday, Laura started the customary routine after a weekend with Steve: she woke at 5:00 AM, dressed quietly, and tried to kiss him goodbye without disturbing his sleep but Steve rolled over to say, "Don't call tonight. I've fallen behind and now it'll be worse because all I'll think about is you."

"Okay; I promise to go back and shove things forward in that shitty little town." She arrived in Fallsbridge with barely enough time to change; the first thing she did from her desk was call Violet, verify the meeting with Marsethe, and agree to meet for dinner.

The day turned out to be a drag until Al stopped by late in the day. "When can I expect a bill?"

"I forwarded a worksheet to Burlington for processing."

227

"How many hours at what outrageous fee can I expect?"

"I reported 20 hours at $150 per."

"That's all? You put in a hell of a lot more than that."

"I'm glad you think it's fair."

"Fair? Shit; I got my girls back, my life, and my job."

"I could send an amended invoice if that would make you feel better," Laura chuckled and gestured toward the door. "Sorry but I have a dinner engagement."

"Too bad; I planned to ask you to join me for dinner in a faraway place like Honolulu or Tokyo."

"Oh, how I'd love to escape this shitty little town."

They crossed the green toward the inn as Al reported he returned to full rotation. "If you need me, call my office number days or home number nights; cell coverage is too spotty."

"Don't I know it! Every time I need to talk to someone in Chittenden County, I use a New Hampshire pay phone."

"Another way is to keep an eye out. I love to show up unannounced so the elders get frazzled at the sight of me." He turned serious and faced her. "Earlier today a reporter called about my return to active duty, which raised questions about the secretiveness surrounding the disposition of the case. If she's any good at her job, she'll dig into public records and sniff out talkative clerks. It'll be public knowledge as early as tomorrow. Did you fess up yet with these freaks you got me off?"

Laura admitted no but would do it that night. She nodded goodbye, pushed the heavy door open, and smiled as Glenn hurried over. When he heard she planned to meet Violet, he looked disappointed but recovered quickly. "I'm glad you stopped by. The Essex County Business Cooperative has its quarterly meeting tomorrow night so once Muriel takes over set-up, I'm free. I thought we could drive to Newport, have dinner, and see a movie. I can't recall the last one I saw one in a theater."

Laura shrugged, "I fell behind on Mel's patent application so how about Saturday? We can meet here at 4:00."

Dinner with Violet was fun; she had a sly sense of humor and away from her family, a bawdy one at that. When Violet confessed she always felt giddy after an afternoon with her lover, Laura glanced around. "Aren't you the one who warns me to keep my voice down?"

Violet shrugged, "Love terrifies the CFEL, not sex."

Laura moved her chair closer, lost balance, and landed on her wrist with a groan. Glenn rushed over to ask if she fainted and Laura laughed, "No, Violet said something unexpected and I got distracted."

Before she knew it, Violet pulled her car around and Glenn escorted her outside. They drove the equivalent of one city block to the doctor's office. All the way in and onto his examination table, Laura argued, "It's the heat, humidity, and sip of wine on an empty stomach."

Marsethe checked her wrist and wrapped it. He listened to her lungs and heart, took her pulse, and studied pupil response to a light. "Years ago when Sweet Lynette's mother Marie Marceau experienced balance problems, I suggested a series of tests to confirm or eliminate an inherited disorder. Lynette declined the offer for your family but..."

"I'm fine," Laura interrupted.

"You know of my interest in family history and..."

"I said I'm fine!"

"Okay, then let's agree at times of dehydration, water and fruit juices are preferable to wine, yes?"

In the end, Laura and Violet never finished dinner, Glenn never returned for rush hour, and he joined them. Laura soon discovered she wasn't the only one who saw the full scope of his work for the first time. With theatrical flair, Marsethe unrolled and displayed the first of three charts. Laura studied what appeared to be a genealogical history spanning seven generations of one family: first names with dates of birth by year, interconnecting lines, notes. She focused on a confusing section where one female seemed connected to three sets of initials. She skimmed the bottom of the chart and noted small numbers with additional letter references. She expected to find a key to the symbols and ran her eyes across every inch but couldn't find one. She straightened up. "Mel, during your sermon, you said the CFEL began a fourth generation."

"I admire your attention to detail! Yes, that's what I stated." He pointed to a series of black lines and explained he gathered pertinent information verbally or from town records and birth certificates, while color lines indicated a direct intervention to amend the bloodline. He unrolled the second chart and spread it out.

Laura studied red, green, and blue lines. "This may sound stupid, but how does one intervene directly?"

"Scientific intervention leaves little chance of error."

"But what does that mean?" Laura repeated.

"At another time we'll see more," Marsethe whispered and Laura shivered at the intimacy in his voice: the same voice she heard in his parlor one afternoon, the same voice she heard in a dark bedroom one windy night, the same voice that promised there'd be no pain, the same voice that whispered lies of love. She felt the blood rush to her head, feared she'd faint, and steadied herself by touching a table. No one noticed.

Glenn touched a rolled-up third chart. "What about this?"

Marsethe grabbed it, refused to unroll it, and at repeated requests, sneered, "Glenn, Family Y would be known to you instantly! Discretion in research is required."

Marsethe insisted they sit and used a laminated wall board, wipe-off markers, and pointer to present material in as organized a lecture as any she attended in college or law school. Laura found his information fascinating and listened to explanations of dominant and recessive genes, inheritable traits, the matrix, and markers. Laura thought of the child she yearned to create with Steve. His eyes were blue, hers brown; his body round and sturdy, hers long and slender; his fingers long and tapered, hers short and stubby; his talents in music, hers in language; he tanned with hair lightened by the sun, she burned and freckled with hair always black. Laura returned full attention when Marsethe's tone shifted as he presented material in a dry, factual tone and drew x's and y's familiar to her from biology coursework with a concise explanation why the male and only the male determined gender of offspring. He drew an unusual configuration and stated, "At times, males are born xyy and research indicates a second y often present in death row inmates. Such knowledge will be of use to law enforcement in the future, since existence of a second y suggests antisocial, aggressive, violent, and criminal behavior."

Laura squinted, "If I understand theories of heredity correctly, wouldn't that be called a predisposition?"

Marsethe chuckled, "I would imagine someone with an interest in law enforcement would see value in such knowledge."

Laura shrugged, "What if it led to profiling?"

Violet interrupted, "I don't understand any of this."

Marsethe ignored her and continued with a presentation of the double matrix. "Many genetic functions remain unmapped and in light of miraculous discoveries every day, I will never again question use of the word *quality* in reference to the sperm and eggs of others." He stared directly at Laura and laughed, "It is true you hear your offensive word again but simply because one is able to reproduce does not mean one has the right to do so to the agony of us all."

Laura swallowed hard. "What do you suggest: sterilization of an imperfect adult or abortion of an imperfect fetus?"

"I fail to see how your question deserves an answer."

"It does! No one has the right to intervene into private lives."

Marsethe's voice rose as he leaned forward and pointed his finger at her abdomen. "Within you lie millions of quality eggs. Why question something which does not affect individuals like you, Glenn or Violet? Do we debate a principle here?"

Laura noticed how uncomfortable Violet and Glenn looked and smiled. "Even as a kid, Mel, you knew I loved a good debate."

His eyes softened. "That you always did, Little Miss."

Laura concentrated on every word about genetic selection and studied the chart. "Is this known as eugenics?"

"Yes!" Marsethe turned to write on his laminated board and explained, "Eugenics: the science of improving the human race by controlling hereditary factors is derived from the Greek *eugenes* as in well-born—a worthwhile endeavor."

Laura sighed, "That depends on methods," and watched Marsethe tape a second chart of Family K on the wallboard.

He pointed at one square after another. "Had these fertile idiots in Generation 2 tripped along their natural path, the result as we begin Generation 4 would have been countless heathens and lowlifes."

Laura cleared her throat. "How was the path changed?"

Marsethe tapped the pointer at every male in Generation 2 and all but four females. "First, I disabled every male's ability to reproduce; second I performed tubal ligation after birth to all but four females with surprisingly high IQ's; third, with carefully-selected sperm I inseminated fertile women artificially; and fourth, the resulting products were bright, healthy children rather than rejects."

Glenn asked, "What do you mean by disabled?"

Marsethe rushed through an accurate drawing of male genitalia. "In the 60's males saw birth control as a female issue; vasectomies are commonplace now but not then. The vas deferens is this convoluted duct through which sperm is transported from the testicles here to the ejaculatory duct of the penis here. A surgical slice at this point and voilà! Not one spermatozoon escapes."

Violet leaned close to study the chart. "Was disabling or tube-tying voluntary? Did people know what would occur?"

Marsethe nodded. "If you don't believe me, do research. In Vermont and many other states nationwide, social agencies supported sterilization of known undesirables. In fact, many state agencies paid for procedures as a method to cleanse their rolls of systemic neer-do-wells."

Violet sighed, "That's disgusting."

"Is it? If you were older, you'd recall the dismal population inhabiting these square miles we're now proud to call home. Imagine families with eight or nine children yet no toilets or running water, no fresh fruit or produce nine months a year. Imagine, too, enough time and seclusion to produce yet another undesirable."

Violet shook her head and repeated, "That's disgusting."

Marsethe laughed, "No, it turned out to be costly. Again, do your research and see how North Carolina and California now pay dearly in victims' fees for mistakes of the past."

Laura asked, "Because the public discovered the truth?"

Marsethe sputtered, "No, truth was always known by visionaries but pioneers of select breeding kept records on paper for do-good muckrakers to uncover and share with the world."

Laura recalled Claudette Theriault Adams' statement: *"With a husband and child at home, I conducted research in person, left them behind, presented myself to the CFEL doctor, and submitted to tests and scheduled assignations with Brian."* When something squeezed her shoulder, Laura jumped and stared into amazing blue eyes. "Are you among us?"

Laura nodded and realized they reached a perfect moment to disclose the settlement of Al's case. "Sorry I wandered off; but um when I spoke to Al Wilkers about the settlement of his case, I learned his and Frannie's baby is due soon. Were they hand-picked for each other or...?"

Marsethe slapped his pointer on the table. "This is news to me and the elders. How was the case settled?"

Laura shrugged, "Charges were dropped for lack of conclusive evidence," and at Marsethe's glare, added, "The judge found Tina's testimony incoherent. Mel, you didn't answer my question."

Marsethe confessed upon his expectation of excellence, the elders endorsed a Wilkers-Stenzola coition. His eyes sparkled. "One man's seed, mother and daughter eggs: a race to conception, so to speak, similar to that of thoroughbreds, yes?"

Laura studied her knuckles. "A sad story if you ask me."

Marsethe knelt on the floor beside her and in the voice that hurt so deeply, whispered, "Your generous heart shall make you a fine mother someday." He stood and continued, "I'm saddened that as the moment of birth draws near, the Wilkers-Stenzola specimen appears at risk. I suggest we reconvene in a week since some say knowledge is rewarding in and of itself, but I say with my guidance, you three shall be led into the astonishing science of our 21st Century."

106

Steve left work and wolfed down a cheeseburger, fries, and too many coffee refills. He regretted asking Laura not to call; those Monday night talks got him through anything. He returned to his desk to push paper and felt queasy—enough cholesterol in that meal to fill a week's quota. During his last physical, the doctor warned him to get the number down pronto. Sure, it felt easy to eat garbage but led to body-abusing behavior. He gave up smoking, didn't he? For two years and counting, he downed only one drink, right? He went through the discomfort of a vasectomy reversal, didn't he? With a young wife and a shared dream of a baby or two, he owed it to her and those unborn children to be around for decades. After everything else he did, learning to survive on bean sprouts to escort a daughter down the aisle someday felt like a piece of cake.

107

For Glenn, the week moved forward with catering demands, consults with Rita on a new menu design for printing, and hard work required of all small business owners. Still, Saturday couldn't come fast enough. Laura arrived at 4:00 as promised and he felt a surge of confidence at how she dressed and fixed her hair for their date. During dinner, she listened while he talked on and on in what he hoped sounded informed and cultured. He feared he babbled but needed something awkward out of the way. "Um about Mel's drawing the other night—that was too de-romanticized for me."

Laura laughed, "Me, too."

Glenn borrowed Mel's Cadillac Escalade for the air conditioning and the drive felt heavenly even when she leaned against the door. When he told a story about himself, Gil, and Jack as kids, she finally relaxed enough to smile. The movie was a blank, which felt embarrassing. What if Laura liked to discuss plot and dialogue over coffee afterwards? The more he demanded he pay attention, the less he did. As a 37-year-old man in love and willing to say so, it felt useless to worry whether or not he looked foolish. During the return drive, Laura said, "Like books, movies leave impressions and weeks later, I'll recall a phrase or envision a scene so I hope it's okay if don't talk about the movie. Jack's the exact opposite. He dissects eyebrow lifts."

Glenn sighed, "I'm like you; I get tongue-tied."

Glenn asked but Laura declined a glass of wine in his apartment or at the bar. Even though the clock read 10:30 and a new band performed on stage, Glenn felt obliged to take her home when she asked.

In the driveway, she made no move to jump out of the car and actually sat to talk. He imagined something might happen between them if he took it slow. He studied her eyes at every move and first, unfastened his seat belt; second, slid into the middle of the seat; third, put his arm around her shoulder, and fourth, pressed his lips to her temple.

Laura edged away. "Please don't touch me without permission."

Glenn followed her to the door as she fumbled with her key. "Laura, I'm sorry if the way I feel upsets you but…"

"Ask Mel why I'm afraid."

"Laura, I know you were raped."

"There's more. Ask Mel why I'm ashamed to let anyone closer." She slipped inside and closed the door softly,

Glenn returned to the village center, parked Mel's car in his garage, and knocked on the door to return keys. The old man answered in his robe and tsk'd, "Your hair is quite tousled. Please do not confess to a sticky stain on leather."

Glenn sneered, "That's disgusting. I sh…"

Mel laughed, "I see love for a girl who loves you not."

As always, Glenn felt blindsided but his reason for being there outweighed a need to avoid embarrassment. "I think Laura's coming around but when I tried to kiss her, she looked terrified. Why would she say she's ashamed to let me closer?"

Mel opened the door wide. "Ah, that one rests so deeply within herself, it is frightening to watch, yes?"

Glenn followed to the living room and cringed at the doctor's description of disfigurements on the body of a 13-year-old patient. "How'd they get there?"

"She claimed to have suffered an assault."

"She charged you."

"That she did but by her own admission, never saw a face. It wasn't me, Glenn; it could never be me. I could never hurt a child." As the old fool talked, he often closed his eyes and swayed to music in the background. As notes softened, Mel opened his eyes. "I imagine young men still love to move lips across skin on a path to that most responsive of all female places, imagine young men prefer such skin be uninterrupted."

Glenn stammered, "I heard stories over the years and remember how weird the elders got when the Deloranges left but never knew why they left when they did." Glenn headed toward the door for an easy departure if necessary. "Last week I heard there may be truth to Angela's claim her assault didn't occur in your office at all but at your boathouse."

Mel shrugged, "That child is like others who misinterpret an appreciation for their gifts to inappropriate actions on my part. As a physician overseeing maturity, physical exams often feel invasive."

"You didn't answer my question. Did Angela make her claims following a visit to your boathouse?"

"Wherever they occur, physical exams often feel invasive."

"You're sick."

"Am I? Or do I understand Laura has a flawless test: any man who endures the skin of her earns the love of her?"

"Is that what will happen to Angela soon?"

Mel smiled. "How would I know if a beast lurks nearby?"

Glenn repeated, "You're sick," and left. He walked through woods behind the academy to the carriage house and knocked. A beam from a flashlight hit his face as Laura opened the door. "Run out of gas?"

"No; I'd like to talk about what you said earlier."

"Not here; Brian... never mind." With the flashlight, Laura led him into the woods along a familiar hiking path. When they reached the boulder at the river, she turned the flashlight off and stared at a starry sky. "It's different here at night, don't you think?"

He glanced around. "Do you do this often at night?"

She shrugged, "Not since I was a kid."

In light from the moon, Glenn studied her face and said, "Mel will never admit what he did to you and Angela was wrong. If there's any shame, it's for Mel to live with, not you."

Laura took his hand and led him back to the carriage house. His mind raced through possible scenarios, including a recurring dream she'd invite him in. She didn't but at her door, she kissed him lightly on the lips and whispered, "You know there was someone else but if I ever love another man, he will be you."

108

Bobby figured another weekend watching Buerton's house was smart but didn't expect help from other detectives or troopers. With a thin case and everyone stretched thin, he'd conduct surveillance alone, not 24 / 7 but in spurts—on his own time, in his own car, without back-up from assholes who found it okay if one of their own missed an important social event. All day Saturday he parked in the trees in partial view of the lady's property and tried to stay alert. It didn't work. Bobby awakened Sunday morning when sky brightened, rubbed his neck, and studied the house. Perfectly quiet. He watched a car slow to stuff a

Sunday *Free Press* in her box, then a car filled with folks in their Sunday best cruised by. Bobby worked out the kinks in his neck and rolled the window down to gulp fresh air—another hot day on its way for sure. He watched Ms. Buerton come out with a basket of laundry, shake wrinkles out of each garment then clasp clothespins. She moved unbelievably slow and for saying the air felt above 70° already, looked weird in long pants and sweatshirt. She wore sunglasses, too—odd since it was barely daylight. Every time she lifted a new item of clothing, she glanced at a particular window. She looked confused, fearful. Something rang familiar and Bobby recalled Scolarzski's notes: neighbors of the woman Sivalette allegedly murdered a year ago testified they saw her on a number of occasions throughout the weekend her killer was already in her house; one neighbor testified he watched her hang laundry. Bobby gasped, "Damn," grabbed binoculars and studied the window closest to the clothes line. He tried not to blink as he watched for movement. Stillness paid off when he detected a glint of metal behind a screen. When Ms. Buerton emptied the basket and turned away, , Bobby observed a limp. He grabbed his Glock, checked for ammunition, and lifted his cell. "I'm at Buerton's and God damn it, someone else is in the house!"

Scolarzski calmly asked questions then instructed Bobby to remain in his vehicle, keep an eye on the house, and wait for back-up. "I'll dispatch a trooper and head over myself but wait for back-up!"

Bobby dropped the phone, grunted, "Like hell," climbed over the gear shift, opened the passenger door, and rolled to the ground. He crept on hands and knees through brambles, twigs, and branches to reach a corner. It seemed only seconds passed before a cruiser screamed into the driveway and stopped. Bobby groaned, "Why the noise?" as a second cruiser tore around back. Two troopers communicated with arm gestures: one to the back, one to the front. When Bobby dashed from the corner one trooper raised his weapon; Bobby raised his shield and shouted—just enough time and confusion for a man to barge out the back door and tackle the trooper. Bobby rushed to jump on top.

109

At services, Laura joined Glenn in a forward pew. Elder Matthew presented the guest sermon, a confusing fire and brimstone bit about physical, intellectual, emotional, and spiritual laziness. She found it odd how he neglected the need for moral or ethical strength and imagined that was intentional—for the assembled group, it was easier to be told every rule up front. Laura felt the telltale tug, turned, and smiled at

David. She was surprised Reilly was nowhere in sight and remembered she requested vacation time. When David bounced on the seat, arms extended, Laura asked for permission. At Mary's smile and nod, Laura lifted the squirmy angel over the pew and buried her nose in his cheek. David pressed his mouth to hers and blew spit bubbles. When Glenn stared, Laura settled David down but Glenn's look wasn't one of disapproval; he leaned close to whisper, "We could have one of our own."

After services, Glenn invited her to breakfast but she declined. "I signed up to work at the farm later, too, but hope to be excused—not because I'm lazy but feel sick again."

Marsethe overheard and studied her eyes. "Many feel out of sorts in this weather, yes? Rest in bed with music off and curtains drawn."

Laura returned to the carriage house, changed into her ugly yellow nightgown, and collapsed in bed. She heard a knock and opened the door to Glenn. "Here; take this; you'll feel better." He left and Laura devoured the fruit salad, yogurt, and quarter-loaf of banana-nut bread.

110

As two ambulances blew by, Steve braked hard, jumped out, and asked a uniformed trooper, "Jim, what happened?" Steve didn't wait for the answer but ran to Rawlings who winced in pain as one EMT tied a tourniquet around his left leg and another dressed a wound on his upper left arm. As EMTs lifted Rawlings into the first ambulance, Steve watched others load a man who resembled Sivalette into the second.

Rawlings groaned, "I screwed up, Steve, but she's alive."

Jim added, "The victim's in her kitchen, a mess, but coherent."

Steve whispered, "Rawlings, I'll be by the hospital later," headed inside, and cringed at what should have been a familiar face. As an EMT tied a cuff to measure blood pressure, Steve sat and said, "I apologize for having to ask but describe what happened."

"He had a gun and knife; he stabbed one cop in the stomach then Sergeant Rawlings jumped on top. I think he got stabbed, too."

Steve took her hands in his. "How can I help?"

"I'm okay," She insisted but as her eyes filled with tears, she turned to the technician. "I'm sorry; you were right about the hospital. I should go; I'm bleeding in places that... uh, I'm bleeding bad."

111

At work Monday, Laura felt disoriented without Reilly there; when she arranged time off she said she planned to accompany a friend out of state but offered few details. Laura realized she hadn't seen Gil and imagined they were together. Laura spent the day on the kind of activities that required concentration and helped pass time. After what she deemed a productive day, she headed to the carriage house, cleaned the bathroom, ate a light supper, and weeded the garden. Finally, she saw the clock reached 8:30 and flew across the bridge to Littleton.

Steve blurted, "Rawlings completed a long-overdue investigation yesterday, got stabbed twice and…"

"He's fine, right? He'll recover?"

"He'll be fine but limp for a while. I feel like the world's worst colleague because since the incident, all I think about is you. My God, the rape victim herself looked so…."

"Wounded and destroyed?"

"Yeah; how'd you survive such a thing, Laura? And how did a guy like me earn your trust?"

"I waited my whole life for you."

"Jesus, kid, I don't know what to…"

"Don't say a thing, mister. Count the days until I'm home."

August crawled in bogged down by excessive heat and humidity. On the first Monday, Laura dressed for work and stared at how her boobs popped out of her bra; her breasts felt tender lately, sore even. She adjusted and figured *I gained weight*. She turned sideways and noticed a bit rounder belly. *Dear God in heaven, can it be?"* At work, Laura studied Reilly on her first day back and thought *she seems different: more confident, more relaxed, and remarkably more beautiful.* For a change, Reilly preferred not to talk so Laura didn't push. As Reilly prepared to leave, she phoned someone to share a sweet, flirty conversation. Laura couldn't resist and whispered. "I hope you and Gil enjoyed the luxury of privacy."

Reilly asked Laura to follow her outside and on the bench in the green, asked, "I can trust you, right?"

"I'd like to believe by now, you know you can."

Reilly nodded. "Gil looked for another job away from here and I went for a pregnancy test away from Mel."

"And? Come on!"

"I'm due the first week of February."

"You two got married, too, didn't you?"

"There's no way you can know this much."

"I overheard enough the week before you left to put two and two together. I did some digging and discovered Gil registered for a law enforcement conference in New Mexico."

Reilly gasped, "It's not only the CFEL that spies!" looked around to make sure they were alone, and described a small ceremony with two strangers as witnesses, a wonderful week of touristy visits around Santa Fe, job interviews, and a visit to a new doctor. "The best part of all? We registered at the hotel as husband and wife without fear."

"I envy you," Laura whispered.

After work, Laura drove to Groveton and called Essex. "Mom, how'd you know you were pregnant?"

"Skipped periods, tender breasts, bloating, and morning sickness. Honey, are you?"

"Probably not; remember my exam before college? The doctor said with my history, it's unlikely. I never cared before now."

"See a doctor immediately and if you test positive, come home."

"What bothers me is humidity and lack of sleep."

"I'll call my doctor's office and beg for an appointment. So hang up and give me a number so I can call back with the details.""

"Mom, I think I can find a doctor in St. Johnsbury or..."

"No! I recall a graphic description of your uterus and I'm frightened. Honey, you have a husband who loves you! Don't you realize you can't make important decisions alone anymore?"

"Steve can't hear about this yet; I won't raise false hopes."

"Okay for now but give me a number to call you back."

"Um, I don't think this takes incoming calls."

"Okay, hang up and call back in 10 minutes."

Laura waited, looked around, paced, needed to use the bathroom, and dialed. "Any luck?"

"No one can see you 'til Friday at 3:30. It's a half-hour drive from here, then parking, so be here no later than 2:30. If you feel it's easier to get away with a reason, tell those nosy sons of bitches I have a follow-up appointment to a test."

"Is that true?"

"Yes; I fell again last week, cracked my head pretty good, and had an MRI. I see a neurologist to hear an assessment."

"I'm sorry you had to go through that. Did Dad...?"

"John doesn't handle things like this well so Gina drove me."

"Um, that was nice of Gina but I'm hurt you didn't call me."

"Sweetheart, I had another stupid fall."

"Mom, you..."

"Laura, what's done is done."

"All right; I'll see you Friday afternoon."

Laura dialed Steve's direct line to hear a growled, "What now!"

"Hey, mister, can I come home this weekend?"

"You're kidding, right? Don't you know I'd lie naked in poison oak to see you again so soon?"

"I'll be late."

"Not a problem, kid; never will be. Oh, thanks for the card. The weekend forecast includes warm, starry nights, half moon."

112

Gil waited until after the dinner rush to ask for a loan but when Glenn the original let's-do-it-by-the-booker asked questions, Gil stood. "Never mind; I wouldn't have this much trouble at the fucking bank."

Glenn pulled him back to a chair. "Why cash? Be honest."

Gil scanned the area for big ears. "Reilly's pregnant and I want us out of here before that becomes obvious."

"All of you? David?"

"For Christ's sake, of course! A baby needs to be with his mother." At his brother's terrified look, Gil preferred to think Glenn cared enough to worry about him but he knew Glenn didn't want to hear anything that might force him to take sides. Gil stood again. "Bad idea."

"You know how it is; none of us has much cash, anyway, but I know how to get my hands on $12,000."

Gil sat again. "How? I wouldn't want you to have to get a second mortgage or sell something."

"There's no mortgage on the Maidstone but during the winter, Mel noticed the roof needs repair and as the corporation's major stockholder, set up a joint escrow account requiring only one signature for transactions. "

Gil felt torn. On the one hand, he wanted to get his new family far, far away; on the other, his brother would be left to face fury. "Forget it; I won't put you in this position."

Glenn snorted, "You always whine the old man has a soft spot for me. Mel's excited he may get what he wants soon."

"Oh? How are things going in your pursuit of Laura?"

Glenn stared across to the law office. "I know she's fond of me but if God's listening to my prayers, she'll come around."

Gil confessed the rest of his news about marriage and at Glenn's sudden hug, pulled back. "Stupid move, Glenn. I'm sure someone saw so when the old man asks, you asked for pick-up advice. Got it?"

113

Mel unrolled the chart of Family Y, the one he refused to show Glenn. The doctor pulled reading glasses on, moved his fingertips across the middle row, and painstakingly erased the *Laura* notation beside the entry *Gilbert* and switched it to *Glenn*. He took drafting tools and drew a straight black line down for the entry of a first child. As Mel rolled the chart and reinserted it in its plastic sleeve, he recalled Matthew said two brothers sat at a window table that very evening and imagined as when they were boys, Gil and Glenn conspired against authority. He laughed, "So be it," started a CD of clarinet concertos, and lifted the phone to summon Glenn.

"Can't do it, Mel. I have an emergency with a guest who discovered a large spider in her bedding. She raises holy hell so let me take care of her and I'll be there when I can."

Mel hung up and admired his progress on photo albums. During his visit with Lynnandra, he felt impressed by his father's organization of the lifetimes of those Gerald loved. When he returned home, Mel spent hours every evening sorting thousands of photographs in boxes and organizing them into albums. Mel checked the clock, waited patiently, and noticed Glenn failed to knock for 51 minutes. Mel decided to let the insult pass but not without comment once Glenn described the invader. "In the future, learn to distinguish a threat! To the untrained eye, a wolf spider is mistaken for a tarantula, its 1/2-inch body covered in hair like distant cousins. Though common to natural areas in Vermont, your nocturnal specimen will bite if handled or provoked. As temperatures cool, they seek dank areas such as basements or cellars. My guess is she came in on clothing or firewood." In response to Glenn's blank nod, Mel chuckled, "I do love my educator role, yes?" and invited Glenn inside.

When Mel mentioned Matthew watched two brothers wheel and deal that afternoon at the restaurant, Glenn sighed but sat down without a word. Mel suggested he hear it directly before he found out later and Glenn shrugged, "We discussed all kinds of things."

Mel leaned forward. "Discuss this discussion."

"I asked for pointers with women; no big deal."

"I'm disappointed. Laura seeks a man with sensitivity and intelligence not experience. Don't you understand?"

"Yes."

"Fine; we start." Mel led Glenn into the den and pointed to a row of maroon leather albums, touched one, and whispered, "A man with time and interest studies the one he loves from pre-birth to womanhood. The Laura we both love can be uncovered in her entirety here."

Glenn moved close to study labels. "I can look at one?"

"You may look at all." Mel watched Glenn withdraw the first in the series of nine, pleased he had sense to begin at the beginning. Glenn leaned over a photograph of a very young and beautiful Lynette at a picnic, her body rounded and sublimely womanly, a smile upon her beautiful face as she caressed her abdomen. He left Glenn to his privacy and felt no surprise when seven hours later, he wandered downstairs and found the den still lit up, eight albums spread across the desk, couch, and table as the young man studied the ninth.

114

The instant she woke, Laura grabbed her personal calendar, flipped to the back, and counted the remaining squares for August and September—six weeks and three days remained until Steve and she would celebrate their marriage with a public ceremony and reception. As she dressed for work, Laura turned sideways and stared at herself in the mirror. If she were correct, during their celebration they'd announce a new life would enter their world soon.

At 9:00, Laura entered the law office, stunned when Reilly turned away abruptly. Violet sat in a chair primly holding her purse while beside the photocopier Peg, Maria, and Tina Stenzola stood like statues. In her office, Marsethe used the phone—weird enough but when Elder Matthew headed out of the bathroom wiping his hands, Laura gasped, "What's going on?" Marsethe guided her to a chair and turned to speak privately to Peg. Laura stood again and laughed, "Why does my office feel like the circus came to town?" but stopped when she noticed Tina's tears.

Marsethe stated. "Last night there were complications with the Wilkers-Stenzola specimen."

Laura turned to Peg. "What happened?"

"My grandson never whimpered or..."

Laura glared at Marsethe. "Why are you here?"

Marsethe shooed the girls with: "Cross the street safely and wait on a bench like little ladies." He turned back. "The Council of Elders believes when Wilkers hears he fathered a son, a tragedy turns nasty."

"How?"

Marsethe shrugged, "Possibly malpractice or worse; as a former one, you understand cops are distrustful and paranoid."

Laura glanced at Peg, who seemed strangely composed, and thought *Peg knows for a fact he didn't die. Peg knows.* Laura repeated her question. "Why are you here?"

Marsethe responded, "As a respected colleague who aided him recently, we imagine he might accept your counsel more than ours."

Laura fought not to laugh or cry at the predictability—they offered a chance to prove allegiance to the community and loyalty to its doctor—not to mention measure ardor, obedience, and submission to that elusive otherworldliness the CFEL promised its devoted faithful. Laura nodded. "Even in his moment of pain, he'll listen to me." As the group left, she found their conversations odd: weather, lack of rain on the corn crop, and an upcoming guest sermon by Brian concerning the need to attack discipline problems at the academy head on. Laura glanced at Reilly; it seemed obvious she struggled to stay composed and Laura fought an urge to reassure her that the *specimen* was in all likelihood alive, healthy, and sold to the highest bidder. Laura decided not yet, definitely not yet and grabbed her purse. "I need to see Al before he hears about this over an English muffin and coffee."

Reilly's head shot around like a cannon. "How awful! You sound flippant and cruel like Mel!" Laura thought to argue *I only play a part* but felt humbled and escaped.

115

Al took a call from Scolarzski about a micro-cassette tape he found gathering dust on top of a file cabinet. "Laura wrapped a note around asking they be converted to numbers. Granger said he didn't have time to handle it so I had tech guys do it. Any idea why she needs this?"

"No, but I'll pass the information along."

Al hung up and studied the 11 digits: a New Hampshire area code and rural western Coos County exchange, a short hop across state lines. He dialed and heard a woman: "You've reached the home of Joseph and Kristina Logen. Please leave a message!"

Al jotted names alongside the number as a car pulled into the lot, recognized it as Laura's, and went out to greet her. "Steve had your tape analyzed. Why do you need this?"

Her pupils dilated to pinpricks. "Marsethe claims Frannie delivered a stillborn baby boy overnight."

Al shook his head. "No, Frannie isn't due for…"

"Listen to me; I said he claims she did."

Al stared at passing traffic and thought *why so much noise in the world? Why so many people and cars making so much racket?* He felt shocked to climb out of Laura's car; he never felt it move but there they were, miles from his desk. He followed her into a restaurant and heard her order for them both. A coffee arrived and a cup of tea with a wedge of lemon—so annoying to watch her use fingers to squeeze liquid into her cup. He closed his eyes and tried hard to deny he and Frannie created a child in the first place, extra hard to listen to Laura's explanation about a conversation she overheard at a birthday party. *A birthday party?* Weirder than that was her theory about his son. In the end, Al knew where Laura headed and choked, "Don't ask me to do nothing!"

Laura insisted with his help, she'd get inside and sounded confident as she outlined a scenario: "First, I convince them I returned to the fold; second, you appear to accept the infant's death as the will of God; third, your silence buys me valuable time to gain access to records; fourth, I find who has your son; and fifth, the State of Vermont nails the bastards for baby-trafficking. I'm convinced years ago Marsethe did the same thing with my niece or nephew."

"You're nuts if you expect me to sit back and…"

"Wait! You of all people know how methodical he is. Marsethe saw you as an impressive addition to his project but as a grieving father assures no one takes your investigation seriously."

Al studied Laura's face, recognized she believed every word, and thought *Laura presents her theories succinctly and lets me goddamn think.* "Okay, you have two weeks to find evidence; then I go to the authorities."

"Two weeks? You're kidding! It's taken me more than two months to get to this point; I need more time."

Al choked, "Don't ask! In that length of time, a baby becomes attached to who he thinks his parents are."

"Um, how about a month?"

Al tapped his coffee spoon over and over. "One month, counselor, then I shout to the high heavens!"

116

Laura returned to the office and bolted into the bathroom with no time to close the door before she fell to her knees and vomited. At her desk, Reilly grimaced and held her abdomen. Laura rinsed her mouth, washed her hands and face, and leaned against the door jamb. "I'm sorry but my conversation with Al was heart-wrenching."

"How awful for him and Frannie—I mean, they weren't a great couple but were a great match."

Laura forced herself to her desk chair, felt she might vomit again, pulled a drawer open, and stuffed a handful of saltines into her mouth. *There isn't enough time to do everything; what can I hope to accomplish in another month? I need to be with my husband, too, but how can I move an investigation forward more than 130 miles away from one shitty little town?* She closed her eyes to three weird sensations at once: her head throbbed, stomach churned, and boobs hurt. She opened her eyes and grunted, "Hnnh?"

Marsethe stood a foot away, eyes focused on the open drawer and waxed paper sleeve. "Your stomach remains unsettled?"

Laura stammered, "Um. I often vomit when I'm stressed."

Marsethe smiled in his patronizing way. "Reilly informs me the Wilkers deed is accomplished successfully."

Laura nodded. "When I left him, Al seemed angry but not vindictive. He thought the baby was born too early."

Marsethe laughed, "I'm not surprised. Libidinous men see no clues as to onset of pregnancy and thus easily misreport due dates." When Laura squinted in confusion, the doctor added, "Ejaculation is the primary focus; what is important is the availability of a partner for recreational coition, not a budding life carried undetected."

"Are you saying Frannie's baby was full term?"

"If you wish to know of the entirety of my project, are you willing to barter for the privilege?"

"I have nothing to offer except legal advice."

Marsethe leaned close. "No, you have the quality gift of you. Picture how one young man's life might change within a calendar year."

Laura thought *he sets things up too smoothly and gives the only acceptable answer ahead of time*. She stared at her left hand, imagined she saw two rings where they belonged, and whispered, "If I found the courage to enter a new relationship, it would be Glenn."

He grabbed her chin. "Say those words eye level."

Laura felt terrified at how readily he inflicted pain but answered, "With Glenn, I'm willing to try."

Marsethe rambled on about deadlines only he knew existed, then nodded. "I foresee October 1 as agreeable for you to begin an intimate relationship with the town's finest bachelor." Laura's mind raced again. *October 1? Al ties my hands and now Marsethe ties access to his project to a sexual involvement with Glenn? My investigation's doomed. I spun my wheels for more than two months, only to arrive at a point where...* Laura felt pain as Marsethe

245

pinched her cheek. "Pay attention! There is much to be done. I will see to arrangements with Violet and Glenn and expect the third of my Three Little Musketeers to arrive at my lab promptly at 6:30 this evening."

Laura saw no connection between the conversation and what appeared to be an invitation to another visit to the lab. She blinked slowly and forced a weak smile. "I'll be there."

117

Someone shouted he had a call and Glenn raced across the dining area only to hear Mel snort, "You sound out of breath. Did you hope to hear from your dream lover?"

Glenn sighed, "I'm busy, Mel. What can I do for you?"

"Be here at 6:30 to join me and the ladies."

"Laura?"

"And Violet—do not be so insulting and unfeeling like insensitive Brian and overlook sweet Violet."

Glenn studied the wait staff schedule and figured with Muriel off, wiser to stay. He pictured Laura's face that night in the woods and thought *with a slight break in humidity she might not feel so drained and agree to a walk or drive or who knows what?* and answered, "I'll be there."

When he arrived, Glenn found Laura, Violet, and Mel sipped iced tea in the gazebo. Mel held a glass in the air and waved it. "Mr. Busy Businessman honors us with his presence."

Glenn felt embarrassed but followed everyone inside. When Laura stopped to study an 11 x 14" group photograph of a summer picnic, Glenn pointed to a young Peg Stenzola with a toddler in her lap. "That's Frannie; over here's Jack, you, Gil, and me. These two are Greg and Garry, and the tomboy with the filthy face is Reilly as a toddler."

Laura leaned close. "Should I remember Greg and Garry?"

Glenn looked for Mel and laughed, "Thereupon you find reflected the faces of the older Munier G-boys, yes?"

Glenn caught a glimpse of a glare as Mel inched over, touched the glass, and murmured, "The face of every soul I love is reflected here but two. My mother lived far away and one not yet born: Angela—loved already at a mere promise of her conception." He sighed and pointed. "And Little Miss Francesca Theresa Stenzola is a precious beauty, yes?"

Laura turned to Glenn. "Frannie's initials are FTS?"

Glenn nodded and waited for her to continue but she turned back to study the photograph. Mel insisted the three take their seats and proceeded to confuse with a summary explanation of more than 60 years of history of people in the area: who married who, who moved where, who served in war, who came back, who shirked their responsibility to serve, who died from polio, who lost a farm, who died in tractor accidents, and who committed suicide. He unrolled a chart and taped corners to the wall: an inverted triangle with a set of x's at the base and two sets of x's immediately above, the remainder covered with lettering until along the top line, a series of 30 or more sets of initials, letters so tiny, Glenn couldn't read them. He glanced at Violet and Laura, who seemed confused, too. The old man took a pointer and tapped along the top. "All project babies born in a two-year stretch were progeny of one of six members of the first, influential group from Boston: surgeon, college president, physicist, businessman, doctor, and writer; a second generation of project babies followed three years fathered by an equally influential group, some from the first but new members including a minister, politician, chemist, and newspaper publisher."

Glenn leaned closer. "These numbers seem off, Mel. Isn't the CFEL only 40 years old?"

Mel admitted official records placed the formation at 40 years earlier. "However, when I visited years before that, Elder Vincent and I started quite by accident what would soon become a life's passion for two men with a vision of the future."

Violet stood up, moved closer, and squinted at one line after another. "If I read this correctly, there are a few people in Fallsbridge who may not be who they think they are."

Mel shrugged, "Yet infinitely better than would have been the case otherwise, yes?"

When she turned, Violet grimaced. "At my age, it shouldn't matter but it does." She sat and stared outside.

Mel chuckled, "How Violet does love to fuss and fume, yes?" and extended his hand to Laura. "Find yourself."

"I'm not sure I want to," Laura whispered.

"I insist."

Laura leaned close. "I see my initials but don't know what this line here means."

Mel pointed. "It indicates conception occurred during natural insemination. John Delorange is your biological father."

Laura ran her fingers along another line. "Why did you cover this side area with tape? Is there...?"

"Some details remain unfinished."

Laura ran her fingertips higher. "So does that mean...?

"Oh, how our little lawyer loves details! Suffice it to say, Lynette Marceau Delorange lay naturally with John David Delorange, Sr."

As Laura sat with a smile, Mel summoned Glenn forward but he said, "I don't care to..."

"Again I insist! Stand up and come here!" Glenn knew where his initials were: only one section on the chart listed four males as offspring of one female. When Glenn pointed to the lowest of four XY squares, Mel grinned. "You believe you are so smart you need not research further?"

Glenn faced him. "Some people prefer not to know about bodily functions from decades earlier."

Mel tapped his pointer against the box and spoke in a staccato-like voice. "Gregory and Garrett are perfect examples of the sort of specimen which springs naturally from fertile loins of a Rollie Munier. Good-natured and hard-working yet..."

Glenn interrupted, "My brothers are good men who..."

"Are perfect examples of non-intervention, yes? Are the sort of slow, lazy, hard-drinking, blue collar, uncritical-thinking Vermonters who blend into cold, lifeless mountains?" Mel turned his back to the women and finished, "I love you like a son because that is who you are."

Glenn considered his brothers—he and Gil always knew they were different—more than lighter hair or blue eyes, both over six feet tall and slender instead of 5' 8" and chunky. Greg and Garry seemed like a different generation and now Glenn knew why. He studied the old man and found it easy to find fault, damn him, or repeat Mel's insult: *You believe you are so smart?* Glenn felt tears and wondered how his own conception occurred. *Did my mother willingly participate in an affair with the CFEL's doctor? Did she agree to a dispassionate acceptance of sperm in his office? Or worse, did the elders deem her unworthy to know the truth at all?*

Violet whispered, "Your project is an abomination."

Mel laughed, "Would you prefer to be not born, to not have your own blessed three?"

Violet stood. "I prefer not to know my biological father isn't Vincent Mottolla. I'm leaving. I won't hear another..."

Mel pushed her back into her seat. "You came of your own volition, thus are obligated to remain."

Violet stared outside as Mel droned on about attributes which manifested themselves from one generation to the next and focused on David on the right side and Paul on the left. Violet laughed, "My youngest son is not some toy in a Cracker Jacks box who..."

"Enough!"

Laura seemed noticeably quiet and Glenn wondered *is it easier for her to be there? After all, she's who she always believed herself to be, not some genetic hybrid who conveniently meets an arbitrary goal on a chart.* Mel announced that naturally or artificially, within one calendar year he foresaw the birth from the unification of Glenn's seed and Laura's egg, a female specimen to serve as the future mate of David. He pointed to the third tier of the inverted pyramid. "David here, female specimen there, undetermined as yet female specimen here, Paul there which then leads us to our final unification." Glenn tried to listen but his mind raced. *Since Laura didn't argue against the pairing, it's a matter of time before she comes to me willingly. Isn't it? How will Gil's plan to leave with David change the next generation? How will Mel and the elders deal with me when they discover my involvement?* Glenn jumped when Mel smashed the pointer against the desk. "I thought you were ready but see foolish dullards. Go!"

On the steps, the three stood apart yet curiously together. Violet sighed, "Let's take time to digest this."

Laura looked from one to the other. "I'm sorry to have to ask but what did you learn?"

Violet sighed, "I always felt close to Glenn and now understand why. I wish Mel wasn't the reason." She shook her head and ran off.

When Glenn started to speak, Laura murmured, "You don't have to say a word," led him across the green, into the woods along a familiar path. They relaxed side by side on the boulder and as deeply as he craved her touch, he accepted the odd comfort of her silent presence.

118

Laura climbed into bed in her ugly yellow nightgown and considered Marsethe's latest assault: how cruel for Violet and Glenn to discover a shared lineage in such an insensitive way. She shivered at a thought for 20 years Steve loved Mick wholeheartedly yet feared he wasn't the biological father. After hours of tossing and turning, Laura grabbed the note from Al, left and at a pay phone in Littleton, dialed. At a sleepy hello, Laura said, "Is this Mrs. Logen?"

"Yes, this is Kristina. Who's this?"

"Um, you don't know me but my doctor said you'd be good to a baby if you had one."

A long silence then, "How did you get this number?"

"I want to make sure any baby you get will be loved."

Another silence, then: "If you broke the rules, you must feel strongly about this."

"I do; will you answer some questions?"

Laura heard rustling then a man. "That depends."

"Do you have any other children?"

"No; we've been married years and never tried not to, but..."

"Will you love someone else's baby as if it's your own?"

"Ever since we heard it could happen soon, we've loved that unknown child. We'll be good to your baby." After a long silence, he added, "I run a dairy farm and Kristina's a teacher. She already requested a leave of absence for when the baby arrives next spring."

"Um, where did you get the money to pay my expenses?"

He cleared his throat. "Well, let's say of what my father left me, I now own about half the original acres and herd."

Laura closed her eyes and pressed her forehead against the siding of the country store. "You sound like good people."

"I think we are but are you okay with this?"

"I am now. Thanks for talking to me."

Laura hung up and felt saddened any couple might be so desperate, they... She turned, bumped into someone in the shadows, and shoved Gil until he stumbled backwards onto his butt. When he jumped up, he laughed, "I'm sorry I frightened you but I need a lawyer's advice."

Rather than his customary cockiness, Laura saw an unusual look in his eyes—fear or embarrassment—and decided to give him a minute. They sat on the steps of the store and within minutes, Laura heard deep feelings for Reilly and David, desire to take them both far away, and most of all, fear of the CFEL. Laura took advantage of the privacy late at night in the middle of nowhere and reported everything: the phone call to the Logen's, her belief Frannie's baby survived, and the conversation she overheard at Glenn's party. "Um, my former partner with the Vermont State Police criticized me for wild stretches in logic and I pray I'm not taking that path again but it sure sounded like they planned future pairings. I heard a different woman's name matched to yours when they talked large sums of money."

"They know I won't do that anymore but money's rarely an issue since the old man plans everything years in advance." Gil paused and added "Wait; Mel recently proposed upgrading his diagnostics lab, saying things like the *promise of microfluidics technology* to dazzle people like me who have no clue what that means. So far they let him order whatever he wants if it's FDA approved and in hospitals already, but his latest wish list included equipment with a base price tag of $80,000—enough to stop the elders in their tracks. I can't imagine them giving him a green light to..."

"Um, what if he obtained a patent?"

Gil shrugged, "Can't say; this is a man who craves recognition from a world he believes snubbed his genius and sentenced him to the sidelines to watch inferiors surpass him. If he…"

"I help him with a patent application."

"Oh, well, I guess I could see that would mean they'd expect extra bucks coming in but still I don't see how…"

Laura grasped his hand. "Gil, the people I just spoke to aren't the ones who got Frannie's baby. Theirs will arrive in the spring."

"Mel would never do that to me," Gil insisted, paused, then chuckled, "Yes, he would; the old fool does whatever's necessary to get what he wants. I don't know if I should trust your theory but it doesn't matter. I need to step up my plans to leave with Reilly and David but without a job and nothing to sell, I can't be totally irresponsible and need more time to do it right. For god's sake, I'm 39 years old and don't even own my own car! In exchange for my cooperation in any goddamned scheme, they supported me."

"Surely you could…"

He turned with a laugh. "Can you believe Reilly was four the first time she said she loved me?"

"How old?"

"Four; I was 16 and flirted with Rita during a picnic. I put my moves on but it didn't help when Reilly wandered over to say *I'm going to marry Gil someday because I love him.* Can you imagine that?"

"Actually I can," Laura chuckled and studied a cloud of moths flutter around an overhead light. "Let me call my father. He teaches math at UVM and runs a business part time conducting audits and inventories. Recently, he mentioned he needs a manager badly."

"I'm useless at Math."

"My father conducts the audits; he needs someone to run the day to day operations, someone he can trust."

"Why would you go out of your way like this?"

"At first I figured you're just another CFEL puppet but Reilly's love for you changed my mind."

Gil choked, "I'm no more than that puppet you mentioned. I followed you around, took photos, and reported every move."

"I knew that," Laura admitted, stood, grabbed the phone, and spent the next minute conducting a hushed conversation reassuring someone she knew what she asked. She extended the phone. "My father remembers you as Jack's asshole buddy; convince him you grew up."

Gil covered the mouthpiece. "I owe you big time."

"You owe me nothing but you do owe Reilly, David and the new baby everything imaginable. Remember that."

119

Once John and he made arrangements to talk, Gil returned to Fallsbridge. After all he did to thwart her every move, he felt stunned by her generosity, shamed. He found the old man's fixation on her weird but then the old man acted weird with others. He headed to Mel's. "Laura stopped her nocturnal wanderings weeks ago; it's time I quit the patrol."

"While it's true I sense she inches closer to your brother, I insist upon more time to make certain of her sincerity."

"It's a waste of my time, Mel."

"Oh and suddenly you have Pulitzer-winning novels to write or atoms to split?" Gil laughed and followed Mel inside—big mistake; the old man's eyes were slits when he demanded, "I want details of your attendance at a law enforcement conference 2,000 miles away the same week Reilly McGuinn vacations at the Maine shoreline without a mother or son. The elders require receipts from both of you."

Gil pushed himself to a stand. "You've got it all wrong." Outside in his car, Gil figured he had two days to produce something, three tops. He recalled dozens of members—current and past—he followed, photographed, and reported on who experienced changes in status. *Depending upon the indiscretion, penance may be a lost job, singling out during services, or shunning. The only one who routinely misbehaves without consequence? Violet—odd how the CFEL forgives and forgets so selectively.* Gil stopped at the Maidstone and headed to his brother's apartment. "What if I sign a promissory note to repay $300 a month?"

Glenn invited him in. "I've been thinking I can solicit bids from roofing contractors, transfer funds into my personal account, and on the day you leave, withdraw cash. Make haste because I have no doubt he'll hear about the transaction by 9:30 AM Monday if not sooner."

Gil found the conversation easier to get through than he dreamed since usually Glenn openly criticized Gil's lifestyle, but not that night. Gil whispered, "Thanks for not rubbing it in that after years of arguing the exact opposite, I admit you were right all along. There's no room in a decent man's soul for random, loveless sexual encounters. Thanks, too, for your friendship all our lives and help now when things are tough."

As he drove home, Gil pictured another night two years earlier after he left the Maidstone. He headed down the back stairs at the inn and came upon Reilly as she sobbed on the bottom step—a remarkable sight and sound untypical for a girl who knew who she was, where she wanted to go, what she liked and why, and what she expected from the future. Gil stood frozen on the mid-level turn and asked, "What's wrong?"

Reilly stared up at him, smoothed her blouse, and with a noticeable harrumph answered, "Nothing that's any business of yours." He felt struck by how grown up she looked and even with her wet face, how spirited. He studied her as she straightened her shoulders, marched off, and disappeared into the parking lot. That night like many others, Gil stopped at Mel's to demand truth. The perverse old fool grinned and announced the young lady with the monumental crush fulfilled an assignment: she visited a particular guest month after month in the hopes of conceiving a remarkable male. Gil rushed back to the Maidstone and against his brother's wishes, grabbed the register and saw Marschek stayed a few nights every two weeks for a year. Gil left with a vow Reilly would see her four-year-old's wish come true then waited while she carried another man's son. Gil pulled up in front of the McGuinn house and studied the second story window. A figure moved behind filmy curtains and he recognized Reilly's walk, the very same hop-along-on-her-toes bounce he loved to watch when she was little. He pictured Reilly that Sunday at the picnic; she held a slice of watermelon that dripped down her arm onto a yellow sundress. Only four, she managed to stare him down before she smiled and announced her intentions to marry him. Gil stared at the window. "Good night, Reilly. I love you."

120

Inside church, Laura shivered during a half-hour service as hundreds of voices sobbed, whispered, and choked. None sang. As Elder Matthew spoke about how often God called young angels to His side, Laura watched Frannie bend at the waist and Peg prop her up. Al stood in the back, in the shadows, and clasped his arms against his chest tightly. In the cemetery, Laura encouraged him to lean against her; he felt hot, on fire. When she overheard someone whisper a closed casket because of an autopsy, Laura imagined it was closed because it was empty. That seemed impossible—clearly, pallbearers handled weight and Frannie didn't fake her grief in sunlight too blinding, clouds too majestic, sky too blue, and scent on a breeze too sweet. At the sight of an impossibly small casket lowered to the ground, her knees buckled and her arms dropped away from Al. She envisioned herself rolling into the gaping hole but hands grabbed—Al on one side, Glenn on the other. The pervert himself knelt on the grass to fan her face. Laura climbed to a shaky stand and stared at the sight of pale faces—too many sad faces for one place.

Laura insisted Reilly take the rest of the day off and headed to the dark law office alone. Despite the painful memory of the funeral, her anger was like adrenalin. She attacked the work and discovered her determined approach led to a high level of productivity. Even a first draft of the patent application stood ready for Marsethe's review. By midweek, Reilly noticed the volume of completed work and commented. As shallow as it sounded even as she spoke, Laura whispered, "Life does go on." Laura reorganized file cabinets and answered backed-up mail. She drew up two wills, guardianship papers for a family with three children, followed up copyright and trademark applications, and prepared a pre-trial statement for the judge assigned to the Browne marijuana cultivation case. Laura met with a new client: a 16-year-old student expelled from the Fallsbridge Academy following three previous suspensions for smoking, swearing and overall *unsociable behavior* who faced a hearing before the headmaster and steering committee. The father argued they fought for a matter of principle. "I said no to them one too many times, so they retaliated against my boy instead."

Laura directed her questions to the son. "Pete, how often did you swear on academy grounds?"

He shrugged, "A few times."

"How often did you smoke?"

Another shrugged, "A few times."

"Alone?"

"Nope; always with other guys."

"And you knew the academy rules of conduct?"

He snorted, "Of course; they tell us often enough."

"Who else was suspended or expelled the same day?"

"No one; only me."

"I'll research further but in the meantime, to show your commitment to education, enroll in the nearest public school."

When Reilly brought the mail in, Laura checked return addresses and found an envelope from the Chittenden County District Court. She ripped it open and read a letter signed by the clerk to the judge assigned to the Orsini case. Laura read a request—not an official summons—to appear in closed session the following Thursday at 9:00 AM. She sighed, "Shit, shit, triple shit." When Reilly peeked around the door jamb, Laura held the stationary in the air and groaned, "I bet she walks!" Reilly inched in, sat in the client chair, listened patiently, and offered comments and reassurances. In the end, Laura knew she had little control over what would happen. She would testify and trust the system worked. Laura refolded the letter and whispered, "How are you feeling?"

Reilly nodded at the door and outside said, "I feel better in cooler weather and reassured because I'm into my second trimester."

Laura took advantage of the younger woman's eagerness to share and asked questions about pregnancy, childbirth, breast-feeding, and the question most on her mind: "Is it safe to have intercourse?"

"It is until the seventh month but by then, a woman's so big it isn't fun anyway." Reilly chuckled and looked around. "Um, Gil's been thinking about moving away but I won't encourage him! Everyone knows how it works—if we run, we're in constant fear the CFEL follows but if we stay, we can predict the consequences."

"Ah, yes, the famous *everyone* but Gil may be right to…"

"He isn't! Laura, it works like this: during services, the elders preach about animal behavior and in private threaten to take the new baby away but because Gil's the father, Mel intervenes, the elders forgive us, and we have everything we want right here."

Laura considered leaving things alone but said, "An infertile couple in Coos County's been offered a healthy baby in the spring."

"Everyone knows Mel helps women who can't conceive or carry full term. I know a woman in Groveton who…"

"I haven't fit all the pieces together and may never but know this: I overheard a conversation between Marsethe and Elder Matthew as they planned a future pregnancy between Gil and another woman as *quality* during the same conversation about large sums of money."

Reilly sighed, "I believe Gil hasn't been with anyone else in…"

"I'm sure that's true but what if Mel has other ideas?"

Reilly pressed a palm to her abdomen. "Those old fools will soon discover I am **not** Frannie."

Laura nodded. "Gil and I talked about you guys leaving and…?"

Reilly laughed, "I think I know what you want to know. If we believe it's as bad as you suspect, and if Gil convinces me the only way to proceed is to leave, Mr. Delorange asked him to start in two weeks."

Laura grabbed Reilly's hand. "If I'm wrong, I apologize but if I'm right, it'll be wonderful to have you guys there."

After work at the carriage house, Laura packed a weekend bag and filled a cooler with vegetables from her garden: tomatoes, cucumbers, eggplant, and green peppers. As she packed her car, she saw Brian trim bushes and asked for an appointment to discuss Peter Herroux.

Brian nodded. "Don't spend a lot of time preparing to defend a little shit who thinks he can say and do anything he pleases."

Laura thought *like all CFEL-bred males* but said, "Gotta run; my mother has an outpatient procedure and can't be late!"

Out the kitchen window, Violet gasped, "What?"

"Mom fell without warning coming out of work, not for the first time. She had an MRI and meets with a neurologist about the results." Violet came outside to talk but Laura waved and left.

Though she exceeded the speed limit, Laura pulled into her parents' driveway a half hour later than planned. Lynette hobbled out using a cane and without even saying hello, chastised her daughter all the way through Essex into Winooski and Burlington. When they finally parked and entered the office, they were 15 minutes late and Lynette started all over again. "It's Friday afternoon, some people have plans, and it was hard enough to get you in on short notice. Honey, I thought you understood this visit's important."

Laura hugged her mother. "I do, and I love you, too."

Laura was pleased her appointment was with the same doctor she saw before she started college. Even though the gynecologist was female, Laura found the examination horrible and struggled against every poke, prod, push, and pull. When she finally relaxed, Laura decided Dr. Hensen was gentle and respectful; in fact, all her torture tools arrived warm. A file was open on the side table and more than once, Laura watched the doctor compare her records at 18 and 34.

"Laura, I see after an earlier pregnancy, you..."

"If I am pregnant, this is my first."

Hansen studied her notes. "You have extensive scarring."

"Some faded but there are new ones from when I was shot."

Hansen scanned the notes again. "I wrote some scars were likely from a caesarian section."

"No, the scars are from a rape. I guess I didn't do a good job with my history but I had trouble even thinking about it."

Hansen poked and prodded a little more. "Your bladder feels nice and full. Why don't you leave a sample?"

Laura sat up. "Am I pregnant?"

"With your history, I hesitate to say until I review test results but it feels like you carry a 10 to 11-week fetus." Laura tried to concentrate as Dr. Hensen talked diet, exercise, blood pressure, and prenatal check-ups. "If the test's positive, I recommend you schedule an ultrasound and if the father cares to participate, he's welcome."

Laura nodded at every word. "Um, is intercourse okay?"

Hensen smiled. "As long as there's no bleeding or pain, a pregnant woman can enjoy every facet of being female." The doctor closed the file and added, "I'd like to pursue a personal topic. In my notes following your first visit, you declined birth control information and expressed disdain for men and sexual activity."

"That was true when I was 18 but things changed."

A slight squint then, "All right; I'll call with the results."

"Um, that's tricky so can I have them mailed to the address I gave the receptionist?" Alone again, Laura grabbed her clothes and found her hands trembled so badly, she couldn't hook her bra. She heard a knock, watched Lynette peek around, and asked for help as she choked, "Mom, I might be!"

During the drive back to her parents' house, Laura asked about her mother's follow-up with a neurologist but Lynette answered, "That's not until next week; I threw that out there to give you something to tell those snoops and get you here today."

Laura nodded and explained she took a tour of Marsethe's lab to hear about his research. "Um, if I'm pregnant, I wonder if..."

"Honey, don't pay attention to anything that man says. People there think he's brilliant but he's twisted."

Laura chuckled and turned. "Trust me, Mom; I know that but he mentioned he offered genetic counseling years ago when Mèmère first started having problems but you..."

"His theories are junk medicine, Laura."

"I don't know, Mom; some of his ideas make sense and with my history, I wonder if Steve and I should consider..."

Lynette turned and snorted, "Marsethe and his cronies spout outrageous ideas! At one time, I thought you saw that, too!"

"Um, really, I don't mean to upset you with questions but I have odd dreams about when we first moved from Fallsbridge and..." Laura studied her mother's scowl and whispered, "Sorry; let's just dream there's another grandchild on the way, okay?"

"Yes, please; Laura, believe me—any child you have with a man as wonderful as Steve will be miraculous."

121

Steve left work early; at home he changed into baggy shorts and t-shirt and wandered out to the deck. He heard cars pull in at the bottom of the driveway but just as quickly pull back onto the road and accelerate.

After seven false arrivals in an hour, he began to worry. *What if Laura couldn't get away? What if she arrived before I did without a key? What if she got involved with her parents and forgot about me?* He heard an eighth vehicle pull in and smiled at the thought *Laura's the only one in too much of a rush to come to a stop before grinding into first.*

The evening felt miraculous: they packed her vegetables into the refrigerator; barbecued, ate, and cleaned up; picked out a movie and dozed on the couch; stretched out on top of clean sheets to make slow love, and talked for hours. On Saturday they had pizza at Zachary's and saw a dumb comedy at Sunset Drive-in. On Sunday they worked in the garden and broke for Creemees at Joe's. At the end of the day, Laura came out of the shower in a clingy purple number and raised her arms. "Study carefully, Sergeant, and puzzle this out."

Steve's fingers fumbled until he grinned. "Come closer, kid. I've had fantasies about pull-apart numbers."

The next thing he knew, daylight filled the room. As Laura climbed out of bed, he studied how gracefully she moved and thought *you look different.* She giggled, "Does that look mean you're having an erotic flash, mister? Because I could crawl right back in and…"

"Last night, I thought your breasts felt bigger."

Laura stared down. "Nah, they're still nearly invisible."

"I see you filled out in your hips, too—more womanly."

"Are you saying I used to look like a boy?"

"I know you say it's unlikely, but could you be pregnant?"

"Um, I came home this weekend for two reasons: to be with you and see my mother's doctor but Dr. Hensen wouldn't say without seeing test results. She did say I feel about 10 to 11 weeks along."

Steve reached for her hand and tugged until she assumed the nesting position. "What if you are? Will you go back or stay home?"

Laura insisted Granger would need to find another patsy and proceeded to talk a blue streak about diet, exercise, and prenatal care. "Because of scars I'd need a caesarian section."

"But if…"

Laura chuckled, "I'm the world's biggest worrier so if I trust everything will be fine, you can't worry."

Steve lay in silence and whispered, :In another month, we might hear a second heartbeat or detect fluttery movements of a growing life. I can hardly wait to see you in five months."

Laura stammered, "It may never happen for us; promise that won't make a difference."

"I promise; I have all I need now. A year ago I only dreamed I'd get this close to you but honey, if you are pregnant, come home."

"I will; I promise."

As she dressed, Laura talked a blue streak about where she felt she made progress, how she planned to proceed, and what she hoped to accomplish. In the end, Steve felt exhausted and craved more sleep; the best he could do was whisper, "Focus, kid; don't turn a confusing mess into something only you see as a conspiracy."

Laura grabbed car keys, leaned over for a quick kiss, and chuckled, "Will do Sergeant; thanks for the reality check."

122

The drive back felt worse than ever. At work, Reilly buzzed around organizing her departure. Laura watched—*good God, ten more days and no more Reilly*. Laura studied Reilly, who seemed spectacularly beautiful: young, in love, carrying the child of a man she adored, about to start a new life in a new locale and at 22, already the mother of a wonderful little boy. Laura recalled Steve's plea she focus and in her mind, outlined what might force the issue so she could go home: *convince Marsethe to grant access to his records or find proof the elders aided and abetted a rapist.* By Wednesday, Laura felt frantic, decided it would happen soon or never, and grabbed the phone. "Dr. Marsethe, this is Laura Delorange."

"I heard from Violet our Sweet Lynette is fine, yes?"

"Um, another confusing episode; she sees a specialist soon."

"Aware of family history, it would seem prudent for her to consult with me."

"Um, thanks; I'll pass your offer on. The reason I called is in review of instructions for a supplement to the patent application, I…"

"Need access to my field notes?" he interrupted.

"Um, I think so; I'm not sure."

"I've waited long enough for recognition and insist you begin promptly. You may stop by any time day or night."

"What about when you're seeing patients?"

"I shall be proud to work around you or beside you, my little researcher."

Laura chewed her lip. "Will I have access to everything?"

"You have my permission to examine the entirety."

"Why don't I start this weekend?"

"Is there a problem with tonight?"

Laura needed to prepare for her visit to Chittenden County Court but decided she spent enough time reliving the Orsini fiasco. "I can make it at 6:30."

"That is acceptable."

123

Gil bought a Burlington *Free Press* and with a pocketful of change, headed to a pay phone. He dialed one number after another and learned one fact about college towns: *rental units are expensive and as students return, impossible to find.* He made appointments to check two in surrounding towns and hung up with a stabbing sensation: *the old man expects receipts soon.* Gil stopped by the law office and asked, "Can I speak to your boss without an appointment. I need help finding an apartment."

Reilly peeked around the door and a moment later, Laura invited him in. He felt ridiculous as he pulled a chair close to the desk to whisper, and opened the paper to the classifieds, "I'm stumped."

"Do you need help with which areas to avoid?"

"I need help, period."

"I have an idea." Laura said and suggested they find a pay phone. After they crossed the bridge to Groveton, Gil handed her a fistful of coins and she dialed. "Mrs. Bennett? Hi, this is Laura. Yes, I'm doing fine in my new job; um, no, not yet but..." She glanced at Gil. "About my old apartment? I know you said you'd never rent unless you knew the person but would a reference from me help?" Another pause then, "Their names are Gil and Reilly Munier. Um, no, no dogs or cats. They do have a toddler named David and another on the way." A brief pause and a sighed, "Oh, David's very sweet; you'll love him, too." Laura finished the conversation and handed him the phone to work out the details.

124

Laura felt nervous when Violet couldn't accompany her and considered asking Glenn; no, Marsethe wouldn't ruin his chances with weird behavior. Would he? She presented herself at 6:30 and after the customary social niceties, Marsethe deposited her in his office. He briefly explained his filing system and suggested she start with the section labeled *Initial Pregnancies Post 35*. She looked up to ask a question and discovered him gone. She gravitated to certain names and read information about Gretchen Beaudon, some of it familiar from Caroline's story. In the file a notation: *After failure to conceive during 19 years of marriage, artificial insemination #4 successful in office with live sperm sample from D3.* Further along, Laura discovered an entry concerning a female identified only as Cassandra; with the sperm from D1, at 35 she produced a perfect female specimen and at 38, a second perfect female. What seemed different from many other entries was the notation: *Natural insemination.* Laura chuckled at the realization D1 performed live and in person on occasion. Laura scanned dozens of files with notes she didn't understand and wondered if his statistics were scientifically gathered and analyzed; the data did seem well-organized. She put charts aside and returned to the file cabinet. She noticed flecks of paper in the bottoms of stretched-out file folders—paper clips, staples, and balls of dust, too, apparent at one time cabinets held more. She checked other drawers and noticed one after another the same—for saying the space was spotless, it seemed likely drawers were emptied quickly. Laura wandered out and found Marsethe in the kitchen as he cut lemon wedges for iced tea. She climbed onto a bar stool and mentioned the condition of his hanging file folders. He chuckled, "My little detective, it is certainly true I transferred much of my work onto CDs. I will retrieve one for your research. Wait here."

Laura watched him enter the first room at the top of the stairs. When he returned, Marsethe directed her to his lab and computer. Alone again, she studied the room's austerity, lack of color or plant life, huge refrigerator, and rows of locked storage cabinets. There were only 12 files on the CD but Laura knew enough about computers to check for others on the hard drive. She called up the directory and felt startled as the list scrolled for pages. She glanced over her shoulder and at the end, noted there were 14 folders and 117 files stored on C Drive. Of them all, the D1 folder consumed the most space. She licked her lips, checked the back of the PC for a modem connection, and grinned when she recognized the symbol. She stared over her shoulder again and crept along the white tile floor. As no computer expert and unsure how to use a phone line if she found one, anyway, Laura crawled under the table, touched a familiar rectangular shape feet from the computer, rested on her haunches, and grunted, "Okay, Sherlock—now what?"

125

Al felt startled when someone pulled in so late and even more so when it turned out to be Laura. She rushed in and asked about computers, storage, and modem lines. He pointed to a computer. "Here at home all I do is switch it off if one of the girls forgot; at work, I know how to log onto a database." He handed her two hand-drawn maps showing where he discovered bugs.

Laura gasped, "I knew about the office but *three* at the carriage house? And this one's so close to the bathroom!"

"I'll check your car, too."

Laura collapsed on a chair. "I'm useless, waste time, and go nowhere fast. It's time to call Granger and admit defeat."

"No, you need to focus." Al stood at the bottom of the stairs to call, "Sandra, come down? I have a colleague with computer issues."

Al introduced his oldest daughter and as the women huddled over notes, headed out to check her car. It seemed clean but went inside to recommend Laura have a mechanic inspect the underbody. Laura nodded halfheartedly and continued with a description of what she found.

Sandra listened intently. "That's a poorly protected system but I can accompany you, see things first hand, connect the modem, navigate, and turn the monitor off but not the CPU, and direct data elsewhere for collection." She glanced at them and laughed, "Come on! You know I can do this with my hands tied behind my back and eyes closed!"

Laura answered, "No, too risky; an unauthorized search is one thing but out and out theft of data is…"

Al shrugged, "He gave you access to gather information"

Laura sighed, "Sorry but no; I won't cut corners with the law."

Al again: "That's awfully black and white, counselor. You have permission to be there and need something solid; otherwise this could take forever."

Al watched her expression shift. "Um, I admit I'd like to go home but need time to think." Laura headed out and Sandra followed, keeping up a steady stream of conversation. Al loved how his daughter got absorbed in things but saw how desperate she was for contact.

126

Steve checked the clock: 1:20 AM. He heard an odd sound again, climbed from bed, and grabbed his Glock, In the kitchen, he heard what sounded like someone picked the lock. As the door squeaked open, he shouted, "I'm armed!"

A giggled, "I'm home!"

Steve lowered the gun. "Did we get the results?"

"Um, I forgot to tell you I asked they be mailed here."

"Sure; makes sense."

"Um, I also forgot to remind you about my testimony in the morning—funny how someone so central only months ago seems far away and less important. Stephanie…"

"That name isn't spoken in our home," he interrupted.

Laura took his hand. "Are you too tired for romance, mister?"

Steve nuzzled her neck. "After that shocking arrival, I admit I'm wide awake. Follow me, Mrs. Scolarzski."

127

Once Steve left for work, Laura dressed in her white blouse and navy blue suit. She rushed downtown and cursed parking. Inside the courthouse she sat at a conference table in judge's chambers as the state's attorney led her through autobiographical and career questions. For over an hour, Laura testified and stated yes, Ms. Orsini was investigated by detectives in Troop A for the murder of Ian MacClure in October of the previous year; yes, Laura had a brief, personal relationship with the murder victim; yes, the charges against Ms. Orsini were dropped for lack of conclusive evidence; yes, she feared her partner Sergeant Steve Scolarzski was involved with the suspect; and to the most damaging question: yes, she was reprimanded by her lieutenant for continuing the investigation illegally. Laura concluded with a summary statement: "It all boils down to simple facts. Stephanie Orsini chased me along Routes 117 and 289, threatened me with a handgun, and fired three shots willfully. The first hit my knee, the second a guardrail, and the third my lower back. Ms. Orsini drove off and left me to bleed to death in the snow."

The defense attorney skillfully restated basic facts until Laura's behavior between August and March sounded unprofessional and irresponsible. He twisted her interpretation of events and asked if Laura behaved not from indignation a suspect skirted the law but from petty jealousy. "Isn't it also a fact your body was discovered shortly after you left the bed of your lover, Steve Scolarzski?"

"Yes, but that has nothing to do with why we're here."

After the judge asked questions about the timing of events that snowy March morning, he excused her. Laura waited in the corridor and asked the state's attorney how he planned to use other evidence recovered at the scene of the shooting, the handgun recovered from the river, or witness testimony from a driver of a pick-up. The state's attorney reminded her they met in judge's chambers, not court. "We're here to determine if charges move forward to trial or Ms. Orsini remains in state custody. Her attorney found three renowned psychiatrists ready to testify she's not a criminal in the purest sense of the word."

Laura chuckled, "Beautiful—my attacker spends a few months in medical custody but never a day in prison." She shook her head slowly and finished, "I don't care where she is as long as it's far away from me and the people I love."

Laura felt a chill as the defendant passed with two armed guards. Stephanie Orsini turned and smiled, "Laura, you look wonderful now that you're rid of a filthy beast. Say hello to Rick for me? Oh and tell him his baby and I are well."

Laura turned to the state's attorney and laughed, "No one ever claimed this case was pretty."

Laura walked to her car and found nothing funny about the situation. Stephanie Orsini looked a month or two from delivery and heard from her mother Gina and Rick didn't speak regularly, and though Gina still came around, only when Rick was gone. Laura drove to the station and figured at least one of the guys noticed her arrival. Correct; when she reached the door, Steve waited. "How'd it go?"

"Not great," she shrugged and asked who was there; at the names Barber, Macrae, and Sigler, she headed inside to report details of the hearing to the very detectives outsmarted the first time around.

Steve prepared a magnificent dinner but the evening lacked its customary comfort. Laura blamed it on the meeting in judge's chambers, the iffiness of the outcome, the unfocused Fallsbridge investigation going nowhere, Stephanie Orsini's glowing beauty in pregnancy, and Laura's dread fear her dreams of motherhood were just that—a dream. All of that felt awkward enough but since neither felt in the mood for romance, they argued about when she'd be home for good.

During the dreaded drive back, Laura strategized how to get the old bastard legally. If she took Sandra Wilkers up on her offer, Laura could take her along to work with the data. She figured all she really needed were three names—three reliable people without prior arrests, three unimpeachable witnesses, three sworn affidavits. If she couldn't get Marsethe for sexual assault, she'd nail him for baby trafficking; if she couldn't get CFEL elders for aiding and abetting a felon, she'd nail them for gross misuse of their tax-exempt status. At 8:10, Laura entered one shitty little town and smiled when the blue flashing lights pulled into position behind her. Gil stopped at her open window as she passed the paperwork. He pretended to read and reported he met with Mrs. Bennett the day before. "What a great apartment! I think Reilly will feel your presence which will help her adjust to living away from home for the first time in her life." Gil scanned the area and leaned in. "It's only a matter of time before Mel knows so we can't wait another week. We'll come by tonight after dark to say goodbye for now."

"Reilly won't be at work today?"

"She's packing." Gil returned the paperwork and left.

Laura managed to get through a horrible day. She missed Reilly already and the afternoon turned out hot and humid again. When she prepared to leave the office, she called Marsethe to ask when she could stop in over the weekend. "I need additional information for a detailed section of the application."

"I will be out of town—a family emergency."

Laura closed her eyes to another obstacle to progress. "I'll wait until it's more convenient."

A long pause then: "It is I who requested your assistance and I who want this done. If I leave a house key with Glenn, you can work without my nuisance presence underfoot for however long you need."

"Rick's fiancée is my weekend guest so I wouldn't be alone."

"I cannot envision Master Richard as a young man!"

"If you think back, Mel, you'll realize he's almost 21."

A long pause, then: "May I ask a favor?"

"Um, what kind?"

"I confess to an intense desire to meet the young lady. I shall expect both of you this evening at 6:00 for dessert."

"Um, I don't know what time she'll arrive; it could be very late."

"Upon such a momentous occasion, late is fine."

Laura raced across the bridge and called Al to beg for help in prepping Sandra for two different roles. As they worked out the arrangements, Laura suspected he got a great deal of satisfaction out of one request, confirmed when he finished, "I'll let her wear her mother's diamond. In situations like this, Detective, props help."

When Sandra arrived an hour later, Laura whispered, "Be careful; this place is bugged." Laura talked casually about the weather, where Sandra searched for a wedding dress, and of course, Rick. Sandra played along nicely and provided imaginative details about shopping expeditions with her sisters. As she spoke, Sandra took a sheet of paper and wrote: *What else do I need to know?*

Laura wrote: *We'll visit Marsethe tonight briefly. You'll stay the night and in the morning, we'll go back when the house is empty.*

Laura offered to drive but Sandra insisted they walk. On the way from the carriage house to the village center, they cut through the academy grounds and Sandra admitted she heard many things from her father, Peg, Frannie, Maria, and Tina. "But it's better to see things close up." Laura was struck by how mature Sandra seemed as she detailed her life's plans. In the fall, she'd enter as a freshman at UVM to study statistics and math and go right through a master's program in advanced statistics. Sandra figured if she focused on her goals, she'd be ready at 24 to apply to a local police department. After a few years' experience, she'd apply to the Vermont State Police. "My father says I over-organize everything but I intend to be the first woman to climb all the way to the top of that male hierarchy."

Laura offered her own facts: she attended UVM, earned an undergraduate degree in psychology, and went directly to Columbia Law. After four years as assistant DA in Queens, she became a patrolwoman in Essex Junction and finished the Vermont Police Academy. "Two years later, I took the VSP exam and envisioned myself as the first female state police commander or youngest elected federal judge."

"So why quit and come here?"

"This may sound unbelievable but I almost died."

Sandra admitted she knew some of it. "I follow the story in the paper and... I'm sorry I brought that up."

"No problem; that part of my life is ancient history."

Sandra mentioned her father and Steve Scolarzski were friends for years. "One summer when Mrs. Scolarzski and my mother were both still alive, we went to a picnic on Maidstone Lake. I was four and Mickey was five or six. I thought he was so grown up! Mickey fell asleep on the blanket and cried when I kissed him."

Laura studied Sandra's grin. "He wouldn't mind now."

At Marsethe's, the old man studied Sandra's ring. "Your fiancé exhibits fine albeit old-fashioned tastes in both jewelry and women, yes? I approve." Marsethe behaved in a pushy manner as he touched Sandra's face, studied her eyes and teeth, and commented on her appearance and general health. Laura felt appalled when he turned her around and studied her behind. "Although you possess exceptional height, lovely skin and beautiful hair, you must lose 10 to 15 pounds before a first pregnancy makes your slender frame increasingly difficult to maintain, yes?"

Laura followed them on a guided tour, listened to their conversations, and felt pleased at how well Sandra stayed in role. When the group reached the kitchen, Marsethe made a production out of lemon bars and lemonade garnished with fresh mint sprigs. Finally, Marsethe announced, "Little Miss Gina Farrusco, I find you a perfect match for our Master Richard Delorange." With a quick flip of his wrist, he dismissed them with a wish, "Enjoy a sisterly weekend."

Dark when they reached the carriage house, Laura noticed an unfamiliar car. She recognized Gil's stance and Reilly in the passenger seat. Laura handed Sandra her keys and whispered, "I'd like a minute alone with friends." Laura felt embarrassed at how sappy everything became: she and Reilly cried and David, who awakened in his car seat, giggled and extended his chubby arms. Laura unbuckled him, lifted him against her, and groaned, "I'll miss you so much, little guy."

When Reilly wrapped her arms around and tugged Gil into their tight circle, he sighed, "If Brian's home, we're up shit's creek."

Laura nodded. "You'd better get moving."

Gil leaned in. "Let me show you where the bugs are."

"I know about one in the door jamb near the kitchen, one in the phone, and one in the molding near the bathroom."

At first Gil seemed stunned but laughed, "I warned Mel you were too smart for his tricks, but why is Wilkers' daughter here?"

"Crap! Who else might recognize her?"

Gil climbed into the driver's seat. "I'd guess only Peg, Frannie, Maria, and Tina." Gil leaned into the back to check David's car seat, whispered something, and squeezed the little boy's calf. Laura's throat tightened as she thanked God David would have such a man in his life. She studied the main house; all the windows dark—no music, no voices—and thanked God for that small favor.

Laura found Sandra looking at CDs and asked to hear about her, her sisters, mother, father, friends, school, and boyfriends but knew to keep her voice low while music played its role. Laura sat next to Sandra and reminded her place was bugged. In hushed tones, the two talked about everything imaginable until Laura noticed it was midnight and suggested they get rest. She turned the stereo off and silence filled the room as Sandra settled onto the couch. After a long silence, Sandra sighed, "I'm scheduled to report to UVM for Orientation in a week and I'm nervous." Laura detailed dining locations, various residence halls, how warm or cold they were in winter, their accessibility to class buildings, and which walkways to avoid once surfaces turned to black ice.

In the morning Laura took Sandra to the Maidstone for breakfast and from Glenn's reaction, knew he never saw her before. Laura took the house key and the two women walked over to Marsethe's. Laura led Sandra into the lab with the PC and watched her take out a small tool kit. As Sandra started to crawl underneath, Laura left to wander through the entire house to make sure it stood empty of a pervert's presence. She focused on the room at the top of the stairs—the one she watched him enter when he brought back CDs—and found more. Beside his display board, she searched closets, shelves, corners, file drawers, and desk for the rolled-up charts she asked to study closer but he refused to share. More than anything, she wanted to see her family's details—no luck. She wandered into a room which looked and felt very different: cozy, displaying a sentimental side of one weird old man with a handful of photos of him with his deceased wife, a few of dogs over the years, and one each of Glenn, Violet and a younger woman Laura didn't recognize. She checked the spines on hundreds of books: most were medical but a few were fiction classics. She noticed an entire bookcase filled with photo albums, pulled one at random, settled into a chair, and stared at one page after another of photographs of Angela: at school, picnics, in a chorus, the medical lab, and with the old pervert himself at a holiday dinner. Laura stared at a half-filled row of royal blue albums and noted all were labeled *Angela*. The row below contained a single red album labeled *Abigail*. The shelf two rows up was half full with forest green albums labeled *Francesca*, And the row above three-quarters full of maroon albums labeled *Laura*. Second from the top was almost full with yellow albums labeled *Caroline*, and the top row full with white albums labeled *Cassandra*.

Laura pulled a maroon album, stunned to see his collection more complete than that of her parents. The last album in the line had pages of photographs taken since she returned—normal and boring: at her desk, at the restaurant, at the snack bar, in the bleachers at a woman's softball game and a surprising one of her talking to Glenn on the boulder near the river. She flipped backwards and saw photos of leaving the hospital with Steve. The most recent photo was the most surprising of all: she hugged Joyce in the doorway of the restaurant after the anniversary party.

Laura pulled a single album labeled *Abigail* which began with a woman's pregnancy, Christening ceremony, picnics, birthday parties, a toddler in a Halloween costume, and the same girl happily unwrapping Christmas gifts. The final entry? a toddler of three or four in a curly ponytail playing ring toss at a cookout. Laura tugged it out of its plastic sleeve and read a date of three weeks earlier. She replaced it carefully— stunned at a realization Marsethe planned his attacks years in advance.

Laura returned to the lab, relieved to hear Sandra announce, "Five more minutes and we are out of this tomb!"

128

Al studied how pale Laura looked and fixed a tall glass of iced tea with mounds of ice for her and a matching one of cranapple juice for his daughter. He sat back and watched Sandra fool with the PC. She said something about subdirectories, typed like a maniac, and grinned when like magic, the printer started. Laura turned to him. "Did you meet anyone named Cassandra or Abigail?"

"Let's see; Peg introduced me once to a woman named Cassie who I think works for Matthew in his building supply company but I don't recall an Abigail. Why?"

Laura stared as pages fluttered into a box Sandra placed below. He repeated his question a few times but Laura sat silently, sipped iced tea, and watched the printer, pages, and Sandra. Finally, Laura faced him. "Request the state ME exhume the casket supposed to hold your son. I'll prepare everything but a request for exhumation should come from you. He was—no, he is—your son, but not yet; I need a few days."

Sandra reloaded the printer and Al watched what had to be the 50th sheet of paper spew out of the goddamned machine. He turned to observe an unusually strong-willed expression on Laura's face and answered, "I'll do whatever you recommend, counselor."

129

At the carriage house, Saturday night was the opposite of Friday: no joking, funny stories, or discussions of favorite music. Sandra listened to music with headphones on as Laura scanned pages to allow her mind to wander freely through charts, biographies, and summaries of intervention techniques. When something brushed her shoulder, Laura jumped and saw Glenn nod at Sandra. "It looks like Gina's in a world of her own."

"Aren't we all?" Laura laughed and grabbed loose pages.

"What are you working on?"

"Um, Mel's patent application?"

"Here; I brought walnut brownies. Will you two be at services in the morning?"

"Nah, I want to spend time with my future sister-in-law."

"Please reconsider. I'm guest speaker and my focus is on God's wish for strong, well-matched marriages. Seems appropriate, don't you think, since she'll marry Rick?"

Laura whispered, "I'll try," and peeked from behind curtains until his car disappeared. She rushed over to Sandra and lifted an earphone. "Can you keep a confidence?" When Sandra nodded solemnly, Laura jingled her car keys and indicated the door. They headed to the village center and spent the rest of the evening at the law office. Laura handwrote a basic statement and asked Sandra to create a shell form on the computer. Laura reviewed all the printed pages from Marsethe's files, highlighted names and dates, and passed 11 to Sandra to enter into a database. Laura double-checked each as it printed and prayed of the 11 *unusual incidents* in the past 29 years, two or three women would sign a statement that at or immediately following delivery, an infant cried: irrefutable proof of no stillbirth.

Sandra studied the mound of paper, lifted one and pointed: *Stenzola male, 1:17 AM, August 19, 6 lbs 11 oz.* "Can I see if...?"

Laura choked, "Sorry, no; it's too soon and what if I'm wrong? Please be patient, okay? Let's get some sleep."

130

Mel pulled into his driveway at 8:11 AM, enough time to shower and dress for services after a 42-hour punishing trip back and forth to Louisiana. Despite a decision in July never to return, when news came of his mother's passing, he felt a need to say goodbye to her and bid adieu to members of his pathetic family forever. Med felt shocked when lovely Miss Elisabeth Grunwald attended and appeared shy—not awkward as anticipated. When she approached him at the cemetery, he allowed her to set the tone and what a tone she did: "After your generous offer, I'm ashamed I tried to turn a professional relationship into a personal one."

Mel insisted, "No apology needed. I renew my offer of a place to live, employment, advanced education, and if I may be so bold, eternal friendship from a tired old man."

Over lunch, they decided he would see to travel arrangements for a scouting trip in September to determine if a permanent change might be agreeable. She confessed, "I'm tired of my life here," and Mel felt shocked again. How could such a perfect specimen be lonely?

During the return flight, Mel organized information Gilbert collected, the quantity astounding yet quality horrifying: useless reports and faded photographs yielding little return on investment for a skilled law enforcer's time. Whenever the discussion of discontinuing surveillance arose for debate, elders decided unanimously to continue. Glenn wished to believe their beloved Laurette Marie returned to the fold, but wiser minds suspected pure fantasy: proof of possible duplicity in the name of her visit to a certain journalist in Gilbert's motor log.

131

Laura and Sandra settled into an empty pew near the back and watched Glenn fuss behind the pulpit. When he noticed them, he jumped down to lead them to the row he traditionally shared with Marsethe. When the old pervert himself slid in beside her as organ music began, Laura thought *Heavens; that was a short trip!* slid closer to Sandra, and focused her attention on the services. It sounded much as she remembered until Glenn spoke. Laura heard a sweet sermon about honesty and fidelity, the nature of love and beauty of marriage, dignity of behavior and purity of monogamous passion, wonder of conception, and miracle of birth. Not one second of fire, brimstone, or eternal damnation in over 15 minutes. Glenn continued: "I found multiple references in the Old and New Testaments how to find the Kingdom of Heaven. We can be kind, loving, fair, generous, and truthful. Yet as members of the Community for Expansive Love, all their lives women are directed to surrender personal will and function in silence while all our lives, men are told they are privy to the answers." When Glenn paused, Laura looked where he looked: at lined brows on men, smirks on women. Glenn finished, "I found no reference in the Bible that in order to achieve the Kingdom of Heaven, followers of our Lord Jesus Christ must be miserable every step of the way." Laura studied her knuckles and thought *with its endless rules the CFEL demeans the common sense and good nature of members and doesn't trust its faithful to decide what's important.*

Marsethe slid sideways. "Share your reaction?"

"Um, inspiring?."

"Glenn Munier took liberties with the Word, yes?"

Laura stood and squeezed by. "Wonderful, though. "

On the church steps, Glenn invited a group to the Maidstone for breakfast: Elder Matthew; Rita and Angela Lezzaro; Violet, Brian, Ben, Joanna, and Paul Lemphier; Caroline and Gretchen Beaudon; and Mary McGuinn, who thanked him but preferred to go home. Finally convinced to accompany them, her initial hesitation seemed well-founded when the group reassembled in the dining area and Marsethe asked the whereabouts of her daughter and grandson. Laura cringed when the old man studied everyone at the table and bellowed, "And for that matter, where is Gilbert Munier this fine morning?"

Glenn carried a carafe of coffee from the kitchen and knelt on the carpet beside the doctor. "Let's discuss this later."

"I'm away for hours and..." Marsethe pushed himself to a stand. "No; we discuss this now." With a flip of his wrist, Marsethe summoned Matthew to follow and the three headed out of the dining area, up the stairs, and along the mezzanine to the living quarters,

132

An hour later, Glenn crossed the green with a deep sense of regret. He handled the conversation with Mel and Matthew horribly, like some dumb hick. He should have known those two suspected Gil, Reilly, and David were gone and suspected his involvement, too. How idiotic to head into a discussion under a flawed assumption he had the quick-wittedness to take them on? The two vindictive old men even started up on Laura and laughed at his inability to work his way into her bed. Matthew insisted Laura was a cop to fear even more than Wilkers—sent to take over his failure and never to be trusted. After close to an hour of Matthew's list of offenses the elders attributed to Laura—second only to those ascribed to Claudette Theriault Adams years earlier—the only bright spot was when Mel said, "Perhaps our paranoia is excessive; might we consider her contributions to *Nature's Bounties* and my patent campaign as proof her loyalty grows and her return home still unfolding?"

Glenn reached the final turn in the path and paused to watch Laura fuss with her kayak. As she rubbed mud off the sides, she turned with a gasp, eyes full of undisguised terror. "You scared me!" Then a quick smile and, "I had a heck of a time getting this here, Glenn. Halfway, it felt like I lugged a ton! Rick always thought I was stupid to get a two-seater since I usually go out alone."

Laura continued nervous rambling until he sat on the boulder and reached for her hand. "I need to ask a favor." Though she nodded, he noticed her pupils dilated to pinpricks. "Mel threatened to charge me for embezzlement if I don't complete an assignment. Mel's willing to let this rest if we become intimate."

"Oh, um, I could lend you money to pay him back."

"I suspect you don't know the amount I loaned was $12,000."

"Oh; yeah, that's a surprise."

"I'd like to spend one night with you."

"Oh God, no; I'm terrified of men."

"It would be for show only—a way to get them off my back and leave us to what I believe would evolve on its own. anyway."

"I can't imagine…"

Glenn interrupted, "Please; I promise I wouldn't expect anything beyond sleeping in the same room."

Laura muttered, "All men terrify me and this can't be…"

"I ask for one night in the same room." Glenn watched her struggle to respond and couldn't tell if she felt focused or frightened? *Could Matthew be right? Might she be a substitution of Wilkers?*

Laura shifted her attention to the kayak and river. The color on her face returned to normal and her voice sounded confident as she said, "Bear with me once we're on the water. I take frequent breaks because even five months after the shooting, I'm easily exhausted." Glenn let her surprising change in demeanor go unmentioned as they paddled, floated, and relaxed in the shade of trees. She wore a hat and rubbed sunblock on yet turned pink in an hour. She asked about the academy and new people she met. "Um, do you know someone named Abigail who's four or five?"

Glenn thought for a moment. "I think Angela has a cousin who was baptized Abigail. She goes by Abby, though. Why?"

"I overheard the name somewhere." Laura peered out from under the brim of her hat. "Will you join me for dinner?"

Glenn studied her warm smile and imagined her shyness might be a highly polished, perfectly evolved skill. What if Matthew was right? What if she misled them from the day she arrived? But what if the old fool was wrong? Glenn saw she waited for an answer. "Sure; cooking by someone other than Carl is a rare treat."

Laura jumped out of the kayak, dragged it to shore and struggled to lift it until Glenn insisted since she got it there, he'd get it back. They meandered through cool woods, came out of the far side of the tennis courts, and heard screams. Brian and Joanna ran between the carriage and main houses with pots and pans while Violet shouted from the kitchen. As they neared the cartoonish scene, Glenn predicted those two were seconds from tragedy. He was right; they slapped at clothes as a skunk waddled off with an eggplant in its teeth.

Laura laughed, "And I thought a raccoon raided my garden!"

As the odor wafted over, Laura bent at the waist and gagged. Glenn dropped the kayak and grabbed. "Hey, hey, I've got you." She felt limp and he shouted, "Violet, bring a car around!" During the drive, Glenn held Laura close in the back seat. As he carried her upstairs to a vacant guest room, he considered it might be something worse than too much sun and called Mel. Glenn waited for the doctor and figured with the residual stench at the carriage house, she might agree to spend the night and in essence, buy him and Gil critical time.

When the doctor arrived and checked her pulse, Laura opened her eyes and gasped. "I fainted?"

"That you did my sunburned beauty."

When Marsethe opened his bag and lifted a needle, Laura groaned, "No way!" and bounced upright.

"All right, but please rest."

"No; I want to go home."

Violet laughed. "Did you forget the skunk? Brian, the children, and I plan to take Glenn up on his offer to stay here tonight."

After more debate, Laura allowed them to coax her into staying, too. They left her to get rest and after a few hours of checking every so often, Glenn returned with a tray with iced tea, thick wedge of quiche, peeled orange, and slice of lemon meringue pie. Laura picked up an orange wedge and sighed, "Glenn, this is wonderful but too much food. I've had sun poisoning before and my stomach will be unsettled for days."

He placed the tray on a small table. "Eat what you can."

Laura sliced through the sturdy egg mixture to uncover ham chunks, melted cheddar, and chopped spinach. After the first bite, she sighed, "I guess I have an appetite after all. Thank you."

As Laura ate, Glenn opened the closet door. "Let's find something for you to wear."

Laura laughed, "Where'd you get all that?"

"They're left behind by guests. I try to return them by mail but often can't." He turned with a sly grin. "Even an inn out in the middle of nowhere attracts its fair share of John and Jane Does."

Laura thanked him and suggested he leave while she changed. Glenn returned to his apartment, embarrassed by how often he tried to break her reserve only to receive clear signals his attention remained unwelcome. *All my life, pride stood in my way but what does a man have but his good name, self-respect, and dignity? Whenever Mel sent others on assignments, I refused to go. As the first of a new generation of babies arrived, I felt shocked at how little interest Gil or the others displayed for the lives they created with someone else's wife, daughter, sister, or girlfriend. The Master Plan. Really, all that fancy title does is mask dishonesty.*

Glenn recalled the conversation with Matthew and Mel about the cult book and the unwanted notice it drew. After its publication, the elders were livid and for more than a year waited for the authorities to lose interest and until they did, no young men were fanned out like thieves in the night, no hasty deliveries made to couples in northeastern Vermont, western New Hampshire, or southern Quebec. Glenn recalled Mel often labeled the babies *specimens;* on occasion, he called his carefully-planned infants *products—not unlike the award-winning hybrid corn grown on the community farm?*

When Glenn heard a knock, he imagined someone tapped a bag on the wall or parents checked on children in an adjoining room. When he heard a second, he expected the night manager. "Yes, Leo?"

"Um, it's Laura. I'm sorry if I woke you but I can't sleep."

Glenn opened the door a crack. "I can't, either; give me a minute to find a robe then if you want, come in."

Glenn started a CD, joined her on the couch, and enjoyed every minute she talked about Jack, Rick, her parents, UVM, Columbia, and police work. She listened to future plans for his business and critiqued a marketing brochure Rita designed to market the Maidstone as a tourist destination. She even went so far as to recommend strategy. "Consider advertising in *Vermont Life, Vermont Monthly,* or *Yankee Magazine.* Rita spoke to me about print materials included with the *Nature's Bounties* packet, and if this is any indication of her skills, I can't imagine the elders won't approve the expense. Um, I know there's little chance technology will explode here overnight but you might consider a web presence, too."

Glenn shrugged, "We're so remote it would be expensive. Besides, technology groups find it impossible to work with the elders."

Laura laughed, "I'll bet if enough money changed hands," but stopped to add, "I enjoyed your guest sermon. Um, tell me your honest feelings about women."

Glenn shrugged, "What I said is how I feel: I want a partner in life, not a pawn."

"Good to know. I'm aware you helped Gil leave and suspect you also know there's a baby coming."

"I do; Gil also told me about a civil ceremony, job interview, and scouting an area to see if Reilly could live so far from Vermont."

"Still you decided to help? I find that amazing and why I'm here. What kind of proof do you need we spent a night together?"

"I don't know, really. Maybe one of the housekeepers verifying they saw you here first thing in the morning?"

"How about room service? Whoever delivers would see me."

"Yeah, that'll work," Glenn answered, called down to the kitchen for two servings of Nutmeg-Maple Cream Pie and carafe of herbal tea. When the order arrived, Glenn insisted, "My guest and I don't want to be disturbed for the remainder of the night."

Glenn offered wine and Laura accepted. Much later—after a few refills and more gratifying conversation—Laura jumped to her feet and escaped. Glenn replayed everything in his mind: *I didn't make the first move. Laura snuggled close. Laura wrapped an arm around my waist and drew my hand to her breast. Laura slipped her hand inside my robe, stroked me gently, and whispered. "I'm ready, too. Please enter me?" Why did she bolt from the room when she heard me thank God for answering my prayer?*

133

Laura dressed in reeking clothes, snuck out the back, and chastised herself for wine-induced steamy thoughts of Steve. At the carriage house, she detected no hint of skunk but stripped and left her clothes outdoors, anyway. She showered and after a restless sleep, dressed for work and shook her head at her behavior the night before. No more—she'd nail the bastard without involving Glenn.

Laura opened the office and prepared for a meeting with Brian. The Fallsbridge Academy was already in session, its schedule exceeding state-mandated requirements by 35 days a year. Allowing for snow days, the academy ran a minimum of 220 in-session days, its summer hiatus roughly half that of the rest of the state. With a strict and regimented curriculum paired with high expectations came tangible results: academy graduates excelled statewide and frequently nationwide as well. Laura decided to approach Brian with the respect his position deserved. It didn't matter how he got it, how he held it, or how he managed or mismanaged his charter—nothing could be gained by dragging personal differences into the encounter. Brian opted for the opposite and a conversation degenerated into an unproductive debate in which he stated, "Your of your client indicates you condone misbehavior, juvenile delinquency, foul language, and pornography." When she argued she hadn't noticed pornography on his list of crimes against humanity by Peter Herroux, Brian slid an envelope toward her. Laura dumped the contents into her lap and studied a grotesque series of photographs; in a few creatively angled shots, a male appeared ready to engage. Laura held one up. "Content aside, these are of particularly poor quality."

"Most porn is," Brian answered with a smirk.

Laura noted in addition to many noteworthy attributes, the male had large quantities of body hair and a tattoo. She returned everything to the envelope and handed it back. "My client is thin, with fine hair and no need to shave more than once a week. Peter's also tattoo-less, so I see no indication these are of or belong to him."

Brian insisted he never said the photos were **of** her client. "However, the envelope was in his locker."

Laura acknowledged the academy demanded all students sign a blanket statement of agreement to unannounced searches for drugs, paraphernalia, stolen goods, and illegal or questionable items. "Certainly where pornography is discovered is an important detail. However, since my client isn't the only one with access to the locker in question, I see no indication he stored these there."

"So it's to be gamesmanship with fancy phrasing?"

"No, it's the law, Mr. Lemphier—access and liability. I'll order fingerprint analysis on the photos and envelope."

Brian stared for a moment. "To avoid what will clearly become a no-win situation, might we consider a compromise?"

"Exactly what I had in mind," Laura replied and outlined her expectations. "Peter returns with no mention of expulsion on his permanent record; teachers and headmaster provide letters of recommendation to college admissions and scholarship committees appropriate for a student of his standing; and he and his family are no longer singled out for harassment because they're not members."

"That last one is an outrageous allegation."

"Is it? Peter provided names of other students who participated in the same activities; he earned expulsion while they earned detention."

"I want those names."

Laura nodded. "If this matter moves forward, as required by law I'll provide the CFEL's attorney with names I'd call to testify."

Brian smiled. "Your threats hold no water with…"

Laura interrupted, "I also prepared documents for the Vermont State Department of Education. If our meeting ends without accord, I file a defamation of character grievance on behalf of my college-bound client." Laura watched Brian's eyes and saw she hit an appropriate nerve: the State viewed as an unwelcome, unnecessary, and all too frequent annoyance and right behind lurked an equally disturbing sort of vermin: the media.

After a long silence, Brian sighed, "I'll allow the little shit back if he agrees to adhere to stricter disciplinary guidelines."

Laura stood and suggested they meet again Friday. "In the meantime, please review this proposed revision to the current rules of conduct handbook issued to Peter upon his admission to the academy. I'm certain you'll agree this to be fair and just for his senior year."

"What YOU feel? Who the fuck do…"

"Piece of advice: a headmaster at a respected institution like the Fallsbridge Academy might learn to recognize a difference between boys who smoke or use inappropriate language and boys who peddle pornography. That same headmaster might also consider the wisdom of holding students to a higher standard of verbal expression than he himself practices." Laura stood and thanked him for his time but Brian ignored her outstretched hand. "Friday morning 9:30 AM, here—Peter, his father, and me, my client prepared to return to classes."

"Whatever."

Outside Laura turned her face to the sun and calculated what she needed to resolve in four days: a client with a third arrest for DWI, Harvey Browne's marijuana misfortune, statements in need of signatures, and evidence to store with Wilkers. She decided to work 18-hour days if necessary to keep a promise to Steve. Laura rounded a corner and jumped when someone grabbed her elbow from behind. She feared Glenn but faced Angela. "You're never there when I stop by the office."

"I had an appointment here but why aren't you in class?"

Angela shrugged, "Mom took me to a social worker but I hate talking about it because it doesn't matter; you did this, too, right?"

Laura leaned closer. "In case it protects someone else later, we need to talk to anyone who'll listen." When Angela stared at the entrance, Laura recognized the terror in the girl's eyes and recalled how it stung to go to school as if nothing changed, understand she felt different from other girls her age, and hear girls gossip or boys snicker. Laura felt Angela's fingers flutter inside a too-tight grip and squeezed. "In time, you'll feel better about life again. Do you believe me?"

"I believe every word you say," Angela said and headed off.

Laura heard Brian shout out an open window: "As an observant headmaster, I question why a childless adult hangs around my school."

Laura waved. "See you Friday morning!"

At her desk, Laura reviewed records of 11 women who over 20 years suffered a stillbirth hours before another woman's live birth. Connection or coincidence? If Steve were there, would he insist she stretched again? If true, how could she prove it? It was one thing to note similarities in age, ethnicity, educational attainment, hair color, eye color, and religious affiliation, quite another to prove more than biographical coincidence. The CFEL doctor's ongoing interest in heredity was well known, never denied. Perhaps Steve should challenge an investigation into an alleged sexual assault she twisted into a conspiracy.

134

Marie knew she played a hateful game but after years of his shenanigans relished a feeling of control. Ned invited her to a restaurant in Burlington, a place they avoided in the past because dinner for two cost a week's groceries. She almost broke down, not because of the restaurant, prices, or fantastic food but because halfway through dinner, Ned asked, "What happened to those two kids who fell madly in love?"

Marie considered answering, *One stayed faithful and one didn't*, but wouldn't lie; maybe she waited ten years longer to cheat and maybe only once for her compared to countless for him, but both were to blame. She shrugged, "Somewhere along the way, they got lost." During the drive back to her friend's house, Marie confided she found an apartment near work. "I've imposed on others too long."

Ned pulled to the curb. "You have a home."

Marie let him draw her into his arms and heard him whisper his usual promises. She pulled back. "I won't keep living like a pathetic woman with no alternative but to put up with sordid affairs.."

In the end, Ned agreed to everything, right on down to the one he denied for years: leave a number where he could be reached day or night. Marie moved back the following weekend, stunned to see how organized everything looked and watched her husband of 28 years prepare dinner for the first time. Ned insisted Robbie and Erica make themselves scarce and Marie felt awkward alone with Ned but he seemed natural. Later when their connection turned physical, it felt different; no, it felt wonderful, like at the beginning. Afterward, Marie confessed, "I feel euphoric; I know this can't last but…"

"It could if you stopped drinking; you're amazing when you're sober. This is the woman I want to remain faithful to forever."

"I promise to try."

"To get started on the right foot, I recommend a symbolic gesture." He pulled her to her feet. "Show me where you hide your stash; I searched but…"

Marie laughed, "What makes you think I…?" but stopped and nodded. She led him to the laundry room, climbed onto the footstool to pull two plastic quart containers down, and handed them to him. In Melanie's old bedroom, she retrieved a container from behind a box of college textbooks. In the pantry, she pulled an apple juice bottle from behind boxes of unopened cereal. "That's all of it."

Ned led her to the bathroom, poured clear liquid from two containers, and grinned. "Empty yours and flush poison away." After they climbed back into bed, Ned drew her close. "Let's make love again."

Marie laughed, "Twice in one night? My God, Ned, we haven't made love twice in one night in decades."

"I know; I'm sorry." Marie lay awake long after Ned snored, studied his profile, and knew their reconciliation was fragile at best.

135

Steve left work early with another grinding headache only to arrive home to kid carpenters swarming the roof pounding nails. He showered under the hottest water his skin could bear and buried his head under as many pillows as he could find. When he woke, he heard quiet and wandered into the kitchen for leftover pizza. The pile of mail sat on the counter where he dumped it and his heart raced at the sight of a return address: mixed in with junk ads and bills were the results of Laura's test. He started to tear, stopped, and left.

136

Laura loved Mondays because in the evening, she escaped one shitty little town, drove far, far away, and called Steve. To kill time, she headed to the green and studied activity in the park: dogs, Frisbees, baby carriages, and bikes. Shouts from a softball game captured her attention and she headed to the snack bar for a chili dog. She wolfed it down, bought a Creemee, and headed to the ball field. She pulled a wide-brimmed hat on and climbed midway up the bleachers. At the top of the fourth inning, a brunette with a pony tail sticking out the back of her cap smacked the ball hard. As it bounced toward right center, she took off and amid yelps from the crowd, made it to second. From behind, a spectator said, "Good hit."

"Yeah." Laura crunched the cone and licked her fingers.

"Is that the infamous dugout?"

She turned slightly. "Hnnh?"

"Where Aaron Preveau had his way with you?"

Laura turned and squinted into the sun. "Steve?"

"Careful; turn around. Shit, you're blushing. Come on, kid; face the field. I brought something."

Laura watched his hand tremble as he extended a half-sealed envelope, recognized the return address, and grabbed. "Um, the cabin my parents rent for the summer is between Littleton and Woodsville. After Littleton on NH 302 South, it's 11 miles to the entrance to Newman's Campgrounds. Meet me there in an hour."

"Nope; I'm going back; I'm just the mail carrier."

"If I don't meander, I can be …"

"Nope; give me time to get home then call."

Laura smiled over her shoulder. "The dirt road is on the right heading toward the river. Cabin 16's on the water. My parents aren't there but I will be. So will you, mister."

Steve leaned close. "Nope; kid, this is against the rules."

"Like all the other good stuff in our marriage, mister, we open this together." She hopped down the bleachers before he could argue.

137

Steve headed north and crossed near Colebrook. He admired the rustic beauty and wondered if any of the general stores or pay phones along the way were ones Laura used. When he found the campgrounds, Laura ran out and he grunted, "Be careful, kid! No matter what you believe to be the case, be careful." Once inside the cabin, he locked the door and closed the shades. "One of us could have been followed."

"I doubt it; even with Gil gone, I took extra time."

"Maybe so but I fear this is unbelievably stupid."

When Laura reached up to touch his face, Steve flinched and pushed her away. Laura choked, "Are you kidding me?"

"This is dangerous and..."

"Don't ever push me away!"

"I don't think this is wise, Laura, and..."

Steve cringed at the sound of her voice. "Give me a break! Before you, I went anywhere I wanted, did anything I felt like doing, and never worried anything was missing from my life. Boy, do I feel stupid! I'd be better off if we never got involved in the first place. I didn't need to find out what it's like, especially with someone who..."

Steve reached for her hand. "I suspect this investigation..."

"I won't be interrupted! I ache for you, damn it! I ache! I have all this energy and almost let something happen with..."

"Laura, never allow an investigation to..."

"Don't patronize me! I know I'm in way over my head with too much to do before I..." Laura turned away, sat on the bed with her back to him, and ran through confusing details about Angela, Wilkers, Marsethe, someone named Harvey, Violet, and a DWI client named Margo something. "I had dinner with someone and could have... And in this one dream you lit a cigarette and..."

Steve sat on the edge of the bed beside her and took her hand. "You're not making sense, Laura. Why don't we do what you asked before? Let's run through pieces of your investigation, sort things out, and strategize where to go from...?"

Laura choked, "Are you shitting me, Scolarzski? Acting like a fucking police partner is not what I need right now but what really gets me is I suspect you're back there humping anything with a pulse!"

Steve's throat tightened. "Laura, don't."

Laura looked away. "I'll shut up before I say something I'll regret." She moved as far away as she could without actually leaving, grabbed the door handle, and spoke so softly, he could barely hear. "Have I ruined everything? Did I scare you off by how bratty I can be? I'm sorry I said such a cruel and hateful thing but I miss you something awful. I have all this energy and can't..."

Steve crossed the space and wrapped his arms around her. "Kid, I think we just survived our first nasty fight."

Laura relaxed against him. "How'd you know I kissed Aaron Preveau in the dugout?"

"When you gave me permission to look through boxes, that started a ritual of going through one at a time. Some nights were disappointing if I found sweaters or textbooks while others were like hidden treasure. It helps with loneliness."

"Um, have you ever come across anything that made you regret your decision to get married?"

Steve heard a subtle shift in tone and sighed, "You're the best thing in my life but it's taking too long to open this envelope."

Laura tore but thrust it forward. "I'm too nervous. Will you?"

Steve scanned the contents. "It says you provided insufficient information to predict a due date closer than early to mid-April."

Laura squinted. "What?"

"Kid, we're expecting."

Laura bit her lower lip. "I'll be home for good Friday."

"You promised if you were pregnant, you'd..."

Laura bounced to her feet. "I'm so close and four more days is minor, don't you think? Um, there are things I have to do before I come home so I won't be haunted for years about what I left unfinished."

"We should talk about..."

"No more talking, mister." Laura pushed him onto the bed and straddled him. "Tonight, let me call the shots."

"Excuse me?"

"You take your orders from me starting now. Oh, wait." She jumped off, rummaged through her bag, and handed him a gift.

As he tugged on a ribbon, Steve saw her blush. "For heaven's sake, what's in here?"

"Something for your birthday."

Steve tossed the paper aside and lifted a negligee. "I love this color on you." He opened the card, sighed she wrote beautifully, too, and held up two tickets for a September game at Fenway Park. "I didn't know you like the Red Sox."

Laura shrugged, "I don't pay attention really but so many times I heard you debate your brilliance as a Red Sox fan with Ralph's idiocy about the Yankees and thought…"

Steve chuckled, "Come here, kid."

"Not yet." Laura grabbed the negligee and hopped to the bathroom. In record time, she rushed back to straddle his waist and unbutton his shirt. "I'd like to try what I couldn't before."

"Which is?"

Laura pinched his chin. "I'm nervous enough so don't make me spell it out. I might be too terrified."

Steve flipped her over and leaned close. "I'm about to turn 44, way too old for heart-pounding recreation like this." He took it slow and at every new move, asked for permission to continue.

Though she responded, he felt awkward at a sense her body stayed while her mind went elsewhere. When she shuddered and stretched out, Laura murmured, "Thank you for helping me appreciate this body. Now let's see about you."

"It's not necessary for me to…"

"Oh but I think it is."

In the past, he struggled to hold back—like a 19-year-old on fire; not that moment, though. He searched her eyes, tried to slow things down, and squirmed from her touch. "I think I'm too exhausted to…"

"Are you kidding me?"

"I'm tired, Laura, and I'm satisfied to know you…"

Laura bounced up. "What is this? Macho-chauvinist-pigdomism because I'm no longer terrified?"

"Laura, it has nothing to do with…"

"Then tell me what's going on here because…"

Steve touched her lips. "Do you remember a conversation a while back? When you snuggled close, I hesitated because I feared I couldn't finish and you said 'Why can't you understand it's not the sex I crave but your closeness?' Tonight I finally understand what you meant."

"I remember that but don't see what…"

"Laura, forgive my bluntness but tonight's the first time I thought you weren't here with me; any man with the right equipment would suit you just fine. You never once looked into my eyes or…"

Laura laughed, "Nonsense! You of all people know how long I too to be intimate with anyone."

"And I thank God you chose me but tonight felt different."

Laura chewed her lower lip like she so often did and nodded. "Steve, I'm sorry if that's how my reaction struck you because my god, I felt like I left this planet." Laura snuggled close into the nesting position.

The next thing he knew, Steve glanced around and groaned, "Shit! Not good—it's almost daylight and both our cars are outside— Vermont plates." He grabbed his clothes off the floor.

"You worry too much, Scolarzski."

Steve studied her smirk. "And all of a sudden, you don't worry enough. After months of hard work on your part, I show up and may have blown it sky high because I can't get you off my mind."

"That's where I want to be." Laura propped herself on her elbow and watched him dress. As he pulled slacks on, he visualized what she saw: skinny legs that didn't quite match the flabby middle he worked so hard to control but couldn't. Laura rolled out of bed and wrapped her arms around his waist. "Does it bother you when I leer?"

Steve shrugged, "I guess a little, yeah. I worry I might not be able to keep up or disappoint you." He felt tension, pinched skin between his brows, and grabbed car keys. "Continue to build reliable evidence. You know what holds up in court, Delorange."

Laura chuckled, "You sound like a cop again, Scolarzski."

"Yeah? How about I feel like stud service."

Steve expected anger but Laura leaned so close, he counted new freckles on the bridge of her nose. "On a scale of one to ten—with ten outstanding—I give this particular service call a seven: magnificent setting, flawless delivery, horrible departure."

Steve relaxed in relief and buried his face in her hair. "I confess to an old-fangled notion married couples live, eat, watch TV, argue, take showers, and sleep together. I want my wife and our unborn child home, not off in some sleazebag town full of creeps."

"Steve, I'll be home Friday."

"This terror I feel is a first. Damn it, Laura! We have a baby on the way. I don't know why that makes a difference, but it does."

"I feel it, too. It's Tuesday so I'll be home in—" she checked her watch—"let's see, about 85 hours?"

"Promise?"

"I promise. Count the hours, mister, until we can argue and fuss 'til we're blue in the face or the cows come home.'"

Steve watched her drive off but never felt the customary relief; her voice, body language, unfocused eyes, insatiable appetite for physical contact, and mood swings terrified him. When she left, she seemed steady—not her usual self but calmer—but at 130 miles apart, how could he help her stay focused? Steve headed out, found decebt cell coverage, and left a message for Wilkers: "When you get a chance, check on Laura. She's due back Friday but something's not right and I... just check in, please. Thanks."

138

Mel felt insulted Brian didn't have the sense to report on his own and drove to the academy. It didn't take long to discern the fool failed in his assignment. In fact, Brian turned argumentative and freely admitted he took only four new photographs: one when Laura fell asleep at the green, another in line at the snack bar, a third as she wiped ice cream off her blouse, and a fourth as she talked to some guy at the softball field. Mel perked up at that. "Describe him."

Brian shrugged, "Some guy I never saw before sat behind her, probably a parent from the Lyndonville team."

Mel leaned across the desk. "I said describe him."

"About my height and age, light hair, a little pudgy around the waist, and not a snappy dresser. Nondescript, Mel."

"Did you follow him when he left?"

"No, Violet had people coming for dinner and..."

"Describe his car! Did you get a license plate?"

"Are you kidding? I'm not Gil!"

Mel sighed, "Okay, okay; where's my camera?"

"At home."

"The film?"

"I took it over for processing."

Mel leaned across the desk. "Film gets turned in at the pharmacy like a picnic or party? Like I care to wait? Look at these Gil took before he left." He slapped dozens of photos down and watched Brian study Laura, her family, coworkers, and friends. "Although she appears to rejoin us, I fear someone tugs her back. First pay phones, now visits home for picnics and parties. Her former lover may be her lover still to explain her disinterest in Glenn. Look closely: is that man's face here?"

"I don't recognize anyone here as the guy."

Mel grunted, "Of what use are you?" He returned to his office, called Vince, and insisted he confiscate a roll of black and white film from the pharmacy drop-box. "I find I'm surrounded by idiots! If I cannot find someone to use Gil's equipment, I'll teach myself!"

285

Mel called Glenn to demand he stop by. Once again he took his time and made no excuse for a delay. Mel allowed the rudeness to pass and extended an envelope of Gil-produced quality photos. Glenn scanned contents. "Why is this necessary? I trust Laura."

"With the gifts made available to members, our community has a need to assess sincerity; all rewards are earned." In response to Glenn's continued petulance, Mel reminded Glenn of his involvement in Gil's departure. "The elders and I are distressed David is no longer among us to seed the future yet here I provide an opportunity to make amends."

"You place too much emphasis on one or two people to..."

"No! This is not an arbitrary decision of a foolish old man! Mary and Reilly were carefully planned and David's existence proves I'm capable of designing a perfect human. That wondrous male will spend his future alongside yours and Laura's first female specimen."

Glenn lowered the photos to the table. "Some of these go back years, Mel, and she's done nothing to..."

"Then prove me wrong! Laura conspires with known adversaries like Wilkers, Browne, and Herroux and in no time, may spread defamations further. Who's to say she didn't plant negative thoughts in Reilly's susceptible mind? If you're so convinced of her sincerity, take this opportunity to wipe the slate clean because one way or another, you'll pay for a decision to confiscate funds." Mel pointed at Gil's printing on the back of one group photo in particular: *Delorange yard, Essex Junction, July 23, John Delorange Sr birthday - Laura Delorange, Ned and Marie Sigler, Roger and Helen Macrae, Ralph and Joyce Barber, Steve Scolarzski, and Rick Delorange.* In the next, Glenn stared at Scolarzski's arm draped casually over her shoulder and Mel hissed, "I suspect last night idiot Brian took photos of her with this very man, not only her former lover but current."

Glenn sighed, "I don't believe that."

Mel stabbed his index finger in the air. "See how he touches your angel, as if in such intimacy, he lays claim to every inch? See how she accepts his pawing?"

Glenn studied Laura's face. "So she feels comfortable with them." Glenn lifted one. "See this one? She hugs this guy Barber."

"You see Laura through rose-colored glasses and that I accept but it's to your advantage to know the truth of why she's among us."

"I don't like where this is heading; just because Gil's gone and Brian didn't work out doesn't mean I'm capable of doing what Gil did for you and the elders. I'd come back empty-handed."

"As usual you sell yourself short. Gil learned skills slowly, too. Think, please: what is the only method of infiltration likely to succeed?"

Glenn shrugged, "Knowledge?"

"In a way; think further."

"I don't know; just tell me what you're getting at!"

Mel whispered, "One must find a back door to information. Study these faces and read Gil's reports. When you determine the point of entry into a tiny circle of friends, let me know." Glenn nodded and started to read Gil's copious field notes.

139

Laura cringed at a desktop cluttered with folders of assorted work in-process—too much to handle by Friday. She prioritized those she planned to complete, those to move forward in a legal process, those to hand to Wilkers to complete, and those to send to Burlington for later. She started with a review of the academy handbook issued to students, jotted notes, and called the Herroux house to schedule time to prepare for the meeting with Brian. She called the client arrested on a third DWI and reached her sister, who reported Margo recently married and moved to Arizona. Laura sighed, "Did Margo forget charges are pending? Does she understand the ramifications of leaving the state without...?"

"Miss Delorange, my sister doesn't think, period."

"When you hear from Margo, ask her to call me. I think I can get an extension on her appearance."

Laura prepared August figures for client billing: preparation of wills and guardianship papers, copyright and tax research for the expansion of *Nature's Bounties*, appointments with clients with cases pending, and new contacts seeking representation. Without counting hours spent on Marsethe, she had 132 billable hours. Without Reilly's help, she did her own typing, filing, and data entry for two non-billable hours entered as *office maintenance*. When she couldn't procrastinate further, she retrieved statements for Camille Beaugiere, Caroline Beaudon, and Frannie Stenzola, snapped them into her briefcase. and headed out. From data and records spanning 20 years, Laura suspected 11 different women delivered a child live only to have the doctor record it as a stillbirth before selling to the highest bidder within hours. Laura feared Camille Beaugiere's signature would be the toughest but where to start. Laura found Camille's cottage in the same block as the Maidstone Inn, across from the green and band shell. When Camille opened the door,

Laura whispered, "Hello, I'm Laura Delorange. I believe when I lived here as a child, you knew my mother, Lynette."

Camille squinted but answered, "I knew her, yes."

"I'm sorry to intrude and apologize in advance for..."

"I'm busy so if you're selling something, I..."

"Um, I'd like to discuss a baby you delivered 12 years ago."

Even as she started to close the door, Camille's eyes showed a painful truth. "Go before I call the police."

"Please give me a minute! I'm a former state police investigator who suspects she found evidence of baby-trafficking."

Camille sucked in her breath and opened the door wide. "Come in before anyone sees you here." They sat at the kitchen table and Laura shared notes and theories. Camille listened, read carefully, and corrected minor details and after a few minutes of awkward silence, whispered, "I admit I agreed in advance to have a baby and give it up for adoption, but when I changed my mind, it should have been all right."

"Um, yes, I agree and wish I could share everything but..."

Camille interrupted, "No one believed me; they all said I imagined hearing a baby cry, normal for a mother who lost an infant." Camille asked for a pen, signed, and dated. "I'm relieved someone finally believes me. What happens now? Will I learn where my baby...?"

Laura choked, "It's too soon and I could be wrong."

Camille studied Laura's eyes and nodded. "I wish you luck proving any of this but after 12 years, I can wait longer."

Laura left with a promise to keep in touch, crossed the green to the general store, and watched Caroline wrap center cut pork chops for Elder Vincent, who nodded in Laura's direction. Once they were alone, Caroline listened to Laura explain why she was there, seemed curious about the process but suspicious of a legal-looking document with no charges listed or assurances regarding outcome. Caroline read the document multiple times, signed, and mumbled, "For months, Dr. Marsethe had me pump breast milk into containers he took with him and every time, I felt as if I emptied myself. He said mother's milk couldn't be forced to dry up and I believed him! What a fool, huh? I'll bet he let someone else feed my baby with my milk!"

When Laura swallowed hard and whispered, "I can't make any promises but..."

Caroline interrupted, "If true, this affects your family, too, but I kept this inside all these years, Laura, and know how to be patient."

As hopeful as she felt after Camille Beaugiere, Laura left Caroline with new resolve. She searched for the Stenzola house on the outskirts of the village and arrived as the younger girls jumped off the bus with a million stories to share. Laura found Frannie to be as beautiful in person as photos suggested, Laura explained her visit as, "Fact-finding about the delivery; I'm not at liberty to provide detail about what I hope to accomplish but if details are correct, I hope you'll sign to that effect."

Frannie frowned. "Do you work for an insurance company? Is this about malpractice? That could make life more difficult for us."

"No, this has nothing to do with malpractice but I can't go into any detail at this point. I'm sorry; I think I should leave."

Laura felt Frannie's deep scrutiny. "I saw you at the funeral"

"Yes, I attended."

"Are you the one who got charges dropped?"

"Charges were dropped for lack of evidence." Frannie remained silent and barely looked at the document. Laura considered divulging her real reason for being there since by leaving out details she shared with the others voluntarily, she drifted too far off an ethical path. Laura stood. "I'm sorry; it's unkind of me to bother you so soon after...."

Frannie interrupted, "I taunted Al about a son he'd never meet but I never meant to hurt him." Laura sat again as Frannie pointed at the document. "I remember every detail and most are here." Frannie grabbed the pen, signed, and stood. "I wish you well with whatever you hope to accomplish with details this sad. When you see Al, will you tell him something? Even though Mel sent me, it wasn't all a lie?"

"I'll tell him. Thank you."

Laura drove to Groveton to a pay phone, tried to reach Wilkers at his cell and his desk; no answer. At his home number, she left a message: "I believe I'm done, Al. I really think I'm ready to head home for good and if it's okay, plan to leave evidence at your house until we can review and sort together. I'll be in touch."

140

Mel finished his final appointment and found Glenn in the den surrounded by photos, reports, and nine maroon albums. He looked up. "What can I do to make her look at me the way she looks at him?"

Mel sat down to outline a plan. "First you ask Muriel to manage the Maidstone for a few days; second you announce a buying trip out of town; third you head to Chittenden County; and fourth you uncover truths. Who is your point of entry?"

Glenn pointed to a sad smile. "Marie Sigler is a heavy drinker and lonely, neglected wife."

"And how far are you willing to go for information?"

"I'm not my brother, Mel. I'll listen and reassure this woman but nothing more. When I come back with proof of Laura's sincerity, I want a promise you'll leave us alone. And I mean both of us."

"A promise is made."

143

Marie stared out at a glorious day and decided to call in sick. She headed to the mall salon for a rinse to hide early gray and shopped a little. When she noticed the time, she headed toward the state police barracks to invite Ned to lunch. As she neared, Marie watched him leave and followed as best as she could. When she got caught at a traffic light, she watched Ned swing into a space and roll his window down. A woman waved from across the street, a stunning brunette in red dress and black heels. Marie considered it a mistake—W waved to someone else—until she crossed and leaned in Ned's open window. Marie squealed around the corner and pulled up alongside. "Honey, don't count on much today. Ned's got to be exhausted from recent charity work."

Ned laughed, "It's not what you…"

"I'll bet," Marie snorted hit the gas, and peeled away. She turned onto a familiar side street, pulled into an equally familiar lot, and headed inside for a couple of stiff ones.

Marie almost left—but didn't—when the bartender called out, "Hey, Marie. Where ya been keeping yourself?"

"Nowhere important," she sighed and watched him prepare her usual. "Make that a double," she shouted and settled in.

142

After work Laura trimmed the garden, scraggly after harvesting most of the vegetables though way in back along the stone wall, pumpkins and gourds flourished. September in Vermont: perfect for an outdoor reception and in combination with October, a flawless season for warm, sunny days with cool breezy nights; photographing mountains, lakes, rivers, picturesque villages, and fall foliage; drying clothes outdoors; and deep, restful sleep with open windows. She unplugged air conditioners, stashed them in a closet, and chuckled at how ridiculous she felt when for months, each night before bed, she checked to see if empty cans rested atop the trap door to the tunnel. Laura heard a knock, opened the door, and asked Violet. "Are you avoiding me lately?"

"Believe it or not, I was ordered to stay away."

"By Brian?"

"Him, Mel, and my father... Vince. They say you're a bad influence and asked me to guess why you came back to Fallsbridge." When Laura headed to the stereo to raise the volume, Violet said, "You don't need to do that. Brian's at the academy—something's wrong with the AV system. He asked the elders to approve a new digital set-up but to get the most advanced stuff, they'd have to let tech people in and with Gil gone now..." Violet stopped and laughed, "Bitching about how the CFEL sticks its nose into every little thing is not why I came."

"So, how did you answer their question?"

"I said I thought after you were shot by a crazy woman, you needed our kind of peace and quiet."

Laura grinned. "All true!"

Violet explained after their last visit to the lab, Mel found her revulsion odd. "He came over last night, insisted Brian take the children to a movie at the mall in Newport, and demanded I accept a new reality. He spent hours telling his version of truth; no, he did what he always does: lecture confusing ideas about the natural order of life."

"If this bothers you, don't..."

"I know I'm rambling but there's no other way to get it out."

Laura nodded. "I get like that, too. Go on."

"Mel claims fertility specialists were rare in the 50's. Unless a woman could afford specialists just as rare, if she failed to conceive she didn't have a child, plain and simple. After 15 years of marriage without using any sort of birth control—and I have to assume an appropriate sex life though that's hard for me to fathom between Cassandra and Vincent Mottolla—they turned to a blood relative for help."

"Your mother's name is Cassandra?"

"Yeah, why is...?"

"And Mel and Vincent are cousins?"

Violet nodded. "Their mothers were sisters. Mel claims he slept with my mother for months before my conception—he claims all were at her invitation based upon her menstrual cycle."

"It sounds like she wanted you very badly."

Violet insisted she forgave her mother but couldn't forgive what followed. "Mel admitted after my birth and a few others around the same time—not with him as father, thank God, because can you imagine how

291

difficult that would be to keep straight? No, he found other men to match to patients. He already felt obsessed by inherited traits or timing for male versus female so I guess it's no big surprise he fixated on the fertility of certain village women and sought to influence every conception."

Laura sighed, "Why sound surprised? You saw his charts."

Violet snorted, "He must think I'm a fool to believe he acted as a favor to a growing community, not some negative evaluation or direct insult to husbands. This crazy idea about improving the odds sounds deranged, don't you think? Calling it benign is stupid."

Laura shrugged. "Again, why so surprised? He's consistent with his theories of what leads to a quality life: education, diet, and family history. It's why he's so proud of you, Ben, Joanna, and Paul."

Violet sighed, "As much as I'd like to continue this conversation to make sense of it, I stopped by for a reason. I overheard Mel and Brian and need to warn you: Gil may be gone but Brian follows you."

Laura imagined for three more days, Brian underfoot made no difference. "I'll be fine. Um, now that you're here, can I pick your brain about something personal—something female in nature?"

"Sure."

Laura turned the volume up on the stereo receiver. "I know you said Brian's out but…"

Violet grinned maliciously. "Is this about sex?"

"Um, you know about my history but what you don't know is my former partner was my first consensual experience. Everything felt new and exciting and I couldn't get enough of him. Even now there are times when I remember how it feels to lie with him, and I ache for that again. I'm embarrassed to admit I sometimes touch myself and…"

Violet interrupted "Don't beat yourself up; there's nothing wrong with a healthy libido." At the sound of a car, Violet jumped up and talked on her way by. "Sounds like because you didn't use high school or college to experiment and fine-tune your libido, you're confused. Find a willing partner to love and practice, Laura, practice. You'll get it right."

143

Glenn wrote the night off as a total waste then lost daylight Wednesday catching up on sleep in a dive-motel on Shelburne Road. He missed the unblemished establishments and swept parking lots circling the green in Fallsbridge and wondered how anyone tolerated so much ugliness and disorder in a state as beautiful as Vermont. At sunset he repeated Tuesday night's vigil and parked down the block to watch the Sigler house. Not much activity until a woman dragged two suitcases out to a car. Glenn followed her to a bar off Battery Street and imagined in daytime the view of Lake Champlain might be uplifting. He followed her inside, blasted by a scent of sweaty bodies, booze, and cigarettes, and by country music played too loud on a flashing jukebox. He settled into a booth, studied Marie Sigler from a distance, and found her to be an attractive woman in her mid-40's, good figure, attractive hairstyle, fashionable clothes, warm smile, and from what he could hear, husky laugh. She seemed modest in a way that reminded him of Violet, Mary, and Rita, women whose husbands breezed in and out under an assumption decent clothes, new car, comfortable home, and spending cash were all wives really needed. Marie brushed pretzel salt off the counter and spoke; the bartender nodded and laughed. Another customer slid down a few stools and Marie brushed him off, too. Glenn imagined it would be tougher to get close than Mel thought; simply because she was an alcoholic didn't make her stupid about anything but booze.

Glenn looked around for a waiter or waitress, saw neither, and headed to the bar to order a draft beer and bowl of chili. He studied Marie up close: a few lines around her eyes but pretty. When she caught his eye, the sharpness of hers seemed incongruous to everything he read. Glenn returned to his booth, heard lyrics about lust, and watched couples dance. Glenn patted his pockets for coins, headed to the jukebox, and scanned titles until he recognized one his customers selected when the weekend band at the Maidstone took a break, one with sad lyrics and a great beat: *You Have the Right to Remain Silent* by Perfect Stranger.

When Glenn approached and extended a hand, Marie laughed, "Good choice! My soon-to-be-ex says that all the time." She stood and stared. "Don't you know to pull jeans on when they're still damp?"

"What?"

"They're not tight enough to see what I'll miss if I say no."

Glenn grinned at how right Gil was when he claimed most women wanted to be grabbed, mauled, and fucked, not kissed, caressed, and loved and if a man trusted his instincts, he'd know within seconds. "What if I didn't plan to ask for more than a dance?"

"Then I'd say you're a fag."

After the song ended, Glenn offered her a drink and indicated his booth. When he returned, she ran her hand along his thigh. He grabbed. "That's not why I'm here."

"Okay, then tell me why you are."

"I wanted a glass of beer and bowl of chili."

"Yeah, right," Marie laughed and said nothing of interest until she shifted to complaints about her husband, Glenn felt stunned at how much he already knew from Gil's reports and photos. Marie griped about her husband's infidelities and told anecdotal tales about other familiar names which verified Macrae as a recovering heart patient, Rawlings a rookie, Granger a jerk, Barber a playful clown, and Scolarzski overly serious. "Barber's my favorite but Scolarzski's the one I root for. His first wife was an asshole but I think he'll be happy this time." Glenn recalled the name as Laura's former partner, the man who concerned Mel, the one Laura mentioned recently married someone more worldly. Glenn felt a sinking feeling and fished for details about Laura's former love interest but Marie was too foggy to add much beyond, "What can I say to move our conversation from this booth to a mattress?"

"The name of a new wife might help."

"I can't; I really can't tell you what we promised Steve and Laura we'd keep secret while she's off doing God knows what for Godzilla Granger." To shouts of, "Hey, Mr. Baggy Britches, where are you going? Do you want me to come, too?" Glenn headed east toward home.

144

Thursday morning Laura heard two messages from Al on the office machine—odd questions about topics nothing to do with anything they discussed—and figured he checked to see if she stayed on schedule. She called back. "I'm fine, Al, busy as always. Um, if you'll be at your place tomorrow afternoon or early evening, I'll stop by."

"Okay; I'll see you then."

Laura met with Peter and Thomas Herroux to finalize a revised statement of conduct. "If you felt harassed before, you'll be scrutinized to the nth degree after Mr. Lemphier sees this at tomorrow's meeting."

Peter grinned. "I can be a robot for the next nine months. This may sound petty but in addition to finishing in good standing, I intend to be class valedictorian. Let him try to fudge records to take that away."

Laura smiled and extended her right hand. "I admire your spunk. I'll see you tomorrow morning at 9:30 at the academy."

Laura organized Peter's file, dropped it into her briefcase, and scanned remaining piles—a manageable workload representing ten hours of concentrated effort, twelve tops. She opened Harvey Browne's file and phoned the deputy state's attorney to check on the status of his marijuana cultivation charges. The prosecutor said, "I see from our pre-sentence investigation, your client filed required a application for licensed

294

caregiver. During this transition period in how a new law's interpreted, I'm inclined to keep it simple. If your client agrees to plead out, I'll recommend six months' probation and $500 fine."

"I'll speak to my client and get back to you tomorrow." She hung up, tried Mr. Browne's number, and left a message.

Laura pored over Marsethe's most recent records until she felt convinced she figured out which couple accepted Al and Frannie's baby as their own. Laura planned a drive to Barton but at the last minute, cross-checked details from a chart Sandra created from multiple source files from decades earlier. Though she had too much still to to do before escaping one shitty little town, she couldn't leave the area until she knew for sure if there were another Delorange in their world.

Laura headed west, stopped at a general store for gas, and asked another customer for directions to the home of Ellen and Carl Halleston. The man stared her down, studied her license tag, and grunted, "Who's asking?" Though she knew it unethical to mislead, Laura displayed expired state police identification and the man shouted into the car, "Doris, don't you know some woman named Halleston?"

A woman slid across the front seat. "Yes, Ellen Halleston teaches at the school where I tutor reading twice a week."

Laura nodded. "Could you point me in the right direction?"

When the husband went inside to pay, Doris gave detailed directions then asked, "Did they do something wrong?"

Laura smiled. "No, no, I have a few questions."

Doris glanced toward the store. "I'll bet it's about their baby." Laura didn't need to say another word as Doris offered a gold mine of information. "Everyone at school knew Ellen tried to get pregnant for years without success before she and Carl went through all kind of fertility tests and treatments at clinics in Boston first, then Montreal. We felt real sorry for them and then boom, Ellen comes in one day in April to announce she's pregnant. Oddest thing is the next week I go in and she wears a maternity smock. Just a tiny blip but I figure she's proud as hell! Not much later at the 4th of July picnic, it looks like she skipped months of discomfort—the oddest pregnancy I've ever seen and I've seen a bunch."

"I understand the baby's beautiful."

"Oh yes; I've only seen him a few times at church but Theodore's fair like his daddy." Laura started to ask another question when the husband came out and pointed at the passenger door.

Laura headed north toward Newport Center, stopped at a gas station for directions, and found the Mosgrove Farm. Laura parked beside a roadside mailbox, turned off the ignition, and lifted binoculars. As a group of girls giggled past, one studied the car before she stopped at the end of the driveway, pulled a sandal off, slapped it against her thigh, and hopped along on one foot. Her strategy worked because in seconds, male voices shouted from the distance as two young men jumped off a porch and raced across a field. Laura gasped at one's striking resemblance to Jack's two sons with Sarah or for that matter, Jack at 18. She grabbed her camera, set it for infinity, and snapped. At the sight of the girl's backward glance, Laura started the car and pulled away.

Before the bridge to Vermont, Laura stopped at the general store in Groveton for a meatball grinder and can of soda. As she approached the cashier, she had second thoughts and substituted a pint of 2% milk for soda. At the pay phone, she sipped and chomped and tried Steve's desk first, then his cell, and finally the house. When she got another prompt to leave a message, she said, "I planned to wait until I get home tomorrow night to apologize but can't wait. I must have seemed manic Monday night and Tuesday morning and I can't explain it any better than yes, you're right; this investigation tears me to shreds. That will change in roughly 24 hours. Mister, I love you so much it scares me to pieces and promise the next time I'm lucky enough to lie in your arms, I'll make sure you know I know exactly where I am because that's the only place I ever want to be. Be patient; your wife and baby are coming home."

145

Mel recognized deep pain in Glenn's eyes as he detailed the visit and said, "All is not lost. Think. Where shall we go from here?"

Obviously Glenn misunderstood the question; when confronted with the truth of his beloved's marriage to a nothing outsider, Glenn remained protective and prayed she lived apart from a husband for a reason they didn't see. Mel laughed at the idiocy. "She lives apart not while she searches for answers to questions of eternity, God, love, sex, or marriage, but because first and foremost, Laura is a cop."

"I'm not so sure, Mel. Laura's been..."

Interrupted by pounding on the door, Mel opened it to Carl Halleston who shoved his way into the parlor and collapsed on the sofa. Mel turned to Glenn. "We continue our conversation later; now go."

Mel faced Carl. "The specimen is perfect as promised, yes?"

"That's not why I'm here! Today a woman asked about Theodore but you promised the birth certificate lists us as natural parents."

"It does!"

"You promised no one would suspect anything if Ellen appeared to be pregnant."

Mel laughed, "It's true we rushed the process. Describe her."

"My information's second hand. Elgar Meeks said his wife Doris talked to a slender, dark-haired woman with state police identification."

"Automobile?"

"I think he said red compact, not new."

Mel guided Carl to the door. "All is fine; the elders and I assure you this poses no threat to your parenthood."

Mel considered a multitude of possibilities: someone else, a mistake, an odd coincidence. He remained cautious with record storage to guarantee Laura uncovered details only of his pre-patent project. Hadn't he? Mel relaxed on the sofa with the latest maroon album, thumbed through, and feared Laura might be more clever than he always knew her to be. He summoned Brian, Vincent, Robert, and Matthew— no one else, no new members to an inner circle dedicated to the survival of a beloved community. Brian arrived first and unleashed a new assault: Laura stopped near the farm of a family named Mosgrove. Brian held Gil's camera up and laughed, "I got shots of Laura taking **her** shots."

Mel ordered him to follow him to the cellar. "I moved Gil's processing and enlarging equipment here."

"I didn't know anyone else knew how to use his stuff."

Mel sighed, "Surrounded by idiots, one learns." Ninety minutes later—results far from perfect—Mel and Brian returned to the den.

Vincent arrived to report, "Laura showed up at Beaudon's Store, kept playing with her briefcase, and seemed nervous."

With a full group assembled, Mel summarized what he knew of Laura's recent activities, saw fear in their eyes, and understood only he had the fortitude to proceed. "Brian, spread photos around so they see where she went today. Vincent, you recognize the name on the mailbox, yes?" Mel studied faces and regretted more than ever Gilbert's loss to a female, now up to him alone to plan how to manage a growing nuisance. Minutes into a plan, Mel noticed Matthew and Robert dozed—two fools too old to lead—and faced Brian. "On Sunday, Benjamin advances to adult status; prepare him for this great honor."

146

Laura headed to the law office to organize records into boxes to store with Wilkers. When Harvey Browne returned her call, she summarized the offer, relieved when he agreed to the plea bargain. Now if only Margo Tibbetts would check in, she could close another file. Well after dark, Laura headed off with a trunk-full of boxes and dragged everything into Wilkers' foyer. "We can go through this together later." When he stared at the quantity, she groaned, "You're supposed to help me so pretend to be interested! I want to go home."

Al nodded and invited her inside. Laura collapsed on his couch and drifted into restless sleep. Off and on, she heard him move things around until a chuckled, "This is one shitload of information."

She cracked open one eye. "Yeah, but is any of it usable?"

"I won't know for hours, maybe days."

Laura didn't open her eyes again until Al removed her sandals and whispered, "Go back to sleep; you look exhausted."

The next time she opened her eyes, Laura checked her watch—3:10 am—and bolted up. "I can't! I need to be back before Brian notices. Um, you should know when I met with Frannie, she said 'Even though Mel sent me, it wasn't all a lie.'"

Al's nostrils flared like a cartoon bull. "I did what you said and waited to file a request for exhumation. Get your ass out of there because a court order's due to be carried out Wednesday."

Laura laughed, "No problem! It's Friday and I'm out of that shitty town in hours!"

Laura headed east and at the carriage house, turned ignition and headlights off to coast to a stop without touching squeaky brakes. She jumped out, pushed the door closed gently, and in the dark, bumped into someone or something. She feared Brian, a raccoon or skunk but heard Violet. "I can't believe you lied to me and now Brian's so quiet, I know something's about to happen."

Laura's mind raced through every possibility but only one made sense: Brian was better at surveillance than imagined. He knew something, maybe everything, and likely shared it. Laura grabbed Violet in a hug. "No matter what you hear, our friendship is real."

Laura heard rustling bushes behind her and prayed to see a raccoon or skunk but turned to watch Marsethe wave a flashlight toward the house. "Get the hell inside, Violet Lemphier!" Brian and Elders Robert, Matthew, and Vincent approached as Marsethe hissed, "You failed miserably as a guest in our peaceful village." He aimed the flashlight at a black and white photo of her in her car with her camera, and in a fuzzy background, Samuel Mosgrove Jr. flirting with the observant girl.

"Your photographer needs a better lens," Laura laughed and backed toward her car.

When Marsethe grabbed her arm, Laura winced and Elder Vincent reached out. Marsethe turned to sneer, "I look unkindly upon anyone who attempts to assist. Clear, yes?"

Vincent backed away. "Yes."

When Marsethe shoved, Laura stumbled and fell; she rubbed her elbow and stood. "You violate my privacy and detain me against my..."

"Oh how I adore your little lawyer talk," Marsethe chuckled. "Now allow me to hear my frightened Little Miss again, yes?"

"You don't scare me, Mel."

Marsethe turned and as soon as he issued orders, Matthew left to pack a suitcase and throw personal possessions into a box; Vincent headed to the main house to keep Violet and the children away from windows; and Brian covered her mouth with medical tape and tied wrists behind her back with clothesline. When Matthew returned to toss everything into the trunk of a black Cadillac Escalade, Marsethe faced her with a smile. "Prepare for a short ride, Mrs. Scolarzski."

Laura sucked in her breath, landed face first in the back seat, and knelt, forehead against carpet and shoulder stuck under a corner of a box. Robert squeezed in beside her, pressed his foot on the small of her back, and held her motionless as the car lurched forward. He asked, "Mel, don't we wait for Brian or Matthew?"

"No! Recall the plan! One attends to the carriage house and one her car." Laura felt a hand tap her back. "I found it odd how loyal females misbehaved until it became clear someone's brief presence in our community sufficient to corrupt Violet, Peg, and her daughters, and of Reilly, who stole David and Gilbert from those who need them most. I fear we may discover deep corruption of Caroline, too. Prepare to be punished throughout eternity for shameful behavior."

Laura choked, "Only God can decide that, and you are not God."

Marsethe pinched her neck. "The *Bible* is clear that woman is subservient to man; be subservient, woman." When Laura thrashed her shoulders, Marsethe chuckled, "Don't hurt yourself. Our community of souls requires you healthy during re-education to become a proper partner to Glenn Munier." Laura started to cry and Marsethe soothed, "Better, better; this is the salvageable soul I wish to recover.."

After a short, silent ride, Robert asked, "Can I let her change position? Her chest's smashed on the hump."

"She stays as she is—any subsequent bruising a reminder of my sincerity in this undertaking. In discomfort, she shall acquiesce."

Laura concentrated on vehicle movement to guess its speed but couldn't; unlike hers, the Cadillac took every bump and turn with grace. The engine never strained as it accelerated or raced between gear changes; brakes never squealed. She tried to see but couldn't, the pain unbearable. The car stopped and Marsethe opened the back door to yank her by her hair. "I imagine Sergeant Steve Scolarzski became enraptured of such lovely curls against bare skin, became excited by its scent, yes?" When Laura stumbled and threw a shoulder against his chest, Marsethe dragged her three steps into a cabin. She concentrated on surroundings: thick woods, two narrow paths, a dirt driveway off a dirt road, a trickling sound of water, a red mailbox, a.... Marsethe slapped her face hard. "You are to look only at what I deem appropriate, yes?" He ordered Robert to bring her things, for Vincent to tie her securely inside.

As Vincent led her to a dark corner, Laura sobbed and he glanced at the door. "Violet warned you, didn't she? Why didn't you listen?" As he pushed her onto the mattress, Laura lifted her feet and kicked his chest.

Marsethe slammed the door, crossed the room, and wound for a second strike—harder and more painful than the first. When she recoiled from pain in her jaw, he caressed gently. "Now, now, be cooperative and stay safe." When he turned and shouted new instructions, Vincent wrapped yellow nylon boat rope around her wrists and ankles, and stretched her limbs toward the corners of the metal bed frame. She heard a car door slam and Marsethe went to the window to report Matthew arrived with her car. "Robert, take the Cadillac, follow him, and be certain if the idiot neglected to wear gloves, wipe before abandoning it somewhere public." He turned to Laura with a smile. "I recommend the grocer in Groveton, yes? Park it beside her favorite pay phone."

Robert answered, "Yes, sir," and with that response, Laura finally understood Marsethe exerted power, influence, or leverage over others who at first glance, appeared to be equal.

Despite her best efforts, Laura couldn't stop tears as Marsethe checked knots. "Now the fun begins. We take turns. We watch you, know everything you do, and hear every sound you make. If we feel generous, we allow you to use a toilet instead of soiling your bed. You know the expression: *You made your bed; now lie in it?*" Marsethe turned to the three standing awkwardly off to the side. "Find something to assist, you idiotic Scaramouches!" The doctor wrapped a dark scarf around her head, covered her eyes, knotted too tight, and removed her watch.

Laura choked, "Please don't take that."

Marsethe caressed her chin. "I began to think nothing terrified you but see sightlessness does as will a dearth of information. Consider this: you won't know who's here, what he does, or what he sees."

Laura heard the bed creak and felt a shift in weight as he stood. She concentrated on every word, every sound from inside, outside, or overhead: footsteps, whispers, suitcases dropped to the floor or dragged across, a propeller plane, more footsteps, the door, the Cadillac engine, tires against dirt and gravel. When the cabin fell quiet, she concentrated on a soft wheezing every few seconds. Of them all, only Robert or Vincent breathed with effort. Robert smoked and Vincent didn't but had asthma; she figured Vincent remained, since she didn't smell cigarettes. Worried Marsethe hid off to the side, Laura hesitated but risked speaking. "Elder Vincent, please explain why I'm here."

Moments passed before Vincent answered, "Despite the love Mel feels for you, Laura, the one sin he cannot forgive is betrayal."

"Why would he think I betrayed him?" Laura waited for a response and when none came, attempted to engage him with topics ranging from the successful expansion of *Nature's Bounties* to international markets, fall academy concert schedule, or plans for the Harvest Fest banquet. Through it all, Vincent remained silent. She fought sleep, needed to use the bathroom, held it in until it hurt, and finally dozed. More hours passed before he untied her to use the bathroom. After a car pulled up, someone loaded groceries into the refrigerator and cupboards while someone else used a broom to sweep. When hands began to wash her ankle and wrist wounds, she stiffened and kicked. "Don't touch me!"

Marsethe pulled the scarf off. "A lack of cooperation prolongs confinement."

"How long do you intend to keep this up?"

Marsethe chuckled, "As long as necessary."

Laura felt him clean her wounds, spread a cool ointment, wrap her wrists and ankles with gauze, and apply tape. "Um, someone will notice if I don't show up for appointments."

A chuckled, "Why mislead with an s? There is one, arranged."

"Arranged?"

"If questioned, Peter and Thomas Herroux will report they met with their lawyer and academy headmaster as planned. Unlike you, they value the wisdom of cooperation. I get what I want and they do, too."

Laura considered other approaches but in the end, decided to listen. Whenever one left and another arrived, they spoke outside softly. Though no one spoke to her directly, they did to each other and Laura learned to distinguish them with small clues: seconds between footsteps, clearing throats, deep sighs, and scents. Marsethe smelled like a combination of leather car seats, soap, and mercurochrome. Elder Matthew had rough hands and bad coffee breath. Elder Robert smelled like cigarettes and bacon grease, and shuffled as he walked. Brian smelled of cigarettes, nervous perspiration, and Juicy Fruit gum. But it was Elder Vincent's gentle hands, calm presence, and scent of Ivory soap that convinced her to be patient and pray a trip home only delayed

.

147

Steve left work early and arrived home to a finished addition. He wandered the three rooms, stopped at the hot tub, and laughed when at the flick of a switch, water bubbled. The kid-carpenters installed closet shelves, poles, doors, and exterior shutters and outside, the staining was done. Steve tidied up, dusted, refolded her clothes, arranged them neatly in drawers, checked her nightgown was where it belonged, and imagined in the morning she might agree to shop for nursery furniture. No, too soon; there was no room to assemble a crib or changing table until the master bedroom was dismantled and moved to its new location. He stood back to admire the new look of their home and realized it wouldn't really matter until his wife was there to enjoy it, too. Steve sat on the deck with a can of soda, read the newspaper, and tried to relax. It was at moments like this—waiting with no opportunity to control the outcome—when he craved a drink or cigarette most. He refused to re-start two filthy, expensive habits because his wife said she wanted him around for decades and decades; nice, very nice. He read the paper, fussed with chores already complete, reorganized her shoes, and straightened her clothes on hangars. Around 11:00 PM he turned off lights, stood on the porch, and stared at the road in both directions. Every few minutes headlights appeared on the rural road then passed until at midnight, few cars passed. At 2:00 AM he decided a dedicated professional got tied up with last-minute details and postponed a long drive until daylight. Maybe she couldn't transfer everything to Wilkers or felt too exhausted to drive to a pay phone to let her husband know of a change in plans. Of course, Wilkers! Steve dialed and paced until: "What?"

"Al, Steve; did you see Laura today? I mean, yesterday?"

"Yeah, why?"

"She promised to be home between 6:00 and 7:00. I built in a few hours but this seems ridiculous and..."

"Home?"

Steve stared at his bare feet. "Yeah, home. We're married."

"Married?"

"Yup; Laura actually married this fat old fart in late June."

Al's voice shifted from foggy to alert. "Laura seemed distracted when she left a shit-pile of evidence here. There's so much I haven't gone through a third of it—too much to digest in one sitting."

Steve felt the god-awful pressure and pinched skin between his brows. "See anything to put her in danger?"

"Not yet; hold on." Steve heard background noise until Al returned. "I saw notes about people she interviewed, a log of what she did week by week, bookkeeping records, copies of forms about the CFEL's new corporation, some charts, highlighted county maps, and copies of birth and death certificates. Mishmash of... whoa, now I'm looking at three signed statements from women who... Jesus, Steve."

"What?"

"She thinks she found my son... alive."

"If Laura thinks she did, she did."

A long pause then: "I'll call when I have something but in the meantime, I'll head to Ratsbridge, hang out in the park like all the other perverts, and see if anything weirder than usual goes on."

"Thanks. Remember; call."

148

Marie opened her eyes, tried to sit, and scrambled to the bathroom. She rested on haunches, gagged in heaves, and flushed a disgusting mess away. She imagined the worst passed but no; Ned sat on a chair and turned on a lamp. "Let's talk about three days ago."

Even blinking hurt but Marie laughed, "Days?"

Ned's voice sounded weird. "Yes, days; Marie, this is your worst bender ever. Just what the hell do you think you...?"

Marie snorted, "Aw, did I ruin a romantic encounter?"

Ned repeated his tiresome line: "It isn't what you think, Marie."

For the first time in 28 years of marriage, Marie saw fear. *Of what? He got caught in affairs before and lost no time starting another.* "You're pathetic," she laughed as a lump of something vile worked its way to her throat. She stumbled to the toilet, struggled with the seat, and sprayed cabinet and walls. When Ned followed, Marie kicked backward. "Get lost, you rotten son of a bitch!"

Ned dragged her to her feet and for the first time in 28 years, used body strength to overpower her. Marie expected a strike but he shoved her arms to her side and held. "I met her to say it was over. I promised you and I kept my promise."

Marie felt the sting of his words. *If true, that meant one of them kept and one of them didn't.* When her body wilted, Ned released his hold and guided her to the bed. Marie groaned, "I can't believe it's been days. Oh, God, the kids... what do they know?"

"They're aware; how could they not be?"

"Ned, I don't think I can stop drinking."

He sat beside her. "Yes, you can. I'll help."

"The last thing I remember clearly is packing two suitcases and... oh, shit. I tried to pick up some guy I suspect you know—maybe another cop? I don't know. He seemed to know a lot about all of you and..."

"Marie, unless you left with a stranger..."

"I'm pretty sure I left alone."

"Then there's..."

"Wait; I'm afraid I talked about Steve and Laura."

Ned shrugged, "Steve left work early yesterday because Laura's coming home. Everyone'll know soon enough so don't worry about it. Get some rest while I clean the bathroom."

"No! I made the mess so I..."

"My help starts now." Ned closed the curtains and pulled the sheet up. "I never knew how much I love you until the last few days."

149

Laura detected light behind the scarf which probably meant Saturday morning. Against her own demands she stay alert, she dozed off and on as if her life weren't suddenly bizarre or the situation criminal. When she realized her body now nurtured two lives and needed to stay calm, her eyes filled with tears of joy. Joy? How could she dream of a life yet to come when her life spiraled so far out of control?

Someone lifted the edge of the scarf and she stared into Vincent's kind eyes as he whispered, "Please don't cry, Laura. I promise I won't let anything happen to you." He quickly established himself as the soft, gentle one—the one who didn't just shove a white-bread baloney sandwich at her but took the time to cut up vegetables, peel an orange, or heat canned soup. In no time at all, a routine developed and whether she requested it or not, they untied her to use the tiny bathroom on a regular basis. As soon as the door closed, she yanked the blue scarf off, jumped onto the toilet seat, and stared out a shoe-box sized window at trees, sky, or position of the sun or moon. Once finished, she pulled the scarf back over her eyes and thanked whoever waited outside the door to guide her back to be re-tied. She tried to keep track of passing seconds, minutes, and hours but without her watch lost track whenever Marsethe arrived unannounced to order, chastise, and belittle the others. If she counted correctly, he visited six times that day and it soon became apparent only he could break a rule of total silence as he bullied others into action or asked about her habits. Without warning, he demanded she shower and change into clean clothes. He pulled the scarf off and laughed when she blinked in harsh light. He untied her, shoved her across the room, and because the window was too small for escape, he took no exception when she slammed the door and locked it. As soon as water ran, she climbed onto the toilet seat and stared out at the small corner of the world she could see but not for long: time alone in the shower too precious to waste on a view she memorized already.

150

Surprised to find Scolarzski and Barber there on a Saturday, Ed motioned them to join him in the conference room. "I talked to Wilkers on my way in and…"

Scolarzski interrupted, "Did he have news about Laura, sir?"

"You two know? Why'd I have to hear about this from…?"

Barber this time. "What did Al say?"

Ed repeated the little he knew. "No one reliable's seen Delorange since she lugged evidence to Wilkers' house and left Friday after 3:00 a.m.. A quick check with her family turns up she's not there, didn't call. Friday at 7:17 PM New Hampshire State Police found her car in Groveton, purse in the trunk with keys, credit cards, and cash intact. No sign of a struggle."

Scolarzski looked dazed. "Anything else, sir?"

"Wilkers requested permission from Bill Marschek and John Delorange to search the law office and carriage house. Once he gets it, he and members of his troop will search and report back. Wilkers claims she left a ton of evidence at his house." As he watched his sergeants glance at one another for a third time, Ed pushed himself to a stand. "Why do I have a feeling there's more to this than meets the eye?" When both ignored him, Ed summoned the others. Macrae arrived in 22 minutes, Rawlings 14 after that, and studied details spread around until Sigler showed up 11 minutes later to point at the label: *Community for Expansive Love.* "You mean you called me in on a weekend because the same old Jesus freaks make promises they never intended to keep?"

Ed leaned on Sigler's shoulder until he flopped into a chair. "My detectives don't just up and disappear."

Sigler looked around. "We're all here."

Ed checked his watch. "As of this moment, 32 hours and 23 minutes elapsed since anyone reliable saw Laura Delorange. Okay, this is it, people. I want to know where she went after she left Wilkers, who she spoke to, if she felt frightened, if she went somewhere of her own accord. I want to know about her life there the last few months: if she dated, if she slept with anyone, if she argued with anyone, if she drank, if she took a bribe, if she pissed someone off, if she represented a cretin who got off on a technicality for a despicable crime, if she practices disgusting habits with animals or children." When he noticed Sigler glance toward Scolarzski, Ed shouted, "Tell me what's going on!"

"I don't know if I should mention something but..."

Ed leaned closer. "Mention it!"

Sigler faced Scolarzski. "Marie got rip-snorting drunk the other night and ran into a ditch. Burlington police called and I..."

Scolarzski this time. "Get to the point!"

"She's not sure but may have told some guy your news."

Ed shouted, "Describe this *guy* she may have told what someone's about to tell me!"

Sigler choked, "Marie's always confused after a binge."

Scolarzski mumbled, "Laura believed the CFEL would trust she returned home unless presented with evidence to the contrary. I imagine marriage to me would fit into that category nicely."

"You're married?" Ed glanced around the table and realized everyone else knew except him and Rawlings. *I wouldn't expect to be included in something personal but find it ironic they knew to keep me and Rawlings out of it but not Marie?* Ed chuckled, "Interesting how the circle ripples out farther than anyone expects, huh?"

Barber choked,, "Think they know about the baby, too?"

Ed broke stunned silence with, "How far along?"

Scolarzski cleared his throat. "We aren't sure but figure less than three months, sir."

Ed insisted, "That early a pregnancy won't be obvious. Let's talk about where people with brains go from here."

Ed watched his group settle in to participate in predictable patterns: Scolarzski drifted off into the cosmos; Sigler looked stung by his earlier confession; Rawlings stewed about being left in the dark again; and Macrae worried about physical risk. Only Barber listened, participated, asked questions, offered suggestions, and faced Ed. "Sir, I'd like to go up there and assist Wilkers in any way you deem appropriate."

Ed studied Scolarzski and for the first time in the dozen years he knew the man, detected fear or uncertainty . "I'll call Troop B and make sure they want us involved. In the meantime, Barber, familiarize yourself with what you'll deal with since Wilkers claims she got more."

Barber touched the thick file. "Jeez Louise—there's more?"

Ed nodded and delivered an order he knew would offend. "Scolarzski, stay out of it. You'd only hinder, not help."

For the first time in the years he knew him, Ed heard no quarrel; instead: "With Ralph and Al on the case, sir, I stand clear." When Barber dug into the file like a gopher, Ed headed for a fresh jolt of java, shocked to overhear Scolarzski ask Sigler to bring his wife by for breakfast. "Marie may be ready to talk to another alcoholic about a slow path to recovery."

151

Ralph struggled to be patient as Granger negotiated with Troop B Admin about assistance from Troop A. *Whether they want me underfoot or not, only I can be of use—not that the others lack skills or interest but Rawlings recuperates from a stabbing, Macrae still on reduced hours, Sigler preoccupied by Marie, and my best buddy sidetracked by a missing bride.* Ralph eavesdropped on Grangers' political-maneuvering-face-saving shit and hated the delay. *Shit; I can't wait, won't wait.* He rushed home and Joycie trailed as he stuffed a weekend bag and filled her in with as few details as she'd let him get away with but when he grabbed a toothbrush, she snorted, "I know you too well; if you're prepping for more than hours, it's important."

"I won't be gone long, darlin,' no more'n a few days."

"Where?"

"Across state."

"Where across state? How far across state?"

"That's on a need-to-know basis, darlin." Ralph turned away from probing eyes and called Derby. "Wilkers, stay put 'til I get there."

Joycie gasped, "Laura didn't make it home last night, did she?"

"What makes you think she…?"

"Lately whenever I came around you hide that file but I saw enough: Wilkers? Fallsbridge? The CFEL? Come on! Don't leave me hanging like this!"

Ralph stared at his loafers. "I need to be up there 'til Laura's found, okay? I need to do this for my best buddy of all time."

Joyce nodded. "I know; take care of the man I love, too."

Ralph ran out to the new unmarked V-8 gas guzzler everyone lobbied to get from the motor pool, sped to the interstate, and hit the lights. He turned music off to encourage his mind to sift through proven as well as alleged excesses of the Community for Expansive Love: a private academy with an undercurrent of religious fanaticism in a dizzying curriculum; cult undertones in its emphasis on social behavior; allegations of rampant psychological reward and punishment; and hints of shady record-keeping among small business owners. And then Granger implied the little lady found more? Holy moley, what more could there be?

Ralph's mind ran through a litany of details about Dr. C. Melvin Marsethe he'd obtained during one short hour of phone calls from his desk at a substation in Chittenden County, Vermont. He found it unsettling how much could be gleaned when the right questions were presented to appropriate sources. Seems that after Marsethe successfully completed a medical school internship, he washed out of residency programs in three different states. One hospital administrator in Maryland reported discipline following unauthorized use of medical school lab facilities. Twenty years before Roe v. Wade, he allegedly performed illegal abortions at $100 a pop for college coeds and student nurses. When asked to leave, he moved his services elsewhere until yet again, disciplined and asked to leave. One administrator at a hospital in Tennessee claimed a suspicion a young doctor performed autopsies on extracted fetuses was never pursued or prosecuted. Ralph's research uncovered a chilling fact: though never punished or held accountable, the same doctor visited a cousin in Vermont to lick his wounds and discovered a completion of an internship met licensing requirements for general practitioners. Ralph recalled one conversation in particular: a physician who managed an oncology unit at a hospital in West Virginia labeled Marsethe a genuine genius with an IQ that flew off the charts who also appeared to lack what a review board called *the clarity of personal ethics necessary for practicing physicians*. During 18 years of police experience, Ralph met more than a few geniuses in his line of work—real scary people whose synapses struck like bolts of lightning and twisted every which-way especially when braininess mixed in with psychopathic tendencies or a giant ego. Geniuses who shifted their energies to crime loved to confuse and frighten, skulk and stalk, craft devious puzzles, torture the weak and stupid, and prove they were too smart to get caught. Geniuses were like a salad tossed into the air; if it was windy, who the hell knew where lettuce might land?

Ralph exited I-89 at Montpelier and headed northeast along Route 2. He recalled a classmate in Baton Rouge said, "Mel Marsethe planned to be an internationally renowned pathologist by understanding diseases through the examination of molecules, cells, tissues, and organs." Instead, after many stumbles and setbacks, Marsethe found a village in the middle of nowhere with no competition and few restrictions on behavior—a volatile combination.

When Ralph arrived in Derby, Wilkers jumped in. "I never should've agreed to wait! Marschek gave permission to ransack the law office 45 minutes ago!" Ralph raced down dusty back roads and 15 minutes later, squealed into the village of Fallsbridge, every bit as gorgeous as postcards promised. He followed directions and pulled up at an office. Wilkers picked the lock, pointed at various locations, and cautioned Ralph not to say a word; lights stayed off, too, as they searched drawers, file cabinets, and work areas. "Looks like Laura cleaned it out," Wilkers whispered and pointed to the door.

In minutes, Ralph parked behind a brick school with landscaped grounds, well-maintained sports fields, and a tennis court. "Joycie'd take a cut in pay for digs like these for her kids."

Wilkers laughed, "If this impresses you, wait'll you see the inside." They raced through the woods to the rear of a house. Wilkers picked a lock on the door to a building set back, pressed fingers to his lips again, and pointed to a few spots. "This place is bugged, too."

Ralph moved silently through a nice apartment and in the bathroom found a stained hand towel. "Is this blood?"

Wilkers shrugged, "Could be; can't tell."

"Keep looking; I'll go back and call for a mobile crime lab."

Wilkers grabbed him. "Not yet; trust me—no one in this perverse burg can know we're involved." He went to the kitchen, returned with a plastic bag, and held it so Ralph could drop the towel in.

Ralph crept along on hands and knees and squinted at one weird sight: a stack of soda cans under the bed. He extended a broom handle, swept side to side, and exposed an indentation. He gestured for Wilkers to help move the bed to the middle of the room, exposing a trap door opening down. With flashlights, they peered at a rickety wooden ladder, dirt, and a dark hole. Ralph grunted, "Shit, I hate small, dark spaces."

"I'll go," Wilkers insisted and dropped down. Ralph waited until Wilkers moved back into sight and climbed up. "It's a tunnel that shoots off in different directions about 30 feet in. The floors are dirt but the walls are concrete." They returned to the Derby sub-station to begin an arduous task of deciding what they had, if it had any value, and how to proceed without spinning wheels.

152

Glenn negotiated with sales reps, placed orders, worked with Carl on next week's specials, and approved a mock-up Rita brought over for a new four-color brochure. At 6:00 he seated Matt, Robert, and Brian, handed them the specials menu, and offered to get beverages. They seemed nervous and insisted they'd wait for Mel.

Glenn looked around. "Where's Vince?"

Matthew shrugged, "Needed elsewhere."

Glenn found their presence odd; usually townspeople avoided the Maidstone and live band on weekends—too many tourists in jeans with cameras; too many screaming brats; too many rude questions that proved they thought CFEL members were ignorant hicks; too many chances to be mistaken for quaint or naïve like the Amish of Pennsylvania or the Shakers of New Hampshire; too many opportunities to be labeled as hostile, dangerous, and deadly like survivalist groups in Idaho or Alabama; and too many license plates from New York, Ontario, Quebec, and New Hampshire hogging good spaces. Mel arrived, summoned Glenn, and patted an empty chair. "The elders and I have a proposition in which full participation guarantees your life changes forever."

"What would I need to do?"

"First a vow of secrecy, yes?" Mel slid a sheet of paper.

Glenn began to read but Mel snatched it back. "Need I remind you of a criminal lapse in judgment you may wish to reconsider?"

"I'm sorry; I need to know if…"

Mel sneered, "I should have known you'd expect disclosure in advance! Loyalty is measured in acts of faith, yes?"

Glenn swallowed hard. "I guess I lack the necessary faith."

After what seemed like an eternity of silence, Laura kicked her feet out, drew knees to her chest, rolled hips and shoulders, but nothing worked. The rope held; if anything, it got tighter. At the sound of footsteps on the porch and a key in the lock, she panicked then relaxed at the short, light steps and strained breathing of Vincent. He untied her but left her blindfolded, and guided to the bathroom; a few minutes later, she stumbled out, only to be led back and re-tied. He hand-fed her a chicken salad sandwich and held a straw to her mouth: apple juice. When she tasted bite-sized brownie bits with soft apple wedges, she sighed, "Is this from the Maidstone?" When he didn't answer, she added, "My mother's birthday is September 20th and I beg you to bring me a card to sign the next time you come." At silence, she whispered, "She needs to know I'm alive, Vincent, and you're so kind compared to the others."

A chuckled, "So you recognize it's me. Mel warned you'd try to win us over one by one and predicted you'd start with me." Vincent lifted an edge of the scarf so she could see a smile. "No games, okay? Don't give Mel a reason to change his mind about how we treat you."

154

At his father's house, Mick waited for news when the phone rang: his grandmother calling from Florida with details about her flight. She finished and he blurted, "Laura's pregnant and missing, Gran."

"What do you mean, missing?"

"Dad expected Laura to come last night."

A long silence, then, "I'm on my way."

"Gran, you don't need to..."

"But I do, sweetheart. I'll see you soon."

Mick turned the radio and TV on to wait for news. When something triggered the motion detector light, he checked the driveway for another car, startled to see a young woman at the patio door point to the back. Mick opened the door. "Yeah?"

A smile. "Mickey?"

"Yeah; should I know you?"

She extended her right hand. "I'm Sandra Wilkers, your playpen pal from long ago? If you don't believe me, I could prove it with hours of bad video our parents shot at Lake Caspian." Mick invited her in and she headed into the living room, chatting as she went. "Your dad must be so worried about Laura. My dad called to tell me she's missing. Do you remember my dad, Al Wilkers? I met Laura a while ago and she's great, don't you think? She told me so much about UVM, and God, I hope I had nothing to do with what happened."

Mick squinted. "Why would you think that?"

Sandra shrugged, "I transferred files via phone modem from a doctor's office to a PC at home; later we printed I'll bet 100 pages. Maybe I'm not as smart as I think I am; maybe I'm a hacker-wannabe who didn't cover tracks well enough."

Mick squinted. "You helped Laura with an investigation?"

"I don't know; I worry I didn't help at all or made it worse. I thought I handled the file transfer protocols correctly."

"I think I need to bring my father into this conversation." He called the cell number and briefly explained the situation.

"I'll be there soon but let me speak to Sandra."

She took the phone, said, "Hello?" listened, and laughed, "I can't wait to see you again, too." While they waited, they sipped from cans of diet soda and polished off his father's perennial stash of leftover pizza; this time, though: seven-grain crust loaded with fire-roasted vegetables. Mick enjoyed hearing about her father, younger sisters, interests in music, and hobbies. She detailed her first week at UVM, course schedule, residence hall, and friends. "I'm lucky to be the Vermont Scholar from my high school but I'm still on a tight budget. Um, this house is great, Mickey, but so far from campus! Good thing you have a car because a taxi driver charged me $30 to get here!"

"You took a cab? Wow. Um, I live in Burlington so I'll drive you back." Mick watched her check CDs and thought *She's classy like Laura.*

155

Steve worked through his questions, took notes to pass along, checked in with Ralph by phone, and put everything aside to enjoy the company. He collapsed in bed at midnight and heard them in the living room. How wonderful to see her grown up! He smiled at a memory of her at three or four, pressing Mickey's cheeks between her palms to plant kisses until he squirmed free. When the phone on the nightstand rang, he grabbed to hear Ralph, "Just me."

"You found Laura?"

"Not yet. It's been one weird day, podna: soda cans under the bed, subterranean tunnel, and a shitload of paper that should be in front of accountants. Um, we found a bloody towel in her bathroom and…"

"I'm heading up."

"No; a techie said it's a trace amount; Laura's too smart not to have tricks up her sleeve so let us work without worrying about you, too. Wait a sec." Ralph told someone to cover ears and added, "Your wife puts out a tentative image but she's got bigger balls than both of us. During all that scorching of them sheets, you ever feel em? Sorry; not funny. Wilkers talked to John Delorange about a shit-pile of records and he offered to take a look. Rawlings'll drive up and tote 'em back so check in with the lieut 'n make sure he didn't get lost in the mountains."

"Thanks for the call; now let me talk to Al." A moment later, "Sandra's wonderful! She's here now and gave information about a young man from Newport Center of particular interest to Laura, not sure why. If you have time, check out a kid named Sam Mosgrove, Jr."

At the end of the second day, Laura chastised herself for not taking advantage of confusion the first day. Marsethe or Brian would have been difficult targets, sure, but a swift kick to the groin or back of Vincent, Robert, or Matthew could have been enough for a head start—to where, she wouldn't know until she broke free and reached outdoors. She heard enough to know there were always at least two there—one inside and one outside to let her use the bathroom or feed her, one who stayed and one who left. She heard a car pull in then prolonged discussions on the porch before a replacement entered—someone new. Laura stiffened at different breathing, lighter and shorter footsteps, a subtle scent of powder or flowery soap. *A woman? Or a man who just left a woman?* When footsteps crossed to stop beside the bed, Laura imagined she'd recognize a voice and said, "Talk to me, please?" No one answered, untied her, fed her, or led her to the bathroom for hours and hours, and except for the rustling of pages of a book, made few sounds. Laura fell asleep and woke when she felt someone untie the rope.

Vincent whispered, "I'm sorry; she didn't know the routine."

"Who was that"

"Don't pry."

"Was it a woman?" She couldn't wait for an answer, raced to the bathroom, slammed the door, and minutes later exited with a sigh of relief. "It's a miracle I didn't soil the bed."

"I'm sorry. Would you like to join me at the table?"

Laura nodded, excited to spend time sitting up but upset when he re-tied her to the chair at the waist and ankles. Free of the scarf, though, she studied the cabin layout and estimated distances; she concentrated on soft sounds when someone scraped a chair on the porch or jumped from the porch to the ground. Vincent prepared two bowls of cereal with blueberries and milk and poured orange juice. When he sliced two bran muffins, Laura saw the generous amount of raisins and sighed, "Those must be Carl's from the Maidstone kitchen."

Vincent sighed, "Don't pry."

"That was a statement, not a question."

Vincent slid a spoon and butter dish forward. "Use your spoon or fingers, Laura. Mel warned us about knives."

"Um, don't you find it sad how paranoid Mel is?"

Vincent studied her and said, "A photograph of you at the Mosgrove farm gave us all reason to worry." He slid a birthday card forward. "Here; I brought what you asked for."

Though sentimental and nothing like what she'd select for her mother, Laura whispered, "Thank you; it's beautiful. Can I borrow a pen? I seem to have misplaced my purse."

Vincent smiled. "I always found your droll humor charming, Laura, but don't go too far. I'll allow a signature on the inside and address on the outside—no message. Depending on your cooperation, I may even mail it." Vincent ordered her back to bed, re-tied the ropes, but left the scarf on the table. When he leaned out the open door to speak to someone on the porch, Laura stretched and saw trees and more trees. *In more than two days, I heard few noises: no music, no cars, no flowing river or stream, no children playing, no trucks straining to negotiate winding roads and hills into the village. Where the hell am I?* Vincent returned to check the knots, smiled down, and said, "If you continue to cooperate, I see no need to cover your eyes but don't try to take advantage while I'm at services."

"Oh? So it's Sunday morning?"

"Laura, don't pry."

"Will I be alone here?"

A heavy sigh. "You'll never be alone but won't see much of Brian, Robert, Matthew, or Mel—Brian because Mel doesn't trust him here, Robert and Matthew because they experience pangs of conscience, and Mel because he's being watched."

"Watched?"

Vincent tugged hard on ankle knots. "Wilkers and another officer loiter in unmarked cars, a woman checked into the Maidstone, and two men into a bed and breakfast in East Haven. They eat together at the diner but stay in the background. Mel insists they're FBI."

"You said Robert and Matthew have pangs of ..."

"And you wonder about me?" he interrupted. "I have them but to leave you alone with Mel is foolish." Vincent stood and headed to the door. "Without proof of a kidnapping or demand for ransom, outsiders will leave but until then, it's important to keep you healthy. Mel plans to begin his consult soon so if you wish to end this detention sooner, you..."

"What do you mean by consult?"

"Mel will continue what Lynette denied years ago."

Laura licked her lips. "Um, what should I expect?"

"From other instances like this, I recall general exams, interviews about family history and illnesses, and a blood test. Without vital records for the years you were away from our protection, Mel will attempt to update your immunization record. His is a thorough investigation not unlike what I imagine you produced in your former line of work."

As Vincent headed toward the door, Laura struggled to sit. "Wait, please! Um, I need to hear more about this consult."

Vincent turned and gasped, "Don't do that! Mel will be furious to find you bruised and bloody! He'll hold me responsible!" He came back and sat to adjust ropes. "I worry about what we did. I worry about what might happen." Vincent checked his watch, groaned, "Unwise to be late," and jumped to his feet.

Laura watched him go, heard a car door slam, engine start, and tires crunch on gravel. *If he'll be late at 14 minutes before an hour by car, I must be within five miles of the village. Figuring he plans for time to park and walk, likely within three. First, I need to get mobile, and second, get past whoever waits on the porch.* She bumped her behind up and down but stopped when the ropes cut into wrists and ankles so deeply, she feared further loss of blood might harm her baby. *Still, with what I see staining the sheet, I pray it's enough to postpone a consult. If nothing else: I need to think smart, not physical.*

157

Steve regretted inviting the Sigler's for breakfast, checked the refrigerator for ideas, and grunted, "Shit."

Sandra wandered into the kitchen. "If you have bread, eggs, and milk, I'll make French toast." When Mickey wandered in a moment later, Steve stared and Sandra laughed, "Nothing x-rated going on here. I fell asleep watching a DVD and Mickey was kind enough not to wake me. Hope it's okay I'm still here."

Steve smiled. "Better than okay."

"Show me where to find a griddle, please."

"No, you don't need to cook for us."

"My offer has nothing to do with gender expectations and everything to do with thanks for hospitality."

"Okay, but actually there'll be three of us and two Siglers."

Sandra laughed, "Wow, I know the name Sigler, Ned right? After years of Dad's dinner chatter, this feels like family."

Mickey asked, "Does that mean we'll see more of you?"

Sandra shrugged, "I believe that's up to you."

Steve thought *On that note I'll make myself scarce* and left to shower, shave, and dress. In the bathroom mirror, he studied chin stubble and thought *I'll let this grow until Laura returns—a stupid symbolic gesture but important.*

When the Siglers arrived, Steve watched them try to place the pretty young woman and laughed, "She looks just like her mother."

315

Ned squinted. "Is this one of Wilkers' baby girls?"

"I'm Sandra, now a student at UVM."

After a fantastic meal, Mickey and Sandra entertained the Siglers as Steve loaded the dishwasher. He found it funny how at Mickey's age, nothing seemed as important as impressing the opposite sex. "Not that it changes when you're 44; it just takes a back seat to..."

From behind, Marie asked, "What?"

"Sorry; talking to myself." He offered Marie a second cup of coffee and pointed to the deck. "Let's talk in private."

She looked around. "Should I get Ned?"

"Only if you can't do your own talking."

Marie nodded, followed, and—no surprise—started with niceties: "How are you? Mickey? Your family? The job? The garden?" Necessary buffer between breakfast and serious talk.

Steve smiled. "Enough chitchat?"

"Get mad and yell, anything, but don't be kind."

Steve studied her sad eyes. "Tell me what happened."

Marie ran through a scenario familiar to someone who once had a hell of a time with alcohol, too: dive joint, raucous laughter, smoky haze, search for a good time, loud music, comforting touch as two strangers danced unusually close. "I saw Ned with another woman and... shit, if the guy hadn't disappeared, I'd have gone to bed with him in a heartbeat."

"Marie, describe him; any detail you can think of, no matter how insignificant you believe it to be."

Marie described her drinking partner as 6' 1", brown hair, blue eyes, and fair complexion. "Slender but not thin; when we danced, his arms and shoulders felt like he works out to achieve a chiseled effect. Overall, nice looking."

"Can you guess his age?"

"I'd say mid to late 30's?"

"Did he give you a name?"

"It didn't seem important at the time and I didn't ask."

"Would you recognize him in a photograph?"

"I might; do you have some?"

"Not yet; Rawlings will bring some back from Fallsbridge."

"He never said he came from out of town. He said he noticed me once before and needed to work up courage to ask me to dance."

Steve felt the deep pain of recognition and sighed, "Did you ever see this good-looking guy before then?"

"No but that doesn't mean... Oh, you should be mad."

"I won't lie; I'm disappointed in Laura and me for thinking we could talk and in you for not treating yourself with more respect."

"I have no right to ask a favor but will you go to a meeting with me if I work up the courage?"

"Call it by name, Marie."

She laughed nervously. "Will you go to an Alcoholics Anonymous meeting with me? Ned offered to but I don't care what Ned thinks any more. I need to do this for myself."

Steve thought of Denise, their sad and lonely marriage, and the critical part his drinking played in its demise. *Despite regrets, if given the opportunity I wouldn't go back for all the gold on our planet because if I did, I'd miss out on Laura.* "Marie, don't make a hasty decision. Things that seem obvious when we're drunk or hung over, take on clarity when sober."

158

Al parked in the post office lot as hundreds of CFEL members flowed out of the church. He lifted binoculars and recited names while beside him, Ralph jotted them until 15 minutes later, clusters broke apart and people headed to cars or crossed the green to the Maidstone. Al scanned the sheet and found it odd all his best guesses listed: Mel Marsethe, Vincent Mottolla, Matthew Purcareau, Robert Decarreau, or Brian Lemphier. "Damn; looks like they got new recruits."

159

Monday morning turned into a major drag: Laura remained missing, Mickey and Sandra headed back to UVM. With eggs and orange juice used up, an empty cereal box, and overripe banana, not much to eat. To make matters worse, Steve couldn't find clean underwear and keys hid. It was just as bad at the station: Ralph stayed gone, Macrae and Sigler argued like spinster sisters locked in an attic, Rawlings looked as if talking to the husband of a missing colleague were a fate worse than water-boarding, and Granger made a thousand phone calls without once filling his sergeant in about the status of an investigation.

Steve waited an hour before knocking, "I wonder if…"

Granger waved him in. "Rawlings brought a ton of financial records back and turned them over to John Delorange. He spent the night poring over them and contacted a colleague at the IRS which won't pussy-foot around bullshit personal rights like we do."

"Does any of it hint at why Laura's missing?"

Granger shrugged, "At first glance it seems Delorange trawled murky waters and snagged a shark. Besides impressive numbers from legitimate enterprises via something called *Nature's Bounties*, it appears for decades Marsethe worked with infertile couples to facilitate conception but if that failed, ignored adoption laws and sold healthy, white infants from members. A quick scan indicates he brought in big bucks: more than $3 million peddling from two to four a year. But here's where it gets interesting: to cover such a sizable illegal income, the church issued receipts to spread those amounts out. Think of it this way, Sergeant: the IRS gets to focus its energy on small business owners who year after year failed to report actual income on their 940, 941, or 944's. If that's not enough, they'll focus on little guys who never dropped a red cent into the basket on Sunday yet filed 1040's listing $5,000 or more on Schedule A as charity donations."

"And the sexual assault she went to investigate, sir?"

Granger shrugged, "Tax evasion is easier to prove in court but one way or the other your wife may have nailed those bastards."

Steve felt stunned by a growing awareness Laura was every bit the exceptional investigator he always knew her to be. *Why hadn't he paid closer attention when she talked? Why hadn't he asked questions? Why hadn't he done what he did when they were VSP partners: poke holes, force her to focus, and insist she step back and clarify? If her investigation boiled down to an alleged sexual assault, it seemed likely other members would look the other way, turn their backs, and let their doctor dangle in the breeze alone but if in reality, she uncovered evidence encompassing other adult members of the community, it became a different story.* "Sir, Marsethe didn't work alone."

"No shit, Sergeant! They're up to their eyeballs."

Steve knew he needed more information and returned to his desk to call Joyce Barber; he got her home machine, tried her at school, and left a message with a secretary. Within minutes, he answered to hear, "What happened? Are Ralph and Laura...?"

"Joyce, no news yet. I'm sorry if I frightened you. If you still have it, I'd like to borrow your book on cults."

"Sure; keep it as long as you want. Why don't you pick it up tonight and stay for supper? How about 6:30? I hate when Ralph's gone for days at a... I'm sorry; I know it's for Laura and..."

"I understand; I'll see you at 6:30."

Steve managed to get through another shift and at Joyce and Ralph's house later, felt comfortable at a familiar table, relaxing to their favorite easy-listening station, and savoring a home-cooked meal of meatloaf, baked sweet potato, and green beans with almonds.   When Joyce apologized for its lack of grandeur, Steve admitted, "This is great! I pretty much survive on Zachary's Pizza, Al's French Frys, and Dunkin Donuts. Laura hasn't been married to me long enough to learn like many old-time New Englanders, I crave clam cakes and chowder on Fridays and frankfurters, baked beans, and brown bread on Saturdays."

"Laura has plenty of time to learn all that." Joyce leaned forward to squeeze his chin. What's with the facial hair, Scolarzski?"

Steve grinned and scratched his chin. "With everything else going on, I thought I'd take a break from primping, not that primping ever makes a difference."

Autumn

160

Mel finished appointments and headed to the Maidstone for dinner. As he did each day—so unwanted guests could find him easily enough—he sat in a front window to enjoy broiled sole with lemon, mashed potatoes with chive, and baked squash, so delicious he headed to the kitchen to order a plate for Laura. Mel offered generous praise and felt stunned by Glenn's response. "I'm tired of asking the same question. It's been a week since I saw Laura. Do you know where she is?"

Mel chuckled, "I stand before you to applaud another superb addition to your culinary repertoire but am subjected to an inquest?"

Glenn sighed, "If this take-out is for Laura, just tell me."

"We expect assistance without conditions."

Glenn turned in fury. "But I'm not supposed to ask if what you'd have me do is criminal!"

Mel knew he reached a stalemate: diminished involvement from remorseful Matthew and Robert shifted the burden. After only eight days, a change in schedule meant hours with only one there; how long before their guest figured it out and attempted escape? Vincent spent too much time there—unwise to add more because of vulnerability to manipulation. Who could be trusted to step up? Untrustworthy Brian? Emotionally attached Glenn? Certainly not Gilbert—adrift in the arms of a woman? In the past, women were a last resort but Mary went once and formulated unreasonable demands before agreeing to return. An inquisitive Violet, Rita, Caroline, or Peg posed assorted risks and now Glenn demanded full disclosure? Too much. Mel took a deep breath. "I'm sorry but loyalty is measured in acts of faith which you clearly lack."

At home, Mel sat in the den and listened to Ravel's *Songs of Madagascar* until dark. He left lights on as if he relaxed inside, waited a half hour, grabbed a flashlight, and escaped out back on foot. More convenient would be to enter the tunnel through the pantry but the second night of her confinement for reeducation he distinctly heard a sound as if someone lingered in the distance.

Mel arrived at the cabin, heard Vincent's summary of events, and dismissed him. Mel turned to his guest. "First you enjoy dinner, then a medical consult." He sat beside her on the bed to loosen the scarf. "I sincerely apologize if this magnificent meal is lukewarm."

Laura struggled to sit upright. "Can I sit at the table? I need to move around and my back aches from this soft mattress."

"As long as you promise to try nothing, I'll let you." Mel loosened the ropes, cringed at bloody bandages, and removed them carefully. "What have you done now, foolish child?" He opened his bag, removed ointment and fresh bandages, and dabbed. "Move around less, yes? Give your strong body time to heal." Dressing changed, he led her to the table with a warning: "Remember: try nothing."

Laura hobbled to the chair, savored her dinner, and leaned back. "How do you get others to do whatever you want?"

Mel chuckled, "It appears you suffer from a very human tendency to attribute multiple characteristics based upon a single aberration. If a man feels the inveiglement of youthful enchantment, he must therefore be evil in all things, yes? He deserves no esteem or respect because he falters and stumbles as all human beings do. In reality, the community does my bidding because it sees the wisdom inherent in my design. On the other hand, you question simply to question, argue simply to argue, yet fail to see, hear or learn."

A soft sigh: "I know how I am, Mel, so take me back in time and teach as if I never left. Convince me of the wisdom in your design."

Mel hesitated—concerned her tone a ploy, rapt attention carefully planned, and ultimate intentions dishonorable. As his protégé years earlier, he saw a promise beyond that of any of the others he selected. Mel studied her eyes and imagined she forgave an unfortunate lapse in judgment. "Need I fear you try to trick me?"

Another soft sigh then: "I wish I'd done things differently, Mel. I wish I'd asked my questions directly."

Mel hesitated again—concerned her tone a skilled investigator's maneuver and her ultimate intentions as ignominious as those of the reconnoiter who preceded her—Wilkers. "Explain which questions perplexed you enough to veer off on your own."

"My family history did, Mel, especially why you covered some sections around my name, Rick or Jack. After reading Caroline's story, I can't help but wonder if…"

Mel pushed himself to a stand. "It's late and I'm weary. Without the Delorange family chart in front of us or your consult results to consider, it's pointless to continue." He escorted her to the bathroom, led her back to bed, retied her ankles and wrists, and repositioned the scarf. When she started to speak, he murmured, "I weary of debates, yours and too many others. Sleep, please; we will continue a discussion another time" Mel relaxed in the chair, accepted the lion's share of service in her confinement would be his alone, and fell asleep.

161

Sunday morning Glenn left the Maidstone, headed across the green, and watched the usual routine: Robert Decarreau unloaded a box from his van and dropped it on the steps of the church, Ben Lemphier carried it into the nave, and Paul Lemphier sat on the bench and inserted that day's song sheet into prayer books and hymnals. Nothing seemed different until Glenn noticed as worshipers arrived, CFEL members received a packet with green inserts from Paul, while non-members received one with yellow inserts from Ben. Services began and though the church looked packed, a few familiar faces were missing: Laura, of course, Mel, and Vincent. With Brian and Robert's assistance, Matt led the congregation with fewer songs and an oddly dispassionate sermon about obedience. Members seemed different, too, strange: Mary McGuinn nosy; Violet and Joanne nervous; Rita and Angela quiet; and Peg, Frannie, Maria, and Tina fidgety, understandable once Glenn noticed Al Wilkers in the back with another guy, probably a cop. Glenn felt surprised to see Claudette Adams, who hadn't been to services in years. Services over, Glenn folded his song sheet, stuffed it in his pocket, and wandered to the back to lift a yellow sheet from an unused hymnal.

Like every other Sunday for as long as he could remember, Glenn joined others on the steps to greet and hug but felt no pressure to invite anyone to breakfast except his mother Ada and his fa... her husband, Rollie. For the first time in his adult life, Glenn found their company awkward as if the truth did not set him free but trapped him forever in a shameful secret. Glenn saw Rollie Munier as a kind, decent, and patient man who never raised a hand to his children, rarely his voice. *Did Rollie know the truth? Did he recognize striking differences between his first and second sons and a decade later, his third and fourth? Did Ada know? Was he the product of an affair or artificial insemination? Worst of all, did it make a difference?* During breakfast Rollie had little to say, Ada even less. Glenn extended a wish they enjoy their meal and called the waitress to remind her not to prepare a bill. He headed to the kitchen and jumped when his mother followed to whisper over his shoulder, "If you know anything, act before it's too late to save that girl."

Glenn choked, "I know nothing." Alone in his apartment, Glenn sat in his bay window and stared out at three small groups in the green. Mostly strangers: so many new faces, such serious, unhappy, businesslike faces. Glenn took the song sheets out of his pocket and flattened them; at first glance, they looked the same but on closer inspection, in the middle of the third paragraph on the reverse side, the green sheet had additional text: *In everything we do, in every conversation we conduct, we must remember this truth: Our Lord decreed woman shall forever, in all things, remain subservient to man or be punished for her sins.*

Glenn headed downstairs and buried himself in mind-numbing preparation for the Sunday dinner rush. He watched Angela come in alone and sit at a window table. He headed over to ask if she'd join him for a glass of milk and slice of pumpkin pie. At her nervous nod, Glenn whispered, "Is something wrong?"

"No," Angela insisted and talked about the Harvest Festival, her new homeroom teacher, and the fact she tested out and moved into ninth-grade classes in Latin, Algebra, and World History. Finally Angela made eye contact. "Laura took three when she was in sixth grade, too, but English Composition instead of Algebra."

Glenn nodded, "Sounds great; is something else on your mind?"

Angela shrugged, "After Daddy died, I prayed Mom would marry you. I wanted you to be my father, too. I love you that much."

Glenn smiled. "I love you, too, but can't marry…."

Angela choked, "I thought you loved Laura but no one who loves her could know where she is and let her be so scared and alone."

"Honey, what makes you think I know anything?"

Angela looked around. "I visited Joanna after services and heard Mr. Lemphier and Elder Matthew make fun of Laura's garden. They said food for Laura comes from here, not her pathetic patch of land."

"I don't think so, Angela, at least not in any organized manner. We do take-out and catering but…"

"I think if you help feed her, that means you're friends with them and don't care what they do. I came here to say if you do, I don't want you as my godfather anymore." Angela stood and left.

Glenn smiled at how Mel demanded, threatened, and punished in a way that left no recourse except defensive anger yet soft-spoken words from an 11-year-old shamed him in a way Mel would never understand. Gil called his brother *Mr. Clean*—an insightful label. For all his life, Glenn believed knowledge of a crime didn't make a man culpable. *Since he only suspected the elders held Laura somewhere, how could a meal or two a day from the Maidstone as take-out, involve him?* The dinner crowd leveled off and Glenn saw Mel at the bar, shoulders slumped and rounded. As the old man sipped a margarita, Glenn wandered in and counted the four fingers Jake held up. He sat and leaned close. "You look tired."

Mel sighed, "I am; may I ask a favor?" At Glenn's nod, Mel slurred a request the village restaurateur provide assistance with the diet of an important guest. Glenn studied the old man's eyes and feared Laura might be ill. On three other occasions during the ten years he co-managed then took over the Maidstone, he refused when asked to assist. He thought *Remember the time Harlen Lezzarro disappeared, later found dead in the CFEL hunting lodge from a single bullet to the temple, ruled a suicide.? Another time photographs turned up of a naked Rob Dennelle and male student; Dennelle disappeared and a week later they appointed Brian Headmaster? And never forget Claudette Adams supposedly resigned her teaching job to move west? A week later, Robert saw her run alongside the river, never to be seen again until a photograph on the back of a book identified her as an investigative journalist.*

Glenn leaned close. "Mel, are your current needs anything like the earlier Lezzarro, Dennelle, or Adams incidents?"

Mel sat there in silence, stood slowly, and slapped the counter. "Adams! Theriault-Adams! Yes! If I wrote Lynette's sister's name as Claire Therault then her name is Claire Therault! How could I allow lazy Gilbert to confuse and distract me? I am a stupid old man who no longer has the concentration required to lead this community."

Glenn listened to the old man slur more complaints and realized he might never have an opportunity again. Glenn squeezed Mel's shoulder. "You look exhausted, Mel, and I'm inclined to help this time but with two conditions: I want to work toward ownership of the Maidstone and for every day I'm involved, you reduce the amount I owe."

Mel hissed, "You may see embezzlement as a loan but I do not!"

Glenn stood. "Find someone else."

Mel grabbed Glenn. "Yes, yes, yes; take a piece of paper, write what you require and I will sign. I wish to sleep in my own bed tonight."

162

Steve re-read the CFEL section in the book and called the publisher. Within hours, Claudette Theriault Adams returned his call and after introductions, admitted the CFEL became her biggest challenge. "To this day, I regret how unfinished I left that section."

"But there's so much there."

"Many former members recanted stories of widespread abuse. The effectiveness of brute force against the small and weak in any group goes without saying but with the CFEL, control mechanisms go deeper. In your work, I'm sure you see victims who feel diminished, powerless, or numb. Like most cults, the CFEL routinely destroys a person's spirit slowly to rebuild it later to serve another purpose entirely."

"That wasn't clear in your section on the CFEL."

Claudette admitted she never published anything she couldn't corroborate since many sources voiced rage toward a group they believed violated them. "I suspect many still feel the CFEL's influence and in fear of retaliation, chose not to stir things up. What amazes me most is something I felt rather than saw or heard. Members escape physically but no matter how they rationalize the experience, where they go, or what they do, the influence is never totally eliminated."

Steve answered, "I know a woman who grew up in Fallsbridge who's reticent in a way that makes no sense."

Claudette chuckled, "I'm not surprised; not many females in such an unyielding patriarchy escape unaffected. Let me FAX my notes about an organization which portrays itself as a community built on a foundation of love for Jesus Christ. It may astound you, Sergeant, how far off the mark they are."

"Thanks; I'd appreciate that. Knowing how thorough your research seems to be, I can't imagine there's more."

"You're not the first cop to pay me that compliment. No, actually she said she was an attorney but..."

"Laura Delorange?" Steve interrupted.

"How'd you know that?"

"When did you see her?"

"Let's see: late June maybe? We spoke at length about what I'll FAX you. What's your interest in her?"

"She's a former state police investigator who disappeared. I'm surprised you didn't see it in the paper or on local news."

"I'm at a hotel in Idaho trying to re-rescue my sister. I know there's a FAX here because I used it already to forward field notes to my publisher. Whenever I travel, I take everything with me—notebook pc, diskettes, and research notes. Twice someone broke into my house and destroyed what they found. I couldn't prove it was the CFEL but I'm certain it was. It never ends with these people; never."

Steve prayed she was wrong and provided a FAX number at the station. "It'll take me 20 minutes to get there."

"Listen, I have a request for when you finish your investigation: I'd like to consult on an update. Ever since I turned my manuscript over to my publisher, there isn't a single night I fall asleep without regret I never had evidence to crack the CFEL's core."

"We'll see but it should be Laura you work with on that."

Steve rushed to the station, caught pages as they spilled out, and focused on pages where she described a seven-day captivity during which two elders repeatedly informed her she'd *remain until her diseased soul was cleansed and made ready for perfect seed*. Why on earth hadn't she pressed charges? No research for a book was worth risking her life.

At home, Steve snuck in quietly so he wouldn't wake his mother, grabbed the envelope of photographs Rawlings brought from Fallsbridge, and studied two grainy ones in particular: in the first Laura felt comfortable enough with this guy Glenn Munier to take a walk outdoors in nightwear; in the second, Laura sat on a boulder and smiled at Glenn, a man Wilkers described as an all-around-nice-guy, the sort of man mothers loved to see daughters drag home, a never-married successful businessman with appealing looks. Steve grabbed the cult book and re-read a section he highlighted: *There are obvious advantages to compliance: favored positions with excellent wages, business success, and group respect. Yet far beyond the reverse side of shunning and exclusion is this: CFEL leadership seeks total control of the lives of members: harassment, intimidation, subversion of relationships, lies, threats of bodily harm, corporal punishment of students, scheduled mating rituals of young men of sexual prime, and harsh discipline of undisciplined youth are examples of the lengths to which these men will go to create the illusion they wish others to see.*

From the hallway, he heard: "Sweetheart, are you okay?"

Steve turned to see his mother's frightened eyes. "Sorry I woke you but will you look at these and tell me what you see?"

Lea studied them. "I see two friends having a conversation."

"Laura's in nightwear, Mom, and..."

Lea lifted a few more and sighed, "Someone could take pictures of you like this with Joyce Barber."

"My heart says Laura's faithful but my mind fills with memories of..."

"Stefan, trust your heart."

"I try, Mom, really I do but..." Steve put the photos away and grabbed his weekend bag.

"Honey, you promised you wouldn't go up there."

"I have no intention of screwing up the investigation. Granger needs someone to pick a prisoner up in Ohio and since Ralph was supposed to, I can make myself useful."

163

Glenn accompanied Mel behind the academy and along the path behind the tennis court through the woods. He hadn't visited Gil's cabin in years and realized its remoteness might be a perfect place to conceal what he dreaded to find. Mel unlocked the door and once inside pointed to a corner. "Observe but remain silent." Glenn's vision adjusted and he saw Laura: scared, bloody, and bruised. She stunk to high heaven, too.

She sobbed, "I'm sorry but nobody's been here all day and..."

"No more!" Mel hissed, untied her roughly, shoved her forward, and threw towels into the bathroom. "Clean yourself!"

With the sound of a shower in the background, Glenn helped change bedding. "Mel, this isn't right. Laura needs to..."

"With attention to diet and health, she'll be fine."

"But she seems so weak and..."

"She's fine; I sense a change in disposition so her seclusion ends soon and she's yours to love."

"You know I prefer it be her choice, not like this."

Mel hissed, "Which is why I wished to involve you sooner! With kindness and caring on your part in her hour of need, it will be her choice. Why is this so difficult for you to understand?"

When water stopped, Mel rushed over to wait by the door. When she opened it, Mel yanked the scarf across her eyes, guided her back, and retied her to the metal frame. "Rest, child; rest safely."

When Vince showed up to take over, Glenn felt reassured by his gentleness in comparison. Glenn followed Mel down the steps, across academy grounds to the back of the old man's house. Glenn saw him safely inside, glad to go home to mull over what he saw, and decide how to proceed. Mel had other ideas and insisted Glenn join him in the living room. "There is a conversation long overdue about Ada Fecteau Munier, a genetic mystery—a seventh generation native Vermonter of French-Canadian, Abenaki, and Scottish descent from a family that never journeyed more than 20 miles from the homestead." Mel collapsed on his couch and laughed, "Remember when you headed to college in Johnson? Ada could not imagine a visit, as if you traveled to Australia, yes?"

"Don't you dare make fun of my mother!"

Mel gasped, "No, no, you misunderstand my admiration for Ada, a miracle who transcended a weak and haphazard lineage. In my practice, I rarely observe such intelligence spring from barren surroundings. I wonder: is Ada the product of an alliance between her mother and traveling salesman or visiting preacher? Fresh seed is often the most potent and breeders of horses and cattle have known such truths for..."

"My mother's not a horse or cow," Glenn sighed.

Mel chuckled, "Why must you hear words literally versus figuratively? Ada is a pragmatic creature who looked beyond her pathetic existence into a growing community and understood Rollie Munier offered little of value to her or her first two sons. After she joined the CFEL, the elders and I rewarded her obedience with assistance to ease a burden of living with such an ignorant man. Our connection is based on love, the same I have for many others."

Glenn pushed himself to a stand. "You're drunk and I've heard enough. I'm afraid if I listen to one more word, I'll hear you admit you're the monster so many claim you are—it's hard enough to accept the fact you're my biological father without..."

Mel grabbed. "Stay! Of everyone around me, it's you and the one you love I wish to understand and accept why I do what I do."

Glenn heard a different tone and sat again. "Convince me I shouldn't call Wilkers."

164

In the morning, Steve volunteered to pick Travers up in Toledo but Granger said, "Why?"

"Sigler and Macrae are up to their eyeballs, Barber and Rawlings busy with Wilkers, and my level of concentration isn't what I'm accustomed to; sir, it's a no-brainer."

Granger squinted, "Maybe this isn't the best time to..."

Steve interrupted, "I need to be anywhere but here, sir."

"Got it." Granger passed the case file and Ralph's travel itinerary. "I'll call the airline with the change."

After check-in at the airport, Steve reviewed Travers' pathetic life: *the man the stupidest kind of career criminal;, a jerk who buried himself in bullshit up to his armpits; a loser who orchestrated ridiculous crimes and failed miserably at all attempts; a fool who graduated from burglary to armed robbery; an idiot who after being released on bail returned to a foul hellhole to pommel his wife and kids; a drunk who tripped unsuccessfully along the 12 steps and felt surprised when he woke somewhere dark and smelly, a week missing from the calendar.*

After boarding, Steve put the case file aside and turned to the Adams book. In the preface he reread what he highlighted in the preface: *Despite outward appearance, authorities in law enforcement, the state department of social services, and the attorney general's office keep their eyes and ears open for the Community for Expansive Love's polished façade to crack and wait for the organization's inevitable blunder on its bizarre path to Heaven.* After take-off, Steve stared at mountains and trees for as far as he could see. Upstate New York and Vermont were similar: both had unusually beautiful views that coexisted alongside cultural problems like alcoholism, domestic assault, high unemployment, unwed teen mothers, incest, wildlife poaching, and marijuana cultivation. He agreed with the author's statement: *Cult leaders seek economically-depressed rural locales not because the land is affordable but there already exists a generations-old ability to mask squalor.*

Six hours after he left Burlington, Steve stared out a hotel window at nighttime Toledo's thousands of lights and imagined he saw more in that place than all of Vermont. He called the Lucas County Corrections Center to solidify extradition details for the next day, ordered from room service, and watched local news and sports. When he felt tired, he collapsed on the bed, closed his eyes, and whispered a good night prayer to God to keep Laura safe. He drifted off as Laura curled up behind him, her toenails digging into his heels. He dreamed her breath lifted the hairs on the back of his neck; he dreamed she pinched his chin and whispered, '*This beard leads to racy thoughts, mister;*' he dreamed when she turned, she cradled him in her hands, drew him inside, and held him tight. Her features blurred and she disappeared from beneath him. He grunted, "Hnnh?" and sat up, surprised to find himself fully dressed on top of an ugly green spread. He stood again at the window and stared out at a city late at night: noisy, alive, and beautiful with its sparkling sky. He remembered other visits to other places to retrieve riffraff headed back to Vermont and imagined he could head out and find something to do; in the past, an easy decision: bars, booze, and broads. Instead, he stripped to boxers and socks, returned to bed, and drifted off. He woke when he heard music from the next room then two voices, laughter, creaking mattress. "Shit," he groaned, climbed out of bed, dressed, and headed into the corridor where he'd noticed a soda machine. He counted the coins in his pocket—not enough—and headed back to his room.

A female voice behind said, "I have change."

He turned to see Meg Barber. "What the hell?"

"I was about to ask the same thing! I'm here for a conference for work but what brings you to Toledo?"

"I'm escorting a sentence-skipper back for your father."

Meg plopped four quarters into his palm and gestured, "They woke me, too. Come join me for a drink and conversation?"

Steve found her presence too much of a coincidence *but only Granger knew his location, right?* "No thanks, I have a long flight back."

Meg chuckled, "We won't get much rest while our neighbors go at it. Come in for one quick drink."

"Really, Meg, no. This is uncomfortable."

Meg took a cigarette pack from her robe and offered him one. He declined—months since he lit up. He watched Meg light hers and shake the match hard; her breasts jiggled and he noticed they were nice and firm. He felt shamed by his thoughts and his throat tightened at the fact that of many horrible habits he once enjoyed, the worst had to be fooling around. He wouldn't be surprised if over the years, Meg heard her father express dismay over how often his best friend engaged in sordid affairs; no wonder Meg grew up thinking Steve's world revolved around casual sex. Meg verified his suspicions when she said, "Dad often joked about the victims in your hit and runs. I'd never feel like a victim if…"

"Meg, I'm not interested."

She took a deep drag. "Maybe not tonight but you should face what you're going through again."

"Excuse me?"

"I overheard Mom on the phone about photos of Laura with some guy; it sounded a lot like when Denise…"

"Enough, Meg, really."

"I'd never do that to you in a million years." Steve visualized one photo in particular: Laura and that Glenn person stood by a door, framed on three sides by bushes and on the fourth by a dim lamp. She stood on tiptoes to kiss his cheek. There were others, too, capturing an intimacy he feared meant more than friendship. Steve was shocked back to the corridor when Meg squeezed his hand. "All's quiet in the next room so join me in what will remain our secret."

Steve pulled his hand away. "No, thanks."

'That wasn't an offer of a drink or conversation."

"I know. Good night."

Meg's voice cracked. "All I ask is one night to…"

"Enjoy your conference." Steve dropped coins in the machine, headed to his room, and left the unopened can on a dresser. *In the past if a woman offered comfort, I didn't look back. It feels good to think I declined because I love Laura but what if part is secrets have a way of sneaking out? How did life get so out of control?*

165

Mel finished his appointments and returned to his living quarters, pleased to discover Glenn left a take-out container of Yankee Pot Roast, Gingered Carrots, and Red Potatoes with Fennel. He reheated the dinner in his microwave and noticed his answering machine blinked from two days' accumulation. Most were routine requests for appointments or refills but two were disturbing. First, his brother Norman indicated he was in Vermont; not in Fallsbridge, thank Heavens, but at a motel south of Canaan. Norman's message was clear: *Violet and I are in frequent contact so why don't the three of us meet for dinner soon?* The second was far more pleasant from Little Miss Elisabeth Grunwald: *Thank you for the airline tickets. I can't wait to see you at the Montreal airport. Do you know this will be my first trip out of the United States? Good thing I have a photo id, huh? If your busy schedule allows, I'd love to see the Botanical Gardens and Olympic Stadium or anything else you think I'd enjoy!* Mel replayed her message and stood paralyzed in the middle of his living room. Nothing felt under control.

Mel heard the grandfather clock chime and realized he was late leaving for the cabin to relieve Robert, the crotchety old fool who spent less and less time every passing day involved in an endeavor he once agreed was necessary. Mel grabbed the dinner and left on foot. When he arrived, he held his tongue as Robert wagged his tiresomely. It was because Mel was so exasperated by the situation that his guest was successful in a negotiation for table time to enjoy her meal. Laura was her usual charming self but after finishing, took little time to pepper him with questions and concerns. Mel chuckled, "So once again we debate the wisdom of my beloved community doing my bidding and I repeat: you question simply to question; you argue simply to argue; and yet you fail to see, hear or learn."

Laura grinned. "Then let me repeat where we left off: take me back in time and teach me, Mel. Convince me of the wisdom of your design." Mel imagined her tone was a ploy, her rapt attention carefully planned, her ultimate intentions dishonorable. He studied her eyes and wondered: did his desire to envelop her in every way imaginable be the reason they faced each other in an isolated cabin in the deep woods of Vermont to negotiate again? If by the grace of God she forgave him, might she truly return home? Laura studied him and added, "I watched my Mèmère Marceau's medical struggles for years and now fear my mother heads in the same direction. I'm curious, Mel: if I choose the father of my unborn child wisely, is there a chance for a different future?"

"Yes! That's why I offered Lynette a consult, a chance to predict and foresee. I knew I was right to select you when you were a mere child. You understand why seeking the right partner for coition is in the long run, the only solution to the rapid decline of our nation."

Laura cleared her throat. "I'd like to see the chart about my family. I found it fascinating but didn't have enough time to study your findings or understand what you discovered about my blood line that projects a match with Glenn would be perfect."

Mel agreed to bring the chart on his next visit. "Perhaps you could help me update with pertinent data of your brother Richard, his lovely fiancé, your brother John Jr, his wife and their two children."

"Jack and Sarah have three now."

Mel sighed, "I fall behind on many tasks but I believe with your help that will change. Now no more talk; we rest."

166

Laura counted inside her head and figured it was Tuesday. Brian hadn't been there in over a week, Matthew and Robert only once every other day, and Vincent less and less often. From time to time, she heard chairs scrape, extra footsteps or multiple voices on the porch when someone else was inside with her, but slowly it seemed the task of keeping watch fell almost exclusively to Marsethe—the one there first thing in the mornings, brought food, exchanged clean clothes for soiled, allowed her to use the bathroom or shower, who tied knots too tight, shoved her from behind if her legs fell asleep again and she took too long to cross the room or return to bed, and never forgot to reposition the scarf. She felt confused by another person who accompanied him once and stood silently beside the bed, so close she could feel body heat, smell body sweat. She tried to peek but the scarf held tight, the room too dark. From the length and sound of steps, she imagined someone younger than Marsethe—perhaps Ben or another too timid to take a forward position. She detected an odor of yeast, imagined it might be Glenn or someone else recently in a kitchen—which would explain the suddenly-improved meals—but rejected that idea: Glenn despised the old man's schemes.

Laura concentrated on her months in Fallsbridge, recalled files and photographs, replayed conversations in her mind, and tried to make sense of too much information with too little clarity. What did she know, really? What could she prove if called into a court of law? Were her months away a waste of time? As was often the case she drifted to sleep with nothing to see, hear, or do. One time she dreamed she stood naked in front of a full-length mirror, caressed her swollen abdomen, and worked vitamin-rich ointment into stretched and scarred skin. Another time she dreamed she couldn't sleep because she felt butterflies inside her abdomen. Another time she dreamed her mother came up behind as she held a nipple to show her how to coax the infant to suck by squeezing his velvety cheeks. Another time she dreamed she changed a diaper, a tiny

333

penis to move aside and bathe around, tiny testicles to clean beneath. Another time she dreamed bloody towels cluttered her parent's bedroom; odd because it wasn't Essex but what other would look familiar?

At the sound of a tree limb crack in the wind, Laura opened her eyes. She felt a flutter and held her breath. *Could that be what Reilly called a quickening?* She concentrated and waited but the sensation was gone. On Wednesday—day 12, she figured—Marsethe arrived to change her dressings. He came alongside the bed to position the blue scarf, summoned someone into the cabin and by the length of steps and gasp at the door Laura imagined a woman. Laura risked his fury with: "I need to exercise after this much time in bed and…"

"Enough!" Marsethe groaned and covered her mouth. He barked orders, the person left, and she waited for a blow. None came. Time passed, two voices spoke softly on the porch, and he let her take a shower. When she returned to bed, he applied cream to her wrists and ankles, and sighed: "Please don't struggle; these wounds need to heal. Like you, I weary of this."

"Then let me go. I won't tell anyone this time."

Marsethe chuckled, "I wish it were that simple." He adjusted the scarf, retied the ropes but not so tightly, and settled into the chair beside the bed. "Quiet now; I need rest."

"Was that Violet before?"

"No, Violet knows nothing of this."

"Was it Mary?"

"No."

"Was it Peg?"

A deep sigh: "Please do not waste time or energy on questions I have no intention of answering."

Laura thought long and hard. "Was it Caroline?"

A long silence then: "Caroline is second only to you,"

Laura heard a shift in breathing and voice: the disorientation between alert and oblivious, that window of time she learned as a child to avoid in the presence of parents, teachers, or brothers if there were matters best left unexplored. 'Is it any wonder Jack loved her?'

A heavy sigh then: "No wonder at all; would it have been so distressing to let them be?"

Laura waited patiently for him to continue and minutes passed before she heard a light snore. She took a deep breath and talked about picnics and cookouts, excursions to Lake Maidstone to swim or canoe, Christmas concerts and Easter pageants, snow sculpture contests and spelling bees, and Halloween decorations along the green. "Do you remember when the Maidstone was only an inn, not yet a restaurant?"

She felt surprised when he answered, "I do. Glenn is a master at menu preparation, is he not?"

"Yes, Glenn is someone who..."

Laura jumped as he yanked the scarf off, towered above, and poked an index finger on her abdomen. "Why is my son not who you desire? Why do you allow an undeserving son of eastern European immigrants to spill seed into your most wondrous of places?"

Laura expected a blow and cringed. "Please don't hurt me."

He moved away to collapse into a chair. "I weary of this."

Laura lay perfectly still, waited, and realized they reached a point of no return. Marsethe? too erratic to predict. The others? not there often enough to protect her. She heard his breathing slow and whispered, "If you're awake, Mel, I'd like to discuss finishing the patent application."

A heavy sigh: "The application is no longer uppermost on my mind, the opportunity to make my mark already gone."

"I disagree. I've had time to lie here thinking of the potential impact your procedure would offer."

He snorted, "Don't attempt to confuse me by appearing to set aside concerns of ethics. It won't work. Enough; I need rest."

Laura waited for a light snore and realized after 12 days—or was it now 13?—she felt too weak to run but too scared not to try. Why hadn't she tried harder the first day or second? It felt like an eternity before Marsethe dozed off, head bobbing softly against his chest between snorts. The scarf off, she studied the room, listened for noises from the porch, and felt looser ropes than before. Her neck ached as she lifted her head to check slackness. She wiggled sideways into a fetal position, got the rope on her left wrist close, and strained her neck to bring it to her teeth. She got the first rope dangling and started on the second when Marsethe towered above. "You dare to trick me while I rest?"

"No, I need to use the bathroom! I can't wait!"

Marsethe chuckled, "Wait? We all must wait! Your recent visit to the Mosgrove farm is why you're here, why I couldn't wait any longer. Had you simply assisted in a patent application, I wouldn't watch inferiors leap ahead to gain patents in a virgin field. It took five years for *23andme* to navigate a process and earn a patent for diagnostic testing tools inferior to mine yet I stand to fall farther behind not because I am relegated to wait in the backwoods of Vermont but because you barged outside the boundaries of professional behavior!"

Laura braced for a strike but the door opened, Matthew entered calmly, crossed the room, and put an arm around the doctor's shoulder. "Mel, we have a reservation for dinner. Tonight's special is Spicy Lamb Stew with Maple-baked Butternut Squash, one of your fall favorites." Laura watched them leave, heard a car door slam and scraping sounds as someone sat on the porch bench before she felt comfortable enough to yank another section of rope to her teeth.

167

Steve headed to work early to enter data about the transport. Finished, he reviewed notes from a 2013 arrest scheduled for trial in district court. Even with customary delays, he felt prepared to testify in that case and others wending their way through a complex system; what he couldn't abide was an investigation going nowhere 130 miles across state. For 11 days, he left messages on office and cell phones: Wilkers, Ralph, Kobel, and other names mentioned in passing. He found response times deplorable until Wilkers returned one on Day 12. "Something's going on, Steve—it's as if a place in mental hibernation woke up."

"More IRS stuff?"

"Could be but I don't think so. Kobel brought in an expert on cults and parades her around to agitate the townsfolk."

"Claudette Adams?"

"Something like that; the FBI doesn't exactly keep us locals informed but Barber and I figure she's here to consult before this circus becomes another disaster like Waco."

Steve rubbed his hands together. "Surely they know the CFEL's different. There's paranoia, sure, but this isn't some doomsday cult armed to the hilt and ready to…"

Al interrupted, "I'm not sure Kobel buys it. I thought we'd enlist Gil Munier as our own expert advisor."

"The local cop? Why?"

"Laura helped him find a place to live and work and…"

"Excuse me?"

Silence and mumbling before Ralph came on. "With how you crawl all over that girl whenever she's home, it doesn't surprise me it never came up in conversation. Your darlin' wife helped this guy escape with a wife, little boy, and another on the way."

"Excuse me?"

"Budster, they're camped out at your bride's bachelorette pad. Oh, and this Munier's working for John."

Steve stared at his organized desk and files. "What if I find this guy and not just say hello but pick his brains clean?"

"Granger will chew our asses but another detective prowling the opposite corner of the state makes sense."

Steve called the Delorange house, John's office at UVM , and the listing for Numerations, Inc.—no answer. He recalled what Ralph said about Munier's family and headed to Laura's old apartment. At his knock, Steve watched a young woman peek from behind a curtain and pressed his identification against the glass. "Yes?"

Steve smiled. "I'm looking for Gil Munier."

"Why?"

"I have a few questions."

As she chewed her lower lip in that nervous way Laura often did, Steve stared into the kitchen where everything looked the same: bright yellow curtains, scratched wooden table, and mismatched chairs. The door flew open and bounced off Steve's shoe as a toddler jumped up and down, arms extended. The mother scooped him up. "Sorry, David's not usually like this. Um, Gil's not here."

Steve struggled to recall everything Laura said about the people she met. Why didn't he listen? Every time she came home, she talked about but he did what Ralph joked: crawled all over her then drifted to sleep, lulled by her presence. Steve's mind sifted through details, pictured photos Rawlings brought back, and figured if she called her son David, the woman in front of him was Reilly McSomething. "Laura and I are married and if you read the *Free Press*, you know she's missing. You're Reilly, you worked with Laura, and became friends. What you don't know is Laura's pregnant and I need to find out about CFEL weak spots."

"I'm not sure they have any," Reilly answered but pulled the door open wide to invite him in.

Steve headed to the living room and at the sight of a wooden mirror he helped hang, felt his throat tighten. The apartment held too many memories of time spent together when they were partners and friends, but not yet lovers, and of course, that rainy day in the spring when he and Lynette packed so Laura could move in with him and stay forever. That's what she promised and a promise was a promise. Steve felt his eyes tear as David climbed onto his lap. Chubby fingers touched wet cheeks as he turned to his mother and gurgled, "Ern?"

"He's very sad today."

Steve muttered, "I know it's a lot to ask but understand I have to try everything or I may never see my wife again."

"Sit, please; Gil comes home around 1:30. I'll put David down for a nap and you'll join us for lunch."

"That's not necessary."

"It is; anyone Laura loves is welcome in our home."

168

Gil pulled into the driveway, noted an unfamiliar vehicle, and imagined his worst fear of the past 12 days came true: unable to stay strong, Laura told the CFEL how to find them. He considered not going inside but inside with the ones he loved was the only place he cared to be. He rushed along and cursed his complacency; since the moment they arrived in Burlington, Gil allowed them to settle in, get comfortable. Stupid—of everyone, he knew better than to think with the CFEL, a game ever ended. Gil rushed in, stunned when Reilly stood with a smile. "Gil, meet Sergeant Steve Scolarzski of the Vermont State Police."

Gil shook the man's hand. "Why are you here?"

His irritation shifted to curiosity then interest as he listened. The most startling disclosure wasn't how much investigators knew about the CFEL but the fact Laura was his wife. Steve finished, "Reilly thinks the CFEL doesn't have weak spots. Is that true?"

Gil glanced at Reilly. "My wife doesn't know the half of it but Laura's one of a group chosen for Marsethe's project long before birth. In Mel's eyes, he never makes mistakes and while that doesn't protect her fully, it keeps her alive."

Steve frowned. "Then why kidnap her?"

Gil glanced at Reilly again. "I'm not proud for 15 years I served as foot soldier but along the way learned where the CFEL stores people while they undergo re-education. I can draw a map and pinpoint..."

Reilly touched his hand. "Why not show him?"

"With a new job, I can't just..." Gil paused and laughed, "I can get time off." For the first time since introductions, he watched Steve smile. Gil grabbed the phone, called John, and explained the situation. He passed the phone to Steve and drew Reilly into his arms. "I'll be home as soon as I can."

"Be careful; don't be seen. Mel gets so strange when anyone defies him, especially chosen ones like Laura or you."

169

Al answered a call through dispatch, surprised to hear Scolarzski: "I'm minutes away from Derby, Gil Munier with me."

"Head to my place; we're working out of my kitchen to keep our distance from the FBI—no big surprise but they don't share."

When they showed up, Munier waltzed in cocky as ever to camp out at the table to scan everything gathered about activities in and around Fallsbridge for 12 days: field notes, time logs, interview transcripts, ground and aerial photographs. After an hour, Munier stood to announce, "They were on to you by Day 2 and switched from cars to feet on day 3; that means she's close—maybe in one of the elders' houses."

Al answered, "Nope; the FBI conducted a house-to-house search and no one denied access or demanded search warrants."

"Okay, how about tunnels like spokes of a wheel connecting eight buildings to the hub: Matthew Purcareau's hardware store?"

"Nope; we found 'em and troopers are in and out 24 / 7."

Munier moved photos around, held a few close, and stated, "Here's the deal: first I lead you to customary CFEL hide sites until Laura's found; second I disclose details about past activities; and third I testify in court. In exchange, I want a written guarantee of immunity from prosecution both federal and state and I want it up front."

Al said, "I can speak for us but the feds are a different..."

"Fine but you could make a call. I never bombed, set fires, kidnapped, raped, or killed; just closed my eyes to crimes by others." Gil pulled sunglasses on, wandered outside, and relaxed on the deck.

Scolarzski groaned, "Shit! Hurry-up-and-wait starts."

170

Gil studied activity in Wilkers' kitchen, heard three anxious voices, and knew eventually he'd agree to help but it felt early. He recalled John Delorange's voice on the phone: relieved, yes, but accusatory, too. Why had it taken almost two weeks to come through for a woman who came through for him? Had he had time to think, his answer would have been: "John, in case you forgot how to survive with the CFEL, I needed a bargaining position: tit for tat, always and forever, amen." When Wilkers and Barber left, Gil watched Scolarzski wander out, sit in the other chair, and smile as if he'd set the game up with small talk. If Gil learned one thing over the years, it was to hold everything inside, display little, wheel and deal, maneuver, and wait. Even a cop like Scolarzski with years of experience eventually showed something: fears, failures, or desires. Gil felt surprised when the other man hit hard, hit fast, and with everything he had from the first sentence: "If Reilly and David were missing, I'd do anything to help you find them."

"No, if you faced prison as an accessory-after-the-fact, you'd stall, too. Anyone investigating the CFEL needs to know they rearrange facts; nothing's as it seems." Gil stared at an area that only a month earlier obviously produced vegetables and thought *Fall comes too quickly in Vermont and after all this ends, Reilly, David, and I can head south before the baby arrives—tough for Reilly to leave everything familiar behind but...*

Scolarzski asked, "You took pictures of my wife, right?"

"Yeah, lots of them."

"I saw a few of Laura with your brother and wonder..."

"What they show?" At a nod, he said, "I took dozens of them together—moments of tenderness because Glenn's in love with Laura but I followed her through five different Vermont and New Hampshire counties to find pay phones, no doubt to call who she loves."

"I hope."

Gil admitted he knew from experience when Mel re-educated a willful woman, if not in the village itself he moved her to other locations: "Vince's hunting lodge in Canaan, the unused fourth floor of the academy, or the Sportsman's Club on Maidstone Lake. I rule two of those out because from aerial photos, they're on foot."

Steve leaned closer. "I have another question: when women are isolated, does Marsethe draw blood?"

Gil shrugged, "Yeah; I picked up all kinds of test packets delivered to the pharmacy for his lab so yeah, it's common Why?"

"Laura's pregnant."

"Oh, well, Mel believes what he feels for Laura is love not a perverse obsession so he'll make adjustments." Gil couldn't say out loud what else he knew: *Mel often rewrites rules of a game while in play. If Laura were pregnant by Glenn, Brian, or me, the fetus would be highly prized. Its existence becomes an issue only when he discovers a selected female contaminated by an unapproved union.* Gil finished, "I imagine the answer to your concern depends on how quickly he gets down to basics."

171

When Al and Ralph returned in 46 minutes, Steve figured at a 20-minute drive each way using a siren, the FBI magnanimously allotted 6 minutes to debate Munier's immunity or VSP request for broader inclusion. Ralph pulled Steve aside. "Relax, podna; Senior Agent Kobel's a federal boundary-freak but promised to call pronto with a decision."

Al's two younger daughters arrived on the school bus and Steve felt struck by resemblances to their mother and older sister. They behaved like Sandra, too: level-headed, polished, mature beyond calendar years—a lot like Mickey at their ages—sophistication proving all four experienced too much too soon. Sheila grilled burgers on the deck while Sharon set a picnic table with plastic ware, potato salad, veggies, and watermelon. Steve cringed at how the group slid into social niceties—even Munier relaxed and chatted with the girls about the start of a new school year. Al and Ralph joined Steve to pore over reports, notes, and photos especially aerial shots of the last 24 hours of townspeople on foot—confusing assortment of mothers with baby strollers, dog walkers, children, and shoppers. Kobel from the FBI called and offered to discuss immunity if Munier turned himself over voluntarily. They arranged a pick-up and 36 minutes later, a vehicle pulled up. Munier faced Steve on his way out. "I overheard everything about foot traffic and if my wife went missing, I'd say the hell with the FBI. Follow up with Angela. Only one thing provokes the CFEL into action: smartass females who don't accept the natural order of the universe created by God and enforced on earth by His chosen few. Mel takes the role of enforcer seriously and if you three know Angela followed Glenn last night, he does, too."

172

Laura lay awake and recalled the last time Steve and she were together in the cabin. She recalled the discussion of her investigation and his practical suggestions. She flushed at a memory of amazing sex and wondered how they allowed such painful arguments or a dreadful departure to intrude. As usual with nothing else to do, see, or hear, she drifted off to visualize them in his bedroom during a March blizzard months earlier. Steve wrapped his arms around her and guided her to the bed where side by side, they sat awkwardly until he reminded her about their dance at the Sigler reception. She dreamed Steve whispered, *Take the lead like you tried to that day, kid. Call the shots and drive me crazy.* Laura dreamed she answered, *Will you talk so I know it's you?* and he talked as he drew her close, talked as he caressed, and talked as he stared into her eyes and entered her gently. Laura woke and whispered, "I'll always remember that look in your eyes, Steve; I promise."

Laura heard a key, watched Mary McGuinn enter with a Styrofoam container, and drop it on the table when she saw the scarf off. "What the...? Mel promised you'd never know I was here!"

"It slid off but I need to use the bathroom now!"

Mary sat on the stool and fingered the knot around Laura's right ankle. "How'd you get these others off?"

"I bit through them but it's tough to get…"

Mary groaned, "They're so tight and wet!" She ran to a drawer and returned with a knife. "Hold still; this'll be slow but should work."

A few seconds later: "Mary, please let me go."

"I can't do that, Laura."

A few seconds later: "How'd he get you to come here?"

A chuckled, "He warned me you'd do this."

A few seconds later: "What did he promise you, Mary?"

"Nothing; damn, where's a steak knife when you need one?"

Laura bounced her hips. "Where's a diaper when you need one?"

With huge, frightened eyes, Mary confessed the night before Elder Matthew saw Angela Lezzarro out late and followed her to the cabin. "He said Angela followed Glenn here!"

"I don't believe Glenn's part of this."

"Stop talking! He's not! I'm not!"

A few seconds later: "You know, it's not too late to…"

"What if it is, Laura? Angela went to school today and though Mel thinks she didn't talk, he sent me here to get you ready."

"Ready?"

Mary struggled with the knife. "I need something sharp; maybe keys'll work." She patted her pockets and groaned, "I walked!" She found a fork in a drawer and dragged it at an angle. "Better; Mel wants you moved in case Angela brings Rita or the police."

Laura choked, "This is taking too long!"

Mary got through one, focused on the next, and groaned, "You're bleeding! Did I cut you?"

"No, that's from before! Keep going!"

When all ropes dangled free, Laura bounded across the room, slammed the door, and minutes later came out laughing, "You have no idea how much better I feel. Thank you."

Mary stood in the middle of the room. "So what do I do until Mel gets here? I can't let you go but…"

"Let me go and I'll tell you where Reilly and Gil went."

Mary laughed, "You had a part in that?"

"I helped them, yes."

"Why?"

"I find it unconscionable two people in love can't marry and conceive a child without fear."

Mary groaned, "They're married? I knew she saw him on the sly and… I suspected Reilly might be pregnant but… Shit! It never matters what I think." She grabbed a pillow case from the bed, tore it into strips with the fork, and tied strips around Laura's bloody ankles and wrists. She took her jacket off and handed it over. "You'll need this; it's raining. Turn right at the bottom of the steps, head toward the river, and follow it to town. Stay off the road because Mel's supposed to drive here to move you. I mean, he said he'd have dinner and get some rest but..."

"Mary, thank you."

"Yeah, okay; when he gets here, I'll stall him; wait at my house and I'll take you to a hospital."

Outside, Laura grabbed the porch railing, inched down, and prayed after 12 days of immobility— or 13?—she had the strength to run. A half dozen steps convinced her she didn't; she limped 200 feet to the stand of maples; once there, a brief rest and a loosening of the cloths at her ankles meant another 200 feet to a boulder, then another brief rest and trek to the riverbank to dip a cloth into cold water to wash her feet. *Where are my shoes?* She struggled until she could move no further, collapsed to the ground, leaned against a trunk, and closed her eyes.

173

Steve argued until his throat hurt until Al nodded. "It's time to ignore the FBI; let's visit the Lezzarro household." When they arrived, a girl opened the door, grabbed Al in a crushing hug, but pulled back when she saw others. Al took the lead. "Angela, I'd like you to meet Sergeants Ralph Barber and Steve Scolarzski from the Vermont State Police. We have a few questions, if you don't mind."

She extended her right hand to both. "I'm Angela Rita Lezzarro and I'll tell you what I saw."

As Angela described activities from the evening before, Steve felt awed by how mature she seemed yet how vulnerable. Al asked and received permission from her mother to take Angela along to identify a location of interest in the investigation. In the car Angela climbed into the back seat with her mother and Al, Ralph drove, and Steve took the front passenger seat. He felt how intently Angela studied him, recalled the police and hospital photographs of the same child, and cringed at a realization her dark hair, dark eyes, and timid smile reminded him of the Laura he saw in Delorange home movies.

Angela whispered, "Are you the Steve Laura said she loves?"

Steve turned with a smile. "I hope I am."

"Then what took you so long to get here?"

Ralph muttered, "He was ordered to stay out of it."

"Don't you know some orders are meant to be broken?"

Rita muttered, "Angela! Don't be rude."

Steve chuckled, "That's what I believe, too."

As they neared the academy, Angela pointed where to park since she could only find the cabin through the woods. She directed every move: "Walk briskly but don't run; if you run, I can't hear if anyone's nearby. Only use a flashlight if you trip, go single-file but hold one arm up to protect your eyes from branches, and don't talk." Ten minutes later she stopped at the edge of a clearing. "It's weird to find it lit up like this."

Al stopped the group's forward movements. "Angela, Rita, stay back; Steve, you too. I mean it! I won't tolerate mistakes. Ralph, come with me." They drew handguns, raced to the porch, and pounded on the door. "Police! Open up!" The man who opened the door looked terrified and Steve recognized him from photographs as Al grabbed Glenn by the arm and pulled him down the steps. Ralph entered the cabin and a moment later, exited with a woman.

Steve raced inside and shouted, "Laura's not here!" With the recitation of Miranda in the background, he saw bloody sheets and ropes strewn throughout the room and collapsed on the steps.

Beside Al, the woman sobbed, "I said I let Laura go."

"Show us," Al said and the woman led them along a different path. Steve noticed lights at the academy visible through trees and heard running water at the same moment Al turned in a circle. "This makes no sense! If Laura wanted to escape, she wouldn't head back to town."

The woman answered, "I sent her this way to confuse Mel. I told her to go to my house."

When they reached the academy parking lot, Al split the group up. "Rita, go home and get your car. Ralph, go with her, take this bag to the cabin, and gather evidence but wait for me there. Steve, here's a flashlight; search the woods. I'll call Kobel and take Munier and McGuinn to them. Come on, let's move." Al turned to Angela. "You should go home with your mother; it's late."

"I have a flashlight and could help Steve."

Al looked to Steve and Rita and at nods, said. "Okay."

As they searched, Steve called Laura's name and felt the quiet peacefulness, breathed in a rich aroma of pine needles, relaxed to leaves crunching underfoot, and thought *it must be magnificent to raise a child in this idyllic setting.* Angela interrupted his thoughts with, "The CFEL thinks a speed limit of 25, or bike paths, Olympic-sized pool, and 21,000-volume library prove how much it loves its kids."

Steve turned with a grin. "And the hell with everything else?"

Angela kicked a rock. "Yeah, especially bratty kids like me."

"I see someone inquisitive, how Laura is, too." Steve stopped when his flashlight illuminated something white. He ran to the riverbank, pulled gloves on, and lifted a dark-stained cloth. He held it to his nose, gasped, "Is this blood?" and turned in a circle. "Laura, where are you?"

174

After his summary, Al added, "Scolarzski was there when..."

Agent Kobel sneered, "The husband was where?"

Al ignored him and turned to introduce Rita. "Mrs. Lezzaro can lead your team to the cabin where one of my men collects evidence."

"One of your goddamn what does fucking what?"

Al nodded toward his cruiser. "I've got two potential witnesses cuffed inside, terrified, ripe for the picking. If you let go of this need for jurisdictional boundaries, you might conclude this before dawn."

"Cop or not, the husband stays out of it."

Al shrugged, "Sure; first I have to find him."

Kobel laughed, "Great, Wilkers, just great. Classic."

175

At the whir of an engine, Laura opened her eyes to dawn and saw a pick-up back out of a driveway. She saw the *Welcome to Fallsbridge: Gateway to God's Northeast Kingdom* sign and 500 yards farther, the Laundromat pay phone. She laughed at the idea *To reach it and use it, though, I need to cross an open expanse unnoticed—not likely barefooted; wrists and ankles ringed by bruises; legs covered with scratches; bandages stained by blood; and clothes streaked with dirt. What if I reach it to find it out of order? What if it works but without change, I can't get an operator? What if I get an operator but no one answers?*

Laura heard rustling from behind: "Miss Delorange?"

Laura braced herself for attack, turned to Harvey Browne, and whispered, "Thank you, God."

"Come on; lean on me for support." He took it slow while offering details about the FBI, IRS, Wilkers, State Police, and Caledonia County Sheriff's Department. At a nearby house, he carried her past tubs of soil and shrugged, "Marijuana once grew there and I should think about planting daisies or something soon, huh?" Inside, Laura's mind raced through a million options and decided: *first the bathroom then the phone.*

176

For the first time in close to two weeks, Mel felt refreshed by seven uninterrupted hours of rest thanks to Matthew's suggestion of a double dose of sleeping aid. Mel rewarded himself with a red pepper and zucchini frittata at the Maidstone only to feel bombarded with idiotic interruptions. First, Robert reported a visit from the FBI with the same tired old questions; a second when Vincent decided to neglect an already-shortened schedule due to sleep deprivation; and a third when Brian whined, "I got home last night to find six women in my living room."

Mel sighed, "With their book-of-the-month and bags of yarn?"

"Don't downplay this! Violet asks questions and...."

Mel held his hand up and watched Matthew cross the parking lot. "I suspect another disruption to a fine breakfast."

Matthew collapsed into a chair. "On my way to open the store, I saw Harvey Browne with Laura. I'll bet she's using a phone!"

Mel chuckled, "I take my time one day and Mary McGuinn fails in a single task?" He put his fork down and used his napkin. "Well, I wish Mrs. Scolarzski luck in summoning her beloved. We have time to visit the Browne hovel and spirit my fallen angel back into peaceful seclusion."

177

After one recorded message after another on house, desk, and cells, Laura thought suddenly of Granger, dialed his direct line and in response to a live voice, laughed, "Sir, this is Laura!"

"What the...? Where are you?"

Laura provided directions. "Sir, do you think you can get somewhere here soon?"

"Shit, yeah, sure. Hang up."

Laura breathed a sigh of relief and turned. Behind Harvey, people milled about: four children between preschool and teens, an elderly couple, and woman Laura's age. After introductions, Laura recommended everyone go about their normal routine. "Nothing draws attention like an entire family behaving out of the ordinary."

Harvey nodded. "I agree. Kids, go back and finish breakfast. The school bus will be here soon."

"Um, isn't this close enough for them to walk?"

Harvey shrugged, "We don't trust the academy; the younger children head to Guildhall and the older ones to Concord."

Laura flushed, "I never realized how hard it must be to stay, especially in winter. I'm not usually this dense and ..."

"You're exhausted," Harvey interrupted, put an arm around Laura's shoulder, and guided her upstairs. "Get some rest in the girls' bedroom while we get you something to eat."

Laura accepted the face cloth and towel offered and stood in the middle of the room. She smelled coffee, toast, and oatmeal, and heard children prepare for school. She drew a warm bath, crawled in, and scrubbed every grimy inch. She found baby shampoo, washed and rinsed her hair three times, and relaxed knowing no one waited outside the door to shove her back onto stinky sheets and to add insult to injury, tie her down. When she came out, she found a robe, pulled it on, and tied filthy clothes into a ball. Laura lay down, stared at puffy white clouds in a deep blue autumn sky, and watched a pair of cardinals land on the sill. To their whistled phrases, she drifted into a sultry dream where Steve's lips touched hers gently and his hands caressed swollen ankles.

Laura murmured, "I love you so much it scares me to...."

"I love you, too."

At the voice, Laura opened her eyes to Marsethe and slid as far away as she could on the twin bed. "Please no more," she gasped and noticed others in the background: Matthew frowned in anger but Vincent and Robert looked frightened. When she heard no sounds from the rest of the house, she choked, "What have you done to the Brownes?"

"Although that hoard is stunted, they know to keep out of business not theirs." Marsethe gestured and Laura saw his minions swing into action: Robert grabbed an arm, Vincent the other, and Matthew shoved from behind to force her down the stairs.

Laura saw the Browne family on the couch—eyes filled with terror—Brian holding mace spray. "You little creep! I should..." As the men shoved her into the kitchen, Laura saw the black Escalade, its back door open like a gaping hole to hell. She pressed bare feet to tile, grimaced in pain, but backpedaled furiously.

Brain raced in, grunted, "Get out of my way!" yanked her off her feet, and sprinted the distance. Exactly like that first morning, Laura landed face-first on the floor of the back seat.

Brian yanked Matthew out of the driver's seat. "We can't sit here in daylight! Give me the fucking key!"

A woman's voice: "That's enough."

Marsethe laughed, "Ladies, to what do we owe this honor?"

Laura heard Violet: "I called Kobel and he's on the way."

Marsethe hissed, "No one listens to drivel from fools who sleep with their own blood uncles."

"She does what?" Brian gasped.

Marsethe snorted, "Take your wife home and beat her senseless."

Four men in dark suits appeared at a corner of the house and stopped 20 feet away. Each held a handgun, arms raised, eye level. One stepped forward. "I'm Special Agent Arthur Kobel of the United States Federal Bureau of Investigation. Doctor, move away from the young lady and raise your hands above your head." When Marsethe stayed put, the agent repeated, "Move away, sir, and raise your hands above your head. Do it now!" Another agent opened a side door to help Laura to her feet.

Marsethe climbed out. "I have no time for this. In two hours, my presence is required at Mirabel Airport in Montreal to retrieve an out-of-town professional colleague."

Kobel answered, "This is more urgent."

Marsethe struggled against cuffs. "I understand a delay may be necessary because—unlike my peace-loving friends and me—you and your colleagues are armed with dangerous weapons. You will discover secular laws yield no hold over the Community for Expansive Love. Our guidance comes from the Lord."

Kobel said, "I suspect you'll learn to respect those laws, sir," and issued orders for his men to lead the others away.

Laura touched Kobel's arm. "One minute, please?" and faced Vincent. "Twenty years ago, you provided him with an alibi. Why?"

"Mel's my closest friend."

"Vincent, he raped me and left me to bleed to death."

Vincent repeated, "Mel's my closest friend."

Laura lowered her head to stare at bruises on her arms and legs, scratches on her hands, and fresh blood on her wrists and ankles. She felt shamed—not because she made such a pathetic sight—but because she confessed out loud, in front of strangers, in front of men. She felt light-headed and swayed as Kobel grabbed. "You need rest, Mrs. Scolarzski."

Laura snorted, "I don't think so! Every time I close my eyes lately, I wake to the most horrible faces!"

178

Steve threw his jacket to the ground and suggested Angela rest, too. "Then if you're up to it, we'll head another direction."

"Ask anybody; I'm up for anything."

Steve noticed movement in the distance and stared across a soccer field. "Does that look like Ralph and Al?"

Angela looked, too. "I think so."

By the way Ralph whooped, Steve knew the mess ended. He lifted Angela, twirled her in a circle, but released when he saw terror in her eyes. "Sorry but Ralph has a unique way of telegraphing good news."

"I'm okay. I love Laura that much, too."

179

Glenn spent time in a room with Wilkers and a guy named Kobel who moved back and forth between rooms in a corridor. He heard and saw enough to know Mel, Matt, Vince, Brian, Robert, and Mary waited nearby. Since Kobel focused on Laura's disappearance, early questions seemed predictable but after Kobel came and went a dozen or so times, his focus shifted to CFEL structure, activities, and business ventures. When the genetics project came up, Glenn freely admitted, "I know little of the science involved and certainly none of the details." Kobel left the room again and Glenn relaxed. *Everything I said is true—over the years, I heard gossip, not the same as planning or conducting criminal acts. Right? All I need to do is answer questions without extra detail; all I have to worry about so far is how much I donated every Sunday and whether or not I reported all profits.*

180

Laura dreamed colored lights flashed, calliope music soared into the air on a cool breeze, and strong arms rocked her like a baby. A woman's voice whispered, "Keep trying; she's coming around."

Laura thought she heard Steve beg for a chance to be the world's best husband, opened her eyes, and studied every inch of a familiar face with its wrinkles and scars; at a sight of a scraggly moustache and beard, she reached to touch and heard, "Now that you're safe, I'll shave again."

"I think I like this, mister."

When someone else touched, Laura gasped and tried to sit. A young woman's face leaned in. "Relax; I'm here to help."

Laura looked around, recognized surroundings as an ambulance, and swallowed hard. "Is our baby okay?"

The young woman smiled. "I suspect you'll both be fine."

Laura pinched a furry chin. "I missed you something awful, Scolarzski."

"I missed you, too, Delorange; welcome home."

181

Steve felt relief at how quickly things returned to normal. After initial tears of joy seeing her alive, everyone who visited the hospital behaved like always: John and Lynette worked themselves into lathers about last-minute glitches in ceremony plans; Ralph promised not to pry for details about her captivity but did, anyway; Kobel and Wilkers came by way too often with questions; Joyce brought catalogs and giggled over sleazy honeymoon items; Rick voluntarily provided a blood sample to verify or exclude paternity of Stephanie Orsini's child; Mickey stopped often but seemed unable to get past the terror of her time missing; Steve felt concerned about Mickey's nervousness until during his third visit to her hospital room, Laura climbed from bed and crossed the room to hug him. "Your father, our baby, and I are fine, so can I see a smile?" They sat and talked until Laura laughed with delight to hear Sandra Wilkers might accompany him soon. Sometimes Steve forgot the mess ended and woke in the middle of night to feel an empty space beside him. He needed reminders—constant fixes—and showed up during all posted visiting hours or at other times snuck in with chili dogs, fries, thick shakes, and god-awful sweets. He enjoyed watching Laura devour everything even though she admonished him to keep their child's nutritional needs in mind.

182

After four days for tests and rehab, Laura left the hospital with Steve—unsure if she should call his place home. *Was it over? Would they move forward, forget all that happened, move on?* Laura appreciated a constant stream of visitors who insisted on seeing her alive and well—a presence of 'others' to provide a welcome break from thoughts, memories, and odd dreams. Slowly she believed their life together settled into a restful routine. Even an odd visit from Meg Barber implying Steve traveled out of state with her while Laura stayed missing complicated an bewildering summer. Though rehab in the hospital helped, she still felt woozy from little exercise for days on end in the cabin and kept a cane handy. When Mick and Sandra visited, Laura encouraged Steve to lead them on a guided tour of renovations: spacious master suite, spectacular views out a new bay window, empty room painted yellow for a new baby, hot tub, and lots of closet space. A quick run to Zachary's Pizza for calzones then Monopoly in the kitchen hinted a return to reality underway.

Once they were alone and relaxed listening to music, Laura felt the need to take another step. "Um, I keep thinking about the last time we were together at the cabin on the river and I want to apologize for how difficult those hours must have been for you."

Steve shrugged, "I'd like to think that's behind us now."

"I'd like that, too, but need to explain what happened with Glenn. There can be no secrets between us."

"Excuse me? Something happened with Munier?"

"I had a couple of glasses of wine and we watched a DVD. Um one thing led to another and we started making out."

Steve squinted. "Excuse me?"

"Um, I must've been half asleep because when I craved more, I reached inside his robe. At his response, I escaped to my own room."

Steve blinked slowly. "What do you mean by his response?"

Laura stammered, "I asked what I always do when I crave you closer: please enter me? At his voice, I fled."

"Nothing happened?"

"Nothing else happened."

Steve sighed, "I understand how yearning becomes so intense but what does that have to do with the cabin?"

Laura shrugged, "Hormones, libido, loneliness, desire? I don't know for sure but when I heard the voice of who held me, I escaped."

"Laura, thank you for being honest; your frankness gives me confidence to fill you in on some of my own concerns."

Laura touched fingertips to his lips. "Can we continue this conversation later? I'm feeling sluggish, about to fall asleep."

Steve smiled. "Sure; it'll give me a chance to work it out in my head, make sense of it, I guess."

They headed to the bedroom and Laura ached to beg him to leave her breathless like many times before. Instead, her mind filled with memories of a conversation that morning at the cabin: *It felt like any man with the right equipment would suit you just fine. I mean, you never once looked into my eyes.* Instead of reaching out, she assumed the nested position.

The next morning, Steve left for a few hours to finish up work he let slide. Laura relaxed in a recliner and stared at striking yellow, orange, and red foliage but to be awake and alone for the first time in days felt terrifying—too much floating around in need of scrutiny. She tried TV, radio, grabbed the Burlington *Free Press,* and headed out to the deck.

The distraction she craved came up the driveway in a navy blue four-door sedan. FBI Special Agent Arthur Kobel provided an update on the status of the investigation. At how cautiously he proceeded, Laura feared he'd report evidence ruled inadmissible because of records obtained without a warrant and interrupted, "Marsethe gave me a key!"

"I know that."

"I had permission to be there!"

"I know that, too. Marsethe never disputed it."

"He asked for my support in a patent application; maybe he didn't expect me to find what I did, but…"

"Let me finish. We filed charges against 14 individuals in federal court: Christopher Melvin Marsethe, Matthew Purcareau, Vincent Mottolla, and Robert Decarreau for kidnapping; Brian Lemphier, Glenn Munier, and Mary McGuinn as accessories after the fact; the first four—along with seven additional members—for felonies ranging from tampering with the U.S. Postal Service, money laundering, and tax evasion. Up in the air is Gil Munier's immunity from prosecution for illegal installation of surveillance equipment."

Laura leaned forward. "Please try to make it possible for him to escape the punishment rightly due the CFEL core."

Kobel nodded. "Who besides Munier would you be likely to offer support testimony if any go to trial?"

"Gil and Glenn Munier and Mary McGuinn for certain; I'd need to review formal charges against any others but that's a start."

"Not Vincent Mottolla?"

Laura licked her lips then shook her head. "Vince is a kind man who needs to face the fact his silence over the years condoned what happened to me and others."

Kobel thought for a moment than added, "Few will get a free pass, anyway. They'll all undergo expanded IRS audits."

Laura swallowed hard. "Okay, here's the question I avoided too long: what about baby trafficking?"

"Be patient; we review extensive records but sorting out accurate from falsified requires time; and DNA testing will be voluntary. If we find what we suspect we will, we'll need people with diplomacy skills to inform some they aren't exactly who they thought they were. "

Laura visualized Sam Mosgrove Jr—Rick, too—and nodded. "Let's hope they have someone to lean on."

Kobel added, "The State of Vermont will become a major part of a complex process because of tax evasion and falsification of birth and death records." He stood, offered his right hand, and laughed, "You're one gutsy lady. Too bad you decided to leave law enforcement; the FBI might've been an option."

Laura nodded. "Thanks; I'll keep that in mind but my focus from this day forward is my husband and child."

Laura watched him leave and for only the second time since Thursday—*or was it Friday when Harvey rescued her from hiding in weeds?*—

Laura sat awake and alone—first the ambulance, then the hospital, doctors and nurses, FBI and VSP honchos, family members, assorted other visitors, and Steve never far away, freely giving every available minute. To be wide awake and alone with so much on her mind terrified her. That morning when Steve explained he needed to catch up on work, it seemed reasonable—he put so many tasks aside when she stayed missing. Steve seemed glad to have her there but something felt different—he seemed on edge, as if he waited for another shoe to drop. *What shoe could possibly be left to drop? Unlike the one I struggle with: a fear dreams of pregnancy and nursing can never come true? I should discuss my unanswered questions with the best investigative mind I know. It won't be easy and I pray the man I love, the man who makes my blood boil, the man who cast off my fear of letting anyone close, and the man I married is the man I believe him to be.*

Laura inched into the new master suite to a trunk at the foot of the bed. She propped the lid open and rummaged inside. In muted light from an autumn sky, she touched few mementos. In her experience? Dangerous to own anything so irreplaceable its loss might break her heart. With a heavy sigh, Laura lifted out her favorite possession: a Thai spirit house. As she polished its ornate design and intricate carvings, she remembered the day her parents returned from an anniversary trip to Southeast Asia.. She recalled her mother's smile as she presented the gift and explained its meaning: *This tiny brass house is a place to contain evil spirits. If it's intricate enough, it holds their interest. If it's beautiful enough, the evil spirits choose to remain inside, and the living family who owns it is spared their evil wrath.* Tears slid down her cheeks, and Laura licked at them absentmindedly before she rushed into the kitchen for a cookie. She recalled something else her mother said: *From time to time, if the living spirits offer a sweet gift, the evil spirits inside feel appeased.* Laura closed the trunk, placed the spirit house on top of the bureau, and prayed evil spirits would stay away until she confided her fears to the man she loved.

Steve arrived home with Moo Shu Pork from his favorite take-out restaurant and proceeded to wait on her again, right on down to black oolong tea steeped in her mèmère's favorite porcelain pot. With only three days left until their formal reception—or four days to go?—Laura knew she had little time to offer him a chance to halt a raging production. "Um, if we're not going to make it together, let's admit that now."

Steve heaped steaming rice onto her plate. "Excuse me?"

"Um, I know I'm damaged goods, not easy to live with, and we've danced around each other since the ambulance ride."

Steve squinted, "I'd say we settled in, got comfortable, and thanked God everything's fine."

Laura licked her lips. "We haven't made love and I know the last time we were together, I was demanding, scary even."

Steve shrugged, "You were a little wired but..."

"Is this distance because of what I admitted about Glenn?"

Again, Steve shrugged. "I admit the fact you got that physical surprised me but I believe nothing else happened."

"Could it be as simple as I'm pregnant and unappealing?"

"You're amazing and at nine months, still amaze me."

"Okay, then what's going on? Why do I feel I've missed something important?"

Steve took her hand in his. "There's something I started to tell you last night, so here goes. I'm not proud of my history with women and need you to know I'll never take you or our relationship for granted. My God, Laura, meeting you is the best thing that ever happened to me and..." He stopped and shook his head. "I need to get to the point and disclose a painful secret. Meg Barber and I have an odd history going back years. When she was a kid, her declarations of love were cute; Ralph and Joyce found it adorable but I felt embarrassed. Over the years, Meg heard her parents discuss me and obviously believed the way to reach me was physical. During my drunken binges, she babysat Mickey for days on end and I can't count the number of nights I slept it off on her parents' couch."

Laura squeezed his hand. "Steve, unless you had physical contact when Meg was underage, I don't need to hear any more."

"Please wait while I describe the most sickening thing of all and what her parents don't know and I hope never do."

Laura felt a flush and dreaded to hear what came next. "Go on."

"One night when Meg was 14 or 15, she saw me uncovered first thing in the morning, and you know how men..."

"I do."

"She saw enough to offer comfort. I was sober enough to stop what she started and leave but what if she wandered down earlier? It could've been very different and for the past ten years, I've waited for her to outgrow what her parents see as a harmless crush."

Laura blinked slowly. "She never has."

"No, and I let it go on too long. I feared if I asked Ralph or Joyce for help, our relationship would suffer."

"Even now she pursues you."

Steve nodded. "She believes my hesitation is because of an age difference or friendship with her parents."

"Meg needs to move on, Steve. Invite her to the reception so she can see you move on with yours."

"Meg's invited but what if nothing changes? She shows up at odd times and I try not to be rude but..."

Laura interrupted. "It can't have been easy to tell me but Ralph deserves to hear it from you rather than someone else. For instance, Toledo might seem suspect."

"Excuse me?"

Laura admitted once when they visited, Joyce left to use the bathroom. "Meg said you and she stayed at the same hotel in Toledo a while ago. At the time, I found her phrasing odd but now see it would have been an outright lie to claim you shared a room."

Steve squinted. "You believe me?"

"It's best to be honest no matter how painful the truth. It's easy to misunderstand; I almost did."

Steve smiled. "Yet you believe me?"

"At first I struggled but in the end, trusted my instincts. I'm a wife who believes every word her husband says. Scolarzski, a lesser man might take advantage of that."

"Delorange, for you I will always strive to be a greater man."

With that statement, Laura believed she could risk waking demons and whispered, "You have no idea how relieved I am to hear that." She placed her plate down to reach for his hand. "Come with me; I want to lie in bed behind you, nestle in tight, and tell you what's on my mind without seeing a reaction."

"Okay."

In the bedroom, Steve pulled covers back and Laura curved in behind him; she draped her arm around his waist. "It's time I tell you what's on my mind: Rick. During my investigation I learned, remembered, or dreamed things that made no sense like Jack in high school, or when someone fell into the tunnel and needed stitches, or my year of home-schooling while in therapy."

Steve twisted his head to look over his shoulder. "You don't need to go into this if it's too painful."

Laura pressed fingertips to his chin and straightened his head. "Don't strain like that; you'll regret it later. I tried to get answers from Mom, Dad, and Jack to help with chronology. I asked Dad to help me sort through dates and locations so I could..."

"You've always great at piecing things together. Remember that break-in at the soap factory? You were the first to see a link to…"

Laura reached up to touch his lips. "Steve, let me do this without distraction. I gave it a lot of thought and need to…."

"Sorry: I'm terrified you're about to ask for a divorce."

Laura's eyes filled with tears. "I can't imagine my life without you in it so divorce is out of the question, for me at least." When he started to turn his head again, she whispered, "I'm sorry this is so awkward; it's unfair to demand you face away, so please turn. I need to see your eyes." Steve bounced and turned, and even in the dim room, Laura saw his apprehension as she continued. "Dad was weirder than Mom or Jack and I never got the answers I needed. Steve, I suspect some of my scars are from a caesarian section."

"Excuse me?"

"Steve, I suspect Rick is my son." When Laura felt his heart pound, she licked her lips. "This is all I know for sure. I was raped in March, Rick was born in December, and I spent the next year home-schooled. Marsethe is obsessed with tracking people important to his project and seemed fixated on meeting Rick's fiancé."

"Forgive me for doing what I always do but is this coincidence?"

"I want you to do what you always do and yes, I wonder how much is coincidence, but may never know for certain without DNA tests. Um, Marsethe hung a poster in his lab with extra squares around my name he covered with post-its but refused to explain. I have dreams where I breast-feed and change diapers and have noticeable gaps in memory of Jack's high school years." Laura collected her thoughts and rushed on with: "There are people in Fallsbridge I remember well and people I should but don't. How's it possible Violet claims she babysat for us all the time but I don't remember her? Even weirder is Jack's annual from Tufts lists him as Class Salutatorian from the Fallsbridge Academy. I recalled Essex Junction because we lived there by then but don't remember a graduation ceremony. Jack could have stayed behind with my grandparents. They were both still alive then and hadn't moved into assisted care yet so…"

Steve smiled. "Don't rush, Laura. Keep going through your process until you feel you've gone as far as you can."

Laura nodded. "Jack was gone during my year of home-schooling. In my mind, I placed him at UVM but how could that be? He was only 16 the year Rick was born."

Steve's eyes darted over every inch of her face. "I respect you see things differently and end up where no one else ever thought to go. What will you do? Talk to your parents again?"

"I tried. They're always vague."

Steve let his breath out slowly. "This isn't something to rush into, Laura. If true, it impacts many lives. "

"I know; like you and Mick, different facts don't change a thing. I wanted you to know this possibility so we have no secrets between us."

"Thank you."

"Does any of what I said tonight change how you feel?"

"About you? Never. I love you and that will never change. About Rick? I love him like a brother already but your parents? That one's trickier but figure whatever they did was out of love."

Laura took a deep breath. "Last thing and I apologize for how much this is all at once but I have a lot to figure out and work through either with you or with professional help. There are too many gaps and I can't fight this feeling I'm damaged goods, stained, and broken. For you and this child we created, I want to be whole."

Laura watched Steve's eyes fill with tears even as he smiled. "We'll do whatever it takes, kid, to stay together forever. Promise me."

"I promise." Laura felt her own tears build and pressed herself against him head to toe. "I'm not suggesting we do anything more than stay like this all night, okay? I've never felt so safe in my life."

Steve sighed, "Kid, we can stay like this for as long as you want. After a summer that felt like a heap of spinach and Brussels sprouts, making love with you again will be dessert."

Epilogue

Laura found it remarkable how thirteen days in the cabin felt like an eternity but nine days waiting for the reception flew by. As for the day itself? a blur. Obviously she was there and conscious because she vaguely recalled speaking vows of renewal and crying when Steve spoke his.

The party in her parents' back yard got lost in fogginess, too, though photographs proved it happened. Jack flew in from Texas but without Sarah or the children. Rick attended and never took his eyes off Gina, who stuck like glue to Lynette. Laura met new people: Steve's older brothers Tony and Paul flew in from Boston and Providence respectively, and Lea's friend Burt followed from Tampa. Michael drove up from Manhattan and as Laura studied him closely, understood why Steve feared Mick might be his biological nephew not son—the resemblance in looks and mannerisms uncanny, but then again, once she met Anthony and Paul, realized all Scolarzski men looked alike. She squeezed Steve's hand to whisper, "I wish I could have met your father."

"Old Max would've been so proud of me for finding you."

The caterer set mounds of food on a long table beside a beverage bar and a disc jockey played fantastic music spanning all five generations of guests. Her father rented a temporary wooden dance floor and it sat smack dab in the middle of the yard, not far from a stand of red maples in fall foliage, a perfect spot for a photographer to position smiling faces.

A small contingent traveled from Fallsbridge in the church van and stayed together in a suite at the Essex Inn: Violet, Ben, Joanna, and Paul Lemphier; Angela and Rita Lezzarro; and Caroline and Gretchen Beaudon. Al Wilkers brought his two younger daughters down from Derby—Sharon and Sheila—who whooped with excitement to be reunited with big sister Sandra. Maureen flew in from New York to serve as bridesmaid, insisting she needed visual proof Laura allowed a man into her life. Ed Granger showed up alone, sat by himself, and studied everything. Roger and Helen Macrae danced cheek to cheek, and Ned and Marie Sigler looked awkward but okay. When a waiter passed through the crowd with glasses of champagne for a toast, Laura noticed Marie shook her head no but accepted a glass of soda from her husband. Steve leaned close to whisper, "That's a long story I'll share soon but the bottom line is: Marie jumped onto the wagon and hangs on for dear life." Bobby Rawlings arrived with a woman named Marsha Buerton, someone Steve obviously knew, too. Again he leaned close to whisper, "Another long story but I think Bobby found a reason to care."

Ralph grabbed the microphone from the disc jockey. "Good afternoon, guests. I'm Ralph Barber, the best man for this swanky occasion to honor my best buddy of all time and the love of his until-now pathetic life. So lift your classes to join me in a toast to Stefan Maximilian and Laurette Marie." Ralph cleared his throat. "Here it is in all life's barest simplicity: Love's grand and all that sappy stuff but nothing deserves our undivided attention today quite like these two wonderful human beings who took absolutely forever to get here."

To a smattering of laughter and clinking glasses, Ralph handed the microphone to Steve, who announced, "Laura and I are pleased to announce a spring arrival of a new member to our family."

To a second round of clinking glasses and applause, Ralph grabbed the microphone and continued, "Now let's get this party hopping." Ralph paired people to dance: Al with Maureen, Michael with Meg, Mick with Sandra, and Rick with Gina. "Kinda hard to find a perfect title for this mix of folks but since our blushing bride is a Moody Blues fan, let's try *The Other Side of Life*." When the song ended, Laura thought Ralph chose well though Gina made a quick escape. Laura looked around and saw Al dance with Sandra until he gestured for Mick to cut in.

Laura watched Steve approach Meg and ask her to dance. From a distance, it appeared what could have been an awkward interaction stayed cordial. After the dance, Meg approached Laura to apologize. "If I'd known about your marriage, I wouldn't have said what I did." Meg stopped, looked around, and whispered, "No, I've been in love with that man for half my life and I'd do anything to be with Steve. Anything."

Laura nodded. "Believe me; I know how fortunate I am."

"Yeah? Well, be good to him because I'm always watching."

From across the yard, Laura heard a familiar squeal and turned to see Gil and Reilly wave as David bounced across the grass, chubby arms extended. Laura scooped him up. "I missed you, too."

Reilly cried and pulled Laura close. "I'm so glad you're fine. I'm sorry we're late but I had trouble finding a dress that zipped."

Laura held her at arm's length. "You look spectacular and I can hardly wait to need expandable fabric."

Gil stammered, "I'm sorry I didn't help Steve earlier but..."

Laura squeezed Gil's hand. "I understand; so does Steve. You were wise to protect your family now you're away from the CFEL. Let's hope Kobel keeps the focus on the real problem."

Gil squeezed back. "I told Steve you're one classy lady."

Laura wandered among bouncing bodies, impressed by how well Ralph assisted the disc jockey in a brilliant program for a diverse crowd: golden oldies, WW II big band classics, country, and soft and hard rock though no heavy metal. When the music shifted to a slow and bluesy *Don't Look Back* by John Lee Hooker, Laura searched for her husband in a crush of bodies. She found him by the trellis with Lea, Anthony, Paul, Michael, Mick, Burt, and Sandra. She made small talk, laughed at all the right places, and finally slipped her hand into Steve's to whisper, "I don't mean to be a party pooper, but this pregnant woman needs to head to bed soon. Otherwise, I fear I may not stay awake for dessert."

Steve turned with a smile and wrapped his arms around her. They headed onto the dance floor and moved in unison together, a perfect prelude to what she hoped would follow. When the song ended, Steve waved to everyone and shouted, "Thanks for being here but it's time to bid everyone good night!"

In the car, Laura leaned against him and asked. "Um, what do you imagine normal people talk about at times like this?"

Steve turned with a grin. "I'm sure I wouldn't know about normal but this person has one thing to say: after everything the two of us went through, life will only get better from here."

They rode the rest of the way in peaceful silence. At home while Steve locked up, Laura brushed her teeth, changed into a new negligee, and folded bedding back. While she waited for Steve to join her, Laura stared at a glint of moonlight on polished brass, pleased at how well the spirit house protected after so many years.

www.ingramcontent.com/pod-product-compliance
Lightning Source LLC
Chambersburg PA
CBHW060008180626
46817CB00015B/182